A Song On
the Wind

By the same author

Rough Heritage
Maid of the Sea

A Song On the Wind

Janet Thomas

WARWICKSHIRE LIBRARY & INFO SERVICE	
Bertrams	04.10.08
	£18.99

ROBERT HALE · LONDON

© Janet Thomas 2008
First published in Great Britain 2008

ISBN 978-0-7090-8674-1

Robert Hale Limited
Clerkenwell House
Clerkenwell Green
London EC1R 0HT

www.halebooks.com

The right of Janet Thomas to be identified as
author of this work has been asserted by her
in accordance with the Copyright, Designs and
Patents Act 1988

2 4 6 8 10 9 7 5 3 1

Typeset in 10/13pt Plantin
by Derek Doyle & Associates, Shaw Heath
Printed and bound in Great Britain
by Biddles Limited, King's Lynn

CHAPTER ONE

The doctor was just leaving, and Kerensa, hovering at the bottom of the stairs as her father saw him to the door, was listening intently.

'How is he really, the old man?' Zack enquired with lowered voice. 'You can tell me straight. You don't have to choose your words as you did in front of my wife and daughter.' He reached down the doctor's cane and tall silk hat from the hall stand and handed them to him.

'Then I'm afraid it's only a matter of a few days, possibly less.' The doctor placed the hat on his head and took the proffered cane with a nod of thanks.

Kerensa's hand flew to her mouth. He was dying! Her beloved grandpapa. A lump formed in her throat as the doctor went on, 'The age is there, you see, and the breathing problems have become more severe. There's nothing anyone can do except keep him quiet and comfortable. I'm so sorry, Mr Treneer.' He held out his free hand. 'Good day to you.'

Through a mist of tears Kerensa watched as the doctor picked up his bag and descended the steps to his carriage. Expecting her father to return upstairs, she rose to her feet and waited for him. But, instead of doing so, Zack made his way purposefully down the hall to his study where, through the half-open door, she saw him sit down at his desk and reach for a pen. But what was more puzzling was the fact that he had a broad smile on his face.

Wiping her eyes with the palm of her hand, Kerensa ran back upstairs to her grandfather's room. He hadn't moved. Propped high on the pillows of the brass bed, his face could have been moulded from candle-wax, and his beak of a nose was accentuated by sunken, hollow cheeks. He could be dead already.

But with a ripple of movement the rheumy eyes blinked and opened. Kerensa perched on the side of the bed and took one of the gnarled old hands in her own. 'Are you all right, Grandpapa?' she asked with a catch in her throat, thinking at the same time what a stupid question it was to ask a dying man. But what else was there to say? 'Can I get you anything?' A flicker of a smile crossed the pinched mouth and his head moved slightly from side to side. Kerensa swallowed hard on the lump which persisted in her throat, for she loved Joseph dearly. She recalled the burly figure with the booming voice who had been the grandfather she had known, now reduced to this... a tear fell on the spotless counterpane.

With a grunt of effort Joseph's other hand moved to cover hers and he took in a rasping breath. Then, raising his head slightly, he whispered, 'You're a . . . good . . . a good . . . child.' Kerensa bent her ear to catch the quavering thread of sound. 'After . . . after I'm . . . gone . . . look after your mother. That father of yours . . .' It was enough, the old man's head sank back in exhaustion and his eyes closed again, although the hand stayed resting on her own. Kerensa waited until his grip relaxed and she was sure he was deeply asleep before she moved his hand, tucking it tenderly under the covers. 'Of course I will, Grandpapa, of course,' she whispered back, wondering what it was that he had been going to say about Papa.

The sound of her parents' voices floated up to her, growing louder as they approached the top of the stairs, and Kerensa realized they were bickering as usual. Then came a heavy-footed thump which sounded as if someone had stumbled. Kerensa caught her bottom lip between her teeth. Papa was drunk again, then. He always spent the evenings down at the public bar, where he drank and smoked and played cards until late into the night, but now it was only midday.

The door opened and in they came, her father swaying slightly but shaking off his wife's supporting hand as they both glanced at the figure in the bed. 'How's he been?' Her mother turned to Kerensa.

The girl shrugged. 'Just as you see, Mama.' Her parents drew away and moved towards the window, talking in low tones. They were discussing arrangements for the funeral – she could hear them – and Grandpapa was still alive! Maybe he could hear them as well. Oh, how *could* they? Poor Grandpapa! Kerensa gave a sob and sank her head in her hands.

As she came down to breakfast the next morning, Kerensa sensed that the atmosphere had changed, and she knew. 'It's Grandpapa, isn't it?' she whispered and her mother nodded and slipped a comforting arm around her shoulders. 'He died in the night, dear. Quietly, in his sleep, without pain. It's all that anyone could wish for in such an old man.' Kerensa hid her face in Celia's shoulder, which smelled sweetly of lavender water, as she added, 'You won't be going in to school today, of course.'

Kerensa nodded and wiped her eyes. Her days at the Redbrooke Academy for Young Ladies in Camborne were numbered anyway. Now she had turned sixteen, she had been wearing her hair up and her skirts down for almost two years, and could hardly wait for her adult life to begin.

'Oh dear,' Celia sighed, with one hand at her forehead, 'there is so much to think about I hardly know where to start. We'll need mourning apparel, of course, and how we're going to pay for that I don't know, as well as the funeral itself. We shall need to do it all properly – your grandfather was a highly respected man you know.'

'Mama,' said Kerensa, as something occurred to her, 'I was just wondering – I know that Grandpapa was a gentleman and came from a long line of Tregonings, but where did their money actually come from?'

'Oh.' Her mother smiled. 'Your grandfather Joseph was a shrewd man and he invested money he'd inherited in mining shares, when the industry was doing really well, and they paid off. He bought this house, Penhallow, with it.' She took a step or two across the room.

'Well, I was born here, of course,' Celia went on.

Kerensa nodded. 'Like me,' she said.

'Yes. And by the time Zack and I were getting married, your grandmother had died and Papa offered us a home with him. We didn't have much money and he was getting someone to look after him, so it worked out very well for us all.'

Her mother turned as the door opened. 'Ah, Zack,' she said as he entered the room. 'I shall need you to go into town and register the – the death.' Kerensa noticed her father's jaw drop.

'But I've got other things to do . . .' he protested, spreading his hands wide and frowning at his wife.

'You weren't thinking of . . .' Celia snapped. 'Surely you could have the decency to stay away from your rowdy friends for *one* day. I need you to see the undertaker and ask him to call, then go to the newspaper office and put an announcement in the obituaries column. And go to the florist . . .' She rubbed a hand over her eyes, 'Oh there is so much to be *done*!'

'Is there anything I can do to help, Mama?' Kerensa, feeling rather out of things, wondered where her place was in all this busy-ness.

'Oh, Kerensa, yes.' Her mother turned towards her and Zack slipped out the way he had come. 'I was just going to have a word with Cook about the refreshments. You can make yourself useful there, dear. I know what a flair you have for cooking' – she laid a hand on her daughter's shoulder – 'and how you like to bake. Follow me.' And she went bustling down the passage to the kitchen, her skirt swishing on the tiled floor.

★

In the breakfast-room of his comfortable home at the better end of Camborne, Silas Cardrew folded open the morning paper and propped it against the milk jug as he buttered a slice of toast.

Then, 'By Jove!' he exclaimed, the knife poised in his hand. He looked at his daughter over the top of the paper. 'Grace, old Joseph Tregoning's passed away at last – well, well.'

'Oh, Mr Tregoning? Well, he seems to have been around forever. How old was he, Papa?'

Silas took a bite and glanced at the page again. 'Eighty years of age.'

'Yes, he must have been,' Grace nodded, holding a cup of tea in both hands, her elbows on the table. 'Because I remember how frail he was looking when he came to Mama's funeral two years ago. Someone said then that he was almost eighty. We must send our condolences to Mr and Mrs Treneer, mustn't we? Would you like me to do that for you, Papa?'

Silas nodded. 'Yes, I suppose we must, although you know how things stood between the two of us.' He glanced at his daughter's demurely bent head. 'You're a good girl, Grace,' he said awkwardly, not used to expressing his feelings, for emotions were nothing but sentimental rubbish. But it was true. After all, she'd been barely seventeen when she'd had to take her mother's place, an age when most girls were thinking of young men and their own future, and he'd never once heard her complain.

'Why, thank you, Papa.' Grace looked up, and he basked for a moment in the delighted smile which spread across her heart-shaped face and lit up her soft brown eyes. 'I know there was this ill-feeling between you and Joseph, but I've quite forgotten how it started.' Grace poured herself another cup of tea.

'Oh, well, we both held shares in Dolcoath mine and I met him first at the count-house dinners. Got to know a few other influential men there, and someone put my name forward to join their exclusive club, but in the end I was turned down.' Silas scowled. 'Then I heard over the grapevine that Tregoning had raised objections and voted against me because I wasn't a *gentleman* by birth. The fact that I was better off than any of them didn't mean a thing.' Through gritted teeth he finished, 'Because I was *trade*, you see.' He picked up his cup and drained it.

Setting it back on the saucer with a force that had Grace fearing for the china, Silas growled, 'Being like he was, I could never understand why Joseph put up with that son-in-law of his – what's his name? – Zachary.'

'What about him?' Grace glanced up and raised an eyebrow.

'Oh, he's nothing more than a waster – never done a hand's turn in his life,' Silas replied. 'Always has money for the cards and a drink, though. I reckon he lives off his wife.' He took a bite and added through it, 'Joseph always did spoil his daughter – I suppose because she was his only child.'

He popped the last piece of toast into his mouth, carefully wiped his moustache and rose to his feet. 'Yes, well.' Silas tossed down his napkin. 'Find out when the funeral is – your brothers and I had better go to it. It'll be expected, and for the sake of the firm and my reputation, I must be seen there.' He handed the paper to Grace and turned to leave.

Over his shoulder Silas added, 'Tell Richard and Jago about the funeral. I think Richard's up in the top garden helping to fell that great pine tree that's rotten. And Jago of course, will be upstairs' – he sniffed and his lip curled – 'tinkling away on that damn piano of his.' He caught Grace's swift upward glance, but she said nothing. 'I must go,' Silas finished, 'mustn't be late at the foundry.'

The day of Joseph's funeral was almost over. Kerensa had been helping Daisy hand round the plates of sandwiches and cakes and pour endless cups of tea. And now she was listening to the talk that was going on around her.

Silas Cardrew was over there, his huge bulk looming over her parents, his booming voice carrying right across the room. 'Nice place you have here . . . always admired it, you know?' And by the way he glanced up at the ceiling, Kerensa knew that he was fully aware of the ancient inscription which was carved on one of the beams. She knew it off by heart. One of her earliest memories was of sitting on Grandpapa's knee with his warm arm around her. She had been playing with his white whiskers as they sat by a roaring fire and he had told her the old story then, the first of many times she had demanded it. Oh, Grandpapa, Kerensa felt the pain in her heart afresh at the thought of her loss.

She glanced up at the ceiling. Legend had it that the original owner of the house had been one Rafe Nicholas, a local smuggler, who had built it with his ill-gotten gains. 'Deep beneath Penhallow's ground,' it went, 'lies a treasure to be found.' With the initials R.N. beside it and the date, 1770. What a lot of people must have looked for it in vain over the hundred years or so since then.

To her right, two elderly men in black tail-coats and splendid waistcoats were talking in low voices apparently about Silas, as they were casting covert glances in his direction. Kerensa caught the words – 'self-made man . . . hard as nails . . . ruthless – dragged himself up, and now . . .' One

9

of the men shrugged.

Kerensa switched her attention back to Silas and strained her ears to catch what he was saying to her parents with such an earnest expression on his face. Fragments of their conversation floated over to her. '. . . if you should be thinking of selling up . . . change of circumstances . . . be willing to take it off your hands . . . fair price . . .' he said, nodding to Papa.

'Oh, Mr Cardrew.' Mama was saying, '. . . no plans to leave Penhallow . . . have lived here all my life, you see . . . Father has willed the house to me, I know . . .'

Other fragments of small talk drifted over and around her as Kerensa stood taking in the scene. She was trying not to scream at the insensitivity of it all. Listening to the banal conversation and the braying laughs, one would think that it was just any kind of tea-party anywhere, instead of the solemn and heart-rending occasion it was for her. Did no one realize that this was a funeral? Had they forgotten so soon that they had just buried her beloved grandfather? How *could* they be so uncaring? She felt her lips begin to tremble, and could not prevent the cascade of hot tears that came flooding down her face.

Sickened, Kerensa decided that she needed fresh air and a quiet place in which to recover. She would take her favourite walk, which led from the back of the house, up through the peaceful fields to the coast. No one was likely to notice she'd gone – they were all far too self-absorbed. She slipped quietly out of the room and out of the back door. Daisy was now clattering dishes in the kitchen as she cleared up, and Celia was still in the drawing-room talking to a few late leavers. As she thought, no one noticed her exit.

Soon Kerensa was threading her way through a country lane filled with all the wildflowers of spring. Creamy cow parsley frothed in the ditches and celandines lying in great golden pools beneath the trees turned their brightly polished faces up to the sun.

The lane sloped up from the bottom of a valley, where the 'red river' flowed – red from the mineral tailings it carried from the mines up around Carn Brea. The banks of the river teemed with noise and activity, and she could see the little figures of the tin streamers, foreshortened at this distance, working with water-wheels and separating equipment, extracting the remaining valuable ore before it was swept downstream and out to sea at Gwithian.

Partway up the steeply rising ground, Kerensa paused, leaned on a fence-post to catch her breath, and looked back down the hill towards her home. Penhallow, solidly built of the local granite, was a large and comfortable family house. It nestled into the hill behind and its grounds were sheltered from the south-westerly wind by a belt of woodland, now brightening with new emerald foliage.

From Kerensa's vantage point the view swept over and above the tin workings as far as Camborne a mile away, whose town clock was just visible over the rise. What a contrast to the rural loveliness around her, she thought, seeing in her mind's eye the grey and utilitarian industrial town. It was dominated to the east by Dolcoath, the deepest and most productive mine in the county, and to the west by Cardrew's Foundry, manufacturers and suppliers of mining equipment. Between the two was a network of tiny streets lined on both sides with the small cottages where the workers lived.

She took a last look over her shoulder at the house, and was struck by how neglected it looked. Fallen stones from the wall littered the weed-grown path to the kitchen garden, and the garden itself was uncared-for and overgrown. What was happening? Why did they have no money for repairs any more? But shabby or not, she loved it with all her heart. It was where she belonged and the only home she had ever known.

Once Kerensa had turned the corner of the lane the slope took her ever upwards until she could feel and smell the breath of the sea ahead. Then over the familiar granite stile and onto the open cliff-top, where she took a deep breath of the salt-laden air and made for her favourite nook.

Jago had done his duty to the Treneer family, shaking hands and making polite conversation until his smile ached, and now at last they could leave. He had travelled from his home on horseback as both he and the animal had needed the exercise. Now needing it even more, he reclaimed his mount from the stable and took the road to the cliffs and freedom. This was more like it. He gave the mare her head and as the great hoofs thundered across the soft turf there was music in their rhythm. To Jago there was music everywhere, in the flying clouds above them, almost in the very air he breathed.

As he cantered along the narrow track the salt-laden wind streamed through his hair and brought tears to his eyes. Exhausted at last, Jago drew the horse up at the steep drop known locally as Hell's Mouth, dismounted and cautiously approached the edge. Far below in the aptly named pit of hell, the turbulent water surged and lunged, forever pitting its strength against the unyielding granite. In its voice he could hear the stirring chords of a great symphony, while from the breeze through the grasses came wafting the gentler notes of a love song, with the melancholy calling of the sea-birds its counterpoint.

Jago stretched himself full length on the ground and lay with his hands behind his head. Since finishing his training in London and returning home to decide what to do next, he had become very aware of the subtle harmonies of the natural world. There was melody everywhere here, in the song of the larks above him, in the squeaks and rustlings of small creatures in the undergrowth and in the mighty heartbeat of the earth itself.

He came to with a start. He must have dozed off! But for how long? Jago sat up in dismay and looked round for his horse, which was nowhere to be seen. Muttering under his breath, for he had not thought to tether the animal, Jago set off to look for it. Then rounding a bend in the path he caught sight of its chestnut rump not far away and heaved a sigh of relief. He had begun to run before he realized that there was someone with the horse. Holding the reins and stroking its nose he could see a small female figure.

'Kerensa! Oh, thank goodness you found her!' Jago exclaimed, as she turned to him with a smile.

'Actually, she found me,' the girl replied. 'She crept up behind me and breathed down my neck. I nearly jumped out of my skin!'

'You managed to escape too,' he remarked with a grin and Kerensa nodded as their eyes met. Her heart turned over at the sight of him. Wavy brown hair lifting on the wind floated around the narrow, sensitive face she knew so well. High cheekbones, a determined chin and lively eyes the colour of bitter chocolate which at the moment were smiling down at her, soft and intimate. Then she felt a gentle finger beneath her chin as Jago tipped up her head. 'You've been crying,' he said softly, wiping her cheeks with a warm thumb. She nodded. The persistent lump in her throat just would not go away, even now.

'Your grandfather of course.' Kerensa lowered her eyes, turning away to sit down on a lichen-covered rock. Jago sank onto the grass beside her.

'Oh Jago, you saw them all back there – nobody seemed to be thinking about him at all, or why they were there.' Kerensa's eyes were on the sweep of the restless sea beyond. 'They were all chattering away about normal things – and – and – laughing too, just as if nothing had happened.' She felt another tear slide down her face and knuckled it away.

'You loved your grandfather very much, didn't you?' Jago said softly, and slipped a comforting arm around her waist. Her springy dark hair, loosened now by the teasing wind, swung around them. It smelled sweetly of salt air and sunshine. Jago looked down tenderly at the small, pointed face as her eyes the colour of a peaty stream looked trustingly into his.

They had first met leaving church when Kerensa had bumped into him in the crowd and dropped her prayer book. Jago had retrieved it, said a few kind words and she had hero-worshipped him ever since. The four year difference in their ages had made Jago almost grown up to her at ten years old. Since then they had met from time to time at family occasions, for Celia had been friendly with Jago's mother before she died. 'Have you finished studying now, Jay?' Kerensa said, and, when he nodded, she asked, 'What are you going to do next?'

'Kerensa, what I want to do more than anything is to be a top-class concert pianist.' He regarded her solemnly. 'And for that I need a lucky break – a good agent or someone to sponsor me and introduce me to the right people.' Jago looked down at his hands. 'But I'm not going to find that in Cornwall.' He paused for a long moment and the only sound was the whisper of the sea far below them and the sigh of the wind through the heather.

'So you're going away again? For good?' Her voice was little more than a whisper. Jago nodded. 'I shall have to get in touch with some contacts I made in London and see what they come up with.' He looked deeply into her face. 'Music is my life, Kerensa. I'd rather die than give it up for some kind of mundane job down here, which is what my father would like me to do.'

Kerensa nodded. 'I do understand, really.' She turned away. And I can understand too, she thought, that when you go back to London and get caught up in the musical world up there, I shall be very far away and you'll soon put me out of your mind.

She gazed into his beloved face, drinking in every nuance of expression – fixing into her mind's eye the way his eyes crinkled at the corners when he smiled, the way his hair flopped in just that way over his brow and how he was always running his fingers through it to keep it back. Saving it all up to feed on when he was no longer with her. Jago Cardrew, she thought, I loved you at ten years old and nothing has changed.

But I know you don't feel the same way about me – maybe you see me as a younger sister, a friend, but nothing more. We share an interest in music, but love...? I don't think so. To prolong the inevitable moment when they must part, Kerensa said, 'How old were you when you decided you wanted to be a pianist, Jago?'

'I've never wanted to do anything else since I was a small child and heard my mother playing Chopin in the evenings after we children were in bed,' Jago replied and his eyes were far away. 'I suppose it was the only time she could practise undisturbed.' He paused and smiled. 'Sometimes,

13

too, if she was playing during the daytime I would sit right underneath the piano, watching her fingers flying up and down the keyboard and longing to be able to produce such glorious sounds.' He shrugged and spread his hands expressively. 'So when she saw how interested I was, I was given lessons.' His face became serious as he added, 'I still miss her, you know. She was the only one who understood how all-consuming music can be.'

'How proud she would have been to see you now,' Kerensa said softly, imagining the sensitive small boy curled up at his mother's feet, drinking in the music with those dark, solemn eyes. They walked on a few paces before Jago said, 'I'll see you again before I go, of course, and say goodbye.' He must have seen the misery on her face, Kerensa thought, as he gave her a sideways look then changed the subject, saying briskly, 'Now, do your parents know where you are?'

Kerensa stopped and clapped a hand to her mouth. 'Oh Jay, no! I just ran out, to – to get away. And I've been up here for ages. I must go back – right away.'

'Well, in that case I suggest that I give you a lift home on Tessa's back,' Jago said. 'Her rump is quite wide enough for us both and it will save you a lot of time.'

'What? Me – ride behind *you*?' Kerensa's jaw dropped.

'Why not?' said Jago, one foot in the stirrup. And, as he swung his leg across the horse and reached a hand down to pull her up behind him, she couldn't think of a single sensible reply.

Kerensa would never forget the exhilaration of that ride. They went thundering along the cliff top, her hair freed of its pins blowing out behind her like that of a wanton. Like a wanton too, she had to wrap her arms around Jago's waist, as it was the only way to stay on the animal's back. Kerensa felt her body tense and the colour flood into her cheeks at the feel of that taut, lean back against her breast, all the muscles rippling, and the thunder of his heartbeat beneath her hands. The speed of their passage pressed her face against his shoulder, and she drank in the heady scent of clean linen and male sweat through the roughness of his tweed jacket.

When Jago alighted at the top of the lane and turned to help her down, Kerensa had to place both arms around his neck and jump as he held her around the waist. Her legs almost gave way beneath her as he released her and she had to grip his arm to keep from falling. Their eyes met and for a moment she wondered . . . but no. She tore herself away and went running down the lane.

★

'Ah Kerensa, there you are – I've been looking all over for you.' Celia met her daughter as Kerensa was coming sedately down the stairs, neat and tidy again, with nothing to show she'd left the house at all. 'Mr Thomas of Grylls and Thomas, is here to read the will. Come along.'

She followed her mother into the drawing-room where the solicitor in a black suit and stiff collar so high that it looked as if it could cut his head off, faced them over a small table and rustled his papers.

Kerensa's attention wandered as he meandered through the introduction and minor bequests, and from her position on the brocade settee beside her mother, she glanced idly across the room at her father. Her attention was caught by the way he seemed to be fidgeting and biting his lip, almost nervously – but of course he couldn't be nervous.

At last the solicitor announced, 'And now we come to the main beneficiaries.' Kerensa sat up straighter and began to listen in earnest. The man coughed, rustled the papers in his hand and turned a page. ' "To my son-in-law Zachary George Treneer" ' Papa glanced up – ' "the house known as Penhallow and all its contents—" '

'No!' Kerensa jumped as Celia sprang to her feet, wide-eyed, shaking her head as if she didn't understand him. 'No, that can't be right. Father always told me that Penhallow would be mine. That he'd left the house to me.'

The solicitor peered over the top of his spectacles, and his brows rose at the interruption. 'But I assure you, madam, it's all here in black and white, legally signed and witnessed.' He frowned, then leaned forward to pass it to Celia. 'You must be mistaken.' While she was examining it he turned to Papa and enquired, 'Did you know anything about this, Mr Treneer?'

Kerensa glanced at her father, who shrugged his shoulders. 'It's the accepted thing, surely – a husband's duty being to look after his wife, and relieve her from all the worry that goes with maintaining a house?' Zack smiled and spread his hands. 'Especially a house of this size.'

The solicitor nodded. 'Quite so. I'm sure your father was only thinking of your welfare, Mrs Treneer.'

Celia stared at him coldly and resumed her seat, still shaking her head in disbelief. Then Kerensa saw her mother appear to gather herself together and her brows drew closer in a frown. 'What about Father's capital?' she asked. 'So far there's been no mention of actual money.'

'Ah yes.' The solicitor laid aside the will and crossed his forearms on the table as he looked earnestly at them all. 'As you may or may not know, Mr Tregoning actually had very little capital left. Over the years it appears, so the accountant tells us, that he had settled a very generous monthly allowance on you personally, Mrs Treneer.' Kerensa glanced at her mother as Celia nodded, her blue eyes huge in her pale face. 'Well, I'm afraid that has to come to an end from this current month.'

Kerensa saw Celia's jaw drop and she seemed to be speechless with shock. They had no money! 'But how?' Her mother's voice rose up the scale. 'What are we going to do?' She glanced at Zack and their eyes met, but he lowered his immediately and turned away. Kerensa with a flash of adult intuition guessed from that exchange of glances where it had gone, and privately called her mother all sorts of a fool.

So they had no money. Kerensa felt Celia trembling beside her and reached for her hand. Papa was sitting like a carved wooden figure, carefully avoiding their eyes. Fury started to boil up inside her as the stark message sank in. What would they do? How would they live? Would Penhallow have to be sold? She gasped. For that was unthinkable.

CHAPTER TWO

Lennie Retallick, agent to Silas Cardrew and his right-hand man, was coming down the steps of The Pick and Shovel when he almost bumped into someone. 'Ah, Zack!' he said, looking up at the tall figure, 'Haven't seen you around for a while. Where've you been?'

'Had things to do, people to see.' Zack grinned. 'Come back in, Len. Have one on me and I'll tell you about it.' He clapped his hand on the other man's shoulder as Lennie's eyes widened. Something really must be up. He'd never known Zack to be so expansive before. Quite the reverse.

Despite the difference in their ages, almost a generation, they were drinking companions of long standing. In Lennie's character Zack saw an eye for the main chance which struck a chord with him. Lennie, growing up fatherless, saw in Zack the charm and urbanity which he envied. 'Don't mind if I do,' he replied, as they went up the steps together.

'So what's all this great secret, then?' Lennie asked, as soon as they were both propping up the bar. He took a swig and wiped the froth off his ginger moustache. 'You're acting very mysterious, Zack. And looking like the cat what got the cream, besides.'

Zack chuckled. 'So would you, boy, so would you' – he raised his voice as he went on – 'if you suddenly became an owner of *property*.' He had attracted the attention of the regulars in the window bay, and a low murmur of interest rose through the wreaths of tobacco smoke above their heads.

'How – what d' you mean – property?' Lennie finished his pint and signalled across the counter for a refill while the going was good, as Zack swivelled round until he was addressing the room in general. 'What I said. Old Joe's left me his house and everything in it.' He lifted his glass in a mock toast.

Lennie spluttered into his drink. '*What*? He's never gone and left Penhallow to you!' His jaw dropped. 'You lucky sod – but why? I thought he never had no time for you, Zack. Thought the world of his daughter, mind, Joe did. Should have thought it would have come to her.' He glanced around the room. Several men were nodding and rumbling their agreement.

'Well, there we are,' said Zack. He held his head high and rapped on the counter. 'Bottoms up, my friends – the drinks are on me,' he announced. The roar of appreciation was music to his ears. This was more like it. At last he had gone up in the world. Where he was meant to be. Someone to be reckoned with. A gentleman – or as good as. They would have to show him due respect now. And a grin of satisfaction spread across his face.

Silas Cardrew opened the door of his office and strolled out on to the balcony from where he could survey his foundry floor. Down there, dozens of his employees were at work. Stokers were feeding the greedy mouths of the giant furnaces, their tiny black figures foreshortened from this height and resembling automatons as they wielded their toy-like shovels. Silhouetted against the bursts of flame as the doors were opened, the scene could have come from some medieval depiction of Hell.

Other men were pouring off the molten metal, hissing and steaming, into the moulds set out on the floor. Silas watched with silent satisfaction. These would turn out parts for mining machinery of every description, from huge steam engines to humble rock borers. Also domestic ware – for Cardrew's were well known for their Cornish ranges.

He gave a grunt, consulted his pocket-watch and raised an eyebrow. Where on earth was his damned agent? Silas thrust his hands into the pockets of his tweed suit and re-entered the office. From outside in the assembly shops came the deafening sound of metal hammering on metal as the great cylinders and boilers were riveted together. Long may it last Silas hoped, thoughtfully stroking his beard. If that dratted man would only get a move on with the order books, he might get some idea of how long.

'Ah, at last.' Silas, seated behind his great desk, turned to the figure in the doorway. 'And about time too,' he growled, as Lennie came staggering in, carrying several large ledgers. 'Where've you been?'

'Had to see to the delivery of that great fifty-ton bob for the pumping engine over to Wheal Ellen. You know I did,' Lennie said defensively, as he dropped his load onto the desk and straightened up. 'Took some time too – had to send for extra horses, see. Needed twenty pair to pull her.'

'Hmm. Well, what are orders like now?' Silas pulled one of the leather-cornered ledgers towards him.

'Don't look too good,' replied Lennie, pulling up a chair. 'I bought the *Mining Journal* too while I was out.' He pulled the paper from a pocket and passed it over. 'Nothing but doom and gloom, it do look like. More and more mines closing down every week, seem to be.'

'Firm's doing all right though – isn't it?' Silas replied. 'Mustn't grumble. Our turnover doesn't depend totally on the mines, does it? Always a good idea never to put your all eggs in one basket, boy.' He gave his assistant a sly wink and tapped the side of his nose.

'Heard a bit of news too, while I was out,' Lennie broke in. His pale eyes regarded his employer's bent head as Silas ran a finger down a column of figures.

'Uh?' came a grunt and Silas straightened up with a look of interest.

'Zack Treneer was down the public, boasting about how he have come into money,' Lennie went on.

'*Money?* Him?' Silas gave a snort. 'Go on – pull the other one,' he said sarcastically.

Lennie picked up the newspaper from the desk and nonchalantly scanned it. ''Tis true,' he replied. 'Old Joe have left his house to him.'

Silas's jaw dropped in total astonishment as he stuttered, '*Penhallow*? To *him*? He never has!' He sprang to his feet and began to pace up and down. 'But I thought they didn't get on – it was common knowledge.' He turned on his heel. 'And I heard years ago he'd willed it to his wife. I was chatting to old Thomas the solicitor – this one's father – once, when we were doing a bit of business, and he mentioned it to me then – in strictest confidence of course – because he thought it was unusual. Well, well, I wonder what made Joe change his mind.' Silas paused, then came to a halt beside Lennie's chair and looked his agent in the eye.

'Lennie, there's a matter I want to discuss with you, and it's nothing to do with work.' The other man raised an eyebrow and waited. 'Something that calls for a little discretion and a certain amount of sleight of hand. Do you know what I mean?'

Lennie raised the other eyebrow. 'Maybe.'

Silas helped himself to a pipe from the rack which stood near at hand, and stuffed it, then lit the tobacco and blew a thin stream of smoke towards the blackened ceiling. 'As you may or may not know, I went to old Joe's funeral,' Silas paused and blew a perfect smoke ring. 'Thought they might be putting the house on the market now – big place for the three of them – so I put out a few feelers. But apparently not.'

Silas leaned a little closer, lowered his voice and said briefly, 'Lennie, I want that house. I want it badly. If I could move into Penhallow, it will be seen by those that matter that I've *arrived*, and they won't be able to turn up their toffee noses at me any more.' He scowled, then his face cleared as he recalled a beamed ceiling and a carved inscription. With all the machinery at his disposal, turning over the ground would be simple. . . .

'Yes, I'm determined that I and my family will be accepted into the middle classes, Lennie, whether I made my money through trade or not.' His bushy brows met in a frown of concentration. 'And between us I think it can be done.'

'So what's in this for me?' Lennie's chin rose and he stared his employer down. 'That's if I even agree to whatever it is.'

Silas glared at him. 'I'll make it worth your while, boy, don't worry about that. Stands to reason. Do what I ask and make it work – then I'll make sure you get what you want.' He sat back with a nod.

Lennie leaned forward and stony blue eyes met flint-grey. 'You know what I want,' came the reply.

Silas straightened and chuckled softly, as his voice dropped to a whisper. 'Now this is what I want you to do . . .'

A few days later Lennie strolled into the public house and made straight for the bar where Zack was propped up as usual. After the initial formalities and with a drink in his hand, Lennie said casually, 'Got an invitation for you.' Zack raised an enquiring eyebrow. 'Silas is throwing a party tomorrow night at the club. It's his birthday. Nothing extravagant. A few friends, he said – a drink and a hand or two of cards – you know. Come, can you?'

'Love to,' said Zack with enthusiasm. 'Just what I need, a bit of fun.' And a chance to see and be seen, he added to himself. Silas's business associates would be there – and prosperous shopkeepers, farmers, builders. People he would now be able to mix with as equals. 'It'll be a chance to celebrate my legacy, eh?'

Lennie clapped him on the shoulder. 'Good man.' He lifted his arm and downed his drink in a couple of gulps. 'Can't stop,' he banged the empty glass down on the counter, 'I'm supposed to be at work. I'll see you tomorrow evening, then.'

Zack raised his own glass. 'I'll look forward to it,' he replied.

A little later Zack was on his way home, inebriated and with a jaunty spring in his step. Imagine Celia's reaction when he came back tomorrow night loaded down with his winnings! Perhaps that would take the sour look off her face for once. All he needed was for his run of luck to keep up the way it had been doing lately, and he would make a tidy killing off that affluent crowd tomorrow night.

Silas stuck his pipe in one corner of his mouth and looked about him. It had been a good party and now having partaken of supper and drunk several toasts to his health, the bulk of the guests were leaving, while the half-dozen or so of his closest friends were gathering around the card table.

And there was the person he was waiting for. He excused himself as he noticed Lennie Retallick hovering by the door, and sauntered over to him nonchalantly. 'Well, have you got it?' Silas demanded in a hoarse whisper. It would be the worse for him if he hadn't. But Lennie gave him a nod and a wink. 'And you've done as we agreed?'

The other man gave him a scathing look. 'Of course I have. I done my part all right – the rest is up to you. Here – take it.'

Silas slipped the small package furtively into his pocket and turned away to shake the hands of his departing guests. Then he strolled over to take his place as banker for an evening of vingt-et-un.

The air was already thick with tobacco smoke and alcohol fumes when Silas snapped his fingers for another round. He had made sure that Zack was sitting next to him and now placed a pint at his elbow. He took a swig from his own glass and when everyone was served, raised his voice and announced, 'Right, gentlemen, shall we begin?' He waited until the rumble of conversation had died away, then added, 'Place your bets now, please,' and began to deal.

A couple of hours passed during which Silas made sure that Zack's glass was never empty, while his own remained virtually untouched. A sip or two occasionally kept up the illusion that he was matching him pint for pint, but as Zack became more and more inebriated, the more stone-cold sober Silas remained. His flinty grey eyes flicked back and forth across the table as luck ebbed and flowed, and fortunes went up and down as rapidly as the cards were being dealt.

'Thish ish all getting a bit too much for me,' Silas slurred with a pretence of drunkenness as Zack won another hand, and with a fatuous smile on his face, scooped up his winnings. 'You're shertainly on a lucky shtreak tonight, boy,' he went on, playing Zack like a fish on a line. 'You'll break the bleddy bank at thish rate.'

Eventually one of the other players threw in his hand and rose to his feet. 'That's as far as I go, Cardrew,' he said. 'Better pack it in while I've still got a bit left, haw, haw, haw!' He reached for his hat and made his way to the door. 'Me too,' said another, scraping back his chair to follow him out. 'Good game, Silas, thanks for the evening – be seeing you.'

'How about you, Zack? Want to shtop while you're ahead? I'll undershtand if you do.' Silas looked with satisfaction at the man's bloodshot eyes and shaking fingers and hid a smile behind his hand.

'Me? Not on your life – never done sho well before – can't shtop now,' Zack said.

'Well, firsht let's have another round,' said Silas, raising a beckoning finger, 'and then how about if we up the shtakes and make it really worthwhile – as you're doing sho well, eh? What do you think to that?' He slopped his drink down his beard in a state of false inebriation. 'Whoopsh, shteady on there, Silash,' he giggled.

'Count me in,' Zack replied, his glass weaving crazily as he tried to direct it to his mouth, 'Oh yesh. Zack'sh your man. Come on, what st -sht ... what oddsh ... are you talking 'bout?'

Silas leaned forward and met the other man's bleary eyes with his own. 'How 'bout I play you for your house – Penhallow – against my f-f-foundry?' There was a gasp of indrawn breath from the other players, then a hush fell as Silas went on, 'New deck of cardsh, sho it'sh all above board – witnesh – witnesses here ... see fair play. Straight 'nough for you?'

Zack was nodding eagerly. 'You're on – I can't loosh – lose t'night. Bring it on, then – let's get going.' He wriggled to the edge of his chair and rubbed his hands together.

'Jusht one shmall thing – musht do it prop'ly – only fair to you – put your name on this, ole man.' Silas pushed a piece of paper and a pen towards him and Zack scrawled a shaky signature, 'Right. Here we are –

new d-d-deck coming up.' He reached into a drawer beneath the table and drew out the cards Lenny had given him.

Silas in his play-acting fumbled with the cards and almost dropped them before he managed to undo the wrapper. 'I'll cut f-first and the highest card wins. Right?' Zack nodded impatiently. 'Get on with it, man.' He downed the last of his beer. Silas split the pack, and his face dropped. 'Oh no! Four of diamonds,' he groaned as he showed it, replaced the cards and sank his head in his hands. And by all that's holy, Lenny had better have done his job properly, or I've lost the foundry. His stomach lurched in earnest as he took in a deep breath and held it.

With an inane grin stretching from ear to ear, Zack held out a shaking hand towards the pack. The silence was almost tangible, even the clock on the wall seemed to pause and hold its breath as he split it.

'*Two of hearts*? No, oh no, it can't be!' Zack focused bleary eyes on the two spots as if mesmerized, then up at his opponent. 'But ... but ...' He stared slack-jawed at the piece of pasteboard again then shook his head slowly, as all the colour drained from his face. Zack goggled and ran his finger around a collar gone suddenly tight.

Silas caught the cards as they tumbled from his hand and hastily thrust them into his pocket, as he let out all the breath he had been holding in a great sigh of relief. Then he reached across the table and placed his hand on the promissory note, trying to suppress a grin of triumph as he slowly drew it towards him.

'*Mine*, I think,' he said.

'Oh Kerensa, there you are.' Celia was sitting at a small table in the drawing-room, studying the household accounts book. She sat back in the cane chair and rubbed both hands over her eyes. 'Have you seen Papa this morning?' Kerensa gave her a blank stare. Her mother was looking terrible, as if she hadn't slept. Normally so immaculate, this morning her blonde hair was looking like a bird's nest, half up and half down, and her black dress had a stain on the front.

'No, Mama, why?'

'He didn't come home last night. His bed hasn't been slept in,' she said shortly.

Kerensa came further into the room. 'Oh?' she frowned at her mother. 'I hope he's all right,' she replied. 'Where do you think he might be?'

'Goodness only knows,' her mother snapped. 'He went to a party last night. I can imagine the rest. I'd guess that he was too drunk to get home and someone took him in for the night.'

'In that case he won't be long, will he?' Kerensa sat down in the chair facing her mother. 'Are you feeling all right, Mama?' she said, reaching out a hand.

'Oh, I've got this cough that I can't seem to get of,' Celia replied, and rubbed a hand across her eyes. 'It kept me awake last night. So now I've got a raging headache as well.'

'What are you doing?' Kerensa asked, with her head on one side. She had never seen her mother poring over accounts and bills before. Usually she left all that side of things to Papa. 'I thought that it's about time that I had a look at our financial position for myself,' Celia said. 'And' – she looked her daughter full in the face – 'it's serious, Kerensa. More serious than I ever thought.' She broke off as a fit of coughing racked her body.

Kerensa left her seat and laid a hand on her shoulder in concern. She hadn't noticed until now, as she felt the sharpness of Celia's bones beneath her hand, how thin her mother had become. 'Can I get you anything, Mama? A glass of water?'

Celia waved a dismissive hand and dabbed her streaming eyes. 'No thank you, dear. I'll be all right. But you have to prepare yourself for a shock, Kerensa.'

The girl widened her eyes and felt her heart begin to beat faster as she wondered what was coming. 'I'm afraid darling, that you're going to have to leave school a little sooner than you would have done.' Celia raised her head and met Kerensa's startled gaze. 'You won't be going back next week after the Easter break. It will mean that you leave now – that you have already left in fact – and not at the end of the summer term as you would have done.'

The shock of it hit Kerensa like a punch in the stomach, and she moistened lips gone suddenly dry. 'Why Mama?' she whispered.

'Because we have no means of paying the school fees any longer,' replied her mother. She raised a hand to her forehead. 'I'm sorry darling, truly I am, but . . .' She spread her hands. 'We're going to have to make other economies too. I shall have to let Cook and Daisy go. We are all going to have to make sacrifices and work a lot harder if we want to go on living here, you see.'

Kerensa struggled to take it all in. 'But I haven't . . . said goodbye or anything. To my friends. I never thought . . .' She had never thought that the pattern of her life could possibly change so drastically in such a short time. One more term – a few weeks – and then her adult life would have begun. She had thought it all lay before her just waiting to be sampled. The parties, dances, the trips abroad that the other girls were talking about. Instead – this! Her head reeled. 'Cook? And Daisy, did you say? But, Mama, how will we manage?' Kerensa stared at her mother's white face, its pallor accentuated by the black of her mourning gown.

Celia bit her lip and slowly shook her head. 'We shall have to,' she replied. 'You're always saying how you love to cook – and you really do have a flair for it, dear. Now you can start cooking in earnest.' Kerensa swallowed on a dry throat and regarded her mother's implacable face. 'I shall have to attempt the housework myself.' The picture that came to Kerensa then, of her gently reared mother clad in an apron scrubbing floors was too much. The hot tears that she had been trying to suppress brimmed over regardless, and her shoulders heaved as she began to sob.

A week passed, then two and there was still no sign of Zack. Celia, frantic with this new worry, had contacted the police, local and county-wide, who had organized extensive searches, checked the hospitals for miles around in each direction, and had spoken to all his known friends, including Lennie Retallick and the men who had been at Silas's party. They had corroborated her suspicions that Zack had been drunk when he left that evening, but no one knew what had happened to him since. The authorities dragged the river and searched the coastline, but it was as if he had vanished off the face of the earth.

'There's nothing else we can do, is there?' Celia said hopelessly one morning, raising a tearful face to Kerensa.

'Only wait,' she replied, forcing a smile, 'and never give up hope. Perhaps we might even hear something today, Mama.'

Kerensa was so utterly weary of trying to raise her mother's spirits, that it was wearing her down, and if she didn't get out of the house soon she would scream. She had to get away from her mother, just to keep sane. Kerensa grabbed her hat and was through the door before Celia could ask her the where, the why, and the when of her hasty departure. Head down and her thoughts miles away, Kerensa headed towards Camborne intending to do a few errands.

It was not a quiet walk, but Kerensa was deaf and blind to the clatter of machinery and the shouts of the tin-streamers about their work as she followed the banks of the river and took the slope towards town. She only raised her eyes when she had to cross over the main shopping street, and was brought back to earth with a start when she heard a voice calling her name.

She turned, and suddenly there he was. Jago, beaming down at her, his face alight with some sort of excitement as he caught her by the elbow and exclaimed, 'Wonderful! Kerensa, you're just the person I wanted to see.

Have you got a minute to spare? Where are you going?'

Still in a daze, Kerensa shook her head and stammered, 'I . . . I don't know. A bit of shopping . . . I just had to get away – for some air,' she finished lamely.

'Good. Let's go to this new park of ours and sit down. I've had some stupendous news! I must tell you...' He seized her elbow and steered her out of the town towards the quiet greenness of the recently opened recreation ground.

'This was a wonderful way to commemorate the Jubilee,' Jago said looking round appreciatively as they sat down on a bench beneath a shady sycamore. 'Camborne's own spot of peace and quiet.' He waited until Kerensa was seated, then blurted, 'Look, I've had this letter.' His eyes were shining as he pulled a paper from his pocket and waved it under her nose before unfolding it. 'Listen to this. It came this morning and I must tell you before I burst with excitement.'

Kerensa's brows rose. This must indeed be important, for she had never seen Jago so animated. He usually kept his feelings well hidden, and guessed that he did so to protect himself from his father's scorn. 'Hurry up, then,' she said. 'I'm on the edge of my seat!'

'I can hardly *believe* it,' Jago said, glancing towards her. 'But this is from my former tutor at music college. He says,' and he peered at the letter as if to convince himself that it was true, 'that Edvard Grieg himself is coming to London to give a recital. As well as that, the maestro is going to hold some master-classes for a few chosen pupils from the college while he's over here – and he's putting my name forward for one of the places! Imagine!' He threw an arm around Kerensa's shoulders, drawing her to him in a bear hug and dropped a kiss on the top of her head.

'Kerensa,' he said, 'this is the opportunity of a lifetime. It could be the making of my career. To be able to say that I was a pupil of the great Grieg himself, however briefly!' He raised his eyes to the leafy canopy. 'Oh, just imagine the doors that would open for me!' Then, noticing at last the bemused expression on her face, Jago gave Kerensa his full attention and his brows drew together in a frown. 'You have *heard* of Grieg, I suppose? You do know who he *is*, don't you?'

'Er, yes . . . yes, I think so.' Kerensa stammered as she tried to concentrate. 'He's . . . Hungarian, isn't he?'

'No. Norwegian,' Jago snapped, and jumped to his feet. He turned on his heel and pointed a finger as he went on, 'He's only the greatest piano virtuoso and composer alive today – and you *think* you might have heard of him? You had piano lessons, didn't you? Good grief, Kerensa, what did they teach you at that fancy school?'

That stung. And coming as it did on top of Celia's recent pronounce-ment about school, it hurt. Kerensa sprang up and seized his arm, bring-ing him to a halt and looking into his face. 'Jago, of *course* I'm pleased for you – I'm thrilled to bits – but we can't all be musical prodigies! How much do *you* know about . . . about . . . cooking for example?' She said the first thing that came into her head, the subject which was so much on her mind recently. Her chin came up and she glared at him.

Taken aback, Jago stared at the fierce little figure, her dark eyes blaz-ing, and felt the smile slide from his face. He shot out a hand and jerked her down onto the seat again, giving her a little shake. 'Kerensa, I – I didn't expect that from you. I thought you would be as overjoyed as I am.'

His reproachful eyes burned into her soul, but she would *not* apologize. She gazed at his stony face and supposed that in different circumstances she would have been more enthusiastic. But the thought that this would mean goodbye to the only person she had ever cared deeply about, whom she had come to rely on and whom she now needed more than ever, was too much. Together with the dramatic change in their circumstances, and Papa's disappearance of which Jago appeared to know nothing, or had forgotten, was unbearable. But bear it she must. Feeling older than he, and overwhelmed with worry, Kerensa bowed her head and linked her fingers in her lap to stop their trembling.

A silence fell before she roused herself. 'When do you have to go?' she asked dully.

'Ah, yes.' At the change in tone of Jago's voice, she raised her head and her heart lurched as she saw the look on his face. 'That's what I wanted to tell you, as well as my news. At the end of the week, I'm afraid. This is the last time I shall see you for a while, Kerensa.' He avoided her eyes, taking his time about folding the letter and replacing it in his pocket.

Shock widened her eyes and sent a tremor through her whole body. Of course he had spoken before of leaving, but for that day to be so soon seemed yet another cruel twist of fate. 'Oh, no,' she whispered. But Kerensa could see the suppressed excitement still lurking behind Jago's eyes in spite of his sober expression and knew that she was lost.

'Don't look so sad, Kerensa,' he said, putting a finger under her chin. 'It won't be too bad. I'll get down for the occasional weekend, and a long break in the summer. And one day, when I've made my name and the money is there' – his eyes were far away in a dream now – 'then we'll travel the world together, you and I.'

Dreams, all dreams. Oh Jago, if only! He was away in his own world already and his eyes were glowing with visions of a golden future. 'In a few years I could be playing at all the capital cities – Paris, Rome, Vienna – oh Kerensa, imagine it!'

Kerensa nodded and swallowed hard. She could imagine it only too well. And could also imagine that to reach such a pinnacle was going to take far longer than Jago in his optimism dreamt of. Meanwhile, she would remain here, fighting her battles, with no one to sustain her through the hard times which she sensed were very near, and he would be far away in another world, a world of laughter and lilting music, of colour and crowds and bustle. Too busy to give her a thought.

Just as they were getting to know each other. Just as she had realized that she loved this man, really loved him, and would love him for the rest of her life. Kerensa stiffened her spine and tilted her chin. 'Then we must say goodbye,' she said, pasting a smile on her face and reaching out a gloved hand. Jago took it in both of his and drew her nearer. As their eyes met, Kerensa breathed in the scent of him, leaned into his warmth and looked deeply into his beloved face. His brotherly kiss on her cheek was light and fleeting as if he was already half in another world, but Kerensa would savour it and lock it away in her memory box. For dreams and memories would be all she would have to sustain her through the dark days ahead.

CHAPTER THREE

Kerensa and Celia were seriously economizing. Cook and Daisy had been dismissed, but with good references. John the groom had been kept on for the outside work, and for the rougher tasks like bringing in coal and chopping firewood.

While Kerensa, a copy of *Mrs Beeton's Book of Household Management* at her elbow, rolled up her sleeves and began to plumb its depths for simple meals that she could prepare for them both. At first it had seemed almost like a game, but the more she read, the more bowed-down she felt with the weight of it all.

She was glad of the occupation however, for she missed Papa sorely and the constant nagging worry about what had become of him was always at the back of her mind. She missed her school-friends as well and worried about her mother, who was so pale and had lost so much weight. Night after night, she could hear Celia's muffled weeping and after a few weeks of this strange new life, Kerensa felt that she had left childhood behind for ever. She had been pitch-forked into a totally alien, adult world for which nothing had prepared her, and which seemed to hold only drudgery and responsibilities.

For a long time Kerensa suppressed the inner feelings that wanted to scream, 'You're my *mother*, for goodness sake! You should be the stronger of us – I need to look up to you – I don't know how to cope with all this on my own!' And went on coping just the same.

'What do *you* think has happened to Papa?' she asked her mother at the end of a particularly trying day.

Celia was sitting at the kitchen table, her chin resting on her hand and a defeated look on her face. She raised tired eyes to Kerensa and her voice held a new tone of bitterness as she replied, 'I think the cowardly so-and-so has run off rather than face us after what he's done with our money.' Her jaw tightened. 'He's hiding out somewhere – maybe he's even left the country. He can't be dead else they would have found the body by now.'

With the first spark of spirit she had shown for weeks, Celia added, 'And quite honestly Kerensa, I just don't *care* any more.' Her expression hardened as she went on, 'And do you know what? If he turned up now I think I would kill him myself with my own bare hands.' Her fists clenched as if she imagined them round her husband's throat.

Kerensa slid into the seat opposite her mother. There was something she had always wanted to know and this seemed the time to find out. 'Mama,' she asked, 'why did you let him live off you all these years? I've often wondered why you gave him your money when all he did was waste it.'

Celia traced a pattern on the tablecloth with her fingernail. 'It all began after you were born, because I felt so guilty,' she said in a whisper.

'Guilty?' Kerensa frowned. 'What about?'

'It was like this.' Celia raised her head. 'I was told I could never have another child. And I knew that Zack desperately wanted a son.' Her eyes clouded. 'I loved him so much then, Kerensa, I would have done anything to make it up to him.'

'But it wasn't your fault!' Kerensa burst out.

'No, I know. But I tried to make up for it all the same, by giving Zack money for his pleasures out of my allowance. I felt I could hardly begrudge him a drink and a smoke with his friends, or a hand or two of cards, could I?' She spread her hands and her shoulders lifted. 'Then it went on from there and I couldn't stop you see, once I'd started.'

'Why didn't Papa ever get a job?'

Her mother shook her head. 'He tried to many times, but he never held anything down for long. "I was born to be a gentleman", he would say with that engaging grin of his, you know?' Kerensa nodded, grim-faced. She knew. Her father could charm the birds from the trees with that lop-sided grin and those twinkling eyes.

'Then he would take me in his arms when he came in with another tale of an unfair sacking, and say things like, "Any time I spend away from you, my love, is time wasted". And I would believe him, Kerensa! I loved him that much.' Her mother's eyes were far away as she added in an undertone, 'The only time he worked really hard was in searching for that mythical treasure which he was convinced he could find, no matter how many others had hunted for it in vain.'

She snapped back to meet Kerensa's gaze as she added, 'His rage when he failed too was terrifying, and after that we seemed to drift apart. Your father took to spending most of his time away from home. Then after a while he moved out of our bedroom because he said he didn't want to disturb me when he came in late.' A tear ran down her mother's cheek and Kerensa, with more compassion than she had been feeling recently, placed a comforting hand over hers.

Celia brushed her other hand across her eyes and her head moved from side to side as she said almost to herself, 'I *still* cannot understand why Father left the house to Zack, and I suppose I never will now.' She met Kerensa's eyes and went on, 'When he knew very well what he was like with money, too.'

Kerensa shrugged and rose to her feet. 'As you said, Mama, I suppose we'll never know.'

'Strange thing about old Zack, eh?' Silas raised his head as Lennie Retallick entered the office and banged the door behind him. 'Heard anything, have you?'

The other man shook his head. 'Not yet. Shouldn't be surprised if he's too afraid to go home and face his wife.'

A thin smile played over Silas's features and he nodded. 'Guess he's holed up somewhere until he thinks her shock's worn off.'

'Been over there yet, have you?' Lennie enquired, his round eyes avid for news.

'Not yet. Haven't told my own family either. But soon, soon,' said Silas and rubbed his hands together.

'Right, then.' Lennie drew closer and faced Silas across the desk as he stared him straight in the eye. 'Now look here. I did what you wanted – and you've got your fine house. Now I want what you promised me. So how about it?'

'You did Lennie, you did. And a fine job you made of it, too. So of course, you shall have what you want.' Silas leaned back in his chair with a sly grin. 'It's the Treneer girl, isn't it? You want her. Well, I'm working on it, boy. Be patient.'

Silas was still grinning to himself next morning as he made his way down the hall and, when he heard the sound of piano music drifting towards him, paused for a moment, then entered the room.

Jago, packed and ready to leave, was getting in a last practice before his departure that afternoon. Thinking himself alone in the house, he had been deep in a Mozart piano sonata, and jumped in surprise as his father entered. The melody came to a discordant halt and he turned abruptly to look over his shoulder.

'Sorry I interrupted you, boy; carry on, carry on.' Silas beamed and came to lean on the top of the piano, tapping his fingers on the shining wood. Jago, open-mouthed, could only stare at his parent. What was up with him? Suspicious, because Silas in jovial mood usually meant that someone was about to suffer for it, Jago murmured some reply and flexed his fingers.

'Nice little tune that,' Silas added, as he hummed a few bars and beamed down at him.

Jago, feeling that some reply was called for, managed to stammer, 'It's – er – Mozart.'

Silas straightened and rocked back and forth as he said with an expansive gesture, 'Maybe all that money I spent on sending you to the Royal Academy wasn't entirely wasted after all.'

Flabbergasted, Jago changed the subject. 'Aren't you going in to the foundry today, Father? You're usually away by now.' Which was exactly why he had chosen to start practising early.

'Later, my boy, later.' Silas took a turn about the room. 'I've got a call to make first. Going over to Penhallow – got a bit of business with the Treneers today.'

'The Treneers?' Jago's brows shot up and it was on the tip of his tongue to ask what and why, but any show of interest might rebound on him, and that just wasn't worth it. He would find out eventually.

'Yes,' Silas replied. 'I'll see you at lunch, my boy. Then I'll drive you to the station, eh?' He strolled towards the door merrily whistling, and Jago cringed as he recognized the mangled version of Mozart's 'nice little tune'.

He rose to his feet and paced restlessly around the room. Amazing to think that tonight he would be in London! Back in the same lodgings he had shared with Hal and the other students. Jago gazed out of the window, seeing not the gentle fold of green fields in the distance, but the bustling streets of a big city, with its noise, dirt and traffic. And one day...he lost himself in dreams of the future.

One morning, Kerensa was struggling to make a white sauce to accompany the fillets of hake which they were having for lunch. The fish was steaming away on the range while she stirred and frowned, pounding at the congealing lumps with a wooden spoon. Oh, Mrs Beeton, she sighed, how easy you make it all sound. Surely even you couldn't turn this sticky mess into the smooth and creamy paste that it's meant to be.

At the back of her mind she could hear the doorbell ringing, but Daisy would answer that, of course. Now . . . this sauce . . . Daisy! Suddenly the penny dropped – there was no Daisy any more, and Mama was upstairs out of earshot. Kerensa pushed the saucepan to the back of the range, tore off her apron and ran down the passage.

She pulled open the heavy front door and recognized the man standing on the top step. 'Oh – Mr Cardrew,' she said breathlessly.

'Good morning Miss Treneer,' Silas lifted his bowler hat. 'Is your mother at home today?'

Recovering her composure, Kerensa opened the door wider. 'Yes, yes, she is. Please come in and I'll tell her you're here.' She took his hat and cane and hung them on the hall-stand, then ushered him into the parlour just as her mother was coming down the stairs.

'I thought I heard voices,' Celia said as she joined them. 'Mr Cardrew.' Her voice rose in slight surprise. 'Good morning.'

He inclined his head. 'Mrs Treneer. I hope I find you well.'

Celia indicated a chair. 'Please, won't you sit down?'

Kerensa's first thought was that he might have some news of her father, so she slipped into a seat in case she missed something.

'Have you – have you heard anything of Zack?' asked her mother, who was obviously thinking the same thing.

'I'm afraid not,' Silas replied. 'However, the reason I have called on you does concern him indirectly.'

'Oh?' Celia's eyes widened.

Silas cleared his throat and reached into a pocket, pulling out a piece of paper. 'I'm afraid this is going to be a great shock for you, madam.' He paused and Celia's hand flew to her throat.

'Yes?' she whispered.

'Yes.' Silas paused and held her gaze. 'This is an I.O.U. – a promissory note, you understand? Signed by your husband. We were gambling on the cards you know, the other evening. Zachary placed a wager and unfortunately for you, he lost it.'

Kerensa saw the little colour that remained in her mother's cheeks slowly drain away and the hand she extended was trembling. 'You – you mean that we owe you money?' Her voice dropped to a whisper.

'Not money, Mrs Treneer, no,' and Kerensa saw her mother relax with relief.

'Please read this carefully.' Silas handed over the document. Celia took it as if it were alive and began to read aloud. ' "Should I, Zachary George Treneer of the house named Penhallow near Camborne lose this wager, on my honour I promise to Silas Cardrew of Bareppa, the aforementioned Penhallow as forfeit." '

She raised her head and looked at Silas in disbelief. 'You don't mean – this doesn't mean' – she tapped a finger on the paper and her eyes widened – 'that Zack gambled away our *home?*'

Gravely Silas inclined his head.

Celia sprang to her feet with a cry, her eyes huge in her drawn face. 'He staked *Penhallow* on the turn of a card?' she whispered. 'Is *that* what you're saying?' Kerensa ran to her mother's side as Celia drew in a shuddering breath, swayed on her feet and the document fluttered to the floor.

'But he can't have – he wouldn't – Papa wouldn't do a thing like that!' Kerensa protested, even as the words and his unmistakable signature burned into her head like letters of fire, scorching it. And the fire shrivelled to ashes the unconditional love she had always given her father, shattering her childish illusions. It was the final step in her growing up.

'I'm afraid he has,' said Silas, rising to his feet and hovering over them like a figure of doom. His voice carried an ominous ring as he added, 'As you can see, Penhallow now belongs to me.'

The words were hardly out of his mouth before Celia gave a moan and collapsed in Kerensa's arms. She gently lowered her to the settee and reached for a cushion as Silas turned to leave. Over his shoulder he said, 'Tell your mother when she recovers, that I require her to vacate my property as soon as possible. Good day, Miss Treneer. I'll see myself out.'

★

It had been just over a month. Four weeks since their lives had been turned upside down, and Kerensa's childhood snatched away from her forever. During the harrowing time since Silas's devastating visit, Celia had become so distraught as to be almost useless and there were moments when Kerensa thought that her mother would go completely out of her mind. Picking things up and putting them down again, weeping and wringing her hands, she drifted about the house like a ghost.

Eventually, feeling as if their roles had been completely reversed, Kerensa lost all patience and resorted to bullying her mother as if she were the adult and Celia a recalcitrant child. And the most frightening part of that, was to see her mother actually doing as she was told.

On the day of their departure from Penhallow, Kerensa took a last stroll through the quiet rooms to say goodbye to the home she had known forever. She leaned on a windowsill and looked out over the grounds. At least no one could rob her of her memories of dreamy days in summer, sitting under the willow tree with a book. Of crisp and frosty winter days when the lake lay still as a steel plate beneath a slate-grey sky, the reeds at its edge as stiff and black as a Japanese painting.

She sighed and straightened up. Already the house felt as if it were withdrawing from her, shutting her out. Familiar objects had become strangers now, somebody else's property. Echoes of her footsteps on the staircase sounded like a person following close behind to usher her out, eager to be rid of her and to take her place. How stupid, she told herself. With a sob she turned and ran down the stairs, and when she reached the bottom took one last look over her shoulder. 'Don't worry – I'll be back,' she whispered to the silent rooms, 'I swear it. I *will* come back – someday, somehow. So wait for me.' She closed the door firmly behind her and ran down the steps without looking back.

Kerensa had had to resort to bullying her mother into action again and had told her flatly that if they were to find anywhere at all to live, Celia would have to sell her jewellery, the only thing of value they had left. There was more weeping and wailing and wringing of hands, but once she had been persuaded to do so, it eventually brought in enough to cover a modest rent for a few weeks if they were careful.

So they had spent hours scouring the offices of estate agents and tramping the streets of Camborne looking for somewhere affordable, but soon discovered that 'affordable' meant nothing larger than a tiny and insalubrious cottage in one of the back streets of the town.

Tired and dispirited, they returned home after another morning of fruitless searching, to find an envelope on the doormat. Celia picked it up and drifted into the drawing-room as Kerensa went down the passage to put away their shopping. 'Kerensa!' called her mother, as she cast her eyes over the contents of the letter, 'Come and listen to this! You'll never guess who it's from.'

Kerensa came running from the kitchen to look over her mother's shoulder and her eyes widened as she skimmed the single page. It was brief and to the point.

"*... should you have difficulty in finding suitable accommodation which accords with your means, I have pleasure in offering you the above property as a personal favour. The rental you will note is lower than the average for a cottage of this kind and I hope you will give the matter your due consideration. Yrs. etc ... Silas Cardrew.*" An estate agent's card was enclosed with the details.

'Oh, what a surprise!' Kerensa took a step back. 'Isn't that kind of him, Mama?'

'*Kind?*' Celia's eyes flashed and she tossed the letter aside. 'The cheek of the man! Not content with turning us out of our home, now he wants to gloat about it!'

'Oh, I don't know. He didn't *have* to send this. It's not as if he's responsible for us. After all, it's not his fault that Papa lost the house.'

'Huh,' retorted Celia, 'I wouldn't trust that man out of my sight. He's too smooth. And his eyes are cold. I think he likes having control over people,' she added shrewdly.

Kerensa was studying the card which had come with the letter and didn't reply. 'But he's right, Mama,' she said, looking up, 'we'd never get a cottage like this for that money – you know what the ones we've seen have been like. And this is at the end of a terrace, it says. So we shall only have neighbours on one side. That'll be nice. I think we ought to take it.'

'Well, we'll go and have a look,' Celia said grudgingly, 'and see what condition it's in, but I wouldn't be surprised if there's a catch in this somewhere.'

'Oh, look, Mama,' Kerensa said encouragingly, stiffening her spine as Celia stared around with despair in her eyes, 'being on the end of the row, there's a little strip of garden too. You'll be able to grow some of your favourite flowers. It won't be too bad here, you'll see.'

She regarded the plot through Celia's eyes. The whole of it would have fitted onto the front lawn of Penhallow with room to spare. By the rows of rotting cabbage stumps, and the smell of them, it was obvious that the previous tenant had used it for growing his vegetables. In one corner stood the privy with its earth closet, modestly screened by a gloomy laurel bush; in the other was a strip of brick paving with a washing line strung above it. 'I'll help you dig it over,' Kerensa went on, forcing a smile to her face, 'and we'll soon have it transformed – the house too – you just wait.'

'Yes dear,' was her mother's only reply, as she trudged back into the cottage.

'Mama, I've decided that I'm going to look for employment,' Kerensa said a few days later, lifting her chin and meeting her mother's eyes as she looked up from the local paper. The newspaper was spread out over the kitchen table of the cottage and the kettle was murmuring softly to itself on the gleaming range. Kerensa had spent most of the morning black-leading the monstrous thing and using brass polish on its many knobs.

Over the previous weeks she had also scrubbed out the whole place and persuaded a local handyman to dab some fresh paint on the worst spots, in exchange for several dinners in lieu of wages. 'All right, my handsome,' he had said, and Kerensa had seen the look of pity in his eyes. It was the pity that affected her most deeply, and she had had to leave the room to hide her tears.

The furniture was minimal, but together she and her mother had hung bright curtains at the windows and placed potted plants on the sill, doing their best to turn the drab surroundings into something approaching comfort. Although compared with Penhallow the place was small to the point of being claustrophobic, Kerensa hoped that in time, Celia might adjust to it. As their few relations had turned their backs on Celia when she'd married Zack against all advice, she would have to: there was no one else to help them.

Her mother just entering the room, stared at her before she replied. 'Employment?' Celia arched her brows. 'You mean that you're thinking of going out to work?' She steadied herself with one hand on the back of a chair.

'Yes, Mama.' Kerensa regarded her mother steadily. 'Think about it. What are we going to live on when the money runs out?' In her new role as an adult, she was brutally frank. 'We have be realistic.' She spread her hands to emphasize her point as she went on, 'We have no income and the rent has to be paid, otherwise we shall have no home either.'

'But what will you do? What can you do? You're only just out of school

– you're not trained in anything . . .' Celia shook her head as if in disbelief, then raised a hand to her forehead.

'I can cook, Mama,' Kerensa said firmly. 'You remarked yourself how
competent I've become since I've been making our meals, do you remember?'

Celia nodded and sank onto a ladder-back chair beside her daughter.
'Yes, but—'

'So,' Kerensa broke in, 'I shall get a position as a cook – or maybe assistant cook,' she said, realizing her limitations, 'if there's one available.' She
raised her chin and stared her mother down. She would never for a
moment let her composure slip and reveal the stark terror she felt of what
she was proposing. But they desperately needed money and this was the
only way.

'You don't mean – you *can't* mean – that you're going into domestic
service!' Celia's horrified look raised her eyebrows to her hairline. 'Oh
Kerensa, really,' she said with contempt. 'How can you possibly sit there
and tell me you're seriously thinking of becoming a *servant*?'

Kerensa realized then how wide the gulf was between them. Celia
would never understand the reality of their new circumstances. Oh, *Papa*!
Kerensa gritted her teeth and thought that she could willingly help Celia
to strangle him. How could you desert us so? When it's all your fault that
we're in this mess! Oh, it isn't *fair*! She bit her bottom lip to stop its
wobble.

But who said that life was ever fair? She had learnt that lesson quickly
enough. Kerensa drew in a deep breath and her spine stiffened. 'Mama!'
She banged a fist on the table and her mouth tightened in anger. Anger
was one way of staving off the tears which were never far away. 'How can
I get *through* to you that we're in no position to be choosy?' She began to
pace up and down. 'That we no longer live the comfortable life we've been
used to. We've come down in the world.' She waved a hand that encompassed the room. 'We are working-class people now. So face up to it.'

'Oh my dear child,' Celia twittered, 'you sound so *hard*.'

Kerensa blinked and swallowed the lump in her throat. Feeling very
much alone, she glared at Celia. 'One of us has to be,' she snapped.

Next morning, Kerensa was going through the unfamiliar experience of
doing the household shopping. They had to eat, and the sooner she
learned what things cost the sooner she would be able to calculate their
weekly expenditure.

But it was a tedious and time-consuming task. Especially at the butcher's, where choosing what to buy from the bewildering variety of cuts of meat on display was a nightmare in itself. Waiting in the queue for her turn, Kerensa scuffed a toe in the sawdust on the floor and studied the diagrams of sides of beef and mutton which decorated the walls. Learn, learn and remember, she muttered under her breath, this is important. Lamb and mutton: best end ... scrag end ... cutlets. Beef: shin ... topside ... fillet steak. ... It was too much, there were so *many*.

The grocer's was easier, but by the time he'd sliced the bacon, weighed out the broken biscuits that Kerensa wanted as they were cheaper, and searched in the back room for a fresh supply of blue paper bags for the sugar, the time had flown, and she still needed to get some black darning wool to mend a hole in her stocking.

She swept all her purchases into her basket and ran down the steps. Wool – she would have to go back to the draper and haberdasher's shop in Church Street. Bustling along with her head down, Kerensa jumped as she heard someone call her by name.

'Nell!' she cried in delight. 'Oh, how lovely to see you. How are you? What are you doing, shopping? Are you on your own?'

'I'm just waiting for Mama – she's posting a letter, then we're going to look at dress materials for my coming out dance. Isn't it exciting?'

'Oh, yes,' Kerensa replied. 'Nell, I haven't seen you for so long.' She smiled up at the perfect English-rose face and golden curls of Eleanor Robartes, her friend from school. Taking in the peach-coloured gown with matching velvet trim, and the fashionable little hat, she wished she had worn something more attractive than her washed-out cotton skirt and blouse. But she'd been too preoccupied to think.

And she was saving her better outfit for the interview about a position, which had been arranged for this afternoon. Far from telling Eleanor about that, Kerensa hadn't even told her own mother. Her stomach did a flip at the very thought of the ordeal to come.

'Well, you just disappeared,' said the other girl. 'One day you were sitting there at the desk next to me, then you vanished and we heard that you'd left school for good. You could at least have said goodbye,' she added in a tone of pique.

'Oh, I wanted to!' Kerensa cried. 'But so much happened after that. Did you know—' She broke off and followed Eleanor's gaze which was fixed with distaste on Kerensa's basket. On the top so as not to squash it she had placed the brown paper parcel of meat, which in spite of her care had started to ooze a sticky trail from one corner. On the wrapper was stamped 'W.F. Rodda. Family Butcher', in large blue letters.

'Oh! Are you shopping for your own *comestibles?*' The other girl's lip curled and she took a step back. 'Why on earth don't you send one of the servants?'

'Don't you know . . . that is, haven't you heard. . . ?' Kerensa felt herself redden with embarrassment. 'Um – we're living, Mama and me, in . . . reduced circumstances now?'

One daintily gloved hand flew to the cupid's-bow mouth and the sapphire eyes widened. 'But of course, how silly of me. I did overhear something when Mama and I were attending Mrs Basset's At Home the other day. Wasn't there some . . . well, some hint of' – Eleanor lowered her voice – '*scandal*, concerning your Papa?' She drew a little closer. 'I didn't hear the full story, because when Mama realized I was listening she changed the subject.'

'Yes,' said Kerensa tartly and glared. 'Well it's been nice seeing you, Nell, but I must call in at this shop for some darning wool before I forget it.'

Her friend's delicately arched brows rose and she smiled. 'You mean embroidery wool don't you, for your Berlin work? Or are you doing gros-point now?'

Kerensa looked stonily into the laughing face. 'No, Nell. I meant darning wool. Black. To mend a hole in my stocking, you see?' She noticed with grim satisfaction how the smile slid slowly from the perfect features and added, 'Now I must go – goodbye.' Head held high and back stiff, she swept into the emporium as if she owned it.

When she came out again, Eleanor was nowhere to be seen. Kerensa glanced up at the town clock. She shouldn't have stayed talking to her for so long really. With hindsight, she regretted being so sharp with her too, but her former friend simply had no idea – and was another reminder of just how much she, Kerensa, had lost.

She hurried up the road and arrived panting at the front door, with just enough time to drop the groceries, tidy herself and leave the house again for her appointment.

Kerensa arrived back an hour later, just as Celia who had been taking a walk in the park, was coming up the road in the opposite direction. But seized by a sudden fit of coughing, Celia could only wave at her daughter as she reached the house first, opened the door and leaned heavily on the frame to catch her breath.

'Mama! Are you all right?' Kerensa took Celia's arm, led her into the parlour and settled her in a chair. 'I'll get a glass of water for you.'

By the time she returned, Celia had recovered herself enough to take a grateful sip. 'I must have walked too far,' she said. 'I'm feeling quite worn out.' She placed the glass on the small table at her side. 'But where have you been, Kerensa?'

Kerensa, still on her knees at her mother's side from where she had proffered the glass, said with a smile, 'I went to enquire about a position, Mama. And I was successful.' She rose to her feet as Celia sat up straighter and their eyes met.

'Oh my dear girl! Tell me all about it,' said her mother.

Kerensa held her gaze as she replied, 'I've been taken on as assistant cook and parlourmaid, Mama.' She paused and drew a breath. 'To the Cardrew family. Of Penhallow.'

CHAPTER FOUR

'*Penhallow!*' Celia had jerked upright to regard Kerensa with horror. 'You can't – you wouldn't – you haven't . . .' Her eyes widened. 'A servant, in your own *home*?' She laid a hand on her daughter's arm and looked reproachfully into her face. 'Kerensa, how can you do it? Isn't it bad enough being a servant at all, without the humiliation, the embarrassment – oh, don't you have any *pride*?'

Kerensa jumped up and faced her mother with arms akimbo. 'Pride won't pay the rent or put food on the table,' she snapped.

'Well, I think it's all very awkward,' Celia said with a frown. 'Anyway, who did you see – when do you start – what are the conditions?'

'One thing at a time, Mama.' Kerensa held up a hand. 'I was interviewed by Mrs Nance, the housekeeper. I should think she's pretty strict. Likes things done properly, you know? Apparently Miss Grace Cardrew is in charge of the household, although I shouldn't think she's much older than me.'

Kerensa unable to keep still, came back to perch on the arm of her mother's chair, smoothing down her skirt as she added, 'Mrs Nance said that these black dresses of my own will do, and that she'll provide me with caps and aprons. I'm to start next Monday. And Mama.' She caught her bottom lip between her teeth. This was the part she had been dreading telling her mother. 'I shall have to live in, of course.'

For a moment the silence was absolute, then Celia whirled around and regarded her daughter with a look of horror. 'Live *in?*' she repeated.

Kerensa nodded. 'It's an accepted condition which goes with the place, you see.'

'But you can't possibly! What about *me?*' Celia cried, one hand to her breast. 'How can you be so selfish!' Her voice rose up the scale. 'Kerensa, you know how much I depend on you these days, how am I going to manage? You never gave me a thought in this hare-brained scheme of yours, did you? And knowing how unwell I am, too.' The tirade ended in a pitiful catch of the throat.

Kerensa ignored it. She would have wept, but the hurt went too deep for tears. She saw for the first time the self-centred, spoilt child who had always lain behind Celia's cool façade. And any respect or filial love she had felt towards her melted away like frost in sunshine. Only duty remained. She would always do her duty to her mother.

But with the loss first of Grandpapa, then Papa, followed so swiftly by Penhallow – and now this, Kerensa felt as alone in the world and as drained as if she had been bereaved four times over. She drew in a breath and held her head high.

'On the contrary, Mother. I was about to say that as I am allowed one half day off a week, plus Sundays. I can come and look after you and the house then. I can do any errands and shopping, any cleaning that's too heavy for you, and the washing too. You'll be able to manage very well.'

Kerensa might as well not have spoken, for far from appearing contrite, her mother ignored her. 'And – and I shall be alone in the house! At night! Anything could happen.' This brought on such a fit of coughing that she was left gasping for breath and sank back into the chair again with one hand to her brow.

Hardening her heart and refusing to bow to this moral blackmail, Kerensa gritted her teeth and ploughed on. 'You have neighbours, Mother. Mr and Mrs Spargo next door are perfectly pleasant and friendly—'

But Celia broke in before she could finish. 'The Spargos?' Her lip curled. 'Pah! John Spargo is a common miner and his wife's a charwoman. You expect me to mix with people like that? Really Kerensa, you surprise me.' She dabbed at damp eyes.

Kerensa swept out of the room. Stay any longer and she might say something she would regret later, for there was only so much she could take. She snatched her hat from its peg and left the house.

'Good morning Miss Treneer.' Kerensa wheeled around abruptly. Deep in her own thoughts, the voice at her shoulder had startled her and she whirled round to look at the man who had spoken. The front doors of the houses opened straight on to the road and he was standing only inches away.

'Good morning Mr—?' she replied hesitantly. 'I'm afraid I don't know ...' But there was something vaguely familiar about those prominent blue eyes and the carroty hair which had been revealed when he raised his bowler hat.

'Retallick, miss, Lennie Retallick. You may remember I attended your late grandfather's funeral.'

So that's where it had been. 'Ah, yes, of course,' Kerensa replied. 'You're a friend of Mr Cardrew, I believe.' Her expression hardened.

The man put his hands in his pockets and rocked back on the heels of his polished black boots. Fascinated, Kerensa noticed that there were blocks on the heels which raised his height. Even so, he was not much taller than she. 'He's my employer, not exactly a friend,' he replied. 'I work as his agent, overseeing sales of Cardrew's supplies to the various mining companies. I also collect the rents on his properties.' His lips parted to reveal yellowish teeth below the ginger moustache.

Mid-twenties or thereabouts, Kerensa thought, as she surveyed the skinny figure, but acts a lot older. The way he speaks sounds false to me, she added shrewdly, like a working man trying to put on airs. The same pretence which makes him add inches to his height. He's a small man trying to act big. She smiled back at him coolly.

'I spoke to introduce myself as your neighbour,' he went on. 'I live at the other end of the street, at No. 26. With the green paintwork.'

'Oh I see.' Kerensa turned to look at the house he had indicated. It was slightly larger than the rest of the terrace, double-fronted and set back from the road. 'Well, how do you do, Mr Retallick,' she said firmly, extending the fingertips of her gloved hand. 'It's nice to have met you, but I must go – I have some errands to do,' she lied.

'Quite so, miss.' He bowed over the hand. 'But if I can ever be of assistance in any way, either to you or your charming mother, don't hesitate to call on me.' He gave a smile which was not reflected in his eyes. 'Two ladies living alone, you know ... no man in the house. Camborne can be quite a rough area when the miners have been drinking, especially at night.'

'You're very kind.' Etiquette demanded that Kerensa should reply with courtesy, so she pasted another smile to her face and added, 'Perhaps your wife would care to come round for a cup of tea one afternoon and meet Mama.'

'Alas, no wife, Miss Treneer.' He shrugged his shoulders. 'I've lived alone since my dear mother died two years ago. She was widowed when I was a child.' The smile flashed again briefly before he tipped his hat and added, 'But forgive me, I'm keeping you. You will remember though, won't you, that I am always there should you need a friend to turn to? And, of course, I shall be calling for the rent money each week, so I'll be seeing you again soon. Good day to you, Miss Treneer.'

'Good day, Mr Retallick, and thank you.' Kerensa feeling slightly unsettled, went on her way wondering what there was about the man that had made her instantly dislike him. He had been perfectly polite, after all, and it would be reassuring to have a friendly neighbour, but even so. . . .

'How did you eventually persuade the Treneers to sell the house, Papa?' Grace asked, as they arrived back at their new home from a shopping trip to Truro and she climbed down from the carriage. 'I know you said that they didn't intend to at first.' She picked up her bag, reached inside the vehicle for the lighter items of shopping and looked enquiringly at her father.

Silas paused. He regarded his daughter's innocent upturned face and did some quick thinking. 'Oh, um, when Zack Treneer disappeared like that, his wife was so upset that she could no longer bear to live there any more.' The lie came glibly to his tongue. Silas had been used to lying and bluffing his way through life, his creed being that if a lie were more expedient, then why tell the truth? Give people what they wanted to believe, tell them only what they needed to know, and everyone was happy.

'Leave those bags, Grace,' he ordered, 'you don't have to carry your own shopping any more. Roberts can bring them in for you.' The man touched his cap as the carriage trundled through the arch towards the stable-yard.

'I'm just going to change my gown, Papa, then I'm meeting Dan,' Grace said, as they walked up the steps together and through the newly painted front door. 'I thought I'd show him over the house, then we shall go for a walk. It's such a lovely day, isn't it?' She raised her face to the sun, now strengthening in intensity as May gave way to early June.

Silas paused in the hall and frowned. 'Grace, there's something I want to say to you,' he growled.

'Yes?' His daughter's eyes widened as she unfastened the strings of her bonnet. She removed it and placed it on the hall-stand, tidying her light-brown hair with her hands as she glanced in the mirror. The eyes looking back at her were glowing softly at the thought of seeing the man who meant everything to her. 'What's that, Papa?'

'Come this way,' said Silas, pushing open the door of the room which housed Jago's piano as well as most of the books which had come with the house.

Silas sank into a deep armchair and gestured with one hand for her to do the same. Grace seated herself in the comfortable chair opposite her father and looked appreciatively around the room at the improvements they had made since they had come here. The room still smelt of new paint. To one side, a polished wooden desk held a globe of the world and a pile of music scores. Bookshelves behind glass doors lined one of the walls and at the bay window hung long curtains of moss-green velvet, looped back with tassels to frame a view of the garden. Oh yes, a painting on that wall would look nice. . . .

'Grace, are you listening?' Silas's voice broke in on her thoughts.

'Oh – yes. Yes, of course I am, Papa.'

'Right. I want you to give up seeing that young man.'

Grace gasped and felt the colour drain from her face as she saw her father's stern expression. 'Give Dan *up*?' One hand flew to her mouth. 'But – but why? We've been walking out for over a year now and you've never said a thing before . . .'

Silas had taken out his foul-smelling pipe. 'That's what I mean,' he replied gruffly through the corner of his mouth, 'that was before. Before we moved into this place, I mean.' He removed the pipe and pointed the stem towards her. 'We've come up in the world now Grace, and I intend to see my children mixing with the gentry – not common mining folk – and being accepted by them.'

'But Dan's not common!' Grace blurted, as her father raised a hand to silence her.

'You see, it's too late for me – everybody knows that I'm a self-made man,' he said. 'But the next generation – you and the boys,' he said, meeting his daughter's astounded gaze, 'will lead a very different life. There's to be no marrying a working man, my girl. Oh no. I'm going to see that you mix with young men of the county set from now on – the cream of the landed classes. You make a good marriage and we shall be right up there with the best of them.'

Silas knocked out his pipe in the empty grate and put it back in his pocket. 'We have plenty of room here to hold gatherings of every kind and we'll be entertaining all the best families from now on. Oh yes.' A self-satisfied smile spread across his face. 'Silas Cardrew has become a man to be reckoned with. You're a lucky girl, Grace. Our way of life is going to reflect my position as one of Cornwall's leading industrialists, and my children will reap the benefit of it all.'

'But Papa, I *love* Dan,' Grace whispered, both hands to her cheeks as she stared at her father in disbelief. 'And he loves me, I know he does. Truly.'

'Pah! Love? The stuff of penny novelettes,' Silas snorted. 'You'll soon find plenty of others who'll love you when they find out how much I'm worth,' he chuckled.

But he saw with surprise how Grace's eyes flashed, and two spots of crimson flared in her pale face. 'And what makes you think that the gentry will *want* to come here and mix with us?' she snapped, her head held proudly high. Silas was momentarily silenced. Was his normally biddable daughter answering back? 'Or be falling over themselves to make our acquaintance just because we've moved into Penhallow?' she added.

'But . . . Joe Treneer was always on first-name terms with the Bassets and the Vyvyans, even after he couldn't afford to keep up with them,' Silas blustered.

Unable to keep still any longer, Grace sprang to her feet. 'The Treneers, Father, were old money,' she said with scorn. 'It goes deeper than you realize – it's the bloodline, and breeding, that counts. Not how well off you are. It'll take far longer than one generation to get us accepted in *that* kind of society, I can tell you.'

They were still glaring at each other when there came the sound of footsteps on the tiled floor outside and Richard poked his head around the door. 'Oh, there you are, Father. Roberts told me you were back. I wanted to ask you— Grace?' he broke off in mid-sentence. 'What's up? Is something wrong?'

His sister, her hand over her mouth, gave a strangled sob and fled from the room, with Richard looking after her in surprise. 'What's the matter with her?' He raised his eyebrows and turned to his father for an explanation.

'Nothing that she won't soon get over,' said Silas dismissively. 'Women! There's no pleasing them.' He looked his elder son in the eye as he rose to his feet. 'I was only pointing out to her that now we've gone up in the world, we shall be mixing with the county set – moving in higher circles, haw, haw!' He clapped Richard on the shoulder. 'You'll be pleased, boy, won't you, eh?'

'I certainly shall,' Richard grinned, with the avaricious gleam in his small eyes that was a reflection of his father's. 'I'm dying to get some proper hunting in – maybe I can join the Four Burrow now.'

Silas beamed. 'Good man,' he said, and deep in conversation, father and son left the room together.

'What you mean – you used to *live* here?' Florrie Scoble the housemaid, had been sweeping the kitchen floor. Now she sat back on her heels grasping the dustpan in one hand and brush in the other as she stared up at Kerensa with her mouth open.

In the centre of the room, at the deal table carefully covered with a protective blanket, Kerensa was doing the ironing. She passed a hand over her hot forehead as she crossed the room to the range and exchanged her cooling iron for a newly heated one. 'What I said, Flo,' she replied.

'But what you doing here being a *servant* then?' Beneath her mob-cap the other girl's green eyes widened. About the same age, the two of them shared a room in the servant's attic and Kerensa was thankful that they got on fairly well, otherwise the situation would have been intolerable. 'Simple. We came down in the world,' Kerensa said briskly, sliding the iron over a starched white cotton apron, not forgetting the ties. The housekeeper was very particular about the linen, as she was about everything. 'But Mr Cardrew was very good to us and let us have one of his cottages at a specially reduced rent.'

'Caw! It must feel some funny to change places,' said practical Florrie, returning to her work. Kerensa nodded. No one would ever know what it was costing her to remember her place. To keep her eyes demurely cast down, not to answer back, and to become as invisible as possible if she should come across a member of 'the family'.

She swallowed hard and nodded. 'I – I just can't put into words how awful it is, Flo. I keep imagining I'm dreaming and that I'll wake up to find everything like it used to be.' Kerensa tightened her lips, laid aside the apron and reached for a pile of stiff shirt-collars. She rubbed furiously at them until the lump in her throat had subsided.

It had felt almost surreal to walk into Penhallow again and feel the familiar walls reaching out to enfold her in their embrace. Familiar, but at the same time completely alien, for its three storeys had been transformed from the shabby-genteel home she had known and loved all her life, into a showpiece for Silas's wealth.

The rooms on the ground floor were crammed with expensive objects.

The drawing-room was cluttered with low tables where ranks of orna-
ments stood upon chenille runners and lace-edged cloths. A bowl of
waxed fruit beneath a glass dome now stood on the chiffonier, replacing
the Dresden china shepherdess who had stood smiling down at her for as
long as Kerensa could remember. She had found the shepherdess in the
dustbin one day, her face chipped and her expression changed into an evil
leer, and had dissolved into tears as if an old friend had died.

Kerensa came swiftly back to earth at the jangling of keys, and turned
as Alice Nance swept into the room. 'Ah, Kerensa. Haven't you finished
that ironing yet?' The tall, black-clad figure hovered at her elbow. 'Yes, as
a matter of fact I have.' Kerensa tossed her head and looked the woman in
the eye. Beneath the starched white cap, gimlet eyes glanced over
Kerensa's work, then met her gaze as the girl silently defied her to find
fault with something.

There was nothing, so she retorted instead, 'Well, we'll have less of
your dumb insolence, miss, and a little more respect,' she hissed. 'You
needn't think you can put on airs with me, or think you're a cut above the
rest of us because of where you come from.' Kerensa said nothing, but
stared her down until the housekeeper sniffed and turned on her heel.
'Well, don't just stand there,' she said over her shoulder, 'go and put it all
away, then you can start making pastry for the pies. Cook will require your
help for the rest of the day.'

'Yes, Mrs Nance,' said Kerensa, replying obediently and biting her
tongue as the woman crossed the room. Much as it went against the grain
to do so, obedient she must be. She needed this place. Kerensa had been
readily accepted by the rest of the staff, who all felt sorry for her and were
all basically friendly except for the housekeeper, who never lost a chance
to find fault, or to put her down with some cutting remark.

'Sour old bat,' remarked Florrie cheerfully under her breath, and stuck
out her tongue at the woman's retreating back. 'How's your mama getting
used to the change, then?' She put her brushes and dustpan away in the
broom cupboard and reached for a duster.

'She isn't,' replied Kerensa and gave a bleak smile. 'I worry about her,
Florrie. Not so much because she hasn't settled, I don't think she'll ever
accept her circumstances, but she seems to be so poorly and weak.' She
frowned.

Florrie looked over her shoulder as she started dusting the willow-
pattern china on the dresser. 'Her cough worse, is it?'

Kerensa nodded. 'Much worse,' she replied, as she gathered up a pile of
the finished ironing. 'Oh Flo, she's bringing up spots of blood now – I

46

noticed her handkerchiefs when I went over there and did the washing.'
She met the other girl's eyes, which were full of sympathy. 'She hasn't said
anything, and neither have I, but I'm afraid...' Her own eyes filled.
Florrie's face was grave and she crossed the room to give Kerensa's arm a
squeeze. There was no need for words for they both knew what that signi-
fied.

When Grace fled from the drawing-room and her father's ultimatum, she
had gone running from the house hatless, for she had not stayed to collect
her bonnet, and heedless of the fact that she was still wearing the elabo-
rate rose-pink gown with its flounced skirt and cream piping which she
had worn to Truro. Stumbling over the rough stones in her haste, she went
rushing down the lane to meet Dan before he should get as far as the
house. They must be alone while she passed on her devastating news.
Brushing a hand over her eyes, she sniffed and scanned the road for a
glimpse of his auburn head and long, swinging stride. There he was! Just
rounding the bend. The sleeves of his open-necked shirt were rolled to the
elbow and he was wearing his favourite waistcoat of brown corduroy.
Grace scrambled up on to a large boulder beside the way and waved.

Dan's rugged face broke into a wide grin as he lifted off his cap and
waved back enthusiastically, before starting to lope down the hill and over
the bridge which spanned the red river. When he was near enough to
catch sight of her expression however, the smile faded and a frown of
concern wrinkled his forehead. 'Grace! What's the matter?' he asked.
'You're looking some upset.' When she threw her arms around him and
broke into fresh sobs, Dan tightened his clasp and patted her shoulder
until she was able to speak.

'It's Father,' she gulped, fumbling for a handkerchief.

'Your father? Ill, is he?' Perplexed, Dan drew back, still keeping his
hands on her shoulders, and looked into her face with anxious green eyes.

'No, no,' said Grace and shook her head impatiently. She glanced over
her shoulder. 'We can't talk here. Come for a walk up through the fields,
and I'll tell you everything.'

He took her hand in his big rough one and Grace clung tightly to it,
dragging him up the winding track which led to the coast. When they
were out of sight of the house, her feet came to a halt as she turned to the
tall figure at her side and her voice cracked. 'Oh, Dan, Father's forbidden
me to see you any more!' she said with a gulp.

'*What?*' Dan's eyebrows disappeared into his hairline. 'Forbidden? But
Grace, sweetheart ...' He clasped her closely to him. 'Why should he?'

Then Grace poured out the whole story as she sobbed against his shoulder. Both were oblivious to the sights and sounds of spring – the ditches overflowing with primroses and bluebells, and the air full of birdsong. Fury was surging through Dan at the shallowness of the man, and by the time that Grace reached the end of her story, he was prepared to march straight back to Penhallow and knock Silas down.

Then she moved and turned her small white face up to his, the brown eyes filled with pain. Dan bent to plant a gentle kiss on her trembling mouth and hugged her fiercely to him. 'Oh, he has, has he?' he snapped. 'Well, we'll soon see about that!' He rested his chin on her soft hair and his eyes were stormy. 'So he doesn't think I'm good enough for you any more,' he growled. 'Well, if I was good enough before, then I'm good enough now. And I've a mind to go and tell him so!'

Grace's hand flew to her mouth and her eyes widened. 'Oh Dan, you wouldn't!'

'Why not?' Dan's chest rose and he frowned. 'Are you ashamed of me, is that it?' His tone was bitter. 'Or are you afraid he'll kick you out of this posh new house of yours?'

'Of *course* not!' Indignation had dried Grace's tears and she stamped one foot in frustration as she shouted. 'Daniel Hocking! For goodness' sake, *think* for a minute, can't you? Listen to me! You go and stand up to him and he'll make sure that you lose not only your job down the mine, but your home as well.'

'But . . .' Dan broke in and she silenced him with a hand.

'What's more he'll make sure that you never get taken on anywhere else in Cornwall. He's an influential man, my dearest, and he never forgets or forgives. Believe me, I know my father. You wouldn't be the first man to get on the wrong side of him or to find himself ruined just for speaking his mind.'

With a catch in her voice Grace added softly, 'And I couldn't bear to see you humiliated like that, Dan.' She took a deep breath which came out more like a sob. 'Even if I dropped everything and came with you no matter where – and you know I would, don't you?' Dan's answer was to squeeze her again as she went on. 'He would hunt us down and find us, because I'm still under age, remember? And by law he could bring me back and have you put in prison.'

Dan's shoulders heaved and his voice was a strangled sigh as he replied, 'Grace, I'd go through hell and high water myself if it meant that we could be together at the end of it, but I love you too much to inflict such a life on you.' Then, putting a finger under her chin he tipped her face up to his.

'So, think about this, my sweet,' he whispered. 'He hasn't forbidden *me* to see *you*, and until he does, I shall carry right on doing just that.'

There was a small silence as they looked into each other's eyes and both struggled to contain their emotions. Then, desperate to bring a smile to that trembling down-turned mouth, Dan put both hands around her waist and lifted Grace off the ground, his eyes twinkling with mischief, as he twirled her round until she gasped.

'Daniel Hocking, put me *down!*' she squealed, and a couple of seagulls flying overhead, joined in with a screech that sounded just like raucous laughter.

Hand in hand they began to walk on over the rising ground until they came to a stile and climbed over, where not far away the stark silhouette of Wheal North, a long-abandoned mine engine house, thrust its crumbling chimney to the sky. The couple had found a nook below a piled outcrop of rock which sheltered it from the wind, and were looking out over the sea, Dan's arm around her waist and Grace's head resting on his shoulder. 'Didn't think you were going to be rid of me that easily, did you?' he teased, tickling her nose with a long piece of grass.

Grace sneezed and thumped him playfully with an elbow. 'But – oh, Dan, I don't know what to think – it's all so unexpected I can hardly think straight at all.' She turned serious eyes to his. 'Because Father does mean it, you know. He's determined that I shall marry into the gentry. So what are we going to do if we're found out?'

Dan picked up a small stone and hurled it forcefully over the edge. 'We'll face that one when it happens,' he replied firmly. 'Until then we're going to bide our time until you turn twenty-one, and then we shall be wed and no one can stop us. Simple as that. You *do* want to marry me, I suppose?' he said, looking sideways at her with a mischievous grin.

'Oh Dan, do you need to ask?' Grace replied, with her soul in her eyes, and tightened both arms around his waist. 'But I'm not even nineteen yet, not quite. Two years is such a long time to wait.'

'So, meanwhile we'll see each other as often as we can, although it will have to be in secret. We'll find a way.' Dan's eyes were on the tumbling waves and the white water bursting in plumes of spray high over the rocks below. 'I don't like deceiving your father,' he said mutinously, 'but I can't live without you, Grace,' he added, with a catch in his voice, 'and I don't intend to. And as long as I'm sure of your feelings for me, I can wait.' He gazed solemnly into her eyes.

'You know my feelings will never change.' Grace leaned into him and her lips met his before she gave a sigh and rested her head on his chest. 'So, yes, we'll wait just as long as it takes, until we can be together for always.'

CHAPTER FIVE

A few weeks later, Grace was sitting at the escritoire in her sunny parlour with the household accounts spread out in front of her, but her thoughts had flown away and she was dreaming as always of Dan. They had continued to meet in secret but she knew it was only a matter of time before they were found out, and worry-lines creased her brow.

Grace nibbled her pen as she gazed out over the lawn, then back at the pile of paperwork. Then, restlessly, she flung down the pen and rose to her feet. She'd had enough for one day. The sun was pooling on the floor like melted butter while outside, birds were singing their hearts out. It was not a day to be indoors.

She left the room by the French doors which opened onto the side terrace, and the sound of an engine and the shouts of men at work came drifting across from the garden. Grace skirted the house and walked around to the back. This side was in shadow and she paused to give her eyes a moment to adjust. She was picking up her skirt to descend the steps to the garden when her attention was caught by the sound of a sneeze. Grace stopped abruptly and looked about her. Half hidden by the wall of the wash house, a girl was sitting on a low stool with a book in her lap.

Obviously lost in the story she was reading, she was oblivious to anyone's approach, until a piece of gravel dislodged by Grace's foot rattled past her and Kerensa jumped up with a stab of guilt, until she remembered that she was off-duty.

'Oh – er – Kerensa, isn't it?' Grace felt a trace of awkwardness. She was not yet accustomed to dealing with the servants at all, lacking the poise and confidence which would come with maturity. She was especially uncomfortable with this one, who was of a similar age to herself and who had such an unusual background.

Their eyes met and Grace smiled at her diffidently as she strove to think of something to say. 'What's that you're reading?' she enquired, seizing on a subject at last. To come across a housemaid with her nose in a book was a new experience – but then, this was no ordinary maid, as she well knew. Surveying the girl, she thought it a pity that their status was so different. Grace didn't have many friends, but to become familiar with a servant was out of the question.

'It's an old favourite of mine. I've read it many times.' Kerensa flipped the book over to show Grace the cover. 'Most of my books had to be sold with the ... when we moved house. But I managed to save a few of them.' Kerensa eyed Grace's gown of periwinkle blue and the frills of lace at her wrist and neck with a look of envy, and sighed. It seemed so long since she had worn anything pretty.

'It's cold on this side of the house,' Grace said, rubbing her arms, 'why don't you go around to the front and sit in the sun?'

Kerensa looked her mistress fully in the face. 'I can't. It's not allowed,' she said briefly.

As Grace stared down at the neat figure, sympathy washed over her. The least she could do, she decided, was to lend the girl some different books to read. She cleared her throat. 'Well, as you are so fond of reading, how would it be if I gave you permission to help yourself to any of the books in our library?' she offered. 'So that you don't have to read the same stories over and over again?'

Grace relaxed as the girl's face brightened like the rising sun, and gratified, she returned her broad smile as Kerensa said, 'Oh, that would be wonderful! Thank you so much. I'll take great care of them, I promise.'

Grace turned to continue on her way, replying, 'You're welcome, and I'm sure you will.'

Kerensa skipped up the steps to the back door and headed for the library right away. She still had half an hour of her break left and was going to make the most of it. Slightly out of breath, she pushed open the door and making straight for the shelves she soon selected a couple of novels to take away with her.

As she turned to go, Kerensa glanced around her. She hadn't been in this room since she had started work here. It had formerly been Papa's study – and she saw with a lurch of her heart that his desk still stood in the same place by the window. She wandered over to it and stroked a hand across the polished top, wondering who used it now. Curious, she opened one drawer to peep inside.

Unfortunately she pulled too hard and the drawer came out completely. It brought Kerensa to her senses with a gasp of dismay. To be caught snooping was enough to earn her instant dismissal. She tried to replace the drawer but in her hurry something must have dropped out and slipped down the back, for there was a piece of paper preventing it.

Kerensa stooped to retrieve it, then slid the drawer back into place with a sigh of relief. She was about to toss the paper inside, when her attention was suddenly caught by what appeared to be her father's handwriting on it. Kerensa closed the drawer and her thoughts drifted back to happier times as she looked at the script in her father's familiar hand.

He had had elegant hands, soft and smooth with long slim fingers. Strong though – she could remember as a child being whisked high in the air and whirled around, screaming in fearful delight.

The brutal reality had come later when Zack had been revealed as the deeply flawed man he really was. Until she grew up, Kerensa had never realized how her mother's attitude to him had been forged by his feck-lessness. However, since his defection and their changed circumstances, Kerensa had understood her mother's bitterness only too well.

Her attention returned to the piece of paper in her hand. Figures, crossings out, doodles and bits of handwriting covered its surface. It was probably rubbish, but it was Papa's rubbish, and a connection with the past. So for sentimental reasons she slipped the scrap into her apron pocket to study later on.

'Hurrah! God save the Queen! Long live the Queen!' Jago, caught up in the throng, found the mood so infectious that he tore off his cap and waved it above his head like a thousand others.

The Mall was packed, filled as far as the eye could see with her loyal subjects who had gathered to help their sovereign enjoy her Golden Jubilee. Beneath a sky of perfect blue, banners fluttered, flags waved and bunting and greenery decorated every lamp-post and building.

'Here she comes, I think. I can see movement in the distance.' Hal standing on tiptoe and craning his neck above the bobbing heads, dug his friend in the ribs.

'I'll take your word for it,' Jago replied, for Hal, over six feet tall and as blond as his Viking ancestors, topped him by a couple of inches. Then borne on the breeze came the sound of music, faint at first but gradually increasing, as Her Majesty made her progress from Buckingham Palace *en route* to the service of thanksgiving in Westminster Abbey.

'God bless the Queen!' shouted someone nearby to hearty cheers from all around, as the state landau drawn by six perfectly matched cream horses, drew level, and when a small gloved hand appeared at the window, the cheers swelled to a deafening roar. Despite his outward air of detachment, Jago could not help but feel a stirring of pride today, in his country, its capital and its monarch.

He had been in London for a month, staying with Hal in the modest flat in Edgware Road which he could now afford. Hal Andersen was a violinist and had just obtained a place in the D'Oyly Carte orchestra at the Savoy Theatre, where the operettas of Mr Gilbert and Sir Arthur Sullivan continued to draw adoring crowds. Jago had been going to as many classical concerts, recitals and musical events as he could, but next week would be the highlight, when Edvard Grieg would be arriving in the city.

'Ma,' piped up a child's voice in front of them and brought Jago back to the present, 'That ain't the Queen. She ain't wearing no crown!' His mother hushed him and turned to her companion. 'Alfie's right though – 'tis a pity she didn't dress up a bit more. You'd have thought she *would* have worn her crown, today of all days, wouldn't you?'

The other woman replied, 'I should say so – she could be any old lady in that bonnet,' and her friend laughed as she retorted, 'Well, perhaps not in one of white lace trimmed with diamonds!'

'Still, it's nice to see her out and about again at all. Remember how long she hid herself away after Prince Albert died, do you? I almost forgot what she looked like. And she's still wearing mourning, even now.'

'Coming to see the show tonight, Jay?' Hal asked, as they picked their way through the throng and could walk abreast once more.

'What is it?' replied Jago. 'Not that it matters,' he added, 'they're all pretty much alike, so I've heard, aren't they?'

As they threaded their way through Admiralty Arch, he replied over his shoulder, 'That's what I used to think. But since I've been playing for them, I've changed my mind. I used to look down a bit on popular operetta, but there's more to them than I realized.'

Jago snorted in derision and gave a chuckle.

'Laugh if you like,' Hal retorted, 'but old Gilbert's lyrics are very clever and the music complements them perfectly. Either one without the other wouldn't hold up, but together they're unique really.' He paused to edge around a couple of elderly men who had stopped in the middle of the pavement to have a chat, and finished, 'We're playing *Ruddigore*. Oh, do come, Jay – you'll enjoy a bit of light hearted nonsense for once – it'll make a change from all the serious stuff.'

'Oh, all right then,' Jago replied with a grin. 'But only on condition you come to the Grieg recital with me. You mustn't lose sight of the serious stuff yourself, you know.'

★

So Jago went to the operetta and soon found himself smiling and tapping a foot to the lively tunes. When he joined Hal backstage afterwards he was still smiling, which his friend immediately noted. 'Ha! Told you you'd enjoy it, didn't I?' he crowed.

Jago nodded. 'It was fine for a one-off,' he replied, 'but I couldn't stand it all the time. It's barrel-organ music, Hal!' He dropped into a battered cane chair and folded his long legs. 'You were trained to higher standards.'

'Higher standards won't pay the rent,' retorted his friend, running a hand through his hair. 'This was the only position I could get.' His face became serious. 'It's not easy to get taken on with an established orchestra you know – dead men's shoes and all that.' He reached beneath a table for his violin-case.

'Sorry, didn't mean to criticize. You've done really well, Hal, better than me.' Jago shrugged. 'At least you've got employment and a regular salary, whereas I'm still studying.'

Hal picked up his instrument and rose to his feet. 'Now,' he said, glancing in a mirror and smoothing back his hair, 'we have a supper invitation, you and I.'

'We have?' Jago's brows lifted.

'Well I have anyway, and I was told to bring a friend. You were the best thing I could come up with,' Hal joked. Jago aimed a kick at his shin which missed as Hal did a neat side-step, and followed him outside.

'Where are we going?' he asked, as his friend set off down the Strand.

'To the Garrick Club,' came the reply.

'What? The actors' place?' Jago shouted, as they dodged across the road, nimbly avoiding the stream of carriages, hackney cabs and omnibuses.

'The same,' Hal said, as they reached the other side in safety. 'My friend George is celebrating. He's obtained a part at the Lyceum. Plus it's his girlfriend's birthday.'

'The Lyceum. That's Mr Henry Irving's company, isn't it?' said Jago.

'That's right. They're doing another run of *The Merchant of Venice* at the moment. Miss Ellen Terry is Portia to his Shylock, of course,' Hal replied and Jago nodded and smiled. The couple's reputation was legendary and it was they who had made the theatre the popular venue that it had become.

'George is playing Lorenzo. I haven't seen it yet but I've promised him that I'll go sometime. Ah, here we are.' Jago glanced up at the imposing frontage of the club and followed Hal up the steps. They left their hats in the care of the hovering doorman and passed through to the bar.

A tall young man with a mop of dark hair raised a hand as they approached through the bar. 'Hal – good to see you,' he said with a smile. 'Both of you.'

'Hello, George. Meet my friend Jay from Cornwall.' Jago's hand was gripped in George's firm one.

'Glad you could come,' he said. 'What will you have?'

When they were served and seated, Hal, leaning one elbow on the small round table between them asked, 'Well, George, what are we doing this evening? You didn't give any details in your note.'

'Ah.' George crossed one knee over the other. 'We're meeting some young ladies for a birthday supper.' He winked at the others.

'Girls? Good-oh,' said Hal with a broad grin. 'Who are they?'

'There'll be three of them. Phoebe and Bess are members of the D'Oyly Carte chorus, so you'll probably recognize them, Hal. The third is a friend of Phoebe's. Her name's Isabella and she's an up and coming opera singer – very talented I believe.'

'A party?' said Jago with a frown as he looked down at his clothes. He was wearing his everyday grey suit with its high-buttoned jacket and matching waistcoat. Thank goodness he had at least put on a clean collar that evening. 'Should I have changed?' he asked, straightening the narrow lapels. 'I didn't realize.'

'No, no, it's quite informal,' George reassured him, although he was got up in a jacket of maroon velvet and an embroidered waistcoat which bordered on the new 'aesthetic' dress. But he's an actor, thought Jago, and Hal's not dressed up either so. . . .

'Whose birthday is it?' Hal asked.

'Phoebe's,' said George. He pulled out his pocket watch. 'We'd better drink up, it's nearly time to go and pick them up.'

'Where are we going?' asked Hal, as they left the building.

'Oh, Phoebe and Bess live in a ladies' hostel, and Isabella is joining them there so we can all go together. I believe she has a place of her own somewhere. Ah, there's a cab.' He extended an arm and the cabbie reined in beside them.

In the darkness, lit only by the soft glow of the gas lamps, it was difficult to get much of an impression of the three girls as they piled into the cab with a rustle of skirts. As soon as George had tapped on the roof of the cab and called out, 'The Limelight Restaurant – Covent Garden,' and they began to move, he made the introductions, but to Jago, each girl's face remained little more than an oval blur.

Once inside the foyer of the restaurant, the girls went straight upstairs to leave their wraps and as they returned, he took a closer look. George was advancing towards Phoebe, as fair as her friend was dark, while Hal strolled towards Bess, gave a little bow and crooked an elbow. Behind them Isabella paused on the bottom stair. Jago glanced up and as their eyes met, a jolt of such magnetism shot through him that he had to clutch at the newel post to steady himself.

He took a gulp of air and ran a finger under his collar, which had suddenly tightened. Tall for a woman and straight-backed, she carried her head proudly high. Set in an arresting face with high cheekbones and firm mouth, her heavy-lidded eyes were of deepest brown, and she wore a shimmering gown of emerald, low-cut to show a tantalizing glimpse of rich creamy skin. Jago dragged in a breath, unable to tear his eyes away from her. Beneath a pert little hat, her gleaming chignon of midnight black seemed almost too heavy for the fragile neck to support. Instantly he longed to loosen those pins and bury his hands in its soft cascade.

Then raising the hem of her skirt, she stepped daintily down the last step and placed a slim hand on his arm. 'Jay,' she purred, revealing small, pearly teeth, 'shall we go in?' Jago held his breath, mesmerized by this vision of loveliness, for she was the most enchanting woman he had ever seen.

Kerensa was sitting on the edge of her bed, looking at the scrap of paper she had retrieved from the desk. It was her half-day off, or rather an exchange of one job for another, she thought ruefully. The cottage would need cleaning and there would be washing waiting for her ... and so it went on. These days there seemed to be nothing in her life except work, and Celia was becoming more and more frail.

Kerensa and the other maids slept in a row of neat, box-sized rooms which had once been an attic on the top floor, and the room which she shared with Florrie contained little more than a couple of iron bedsteads, a wash stand and a wardrobe.

She scrutinized the bit of paper. Silly really, it seemed to be only doodles, she didn't know why she hadn't thrown it away. Pure nostalgia had prevented her, because however slight, it was a link with her old life. There were columns of figures on one side, some scratched out and rewritten, that looked like accounts. And on the reverse, as she turned it over, were some names.

Joseph Tregoning – Grandpapa's name – written several times, the script slightly different each time, varying from Zack's own hand to that of a more old-fashioned style. There were other people's names too. She peered closer – Sarah somebody, oh yes, Harris. And William Roberts, both of these written more than once. Kerensa frowned, then her face cleared. Of course, Sarah and William had been their cook and gardener at Penhallow. This must have been some kind of pay sheet she supposed – the figures, the names. . . .

'Kerensa!' She started at the sound of Florrie's voice calling her and slipped the scrap into the drawer of her night stand. 'Oh, you're still here.' Florrie put her head around the door and seeing her, came into the room. 'I thought you'd be gone, as it's your half-day.'

'I'm just getting ready, Flo,' she replied, rising to her feet and reaching for her coat and hat. Florrie took a clean apron from a peg and went clattering down the uncarpeted stairs as Kerensa picked up her bag and followed more slowly. She glanced out of the landing window, from where she could see Silas and Richard waving their arms and shouting over the rumble of machinery, as they directed the driver of the great steam excavator.

A cloud of smoke was flying from its chimney stack and, as Kerensa watched, it turned full circle on its revolving deck, the dipper arm descended and the shovel took a huge bite out of the flower beds. Standing by with horses and wagons were a team of men carrying away the turned soil. Sadly Kerensa realized that her employer intended to demolish the entire walled garden in his obsessive determination to find the mythical treasure.

With a clutch at her heart, Kerensa watched as Celia's shrubs and lovingly tended plants were being crushed under the mighty wheels. The scene was yet another reminder of a childhood cut too short, and a way of life that was gone forever.

But it was a glorious afternoon towards the end of June and she could not be downhearted for very long. The hedges were hung with swags of wild roses, pink and white, and the scent of warm honeysuckle wafted on the air. Kerensa made her way up the steep hill towards Camborne with the sun on her back.

Celia was in bed when she arrived. 'How are you, Mama?' Kerensa took one breath of the stuffy atmosphere and moved across to open the curtains and pull the window down a fraction, as her mother struggled into a sitting position.

'I had to come up here and have a rest,' she said. 'Nearly wore myself out getting my dinner.' She began to cough. When she was able to speak again, Celia snapped, 'You're late today, aren't you?' as she glanced at the wall clock.

'Same time as usual, Mama,' Kerensa replied, determined to remain calm.

'And it's freezing with that window open,' her mother grumbled, pulling up the covers over her chest.

'No, it's a nice warm day and you know that fresh air is the best thing for your condition,' Kerensa said in a brisk tone. 'Now let me brush your hair and help you downstairs. Maybe we could walk as far as the park if we take it slowly.' She fixed a smile on her face. 'Before I start the cleaning. Oh – I wonder who that is?' She raised her head as a knock came on the front door. 'I'll run down and answer it while you finish this.' She handed Celia the brush and a hand mirror and left the room.

'Oh, Mr Retallick!' He was on the top step, hat in hand. 'Good afternoon, Miss Treneer.' Lennie gave a slight bow and stepped forward. Before Kerensa knew quite how it had happened, he was on his way into the parlour.

'I trust I find you well?' he enquired. 'And your dear mama, of course.' He stayed in the middle of the room, rocking on his heels and fixed her with his pale eyes. A smile played about his mouth as he stroked his thin moustache.

'I'm very well, thank you,' Kerensa replied. 'Mama I'm sorry to say, is not – she's upstairs resting at the moment.'

Lennie moved forward and instinctively Kerensa took a step back. 'Er, won't you sit down?' She indicated a chair and he lowered himself into it as she stayed where she was. 'And to what do we owe the pleasure of your visit?' Her voice was as cold as she could make it. She did not like this man, he was too smarmy by half, and the look in his eyes could only be described as calculating.

'I see you must have forgotten the date, Miss Treneer.' He crossed one leg over the other and cleared his throat. 'I've come to collect the rent money, on Mr Cardrew's behalf.' He smiled thinly. 'I am, as you may remember, his agent.'

'Oh, of course!' Kerensa's hand flew to her mouth. 'I'm so sorry, Mr Retallick. You're quite right – it had slipped my mind. I'll go and get it straight away.' She fled to the kitchen and counted out the money, feeling all sorts of a fool for being so cool to the man. He was only doing his job after all.

'Here we are. The right money and the rent-book.' Flustered, Kerensa handed it over and went to sit down at the table. Lennie rose to his feet and came to sit, not opposite her as Kerensa had intended, but as close beside her as he could get, where he opened out the book in front of him and reached for the pen and ink. The man was breathing heavily, Kerensa noticed, and there was a film of perspiration across his forehead. Well, it was a warm day, perhaps he'd been hurrying to get here.

She moved away as soon as he'd blotted the page, when he pushed his own chair back and rose to his feet. 'There we are, all done,' he beamed, showing his yellowish teeth, and held the book for a fraction longer than necessary so that their fingers touched. 'Thank you, Miss Treneer. I'll be off then.'

There was a brief pause, during which it would have been the obvious thing to offer a cup of tea. But when Kerensa remained resolutely silent, he picked up his hat and extended a hand. To her revulsion it was damp and slick with sweat, and it was as much as Kerensa could do to give it a minimal shake, making a conscious effort not to wipe her own hand down her skirt as he withdrew. 'My regards to your mother.' He tipped his hat and thankfully was gone at last.

Grace was still thinking it a pity that Kerensa was a servant. She had grown attached to the girl and would liked to have made a friend of her. Grace was very conscious of her own lack of female company, alone as she was in a household of men. Her former friends were all married now, they had little in common any more, and until she and Dan...but oh, what a long wait that was going to be.

However, today Grace had an idea. 'You wanted me, miss?' Kerensa's enquiring face appeared in the doorway. 'Yes Kerensa,' Grace smiled. 'You may sit down.' She indicated a low button-back chair upholstered in rose coloured velvet. Kerensa's eyes widened as she did so, and she perched gingerly on the edge of the seat, wondering what was coming. Grace, in a gown of lilac with self-coloured stripes and wearing a cameo brooch at her throat, indicated the paper in her hand. 'I have had a letter from my brother Jago in London.'

Kerensa's heart gave a thump and began to beat faster, but her voice was calm as she enquired politely, 'Oh yes. How is he?'

'Very well, and busy too. This is to let us know that he'll be playing in a gala musical evening at the Royal Albert Hall, no less.' Grace waved the letter in the air and smiled. 'It's a charity concert to celebrate the Jubilee, and apparently many famous names are taking part, giving their services free to raise money for the Missionary Society. Imagine!' Grace's eyes were shining. 'Jago will be mixing with the most famous people in the music world. It's just what he wanted, and I'm sure it'll help him in his career.

Kerensa's eyes were demurely lowered. 'I'm very pleased for him, miss,' she replied.

'Yes, of course.' Grace put aside the letter and leant forward. 'You're wondering why I'm telling you all this. The thing is, you see, that he's asked me – well, all of us in fact, but Father and Richard are not remotely interested – if we'd like to go up to London and attend the concert.' She rose to her feet and with a swish of skirts and a waft of rose-petal perfume, took a few paces around the room. 'I'd love to go, and I have cousins nearby with whom I could stay, but I cannot of course travel on my own. And I was wondering, Kerensa' – she stopped and looked closely at the other girl – 'whether you would be willing to come with me to act as my maid and companion.'

Kerensa felt all the colour drain from her face then return in a sudden tide of excitement, and her heart began to beat so furiously that she thought Grace must surely hear it. 'Oh, oh – Miss Grace,' she stammered, 'I'd love to of course, but . . . but . . .' But there was Mama, there was her work here, and there was also the sneaking thought that the other servants, especially Alice Nance, would think she was getting above herself and make life unpleasant when she came back. All this flashed through Kerensa's mind in the few seconds it took for Grace's words to sink in.

But to go to London! And most of all, to see Jago again! To hear and watch him play in opulent surroundings that she could only dream of. But no – surely she wouldn't be going to the concert, would she? She was only a servant. But then . . . Grace would need a chaperon, even if it was only her maid . . . Kerensa's thoughts raced and she held her hands to her burning cheeks. For how could she possibly refuse an offer like this? A once in a lifetime chance to see something of the wider world! Surely Mrs Spargo could be persuaded look after Mama for a few days . . . even if she had to be paid for doing it.

'I understand you'll need time to consider it, of course,' Grace went on. 'But if you are worried about your place here, I assure you that I can hire a temporary help to cover for your absence.' She met Kerensa's wide eyes.

'When would we be going miss, and for how long, please?' she asked, and caught her bottom lip between her teeth as her thoughts raced.

Grace consulted the letter again. 'The concert is on Friday of next week,' she said, 'so we should really leave as soon as possible. I think a couple of weeks would be about right. Then I could do some shopping as well, and that'll be long enough to leave Father and Richard on their own.' She nodded and carefully folded up the letter. 'So will you think about it,' she finished, 'and let me know as soon as possible?'

'I will, miss.' Kerensa jumped to her feet. 'And – thank you, thank you very much for asking me.' She fled from the room, her heart singing and her thoughts in turmoil.

CHAPTER SIX

It did not take Kerensa long to make up her mind. It had been half made up anyway ever since Grace's proposal, and she had only needed to confirm that May Spargo was willing to look after Celia, before she started packing.

Now, with one day left, Kerensa's portmanteau was already packed and waiting. Richard was to take them to the station in the morning, for Silas had refused to take time away from the foundry to see them off.

'Frivolous nonsense,' he growled at his daughter. 'It's time that young man began to earn his keep. Charity concert indeed! There are plenty of charity cases round here if he wants to play for nothing.' He jammed his hat on his head and swept out. Kerensa, waiting at table could not resist a smile, just as Grace glanced her way. Their eyes met and they both burst out laughing.

The following afternoon Kerensa was dusting the drawing-room when she heard the sound of a vehicle on the gravel outside. Thinking nothing of it, she climbed up another rung of the stepladder and swept the feather duster around the cornice to remove a dangling cobweb.

Then suddenly the door was flung open and Florrie appeared on the threshold, her eyes wide and her face grave. With her hand still clutching the doorknob, she blurted, 'Kerensa, you've got to come right away. It's bad news I'm afraid . . . your mother. . . .'

An icy hand clutched at Kerensa's heart and the duster dropped from her hand. '*Mama*! What. . . ?' She took a step down.

'She's been taken ill,' Florrie replied. 'I'm to tell you that you've to go

home at once because your Ma have had an ahem ... hem ... haemor-
rhage,' she stumbled over the unfamiliar word, 'and she's badly.'

As she reached the floor Kerensa began to tremble. 'Who – who told
you, Florrie?'

'Mr Silas,' replied the other woman. 'Mr Retallick came over to tell him
and then he went on to fetch the doctor. Mr Silas is outside now, waiting
with the trap to take you home.'

When Kerensa arrived, the house seemed to be full of people. As she flew
up the stairs to her mother's bedroom she heard the rumble of male voices
and glanced through the open door of the parlour to see Lennie Retallick
in earnest conversation with the doctor. That irritated her, but of course
he'd been the one who initially raised the alarm so she should be grateful
to him. Silas went in to join them, and at Celia's bedside Kerensa found
May Spargo and her daughter, one sitting by the bed holding the sick
woman's hand, the other bundling up soiled sheets.

May vacated the chair when she saw Kerensa, who sat down and took
her mother's hand in her own. Celia was so pale that her face seemed
almost transparent, the veins in her hand standing out in blue ridges. Her
lips were blue as well, but she gave a tremulous smile as their eyes met.
When she spoke it was with great effort and her voice was a hoarse whisper.

'I had ... a bad fit of coughing,' she said, '... couldn't stop.'

She dabbed her lips as May Spargo said, 'She did the best thing she
could,' the woman nodded, 'she knocked on the wall loud enough for me
to hear, just before she collapsed proper.' She pursed her lips. 'Some lucky
I was in, too. Only that minute got back, I had. Anyway, when I come in,
there she was,' – she lowered her voice dramatically – 'collapsed on the
bed and blood all over the place – sorry, maid,' she nodded to Kerensa,
who tucked Celia's hand back under the covers and moved away from her,
out of earshot.

'Twas some lucky too,' said Elsie, taking over, 'that Mr Retallick was in
our house just that minute. Come for the rent he had, and said he would
go and get the doctor, and fetch you too. Some kind, I thought. A real
gentleman he is.'

'Well, I'm *so* grateful to both of you – I can't thank you enough,'
Kerensa said. 'And for changing the bed, too.'

'Don't you worry about a thing, my handsome,' May replied. 'We'll get
these here sheets washed—'

Kerensa laid a hand on her arm and protested, 'No, no, you needn't do that! You've been kind enough already. I can manage.'

'You'll have enough to do with your ma. She's going to need you around a lot for a day or two.' Kerensa felt something twist inside her, but glancing towards the invalid she could see May was right. She swallowed hard and was scarcely aware of what the woman was saying. 'And there's two of us,' May prattled on. 'Doing a bit of washing won't take long – especially with this weather for drying of it.'

As they turned to go, Kerensa pulled herself together. 'I'm just going to speak to the doctor, Mama,' she said, 'I'll be back in a minute.' With her mind in a whirl she followed the others downstairs.

'I'm so sorry to keep you waiting, Doctor,' Kerensa said, as she greeted him. To her surprise he was alone, but then through the window she noticed the other two men in earnest conversation outside. 'But you do understand that I had to go up and see Mama right away, don't you? I was so worried. Now tell me, how is she, really?' Kerensa sank into an armchair.

The doctor leaned forward, regarding her with kindly eyes. 'My dear young lady, don't apologize,' he said. 'I know what a shock this must be for you, and well, I'll give you the truth about your mother's condition as I see it.' He absently twisted his signet ring as he went on, 'Mrs Treneer is showing all the signs of consumption, I'm afraid.'

'*Consumption?*' Kerensa jumped to her feet and her voice rose an octave. 'But that . . . that's . . . fatal, isn't it?' Her stomach lurched and her head began to pound.

'It can be in some cases, I won't deny that.' The doctor met her eyes and his face was sombre. 'The patient needs light, nourishing foods and a great deal of fresh, dry air. And, as I'm sure you know, there are special sanatoriums for the most advanced cases.'

'But, Mama. . . ?' Kerensa swallowed on a throat gone suddenly dry.

The doctor rose to his feet to pace up and down. 'I'd not be doing my job if I didn't tell you that your mother is gravely ill, Miss Treneer.' He paused on the turn and gave her a long look.

'Gravely. . . ?' Kerensa repeated, feeling herself beginning to shake.

He nodded. 'I'm afraid so.' There was a small silence as she sank back into the chair.

'What can you do . . . what can I. . . ?' Kerensa stared into his kindly face as if he were God. 'Can you help her?'

'I can leave you with instructions as to her diet and care and I can keep her under observation,' he replied, 'but if she remains here, that's all I can do for her, my dear.'

'If she remains here,' Kerensa repeated, her eyes still on his face. 'You mean, don't you, that the only hope she has is to—'

'To be removed to a sanatorium. Bluntly – yes. Preferably to Switzerland, where I hear there is an excellent place. The conditions there are perfect and she could . . . possibly . . . become strong enough to live for many years.'

Kerensa's gaze followed his pacing figure as he continued, 'If she remains here, there will be times when she has good spells and appears to be rallying, but don't let these fool you into thinking she's getting better. Do you understand what I'm saying, Miss Treneer?'

Oh yes, Kerensa understood. Her mother was going to die unless she went abroad to the sanatorium. If Celia stayed at home, Kerensa would be required to nurse her to the end, to look after the cottage, and continue her work at Penhallow as well. And in either case, of course, she would have to relinquish any idea of accompanying Grace to London, either now or in the future. Kerensa bowed her head, gripped her hands together in her lap so tightly that the knuckles gleamed white, and nodded. 'I understand, Doctor,' she murmured.

Grace and Dan had met in their usual secret nook on the cliffs to say goodbye. 'I've got something to tell you, Dan,' Grace was saying. Her eyes were on the restless sea which was rolling shoreward in great crested waves of mint green, scalloped with white. 'You know I was only going to London for a day or two originally.' She turned to look at him as he lay stretched out by her side, soaking up the sunshine. It must feel wonderful after working underground, like being let out of prison, she thought.

'Mm,' said Dan.

'That was the plan,' Grace went on, 'but now Pa wants me to stay up there and do the "season" like young ladies of quality, so I'm going to be away for several months.'

'*What?*' Dan started up into a sitting position and glowered at her. '*Months*, did you say?'

Grace recoiled from the anger in his eyes. 'Oh Dan, I don't want to, of course I don't, but you know what he's like!' She spread her hands wide. 'He's insisting – because he wants me to marry well and rise in society. That's all he can think of; he's obsessed with wealth and power. And you know that until I turn twenty-one, I can't go against his will.'

'I see,' Dan growled, and flung a stone at a hovering gull in temper. The bird gave a raucous cackle like ironic laughter and soared away. 'Oh, Grace, maid.' He seized both her hands. 'You'll have your head turned by all that socializing. You'll be going to the theatre, concerts, dances, mixing with other men who'll all be making up to you. I can see exactly how it'll be.'

Then he flung her hands aside in frustration and jumped to his feet. Standing with his back to the sea he planted his legs firmly apart against the wind and shouted, 'You'll end up paired off with one of those city gents – some prancing toff without a serious thought in his head, I know.' He scowled. 'Once you're away from here you'll forget all about me.' He kicked the toe of his heavy boot hard against a tussock which went dancing merrily over the edge.

Grace ran across the strip of grass that separated them and took hold of his arm, shaking it to make him see reason. 'Dan! Listen to me! Do you really think I'm as shallow and fickle as that? I *love* you, you silly idiot. How could you ever think that of me?' Half laughing, half crying she wrapped her arms around his waist and buried her face in his chest. Dan let out all his breath in a long sigh as he clasped her tenderly and stroked her hair with his big, work-roughened hand.

'Oh, Grace, I love you so much, my handsome. That's why I can't bear the thought of any other man touching you, see.' He tipped her face up to his. 'It's bad enough having to wait for your birthday, without you being miles away for all those weeks.'

'But they will pass, Dan,' Grace tried to reassure him, 'and when I come back I shall be all that much nearer to my birthday, think of that.' She clasped his face between her two hands and drew his mouth to hers. 'And you keep your hands off the bal-maidens while I'm away too, do you hear me?' she said with a smile, to cover the pain of their separation.

It was only after she had seen the doctor out, had thanked Silas and Lennie for their help, and when Celia had fallen asleep, that Kerensa was able to sit down quietly on her own for a minute or two, and really think. And that was when the problems piled in, creasing her forehead into a frown and making her head ache. For how on earth could she find the money to send her mother to Switzerland? It was out of the question. And if she nursed her at home, how was she even going to cover the doctor's bills, let alone an invalid diet?

Kerensa gazed into space and bit a thumb nail to the quick. It was going to cost a small fortune, and they were only just managing the rent and their bare living expenses out of her wages as it was. Plus the fact that her mother was going to need someone in the house all the time, even at night, if Kerensa were to keep her living-in job at Penhallow. And if she lost that, how would they live? At her wits' end to know what to do, Kerensa sank her head in her hands and let the bitter tears course down her face.

She went back to work because she had to, leaving May Spargo temporarily looking after her mother. Kerensa was badly needed at Penhallow, for she discovered that Grace had taken Florrie to London in her place. That hurt. It forcibly brought home to Kerensa just how much she had been looking forward to the trip – a welcome respite from the narrow, careworn life which was all she had now. And she would have seen Jago, if only from the distance in which her position would have placed her. At least her presence would have made sure that he hadn't forgotten her. Such disappointment made a bitter pill for Kerensa to swallow.

With the problem of money always uppermost in her mind, Kerensa decided in desperation to go and see Nathan Thomas, the solicitor who had handled her grandfather's will, hoping against hope that he might have overlooked something, some money, however little, that was still available. At the back of her mind was the forlorn hope that he might even be able to suggest some way of tracing Papa.

'So you can see the position I'm in, Mr Thomas,' Kerensa said, after telling him the whole story.

'Give me a moment, my dear young lady, and I'll go and find the relevant documents.' He pushed back his chair and disappeared into an inner room. Kerensa gazed out of the window at the crowds in the street.

Then with a stab of pleasure she saw that Eleanor Robartes had paused outside the window to adjust a loose hatpin and was peering into the glass to see her own reflection. Kerensa took a step forward and waved. But to her astonishment her former friend looked her in the face then narrowed her eyes, straightened up and hurried away down the street. A lump rose to Kerensa's throat at the brazen snub, but she vowed not to let such pettiness upset her. Stoutly telling herself that Eleanor had not been worthy of her friendship in the first place, Kerensa returned to her seat.

'Here we are.' Sunk in her own thoughts, she jumped as the solicitor came bustling back with a handful of papers tied up in pink tape. He returned to his desk and went slowly through them all before shaking his head. 'I'm really sorry, Miss Treneer, but the business was completely wound up after your grandfather died, and the remaining small sum of cash handed over to your mother. There is nothing more, I'm afraid.' He shook his head and regarded her solemnly.

Kerensa's spirits sank to a new low. She had been hoping so much that ... But, 'There was another matter as well,' she said, as he raised an eyebrow. 'I was wondering whether ... er ... whether you could suggest any way I could go about tracing my father. Are there any legal matters, any papers in your keeping which would provide me with a clue at all? I wondered if there were people or interests of his that my mother and I never knew about.'

The man shook his head again. 'I'm really sorry to have to say no again, Miss Treneer. But there's absolutely nothing that the police haven't already been through – and after this lapse of time – you do understand, don't you?'

'Oh yes, quite so.' Kerensa fingered the pair of gloves in her lap and bowed her head to hide the desolation she felt in her soul. Whatever was she going to do? Maybe the man sensed some of it though, for he rustled through the papers, selected one and held it out to her. 'But this is the will, my dear. I've been thinking that you may as well have it as you'll be next of kin when your mother ... ahem ... well, yes. Here you are – you'll keep it in a safe place, of course.'

'Oh, thank you, Mr Thomas.' Kerensa flipped through the thick pages, remembering the scene in the drawing-room when it was first read. 'Mama never could understand, you know – and she still doesn't – how Penhallow came to be left to Papa. She was so adamant that Grandpapa meant her to have it.'

The solicitor rose and came to look over her shoulder. 'As a matter of fact it was a surprise to me as well,' he said unexpectedly, 'because I remember my father, when he was practising here before me, remarking on it.'

He strolled across to the window, then looked back at Kerensa with his hands in the pockets of his pin-striped trousers. 'It was such an unusual procedure you see – the Married Women's Property Act had only just been passed and I think this was the first example of it that he'd seen.' He returned to his seat. 'So there we are,' he finished. 'I'm so sorry I couldn't be more help to you.'

Kerensa recognized that the interview was at an end and rose to leave, no further forward and with no idea what to do next about the plight she was in.

'Isabella's given me a ticket to see her sing Marguerite in *La Traviata* on Saturday,' said Jago, reaching round to the back of his neck and removing a collar-stud. 'Then we're having supper afterwards.'

'My word.' Hal gave him a searching look. 'She's certainly taken a shine to you.'

Jago discarded his tie and tossed it and the collar on to a chair. They were in the kitchen of Hal's flat one Saturday evening, having a night-cap. 'It's only because I took her to see the Grieg recital last week. She's returning the favour, I suppose.' He leaned his elbow on the table. In spirit he was still back in the Albert Hall. 'He was magnificent, Hal. If I could play his piano concerto like that I would die happy.' The fingers of one hand moved over an imaginary keyboard as Jago hummed under his breath and his head swayed to a beat that only he could hear.

'So you've said – often,' Hal retorted with a twinkle in his eye.

Jago chuckled. 'But I mean it. And I'm so lucky to have had those lessons with him. They were inspirational.' He up-ended his glass and drained it. 'I only wish he hadn't had to go back so soon. But the poor old chap was exhausted – I could see that. And I've learned such a lot in so short a time that my brain hurts. But it was worth it.' He ran both hands through his hair and yawned. 'I'm going to turn in, Hal, I want an early night for once.'

'Ah yes,' Hal said, and gave a knowing wink. 'You're off to spend the day with the fair Isabella tomorrow, aren't you?'

'No,' Jago retorted with a grin, 'the dark one!' Hal picked up a cushion and prepared to throw it at him as he ran for the door and reached it just in time.

'I told you I asked my family up to the charity concert, didn't I?' Jago said, gazing out of the window downriver towards Chelsea Bridge and marvelling at the amount of waterborne traffic plying in both directions. From Cheyne Walk, Isabella's flat commanded a perfect view of the Thames and it never ceased to fascinate him.

Since their first meeting their friendship had quickly blossomed, fuelled as it was by their passion for classical music, and he had become a frequent visitor to her home. At times the place was full of Isabella's many friends – actors and writers as well as musicians. She seemed to keep open house and the place was usually filled with music and the hum of conversation, also sometimes with heated arguments as artistic temperaments clashed. But on this Sunday afternoon they were alone.

Isabella, with her feet tucked under her was reclining on a sofa upholstered in the striped cream and gold brocade which matched the curtains, leafing through a magazine. She was wearing a loose gown of rose-coloured, lace-trimmed taffeta, ruffled at neck and wrist, and her lustrous hair was loose, cascading in rippling waves to her waist. She looked up from the page. 'Um? I can't remember, Jay, did you?' she replied lazily.

Jago turned from the window and perching on the arm of the sofa, pulled out a letter from his pocket. 'Mm. And I've had this letter back from my father. He and Richard are not interested of course.' His lips twisted. 'But Grace my sister will be there as we have some relations in St John's Wood – distant cousins on our mother's side – and she is staying with them at the moment.'

The sun streaming into the room was reflecting the ripples off the water with flecks of gold, which lay in pools on the carpet. Jago looking down at the top of Isabella's head, noticed that it also brought out attractive little highlights in her hair. This was not completely black after all, as he had thought, but more of a deep, dark brown and faintly scented with violets. Isabella tossed her magazine aside and replied, 'You'll have to bring her over here one day.' Lowering her feet which were bare, to the floor and wriggling her toes in the carpet, she added, 'I'd like to meet her. Is she anything like you?'

'Well, only slightly in appearance, but we're quite close as we both take after our mother. She was a cultured kind of person, and musical as well.'

'I see.' She rose to her feet and said, 'Now, it's time for my singing practice. Every day I must practise, as you know.' With the lithe grace of a cat she swayed across the room to the piano and opened the lid. Then extending a hand to Jago she added, 'Will you play for me?'

'Oh – um, yes. Yes, of course I will.' It was not the first time that Jago had acted as her accompanist.

Isabella had told him that she had been born in England of Italian parents and Jago had never met anyone like her before. He was captivated – by her, by her bohemian friends and by their relaxed and informal attitude towards life. Not even as a student had he mixed with people like these, and he was completely fascinated.

Isabella was a magnificent singer, well worthy of her reputation as a diva. As her clear and powerful voice soared effortlessly up and down the scales, and she threw herself into the operatic arias with which she had made her name, his admiration for her professionalism grew. His own hands flew across the keyboard as voice and piano melded in perfect harmony, then finished with a crescendo which left them both exhausted.

'Bravo!' they called out together, and caught up in the thrill of what they had achieved, suddenly found themselves in each other's arms. Both became very still as their eyes met and held, then as Jago's head bent a little lower and Isabella raised her face to meet him, their lips clung together in a long and passionate kiss.

★

A few days later, Kerensa was passing the door of the library when the sound stopped her in her tracks. Music, the most glorious music she had ever heard was flooding out of the room in waves of melody and she was drowning in it. It sang to her of heartbreak, of yearning and of loss in a way that touched her soul and brought tears to her eyes. Jago was back! She listened spellbound until the piece came to an end, leaving her as bereft as if some part of herself had died with it.

Suddenly the door opened and Kerensa jumped as a tall figure stepped out before she could move away. The sheets she had been carrying upstairs on her way to change the beds, tumbled from her arms as she collided with him and with a cry of dismay she sprang to gather them up. 'Here let me,' he said, bending to her aid, as Kerensa felt tell-tale colour flood to her face when their hands brushed. Deliberately keeping her head bent, she fervently hoped that Jago wouldn't recognize her as she muttered, 'No sir, thank you. It's quite all right. I can manage, really.'

But he persisted and, as they straightened up and he passed her the crumpled linen, Kerensa's heart fell as she saw the look of amazement and recognition on his face. '*Kerensa*! But what ... what...?' His eyes travelled over her uniform in bewilderment.

'Mr Cardrew.' She bobbed her head in deference. 'It's a long story. But I work here now, sir,' she said woodenly. 'I must go.' Her feet however were fixed to the floor and she could not resist looking up at the face that had haunted her dreams for half a lifetime. And haunted them still. 'Only I heard the music,' she stammered. 'It was so beautiful that I had to stop and listen. What ... what was it? What were you playing?' His eyes were locked into hers, the deep, chocolate brown she remembered so well.

'It was Beethoven, the *Pathetique*,' Jago replied shortly. 'But what happened? What are you doing ... you've gone into *service*?' He looked her up and down. 'And why *here*?' He ran a hand through his hair as his eyes bored into hers. Kerensa shook her head and lowered her eyes to the floor. 'Get your father to tell you,' she whispered, and turned away.

She was a servant, and this was her employer's son. It was as much as her place was worth to be seen talking to him. 'We can't be ... friends ... any more now,' she stammered as she indicated her uniform. She shook her head and, clutching the sheets with one hand, gathered up her skirt with the other and turned for the stairs, closing her ears to the sound of Jago's voice calling after her.

But he took a couple of long strides and seized her elbow, turning her back into the room, where with one foot he kicked the door shut. 'Kerensa,' he said firmly, 'it makes no difference! For goodness' sake, there's no need for this master and servant thing.' He frowned in bewilderment. 'I don't know what this is all about, but I do know that you're not a servant in the usual sense – how can we pretend otherwise? And when I *have* got to the bottom of it, I should like to think that we could still be – er – friends, anyway.'

The melting eyes were fixed on her face, warm, caring, and Kerensa felt the threat of tears hovering behind her eyes. For so long there had been no one to care for her. That must be why this man could so easily reduce her to a quivering jelly.

She was quite unaware, Jago was thinking, that there were little bits of gold shining in the depths of her solemn brown eyes, and that with her hair standing up in spikes like damp fur where it had escaped from its cap, she looked just like a ruffled kitten. Then somehow he could not resist slipping an arm around her slim shoulders and pulling her to him in a comforting hug.

Kerensa stiffened and Jago saw the expression on her face turn to shock, then deepen into something else as colour flooded her cheeks and her eyes widened. He felt her body go limp and relax into his with a quivering sigh. Their eyes still locked, his other arm slid naturally around her waist and drew her closer. Hungrily, as if having been starved of love for too long, Kerensa sighed and melted into his embrace.

The sound of footsteps in the passage outside brought them to their senses with a jerk and guiltily they jumped apart, both pairs of eyes on the door. Kerensa's hands had flown to her face What was she *doing*? For goodness' sake – this was the son of the household, and she was the maid. Bitterly, she reminded herself of how many maids before her had been seduced by the master and ended up ruined. It was just like some bawdy music-hall joke.

Smothering a sob, Kerensa cried, 'I must go!' and forced her legs into action. She was moving towards the door, tucking up her hair as she went, when Jago reached for her hand. 'Kerensa, I—'

She shook it off. 'No, no, we mustn't – we can't....' With a strangled sob she side-stepped and slipped from the room like a wraith.

CHAPTER SEVEN

Silas was in his office at the foundry, going through the morning mail, when Lennie arrived. He did not exactly slam the door, but closed it firmly enough to distract Silas and make him glance up with a frown from under his bushy eyebrows. His agent also had a frown on his face, and his expression as he greeted his employer was truculent in the extreme.

'What's up with you, man?' asked Silas mildly. 'Got out of bed the wrong side or something?' He picked up the silver letter-opener and slit another envelope.

'You ought to know,' Lennie retorted, turning to hang up his hat on the peg behind the door. 'Still waiting, aren't I?' He came forward to stand in front of Silas and bent over the desk. 'When are you going to come up with what you owe me, eh? That's what I want to know,' he said aggressively. 'Waited long enough, I have, and I want it now.' He leaned both hands on the desk and glowered.

'And you shall soon be rewarded for your patience,' Silas said, with the hint of a smile. 'Sit down Lennie, I want a little chat with you.' Still glaring, the other man did as he was bid and perched himself on the edge of the battered cane chair beside the desk.

Silas steepled his fingers and leaned towards him. 'I heard something very interesting on the grapevine today.' He gave his assistant a level look and slowly nodded. 'Word's come my way that old Smithford is thinking of retiring.'

'Retiring? From the fuse factory? Well, that's a surprise. I thought he was the sort that would die in harness rather than have his business taken out of his hands.' Lennie relaxed now, sat back in the chair and folded his arms. 'Tell me some more,' he added with interest.

'Apparently he's very ill,' Silas said, 'but nobody knew it. Now,' – he leaned his forearms on the desk and fixed Lennie with a level stare – 'we know he hasn't any family to pass it on to – never married – married to his work, he was. So as my informant has inside knowledge that the works is going to be put up for sale; that's where Cardrew's comes in.'

Lennie quirked an eyebrow and nodded. 'See what you're driving at,' he grunted.

'If we can get in on the ground floor before word gets around, we can corner the market in safety fuses and double or even triple our income.' He paused and sat back while Lennie digested the information.

'And what I'm coming to, boy, is this.' Silas waited until he had the other man's full attention. 'How would you like a bit of promotion, Lennie? I've a mind to put you in charge of this new branch when I get it.' Ever confident, he said *when* and not *if*, Lennie noticed, as though the deal was already struck. 'How about it? What do you say, eh?'

Lennie rose from his seat and leaned over the front of the desk, almost nose to nose with his employer. 'I say that's fine by me,' he began, 'but it's still pie in the sky – you don't even know you'll get the damn works.'

Silas's expression changed from self-satisfaction to annoyance and he began to bluster. 'But. . . .'

Lennie silenced him with a raised hand. 'That don't change the other things between us, nor what I said just now. I want what you owe me, and I want it right now.' His pale eyes as hard and cold as chips of ice, were fixed on Silas's steel-grey ones as he glowered at him. 'Well?' he prompted.

'It's like this. All the while that I've been biding my time, I've been looking out for your interests, see? And I've come up with something which I think you'll agree will be worth the wait.'

'And?' Lennie growled.

'And,' Silas replied, 'you wanted that Treneer girl, you said. Right?' Lennie's eyes widened a fraction and he nodded. 'Seems then that fate has played right into your hands, and mine.' Silas paused as a couple of men passed by on the landing outside, laughing and bantering with each other.

'Get on with it, can't you?' said Lennie with impatience, but he relinquished his aggressive stance and returned to his seat.

Silas held up a hand and lowered his voice. 'You know how ill the mother is, don't you? Apparently she's likely to die.'

Lennie nodded. 'So what?' he retorted in bafflement.

'So – she needs specialist treatment, that's what.' Silas tapped the side of his nose with a significant gesture. 'Expensive treatment. She needs to be sent abroad to a sanatorium for a long time – I mean *that* expensive. Are you with me?' Lennie stared blankly back at him and shook his head. 'For goodness' sake, man!' Silas drummed his fingernails on the desk in irritation. 'Where do you think the chit's going to lay her hands on money like that? She's a servant, isn't she?'

He pushed back his chair and rose to look out of the window at the yard below, slowly stroking his beard. Then abruptly he turned on a heel and pointed a finger at the other man. 'But if *you*' – he stabbed the air – 'were to suddenly come into some money, from a legacy perhaps' He gave a sly smile. 'Or by other means – like in settlement of a debt, maybe? Now do you see what I'm getting at?' He rocked back on his heels and waited for the penny to drop.

Then at last a smile like winter sunshine appeared on Lennie's face, and he drove a fist hard into the palm of his other hand. 'Of course! Silas, old man, you're a genius.' He jumped to his feet and clapped the other man on the shoulder. 'And she'll be so grateful and so indebted to me that she'll do anything I ask of her. Right?' He rubbed his hands together in glee.

'That's what I was thinking,' Silas said with a smirk. 'As I said, a reward worth waiting for. You scratch my back . . . well, you know the rest.' And they shook hands as the score was settled.

'Yes, well,' remarked Lennie, reaching for his hat, 'no time like the present I say. I think I'll just call in on my way home from work and see how Mrs Treneer is faring.' A broad grin displayed his yellow teeth like some predatory animal as he added, 'And her daughter too, of course.'

Kerensa had been on her feet since half past five that morning, struggling to get through the morning's work at Penhallow before her afternoon off. Now at home she had been struggling through the weekly wash, and by the time that everything was on the line and propped up with the wooden pole kept for the purpose, Kerensa was so exhausted that she was ready to drop, and could hardly summon enough energy to drag herself indoors and down the passage to answer a knock at the front door. When she did so, it brought her no pleasure to discover who her visitor was.

'Oh, Mr Retallick,' she said unsmiling, as he removed his hat.

'Miss Treneer.' Dapper in a pin-stripe suit and stiff collar, Lennie gave a slight bow. In his arms was a large sheaf of flowers which forced Kerensa to move aside as he took a step forward. Then before she could do anything to stop the man he had swept over the threshold and into the house.

'Do come in,' she said with heavy sarcasm, as inwardly seething, she had no choice but to usher him into the parlour, whipping off her apron as she went and tossing it onto the hall-stand.

'This is a surprise,' Kerensa said, staying on her feet. 'Surely the rent isn't due for another couple of weeks yet, is it, Mr Retallick?'

He gave a smile which did not reach his eyes and replied, 'No, my dear young lady, that's correct. I'm not calling about the rent today, certainly not.' He cleared his throat and held out the flowers. 'No indeed, this is not a business call. I came to enquire after your poor dear mother, and I brought these for her – and for you as well, of course.'

'How very kind of you.' Kerensa stepped forward and took the proffered blooms. During the exchange he placed his hands over hers as he folded them around the large bunch of stems and she could not help thinking that he had deliberately prolonged the clasp for longer than was necessary.

She took a deep breath – he was standing too close, crowding her, and his hands were flabby and slightly damp as if he were sweating. Kerensa told herself not to be so nervous and, resisting the urge to wipe her palms on her skirt, plunged her nose into the blooms as a diversion. Hothouse lilies, their pungent scent filling the room – at any other time she would have enjoyed their fragrance, now however it only seemed cloying and sickly. Laced with quantities of trailing fern, the huge trumpets reminded her of a wedding bouquet.

'Thank you so much, they're beautiful. I'll take them up to show Mama presently, after I've arranged them.' Kerensa laid the flowers carefully down on the table and wondered wearily if she would have to offer him tea. 'Won't you sit down?' she said politely, waving him to a chair.

'And how is Mrs Treneer nowadays?' Lennie placed his hat on the arm of the chair and leaned back with folded arms, his eyes meeting Kerensa's. She perched on a low padded footstool for the simple reason that it was the furthest seat from his, and wrapped her arms around her knees. Hunching her shoulders she gave a sigh and replied, 'Oh, Mr Retallick, I'm afraid that she's very ill indeed.'

Then, against her will, but before she could prevent herself, to her horror Kerensa could feel her eyes filling with tears. Tears of weariness and despair at the hopelessness of their position. For Celia was fading away before her eyes and she was powerless to prevent it. They simply did not have the means to provide her with the care and medication that she needed.

Hating herself for such a display of weakness, Kerensa wiped the back of her hand across her face hoping that he hadn't noticed, and swallowed hard. 'The doctor says she ought to be having special treatment in a sanatorium abroad, but of course that's out of the question.' She shrugged. 'But meanwhile we do our best. She had a few days in hospital and they stabilized her condition temporarily, so she is slightly better for the moment. But I'm afraid that it won't last long.'

'I see. I'm so sorry.' There was a silence during which Lennie eyed her thoughtfully and Kerensa, uncomfortable under his scrutiny, half rose to her feet. She had decided that she really ought to put the kettle on – it was the least she could do as the man was only being kind after all – it wasn't his fault that he repelled her.

But at that moment Lennie cleared his throat and took a deep breath. 'Miss Treneer – Kerensa. I may call you Kerensa may I not, now that we have become friends?' Have we? Kerensa thought in surprise as she inclined her head. 'There is another reason why I called on you today.' His pale eyes met hers and something in their cold blue stare sent an instinctive shiver down her spine. 'Oh, yes?'

Kerensa took a step across the room to break away from the uncomfortable eye contact. But Lennie had risen as well and they met in a corner where the furniture in effect blocked her in, forcing them into close proximity.

'For some time, Kerensa, I have held you in high regard,' he began, thrusting his hands into his trouser pockets and rocking back on his heels with a smug look on his face. 'Indeed, I have come to admire you for the qualities of hard work and fortitude which you have shown since your sudden change of circumstances. And even more so since your mother's demanding illness.' The prominent, fish-like eyes bored into her face for a moment as Lennie fingered his moustache, then he turned on his heel and paced up and down. Kerensa still trapped behind a large armchair, could only listen in astonishment with her eyebrows rising to her hairline as she wondered what was coming next.

'High regard, as I have said.' Hands clasped behind his back now, Lennie turned on his heel and faced her at close quarters again. Kerensa recoiled from the touch of his hot breath on her cheek and took an involuntary step backwards. 'And it occurred to me that we might do very well together, you and I, if you would – er – consent to start walking out with me.' He paused and Kerensa felt her jaw drop, but before she could compose herself enough to reply he was going on, 'so that we could – ah – get to know each other a little better.'

What could she say? That he made her flesh crawl? That the very thought of 'walking out' with him made her cringe? That to have him touch her would make her stomach heave? Hardly. Kerensa racked her tired brain for a way of letting him down gently with such short notice in which to think up a tactful reply.

She took a deep breath and plastered a smile on her face. 'Mr Retallick, I—'

'Lennie,' he said quickly.

'Er, yes. Lennie. While I appreciate very much your regard for me, and
... although you are very kind ... I'm afraid that I – um – don't feel the
same way about you, you see.' She gulped and shook her head. 'I'm so
sorry, but I must say this now because it's not fair to you to give you false
ideas. I know it wouldn't work between us, and could never be as you
hope.' Kerensa clasped her hands in front of her and bent her head as she
twisted them together, as she added, 'And while I'm really honoured that
you should ask me, I'm sure there are lots of other girls who would make
you a far better – er – companion than I.'

She glanced up at him as the silence lengthened, and to her surprise the
man was regarding her with what looked like a calculating stare. Then he
turned away to reach for his hat and his smile was that of a reptile as he
said, 'I'll give you some time to think it over, my dear. I see that I've startled you by springing this upon you so suddenly, but I've been thinking
of you kindly for a very long time.' He clapped the hat on his head. 'A long
time,' he repeated with another stare.

'And I won't be put off with a first refusal, you know,' he added rogu-
ishly as he wagged a finger under her nose and turned to go. Kerensa
released at last, crept out of the corner and followed him to the front door.
When she had closed it behind him, she leaned against the wooden panels
and shuddered.

'*Bravo! Bravissimo!* Oh, wasn't that just *wonderful?*' Jago turned to Grace
with shining eyes, then jumped to his feet clapping and shouting with the
rest of the audience. Isabella had just finished her performance, her bell-
like voice soaring effortlessly to a clear and unwavering top C, before
deftly descending the scale to the final note of her aria. She bowed again
and again then spread her arms in acknowledgement of the applause, blew
a kiss and ran from the stage in a swirl of turquoise satin, to return a few
moments later for a second curtain call, to the undiminished adoration of
her audience.

'Isn't she marvellous?'

Jago resumed his seat with shining eyes as Grace half-turned to him
and replied, 'You didn't do too badly yourself, remember – you had a
standing ovation as well, Jay, after that Chopin prelude. We felt so proud
of you, didn't we, Penelope?'

Their cousin closed her feathered fan with a snap and nodded in agreement. Penelope was much older than the other two, thin as a rail and just
as straight. Clad in purple silk, with a sharp nose and chin, her regal

appearance belied her gentle demeanour and kind heart. Her husband George, who was something in banking – Grace had never fathomed exactly what he did, but they seemed to be very well off – beamed benevolently at the company in general and went back to scrutinizing the audience through his opera glasses.

'Wasn't it lucky that you were on in the first half?' Penelope replied, 'So that you could join us and enjoy the rest of the concert, knowing that your own ordeal was over.' Grace smiled up at her brother and thought how handsome he was looking in full evening dress, his face animated with excitement and his whole being radiating confidence. This is where he truly belongs she was thinking, as she had thought earlier while watching him play. Music is his element – it's what he was born for. Grace sighed. If only Papa could see him now, in this opulent setting, maybe he would acknowledge Jay's talent at last. She must try to get some of this over to Pa when she returned home. Maybe there would be reviews in the papers tomorrow – she would keep those and show him. . . .

In the break before the next item her gaze wandered up and around the magnificent circular building where tier upon tier of boxes, curtained in crimson velvet with their fronts decorated with gilded swags of fruit and flowers, swept to the topmost gallery.

The Royal Albert Hall. How proud the Queen's Consort would have been, Grace thought, and how touched, to be remembered with such splendour. She tilted her head until her gaze came to rest on the roof, where an exquisite domed skylight of painted glass held a star-shaped cascade of gas jets which shimmered like something out of fairyland.

Grace returned her attention to the stage for the last performance, a string quintet who were playing Schubert, and wondered what social events Penelope had planned for the rest of her stay. It had been a hectic round so far, of suppers, balls, soirées, and a visit to the races, where she had been pointedly introduced to the cream of London society and had equally pointedly, attached herself to none of them.

She had a sneaking feeling that Penelope sympathized with her, but nothing was ever said. After the necessary few months that she was forced to stay here to please her father, Grace would return home still single, and he could do what he liked about it for she would be almost twenty-one by then!

The red curtains were coming together now and, as the golden loops and tassels dropped into place for the last time, the audience rose to their feet for the National Anthem. As soon as its echoes had died away and people were beginning to move, Jago rose and picked up his top hat.

'Excuse me, ladies,' he said, 'I must go and find Isabella. We're going out to supper. I'll see you tomorrow, Grace.' He turned to his sister. 'You know Penelope's invited me over for lunch, don't you?' He smiled at their cousin and bowed over their hands in farewell. Then with a swish of his black tails he vanished in the crowd.

'Well,' said Penelope, as they threaded their way towards the exit, 'I should imagine that was a very successful Gala Evening.' She quoted from a poster in the foyer, 'And I'm sure that Her Majesty will be delighted at the amount of money it's raised for the Missionary Society, don't you think?' Grace nodded and picked up the hem of her skirt as they went down the steps. Of midnight blue taffeta with a slight train flaring from below the bustle, the slim-fitting gown had made her feel very grand tonight, knowing that she was looking her best.

What a far cry this round of gaiety was from Cornwall and Penhallow, where there were so few opportunities for dressing up. But Cornwall made her think of Dan and that saddened her. Grace missed him dreadfully and was tired of keeping at bay the eager young men whom she met at the many social occasions arranged for her by Penelope. A pang of pure homesickness hit her at that moment, and she replied absently, 'Apparently it's a charity dear to her heart. Converting the heathen and spreading the Christian teachings around the Dark Continent.' She put up a hand to straighten her tip-tilted confection of a hat which threatened to become dislodged in the crowd, and kept it there as they streamed outside.

'Well, surely it's our duty to do so,' Penelope added, drawing on her gloves as George hailed a cab. 'After all, Great Britain is the greatest and most influential country in the world.'

Grace was still not really listening, but her thoughts had turned to another subject now. On their way home in the cab, she turned to her cousin and remarked, 'Pen, I worry about Jay, you know, he seems so besotted with that Isabella Mancini, and I can't see it working out between them, can you?'

'Really?' Penelope half-turned towards her in surprise. 'I'd no idea they were that close.'

'Oh yes,' Grace replied, 'Jago worships the ground she walks on. But Isabella is completely wrapped up in her own career, and I'm afraid he'll neglect his own playing while he's paying homage to her. She invited me round to lunch the other day as you may remember, and I watched them together. She's too self-centred, Pen. I can see it, but Jay can't, although I dropped some heavy hints to him afterwards as he was taking me home.

79

He won't be told – won't hear a word against her, you know?' She twisted her hands together in her lap and added, 'I'm afraid that he'll ask her to marry him.'

'It's that serious?' Penelope raised an eyebrow.

'Oh yes,' Grace nibbled her lip, 'I think she'll break his heart when she turns him down, as I know she will. He's heading for a big disappointment, Pen, and it's going to hit him pretty hard when he has to come back to earth.'

Penelope placed a gloved hand on Grace's arm in sympathy. 'Perhaps that'll happen sooner rather than later, my dear, if she *is* the sort of person you think. That would be best, before he gets as far as suggesting marriage.'

'I hope so,' Grace replied dubiously and shrugged. 'But no one can order another person's life for them, even if they think they *do* know best.'

A few days later, Jago was sitting on the floor in Isabella's flat, deep in conversation with one of her coterie who were gathered that Sunday afternoon to laze about, to exchange ideas about poetry, painting, music, or the state of the world in general, and to share several bottles of wine. A languid youth, clad in the aesthetic fashion à la Oscar Wilde, was sitting in the window embrasure, reading aloud from his own poetic compositions to a girl who lounged on the floor with her head in his lap, and who was hanging adoringly on his every word.

Isabella, draped on the settee in a flowing gown of scarlet silk, her hair loose and floating about her shoulders, was following a musical score while a pianist in a black velvet jacket with a pussy-cat bow tied under his chin, was softly picking out the notes on the keyboard behind her head. 'I like it, Anton,' she said at last, swivelling her legs to the floor, 'bring it back when it's finished and I might *just* be able to persuade the maestro to take a look at it for you.'

The young man flushed and seizing her hand in a theatrical gesture, brought it to his lips with a flourish and kissed the tips of her fingers. 'Isabella, I adore you,' he said, looking deeply into her eyes.

'Of course you do,' she said with a laugh, withdrawing the hand. 'Silly boy!'

'So I was reading this article just now,' said the girl who was talking to Jago. 'Well, it's still here somewhere.' She fished about underneath a chair and pulled out a rumpled magazine. 'Look, isn't this interesting?' she riffled through the pages and held it out to him. Jago took it and followed her pointing finger to a paragraph headed, *Mr Edison tours the States giving demonstrations of his new invention. . . .*

Glancing down the columns he took in *the latest sensation . . . Mr Edison, the famous inventor of the telegraph, has now developed a recording machine, which he has called the phonograph. . . .*

'Phonograph?' Jago turned to his companion. 'What does it do?'

She looked at him with impatience. 'Read it and you'll find out,' she said with scorn, rising to her feet and shaking out her loose, flowing robe of brilliant peacock hues. Jago raised an eyebrow and went back to the article. *The machine consists of a revolving cylinder which is pierced by two needles, one for recording the voice and the second for reproducing it. . . .* Jago skipped the technicalities and skimmed down the rest of the report. *Mr Arthur Sullivan the distinguished composer,* he read, *is quoted as saying that, 'it is the most wonderful thing I have ever experienced.'* He went on to say that he is *'astonished and somewhat terrified'* by the new technology that makes it possible to record sound. *'Astonished at the wonderful power you have developed; and terrified at the thought that much hideous and bad music may be put on record for ever!'*

'I say, Isabella, look at this!' Jago scrambled up and crossed the room towards her, waving the magazine in his hand. 'I'd like old Hal to read it – he's very impressed with Sir Arthur's work. At least with his music for the Savoy operettas – I don't suppose he's ever listened to the more serious stuff.'

'Oh, I've read that,' she replied, meeting him halfway. 'It's my magazine. It does sounds marvellous. I'd love to hear my voice playing back to me.'

'Not if you sang a wrong note though, you wouldn't!' Jago laughed. 'Imagine – there it would be for ever more and you couldn't change it, no matter how much you wanted to.'

But instead of an answering smile, Isabella was giving him an icy stare. 'I *never* miss a note,' she said with scorn and drifted away from his side.

Jago, feeling hurt and put-down at her reaction to what had only been a light-hearted remark, slumped into the nearest seat. Then, looking about him at the gathering of effete young men and languid women, he wondered for an instant what he was actually doing here. Is this what he came to London for? To sit about wasting time *talking* when he could be doing some useful practising?

Then, as a drift of her exotic perfume told him that Isabella had come back, he turned to see her perching on the arm of his chair. She ran a hand through his hair and as her husky voice murmured close to his ear, 'Darling, I'm so sorry. I'll get rid of these people soon and we can be on our own again,' he knew.

Twilight was falling by the time Jago left the flat. He and Isabella had made love several times after the others had left – the mad, passionate kind of love that Isabella demanded. She had bewitched him, Jago admitted as much. He could deny her nothing, for she aroused feelings in him he never knew he possessed, and Isabella had him in thrall like a powerful drug. She was insatiable; sometimes he felt that there was something predatory about her and that she would eventually drain him dry.

She had obviously had many partners before him, but even knowing this Jago could not break away from her. In the casual, easy-come, easy-go atmosphere of her group such behaviour was accepted as the norm, but it was something with which he always felt slightly uncomfortable.

He leaned on the railings watching the myriad lights reflecting in the rippling water, and doing some hard thinking. There was no denying that London had its sleazier side. Not that Isabella's coterie were sleazy – unconventional perhaps would be a better description – but recently with the ghastly murders of those six "ladies of the night" in Whitechapel by the monster they were calling Jack the Ripper, the underbelly of the city had been exposed, and it was not to his liking.

At that moment Jago felt a sudden need for the freshness and simplicity of life in Cornwall, which he had always thought so dull, and realized that he was faced with a serious choice of options for the future. He could return for good to the quiet backwater of his home where there was no stress, none of the frenetic excitement of city life. But no challenges either beyond playing at local concerts, and stagnate there. Or he could stay on here and pursue a career where fame and fortune were always beckoning just around the corner. But around how many more corners? The plain fact was that he had still to find an agent willing to take him on before he could further that career.

I need to go back home, he thought, straightening, to sort myself out once and for all. Then he glanced back over his shoulder as an idea came to him. Isabella is talking about having a holiday – marvellous – I'll take her with me!

CHAPTER EIGHT

'Florrie! I'd no idea you were back. How lovely to see you!' Kerensa was leaving the room which they shared as Florrie entered carrying her suitcase. 'Is Miss Grace here as well? Already?'

Florrie dropped the case with a thump and sank down on to her bed. Panting for breath she held up a hand. 'Phew! I'm shattered, carrying that up all those stairs.' She rubbed an aching arm. Kerensa propped herself against the washstand and folded her arms as she waited for Florrie to recover. 'No,' said the other girl at last, 'Miss Grace sent me home because Mrs Penelope have engaged a trained lady's maid for her, that's what.'

Florrie prattled on about the wonders of London while Kerensa listened quietly, nodding and smiling while Florrie let it all out; then, as she paused for breath, Kerensa enquired in a casual fashion, 'Did you see anything of Mr Jago while you were there?'

'Oh yes – he used to call in quite often. And that's another thing.' The irrepressible Florrie was off again. 'When I was doing Miss Grace's hair one morning – she've started wearing it in a new style, all puffs and things and I was trying to get the hang of it – she started telling me how she's worried about him.'

Kerensa's heart lurched. 'Worried? Why? Is he ill?'

Florrie shook her head vigorously. 'Oh, no. Nothing like that. But he have taken up with this singer apparently – Isabella something – one of they primmy-donna opera singers, and he's spending all his time mooning over her. Playing the piano while she do sing, and all that sort of thing over at her posh flat. Head over heels in love with her, he is, so Miss Grace said, and she don't think much of it. Afraid that Mr Jago will neglect his own career for hers, see? But, like I said. . . .'

Florrie prattled on but Kerensa heard none of it. Fingers of ice had clenched at her heart and were slowly squeezing it to death. So much for the closeness they had shared so briefly, and Jago's desire to remain 'friends' as he had put it. Obviously it hadn't taken him long to realize the gulf in their positions after all, despite his pretence that it didn't matter. Out of sight, out of mind. There was a certain truth in the old adage.

But then, perhaps he'd really meant what he'd said. That they were *friends*, and it was she making more of the tender moment she remem-

bered, than there was. Just because to her he had always been more than
a friend and always would be, didn't mean that Jago thought like that too.
For he'd never said or done anything to indicate that she was more than a
kind of younger sister to him. A hug, a squeeze of the hand – it could have
meant anything, or nothing. So, Kerensa sighed, if he'd had his head
turned by the cream of London society, it was understandable that he
hadn't given her a second thought when confronted with this ravishing
Isabella woman.

During this time Kerensa had another shock when Celia had a sudden
relapse and was whisked into hospital for a second time.

So Kerensa was at her lowest ebb. Sitting at the kitchen table one day,
her head on her arms as she wept floods of hopeless tears, she hardly registered the knock that came at the door. When she did she was tempted to
ignore it, and only the thought that it might be someone with news from
the hospital forced her to wipe her face and drag herself upright. Then, oh
no. Not *him*!

'Mr Retallick,' she said wearily. 'I'm sorry, I. . . .' But he had smoothly
insinuated himself inside and laid a hand on her arm before she could
finish.

'I heard the news about your dear mother, Kerensa, and came over
right away. Such a sad business.' As Kerensa stood her ground and kept
him standing in the hallway, he removed his hat and went on more firmly,
'I have a suggestion to make, my dear, which will be to your advantage –
and hers. Shall we go in and sit down?' He held out a hand to indicate that
she should precede him, and not being strong enough to refuse, Kerensa,
fuming, led the way into the parlour.

'I'm really busy, Mr Retallick,' she said, in a vain attempt at assertion.
'I'm sorry that. . . .' But he merely sat with his elbows on the arm of his
chair and steepled his fingers as he fixed her with a long look, until
against her will Kerensa took the opposite chair and slid into it.

'I'm not one to beat about the bush, Kerensa. I came to tell you that I
have recently come into some money. An -um – inheritance.' The eyes
held her like a snake facing a mesmerized rabbit. Kerensa shrugged and
nibbled her bottom lip. Did he want congratulations or what? 'So?' she
said icily.

'Therefore I am in a position, if you should so wish, where I can afford
to send your mother to the best clinic in Switzerland.' Kerensa's stomach
lurched and her face must have registered her astonishment, for he
smiled, and went on silkily, 'Where they tell me, for I have made some

enquiries you understand, that she stands a good chance of recovery.'

All kinds of warring emotions were churning about in Kerensa's mind as she took in this totally unexpected news. Indignation was one – the cheek of the man, how dare he make enquiries behind her back? Suspicion followed close behind – why should he be willing to spend his money on her? And finally, what did he want in return? She had learnt long ago that in this life, nothing came for nothing. She narrowed her eyes and said softly, 'That seems a very generous offer, Mr Retallick. So generous that it leads me to wonder. . . .'

He raised his head and their eyes met in a level stare. 'Yes?' The mouth was smiling but the pale eyes were glacial.

'I wasn't born yesterday, you see.' Kerensa held his gaze. 'I imagine that you would require something from me in return for this enormous favour.'

'Oh yes, you're quite right. I would indeed.' Lennie rose from the chair and took a turn around it. Then, coming back to face her again, he towered over Kerensa as she cringed further back in her seat to avoid his hot breath on her face, and said, 'In return for saving your mother's life, Miss Kerensa Treneer, I would require you to marry me.'

'M – *Marry* you? *Me*? Marry *you*?' Kerensa's hand flew to her throat as her gorge rose. 'Wh – why? But that's *preposterous*!' She felt all the blood drain from her face and, seated though she was, still the world seemed to tilt as she regarded the man with horror.

'Not at all,' came the cool reply, as he moved and took a few steps across the room. 'As I said before, I have a high regard for you, but as you rejected me in no uncertain terms, then I'm prepared to take drastic measures in order to make you my wife.'

Kerensa swallowed hard and jumped to her feet to find that her legs were too weak to support her and she had to clutch at the back of the chair to save herself from falling. 'But that's . . . blackmail!' she whispered.

'Quite so,' replied Lennie, with a self-satisfied smirk on his face.

'*Why*?' Kerensa forced her dry mouth to frame the words. 'Why are you so determined on me for your wife when you know that I' – she stopped herself just in time from saying 'loathe the sight of you' and amended it to, 'can never love you?'

Lennie threw back his head and laughed without mirth. 'My dear Kerensa, there are many reasons for marriage – the least of which is romantic love.' He placed his hands behind his back and the pale eyes fixed on her face steadily regarded her like a specimen in a glass case. 'No, I need a presentable young woman who will provide me with a family,' and he ran his tongue around his lips as he looked her up and down. Kerensa's stomach heaved and she had to look away, biting her lip as she fought to quell her revulsion.

'As any respectable man does. In return,' – he waved a magnanimous hand – 'you will be raised from servant status and returned to your rightful place in society – for that alone you should be grateful – plus I'm also prepared to save your mother's life. The way I see it, you should be down on your knees, *begging* to become my wife.' His face reddened in anger as he struggled for words. 'Instead of dragging your heels and thinking that you're too good for the likes of me!' The bland features twisted into a snarl. Kerensa jumped, suddenly terrified, and her hands flew to her face to stifle a scream. 'So think about it!' he snapped, turning on his heel. 'I'll call for your answer at the same time tomorrow.'

'Bu-but I shall be at work tomorrow, at Penhallow.' Kerensa's brain, numb though it was, reacted automatically. 'Excellent,' came the reply and he gave a feral grin. 'I have business with Mr Cardrew tomorrow. A case of being able to kill two birds with one stone, as it were.' Kerensa shivered, then he clapped his hat on his head and twirled his cane as he gave her a level stare. 'Until tomorrow then. Good day to you, Kerensa.'

Silas looked up with an irritated expression as Lennie entered the office whistling tunelessly between his teeth. 'What are you looking so pleased about?' he growled, pushing aside a stack of papers, placing his elbows on the desk and running both hands through his thick mane of hair.

He surveyed his agent through narrowed eyes, noting the new suit of expensive cut and cloth, the rolled gold watch-chain and the hand-made boots. Where *did* the man get all his money from, he thought, not for the first time? Could he be running some profitable little scheme on the side? Silas stroked his beard. He couldn't imagine how, but he wouldn't put anything past Lennie Retallick. Always had an eye open for the main chance, did Lennie. Well, he'd never get rich on what Silas paid him certainly, and he would not have wasted his 'legacy' on new clothes if he was going to use it to bribe that little chit into marrying him, for he would have to put that money where his mouth was, and sending the mother to a Swiss clinic was going to eat up most of it.

'I've told her,' Lennie said succinctly, subsiding into a chair and straightening his nattily-striped tie.

'So that's why you're all dressed up like a dog's dinner.' Silas grinned and tapped a pencil on his blotter. 'Well?' he asked, waiting for the rest.

'Going to get her answer tomorrow, aren't I? Can't see how she's going to refuse though – as good as condemning her mother to death, that is.' Lennie gave a smirk and crossed one gleaming boot over the other as he stuffed his hands in his trouser pockets and leaned back expansively.

Something rustled in the depths of a pocket and he idly pulled out a piece of paper and squinted at it. As he caught sight of whatever it was however, Silas noticed a shifty look cross his face as Lennie stuffed it back where it had come from. He's up to something, I'll be bound, thought Silas, regarding Lennie with a shrewd and level gaze as the other man quickly changed the subject.

'Thought I'd go round to Tolcarne Street today for the outstanding rents,' he blurted. 'What do you think?' he went on; too rapidly Silas thought, continuing to give him the thoughtful stare. 'They Williamses haven't paid for months. Nor the Tregenzas neither.' Lennie was beginning to look uncomfortable beneath the frosty stare, Silas noted with amusement, and at last he gave a nod of assent, whereupon a smirk crossed his agent's pasty face as Lennie relaxed and uncrossed his legs. 'Be getting the bailiffs round soon, they will,' he added, then rising to his feet, he reached for his hat and strode out of the room.

After Lennie had delivered his ultimatum and slammed the front door behind him, Kerensa sank shuddering to the floor and wrapped her arms around her knees. Then she rested her forehead on them and let the tears flow unchecked. She wept that day for everything that had happened to her since her life had changed so dramatically. For her father's defection, for her grandfather's change of heart over his will, for her mother's illness and for their present circumstances which she felt sure had helped to bring it to a head. About Jago's heartlessness she had tried not to think at all, but now it welled up to swell the bitter, overwhelming tide which coursed down her face.

When there were no tears left, she dragged herself to a chair and slumped into it as she tried to take in the choice which faced her, between saving her mother's life, or sacrificing any hope of a better future for herself. Ever.

Kerensa nibbled each fingernail in turn and stared vacantly into space as her head reeled. The man must be unbalanced. For what sane mind could have dreamed up such a scheme? And what sort of marriage did he expect it to be, for goodness' sake, given these circumstances and knowing how she felt about him? Well, maybe he didn't know exactly how she felt, for, out of politeness, she had never pointed out the fact that he made her flesh creep, that she hated his hot breath, his carroty hair and his cold eyes, and that if she were totally honest, deep down she was frightened of him. For she suspected that beneath the suave and bland exterior ran a streak of unpredictability, and an evil temper which when roused could easily turn to cruelty.

Kerensa sat on in a stupor, feeling as if she were being sucked even further down into the vortex which had swept away her previous life so completely in a few short months. In front of her stretched an unknown future with Lennie Retallick, which had her shaking with dread at the very thought of it. Kerensa's shoulders heaved as she gave a shuddering sigh and tried to gather enough strength of mind and physical courage to face up to what had to be done.

Because the *choice* was no choice at all really – deep down inside she had known that all along. For how could she live with herself if she refused to save her own mother's life? But equally, she cried inwardly, how could she live with *him* for the rest of her days?

She would have to, Kerensa thought grimly. For apart from the crucial life-or-death issue, she desperately needed his money to pay the doctor's bills and the mounting hospital fees as well. Her whole being was crying out against the fate which was forcing her to sell herself to the highest bidder.

She could not, of course, tell her mother anything about the predicament she was facing and was keenly aware of the lack of someone to confide in, a shoulder to cry on, but earlier she had told her about Lennie's proposal and what it would mean to them. For she *had* to tell someone or burst. Celia had grasped her hand, her eyes full of tears and replied, 'Oh Kerensa, you don't know how glad I am that you will have someone to care for you especially if . . . when I'm away. What a good man he is – so generous and thoughtful – spending all his money on me like this.' And so it had gone on, for Lennie had laid his plans well and had charmed the mother as only he could, as a trap to catch the daughter. So while Celia rejoiced in their good fortune, Kerensa writhed inside and tried to keep a smile on her face. Now she wiped the back of a hand across her eyes as she entered the hospital.

Her mother was lying back propped high against a bank of spotless pillows whose pristine whiteness served only to highlight the greyish pallor of her face. As she heard Kerensa enter, Celia raised her head and turned towards the sound, and Kerensa's breath caught in her throat. For sometime during the day her mother seemed to have taken another turn for the worse. The skin was now stretched so painfully tight across the bones of her face that the skull beneath that skin was clearly visible, and her eyes were sunk dark and deep in the hollows of that skull. Shock kept Kerensa pinned to the threshold as she gulped back a sob. For if she had not already made up her mind, this pitiful sight would have instantly made it up for her.

Thoughts of having to face Lennie Retallick again and give him her answer today made Kerensa feel like the proverbial lamb on its way to the slaughter as she set out for Penhallow the next morning.

The summer months had slipped by and the October air was crisp and fresh. Where earlier there had been swags of pink and white wild roses tossing in the hedges, now they were bright with hips and haws, and gold and red bryony berries were twining themselves like jewelled necklaces around the stems of the hawthorn bushes. Kerensa's eyes glanced at all this brilliance, and glanced away again without registering the beauty of it, for she was sunk too deep in misery and entirely preoccupied with her own thoughts as she turned up the drive towards Penhallow and dragged her feet round to the back door.

Even though he had been on her mind for the past twenty-four hours, it still came as a shock when later that morning she was sent to answer the jangling doorbell and there he was on the top step, waiting. Her nemesis, dressed in a black suit and bowler, and looking like a predatory carrion crow. Kerensa's stomach lurched and her heart started to pound, but she said nothing and avoided his eyes as she pulled the heavy door wider and he stepped inside.

In the entrance hall he tossed his hat onto the hall-stand, hooked his cane after it and stopped with his back to the front door as he fixed her with a glassy stare and said the single word, 'Well?' Shafts of light from the coloured panes set into the wood flickered over his face, bathing it in an unearthly red glow which to Kerensa's taut nerves seemed to be emanating straight from hell.

She regarded him with undisguised loathing. 'Of course it has to be yes,' she replied. 'You didn't expect anything else, did you?' she added, with a look of scorn. 'Although I hardly think that this is the time or the place to discuss the matter.'

Lennie's face twisted with anger as he shot out one arm and grabbed her by the wrist, pulling her towards him. 'Oh, but it is,' he hissed. 'I've waited a long time to hear you say that, and I'm not going to wait any longer.'

Kerensa's head came up as she tilted her chin until their eyes were on a level. 'Take your hands off me,' she said coldly, 'I'm at work, don't forget.'

Reluctantly he released her and she rubbed the wrist as if it were tainted by his touch. 'Now let me tell you something, Lennie Retallick,' she said through gritted teeth. 'You may have bought my body, but you will never buy the slightest affection from me, let alone love, with this enforced marriage.' She tossed her head defiantly. 'Oh, I'll keep house for you, and do my duty.' Her voice quavered and cracked as she added, 'According to the vows which I shall make.' She paused, then added quietly, 'But you will never, ever know what I'm *thinking*!'

Her show of spirit acted like a red rag to a bull. Lennie grabbed her roughly, twisted one hand in her hair and pulled her round towards him. His face contorted as he shook her like a rag doll and Kerensa felt her teeth rattle. 'One day, Miss High and Mighty Treneer, you'll regret you ever said that!' he spat, and his enraged eyes burned into hers. Little flecks of his saliva spattered against her cheek as he tossed her from him and Kerensa cried out at the pain which shot through her scalp. She tried to turn away, but before she could do so, he loomed over her again and said. 'And this is to help you remember it!' Then, as Kerensa's stomach churned, his wet mouth came down to cover hers in a travesty of a lover's kiss.

Kerensa Treneer became Kerensa Retallick in a brief ceremony in the small Methodist meeting house at the end of the road where, Lennie told her, his mother had been a regular worshipper and he had attended Sunday School. They exchanged vows in the bare, cheerless room with its plank floor and whitewashed walls, without a flower to brighten it or a note of music to show that this was any kind of special occasion. Even the weather seemed to be conspiring in the all-encompassing dullness, having turned to a thin, penetrating drizzle as if it were in mourning.

Kerensa wore a simple gown of self-striped powder-blue poplin and carried a posy of late sweet-peas, the only spot of colour in the room. As she had no one of her own to give her away she was forced to accept Silas's offer, although her heart cried out at the idea, as it cried out at the very thought of aligning herself with the complacent figure at her side, not much taller than she, and who, she noticed, was sweating already beneath his tight collar.

No! In his place there should have been someone quite other – someone taller, leaner, with a shock of dark hair and brown eyes looking meltingly down into hers. There would be flowers, music, silver bells ringing out over the countryside, proclaiming the everlasting love of two people made for each other and destined to be together for eternity. But that was fantasy and the unattainable dream.

Kerensa jerked herself back to the present moment. This was stark reality. She looked about her. There was a stranger acting as Lennie's groomsman and Florrie was her maid of honour, but apart from them, as Lennie had no close relatives, the meagre congregation consisted of one or two men from the foundry and their wives, and some of the staff from Penhallow. Celia had been too weak to attend and May Spargo was engaged in looking after her.

Arrangements with the Red Cross for her mother's trip to Switzerland were under way, but Kerensa realized that Lennie was making sure she kept her side of the bargain before completing them. Of course, as he had taken pains to point out, there would be no honeymoon for them – he wasn't made of money and if it were to be spent on Celia, then what did she expect?

So, after the ceremony, the new Mr and Mrs Retallick walked the short distance to Lennie's house where they were to live, dispensed a few cups of tea and biscuits to the guests who had bothered to come back with them, then the front door was firmly closed against the outside world. Later, Lennie went off down the pub to celebrate with his drinking companions and Kerensa was left on her own to get used to her new life.

She had hardly been inside the house before, certainly not for any length of time because she had tried to avoid doing so, but she had gained an impression of dark stuffiness and the smell of old dust about its interior. As she wandered through the place while Lennie was out, she realized that her first impressions had been correct.

It was typically the home of a single man. Dingy brown velvet curtains hung at the downstairs windows, faded into stripes along the folds where the light caught them. The walls were also brown as far as the dado rail, above which hung heavy maroon wallpaper, and while the parlour was furnished with an ancient settee and sagging chairs in balding plush, in the dining-room was a vast oak table with six chairs, all holding the dust of ages on their ornately turned legs.

Kerensa getting more dispirited by the minute, turned up the stairs and surveyed the bedrooms. The furniture in two of them were covered in dust sheets. She would investigate those another day. In the room where Lennie slept, the fug of old alcohol fumes hit her as soon as she opened the door. With one hand to her nose Kerensa crossed the room and struggled to open the heavy sash window, which was obviously not used to such treatment and shrieked in protest. Fresh air blew the dirty net curtains inward and Kerensa sighed as she leaned on the window-sill and propped her head on her hands. It was going to take her months of work to get the place habitable by her standards. But she was well used to hard work. So, first things first. She straightened up, left the room and went in search of clean bed-linen.

Surprisingly, the airing cupboard was stocked with fairly usable towels and sheets. Presumably Lennie must use the steam laundry, as she had noticed that his shirts were always clean. Kerensa heaved a sigh of thankfulness for small mercies as she changed the bed and shook up the pillows in preparation for her husband's return.

This she had been dreading – the moment when they actually climbed into bed, put out the light and she was alone with him. But as it happened, Lennie was too befuddled when he returned that night to do more than wrap his octopus-like arms and legs around her and breathe stomach-churning fumes into her face, before falling heavily asleep and snoring loudly throughout the night. While Kerensa having heaved his inert form over to the other side of the bed and as far away from her as possible, wept weak tears of loneliness into the noisy darkness.

Soon after she had arrived at work the following morning – for Lennie had changed his mind about lifting her out of the servant class and had graciously allowed her to keep her place at Penhallow for the money it brought in – the servants were called together in the kitchen by Alice Nance. Like a general surveying his troops, Kerensa thought.

'Miss Grace will be returning tomorrow,' the housekeeper announced, 'and I want this house looking spotless from attic to basement when she does.' Her sharp eyes looked them all up and down. 'Kerensa, you are to attend to the dining-room – the furniture needs a good rubbing-up. Then give the drawing-room a thorough turn-out. There are plenty of damp tea-leaves saved, so sprinkle them liberally over the carpet and give it a proper brushing, mind.' Kerensa nodded and the stiff figure moved on.

'Florrie, the bedrooms, including the guest room.' The girl's eyebrows rose and, as Alice Nance passed, Florrie exchanged a look with Kerensa, who shrugged. She had no idea who the visitor was, either. Jago? The thought came and was banished as quickly. Even if he came to escort Grace home, he had his own room. 'Cook,' the housekeeper's imperious voice rang out, 'we will discuss the week's menus if you please.' She looked over her shoulder as she turned to leave. 'To your work, all of you,' she commanded. 'I shall be around later on to inspect what you've done.'

'Of course,' said Florrie under her breath, 'and she's probably hidden a half-crown under the mats to make sure we take them up, too.'

The cleaning orgy took longer than one day and Kerensa was still in the drawing-room with duster and brush, when she heard the carriage draw up outside. She stood on tiptoe and glancing through the window saw that several people were alighting.

She had been deep in thoughts of Lennie, her mouth twisted in contempt. For as he had pointed out, if he were to spend his windfall on Celia's treatment, they would need her wages to supplement his income. So her position had changed little – she was still a skivvy in the only place she ever called home, although as a married woman now she no longer had to live in.

But now she jerked back to reality. There was Jago! At the sight of him her heart began to thump in the old familiar fashion, in spite of her present despondency. He had halted to help Grace down the steps and Kerensa was about to turn away from the window when her attention was caught by a third figure. Meanwhile Jago had taken a portmanteau from the carriage, placed it on the ground and straightened up, and was holding out his arm again. Then a daintily gloved hand appeared and another woman made her delicate way down the steps. A tall, imposing woman, expensively shod and clad in the latest fashion with bustle, train, feathered hat and parasol. Kerensa's hand flew to her mouth. *Isabella?*

CHAPTER NINE

It *was* Isabella! Kerensa swiftly crossed the room, her duster still in her hand, and pressed her ear to the crack in the door. It was a Saturday and Silas was at home. First inside was Grace.

'Hello, Papa.' There was a pause where Kerensa could imagine her reaching up on tiptoe to give him a peck on the cheek. 'It's so *lovely* to be home again!' An indecipherable growl from Silas, then the reply, 'Of *course* I had a wonderful time, but it's been so long and I was getting homesick for Penhallow and' – her voice dropped as she murmured – 'for

Dan. I missed him dreadfully.'

'Nothing's changed then?' Silas's voice had a rough edge to it. 'I thought you would have forgotten all that nonsense by now and found yourself a young gentleman. Especially after what I said to you before you went.'

'Oh no, Father.' Grace's voice held a new note of confidence and Kerensa's brows rose. 'I met many young men in London, but not one who could hold a candle to Dan. He's the one for me and I'm prepared to wait for him as long as I need to.' Good for you, thought Kerensa, clasping the duster to her with both hands.

'But—' Silas was beginning to bluster when Grace added, 'Here comes Jago, with someone he wants you to meet. I'll see you later, Papa. Take that case upstairs, Roberts, please,' she added, and her voice faded away into the distance.

Greatly daring, Kerensa opened the door a fraction so that she could peer through the crack. Isabella was standing directly in her line of vision, and she could see the black upswept hair beneath the smart hat, the strong features, dark, flashing eyes and the head held proudly high. Dainty feet in high-heeled kid boots peeked from under her travelling costume of pearl-grey alpaca, its skirt ruched at the back to fall in a becoming drape to the ground.

Jago stood beside her and she had one gloved hand on his fore-arm. 'Isabella has come back with me for a holiday, Father. I've been telling her so much about Cornwall that she decided to come and see it for herself.'

'Delighted to meet you, my dear.' To Kerensa's amazement Silas was bending over her hand with a dazzling smile. Kerensa gritted her teeth. What was there about this woman that seemed to have men both young and old falling at her feet? To her disgust, she could see that Jago had a hand beneath Isabella's elbow as if she were a piece of Dresden china, as they walked down the hall and out of sight. Kerensa's face fell and with a heave of her shoulders she turned back to her neglected dusting.

Week followed dreary week as Kerensa struggled to come to terms with her new role as Lennie Retallick's wife. Gradually she began to know him better, and with knowledge came a certain amount of power. He no longer frightened her, for she had discovered that most of his threats were bluster and he was far too conscious of his public image, and the fact that she could spread tales about him to the neighbours, to actually ill-treat her.

But she soon found out that the shade of the departed Mrs Retallick was never far away. In fact she was still everywhere in the house. Lennie came across Kerensa one day taking down the curtains for washing and when she had innocently remarked, 'These are so faded, I think I'll get some material in the market and make up some new ones. The room badly needs decorating too, don't you think?'

But Lennie's face had flared brick-red as he slammed a fist down in temper, and barked out, 'No! You most certainly will not. Mother chose those curtains and this paper; this was her favourite room and I absolutely forbid you to tamper with it.'

Kerensa discovered that it was the same about any changes she wanted to make. To all intents and purposes 'Mother' was still living here and her word was law. So, apart from cleaning the house thoroughly and washing all the furnishings, Kerensa mentally shrugged off the whole thing. She couldn't care less; whatever she did to this place it would never feel like her home, so if he wanted to keep it as a mausoleum he could.

Kerensa had brought so few of her own belongings with her that they hardly made a ripple on the surface of the house, so she persuaded herself that it really didn't matter either way, because Kerensa found that the one thing she had dreaded most of all turned out not to be so dreadful after all. Although she dutifully shared a bed with him as she had promised, she had discovered that Lennie was actually incapable of anything beyond a few gropes and fumbles when he had been drinking, which he did most evenings. She wondered whether the shade of Mother which lingered so potently in the atmosphere had something to do with it, but as long as he left her alone she could only be grateful to the old woman for staying around.

So although Kerensa continued to use the sponge and vinegar which she had learnt about from the other maids at work, she found them to be unnecessary, and continued to live in the curious state of being married in name but not in actuality. And as long as she didn't think too much about the sadness of that state, she could live with it. At times however, the disturbing thought would surface that before they were married Lennie had said he wanted children, and Kerensa wondered whether she was being overly optimistic.

Meanwhile her work at Penhallow kept her away from home a great deal and her husband spent so much of his time either at work or with his cronies, that thankfully she didn't see a lot of him. There was also some mysterious business which kept him occupied in a building which he owned in a small field across the back lane. The pony trap was kept there and the animal stabled, but as Lennie never mentioned the subject Kerensa did not bother to enquire. She assumed he had some kind of workshop because she had found that to give him his due, Lennie was quite a good handyman, which came in useful when things around the house needed fixing.

One day, however, Kerensa had to go and seek out her husband with a message from the foundry. She could see Lennie through the window, moving about inside the building as she made her way through the gate and across the field. She was wearing soft shoes which made no sound on the grass, and when she pushed open the door and spoke to him, it was obvious by the way he jumped, that he had not heard her coming.

Kerensa widened her eyes in surprise and stared at him, for a look of pure guilt had crossed Lennie's face. It was gone in a flash as he swore and bundled some papers into the drawer of an old cupboard behind him. Turning a key in the lock and quickly pocketing it, he glowered at her and roared, 'What the hell do you think you're doing, woman, creeping up and spying on me like that, eh?' His face reddened as he added, 'I told you never to come down here, didn't I?' He stabbed a finger at her. 'This is my private workshop and I will *not* be disturbed. Haven't I already made that clear?'

Kerensa gasped at this unexpected attack and took a step backwards as Lennie's furious eyes bored into hers and he raised a fist as if he meant to strike her. She rallied then and snapped back, 'For goodness' sake, I only came down with a message for you from the works. And I most certainly was *not* creeping up on you, I just happened to be walking on grass which,' she added with scorn, 'does not normally make a great deal of noise.'

Lennie calmed down and lowered his arm. 'S-Sorry Kerensa,' he blustered, 'it's just that you made me jump so. It's very quiet here, you see, and my thoughts were miles away. . . .'

'I see.' Her voice was icy. 'As to why I'm here, *spying* on you, as you put it, Silas sent a boy to say that you're wanted at the foundry. Some sales rep is waiting to see you, and it's urgent.' Lennie muttered a smothered curse, rolled down his shirtsleeves and reached for his jacket.

Kerensa cast a curious glance around the place, but there was nothing that looked out of place. A work bench ran around two sides, with rows of tools hanging above it, and apart from the sagging old cupboard and the chair, that was all. As she left, she could hear the pony moving about in its stall on the other side of the partition wall. Lennie carefully locked the door and disappeared round the corner to harness the animal and ride into Camborne to answer his summons.

Jago had persuaded Isabella to come out for a ride one morning, during which he intended to take her across the moors and along the cliff path to show her the magnificent coastal scenery. Isabella had taken some persuading, as her idea of riding was a leisurely parade up and down Rotten Row in order to see and be seen by fashionable society.

However, she had eventually consented and they had ambled up through the fields until they were now approaching the coast. 'This is what I miss most when I'm in London,' Jago remarked, as they walked their horses side by side along the cliff top. A crisp off-shore wind was whipping up the waves far below and the white horses of his childhood were kicking up their heels as they galloped shoreward in a froth of jade-green and white. 'Don't you think it's magnificent?' he asked, as he turned a glowing face towards her. Isabella was holding one hand to her hat, a dainty, tip-tilted confection of olive-green felt, decorated with the wing of an unfortunate pheasant.

'Mm.' came the non-committal reply. 'Is it always as windy as this?'

Jago laughed. 'Usually,' he said, 'yes. Bracing, isn't it? Come on, let's go!' He put a hand beneath her booted foot and helped her to mount, then flung himself into his own saddle. 'I'll race you to that stand of blackthorn bushes at the next bend.'

Before Isabella could reply, he was off. Leaning low over the horse's back, he set it at a canter and was soon way ahead of her, reaching the finish before she was little more than halfway. When she caught up, her mouth was set in a pout and her hat was dangling by its elastic at the back of her neck. 'That wasn't fair!' she exclaimed, 'you hardly gave me time to start and you know I'm not used to this mare of Grace's.' Her mouth drooped into a sullen pout as she slid from her mount and joined Jago where he was sitting on a flat rock, looking out to sea.

'Sorry.' he said good-naturedly and reached out a hand to pull her down beside him as Isabella tried in vain to tidy her loosened hair, 'Just look at that view though – isn't that something worth seeing?' The day had started with a dusting of frost in the valley, but now the sun was shining and an exhilarating breeze was tossing puffs of cotton-wool clouds through a clear blue sky.

Isabella had hunched her arms around herself and was sitting with her back to the wind and to the sea. She took a brief look over her shoulder as he waved a hand that encompassed the wild waves tossing in the cove below, and the panorama of magnificent headlands stretching away fold upon fold to each side of them. 'I'm cold,' she said and shivered.

The smile slipped from Jago's face and he fell silent. For a moment a memory surfaced in his mind. A memory of another visit to this same spot, it seemed like aeons ago now, and of the child-woman he had found here in tears. She had loved the place as he did, had revelled in the sharp, pure air which had swept their breath away. He had cantered then along this same path with her clinging tightly round his waist, her cloud of dark hair streaming out behind them.

Kerensa. He had forgotten the freshness of her, the innocence, the honesty. But then he remembered how she had distanced herself on his last visit, had obviously wanted nothing more to do with him, and his mouth hardened.

Jago glanced at the sullen face beside him and sighed. To be fair he supposed he couldn't blame Isabella. She was a woman accustomed to being indoors, to city life, with its crowds and bustle. He should have realized that she was not cut out for the country. 'Sorry, Is,' he apologized again and reached for her hand. 'We'll go back now.'

She ignored the hand and scrambled to her feet. 'Don't call me Is,' she snapped, 'I hate it.'

Determined that he would not apologize for a third time, Jago stayed silent. They rode back still in silence until they reached Penhallow, and coming upon it from the rear, they followed a path which Isabella had not yet seen. Pausing as she took in the devastation of the garden and the great steam excavator which was still churning its way through the estate, her eyes widened as she asked, 'What's going on here? Are you having some building work done?'

When Jago explained, her eyes opened even wider. 'Buried treasure? Are you serious? How exciting!' Her face had lifted for the first time that day, Jago noticed. 'It's Father's obsession,' he replied. 'I'm afraid he's an avaricious man and he's convinced himself that the legend must have a grain of truth in it, so,' he shrugged, 'he's prepared to level the whole place if necessary. Richard's just as bad as he is and keeps urging him on. So far they have turned up precisely nothing.'

As the riders turned into the yard, Lennie was just leaving by the back door. He had been closeted with Silas in the study for some time, and had come through to the kitchen to tell Kerensa that he had been called away on business in Truro and would not be home before evening. Kerensa nodded and shrugged. It was nothing to her. Rebelliously she thought to herself that she wouldn't care if he never came back again.

For recently her worst nightmare had been realized after all. Lennie had come to bed sober for once and had at last set about making her his wife in fact as well as name.

'Leave it,' he'd said gruffly, as she reached across to turn down the wick of the oil lamp, 'I want to see you. Take off your nightgown.' But before Kerensa's trembling fingers could unfasten the row of tiny pearl buttons, he had seized it and she heard the fabric rip.

Kerensa gasped with shock as he jerked the garment over her head and glanced up at her husband in dismay – and fear, as she saw Lennie pass his tongue over his lips and look her up and down, as if he were mentally ravaging her flesh with his hot, greedy eyes.

'No!' she cried, and tried to cover herself, but he silenced her by bringing his wet, open mouth down on hers, while one of his clutching hands caught painfully at her breast and kneaded it with hard, eager fingers. Then he slid his other hand underneath her body until he was gripping her so tightly she could hardly breathe. Terrified, some atavistic instinct made her bring her knee up to try to force him away, but this only excited him even more.

Lennie, inflamed with lust, rolled completely on top of her then and Kerensa's cringing flesh felt the full weight of his body, pressing her deep, deeper into the feather pillows. She was suffocating . . . his hot mouth was all over her, sucking, licking, biting, until at last he forced himself inside her like a rutting animal, grinding his way in to violate the most intimate parts of her body until she screamed aloud at the agony of it.

All this came back to her in a wave of revulsion as she lingered on the step for a moment to take a breath of fresh air. It was stiflingly hot in the kitchen, as Molly had both ranges blazing away as well as the big boiler in which she was preparing the Christmas puddings. With hindsight Kerensa realized that her husband, like most inadequate men, was a bully. Last night had proved it, when Lennie had revealed himself in his true colours. Now she knew what to expect, and next time she would be prepared. Kerensa tilted her chin and gave him a hard stare. She was determined never to suffer humiliation like that again.

'Well, get going then,' she snapped, as Lennie leaned forward to give her a peck on the cheek. 'And stop that. I've told you before – don't touch me in public!' she hissed, scrubbing at her face with a handkerchief. Lennie's face darkened and he grabbed at her shoulder, twisting her round to face him. 'You're my wife and I'll kiss you when I want, wherever I want,' he shouted, 'and don't you forget it!' Suddenly he flung her aside and Kerensa caught her head on the door frame with a sickening thud which made her see stars. She gasped as the sky tilted, before collapsing senseless to the ground.

At the same moment, Jago and Isabella arrived in a clatter of hoofs and reined in their horses, preparing to dismount.

'Kerensa!' Jago dropped the reins and strode to her side. Placing one hand around her shoulders and the other clasping her waist, he was attempting to raise her when Lennie shouldered in and began to pull her from his arms. 'Leave her to me,' he growled, 'I can take care of my own wife, thank you. Kerensa?' He took her by the shoulders and shook her, slapping at her face to bring her round.

Kerensa opened her eyes and gradually began to focus on the faces around her. 'J-Jago?' she said weakly, and extended a limp hand. He bent down on one knee, ignoring Lennie behind her who was attempting to drag her to her feet.

'*Wife?*' he exclaimed, 'You mean that you're . . . you're married to *him*? But you can't be!'

Even in her weakened state Kerensa registered the shock, and pain? – she would like to think so – in his eyes, as she nodded. 'I had to,' she whispered.

'*Had* to?' Jago echoed and she saw with a stab of anguish how his face twisted and his former expression of concern turned to one of disillusion, disgust and finally contempt as he sprang to his feet as if stung.

'Jay, it's not . . .' She tried to tell him of his mistake, but Lennie was hustling her to her feet and straightening her clothing as if he owned her – which he does – oh, Jago, he does! Her eyes pleaded for understanding, but there was none on his stony face and he was turning away; he was going. And, as she stood looking after him helplessly, Isabella's fluting voice came drifting over them all. 'Oh Jago, come along, darling, leave the woman to her husband, for goodness' sake. She's only a servant, after all.' She clung possessively to his arm, her gaze locked with Kerensa's and she too, gave her a look of contempt as she pulled him away.

She was too weak to call after Jago to try to explain, to tell him that no – oh, no, it's not what you think, come back, come back to me! But in her mind Kerensa did all these things. Anything to blank out that contemptuous expression on his beloved face, the last thing she had seen of him as Isabella urged him away.

'Are you all right now?' Kerensa swung round and met the shifty eyes of her husband. They were full of guilt, so he must have realized he had gone too far. Ignoring him, she merely glared, turned on her heel and swept into the kitchen slamming the door behind her. Fortunately it was empty and she could sink into the comfortable rocker and bury her head in her hands.

She wept some bitter tears then, wept until a tiny voice inside her head suddenly spoke up and told her sternly that this was getting her nowhere. Don't sit there wallowing in self-pity, it said, *get even with him*! Kerensa straightened up, wiped her eyes and thought about this. Yes. What she needed was some hold over Lennie if she were to take him on at his own game. Something with which *she* could blackmail *him*, and, as she thought more deeply, a slow smile spread over her face, for Kerensa had an idea.

Lennie *did* have a secret, didn't he? There was something in that shed of his which he kept hidden, she was sure of it. Both hands to her cheeks, Kerensa thought back to the time when she had 'crept up on him' as he had put it, and the look of pure guilt which had suffused his face when he had seen her there. Her eyes widened. Yes!

So she bided her time and watched. Watched what he did with his keys, where he left them at night, and waited. Their house had only two entrances and they both had a key to front and back doors, as they came and went at different times. Lennie also had another key on his ring which opened the small safe in which he kept his money and their personal documents. Kerensa had not been entrusted with a copy of that one. So when he put down the ring of keys on the night stand as he did when preparing for bed, she studied it, noting the extra one and making a mental picture of its scrollwork and design so that she could recognize it by touch, even in the dark.

Over time, Lennie continued to claim his marital rights and invade her body, but never to rape her as brutally as he had that first time. Kerensa wondered if he had shamed even himself that night. Now she was learning to steel herself against his proximity by distancing herself in her mind. She would try to think of something pleasurable from the past, and this was usually by reliving that glorious day on the cliffs so long ago, when Jago had taken her up on his horse and they had galloped beside the galloping sea. If she could immerse herself in memories she could somehow get through the nights.

Kerensa waited for a few days until Lennie came home one night in a drunken state, fell into bed as if pole-axed and was soon snoring heavily, then crept from his side and carefully, oh so carefully, lifted the ring of keys. She tiptoed across the room, holding her breath as a floorboard creaked, then, with her heart pounding, reached the wash-stand. With enough light filtering in from the gas lamp in the street outside to see what she was doing, Kerensa pressed the key of the shed firmly into the bar of wet soap which earlier she had placed within easy reach. Then she took a second impression for safety's sake, replaced the soap with a new bar and crept back to bed, hiding the evidence behind the furniture until she could remove it first thing in the morning.

At the ironmonger's the next time she went shopping, Kerensa produced the perfect image which had been cut in the soap and with her sweetest smile looked guilelessly into the man's face as she said, 'My husband would like to have a key cut from this mould, if you please. This method may be a little unusual, but he asked me to say that he cannot spare the original as it is constantly in use.'

The ironmonger bowed over her hand as she relinquished the soap. 'Of course, madam. Tell your husband that this is an excellent impression and it'll be no trouble at all. I'll have it ready for him by tomorrow morning.'

'Thank you. He'll be most grateful.' Kerensa treated the man to another dazzling smile, and this one stayed on her face until she was some way down the street.

She waited until her next half-day and made sure that Lennie was at the foundry and not likely to come back for an hour or two, before slipping down the back lane and into the field. The key turned perfectly: with a last look over her shoulder she pushed the door open and was inside at last. Closing the door carefully behind her and making sure she was well away from the window, Kerensa went straight to the drawer that Lennie had been at when she had surprised him. It was locked of course, but she had been sharp-eyed enough to notice where he had hung that key before they had left – in the corner behind a row of tools. Yes! There it was still.

The drawer was full of papers. Bills? Receipts? Invoices? They looked formal, and disappointingly boring, like business communications. Kerensa had had no idea what she was expecting to find, but it was something more interesting than these. Careful to keep them strictly in order, she scanned one or two.

Then a letter caught her attention and she paused to read it more closely, looking at the heading first.

Derbyshire Detonators Ltd. For the finest in Safety Lighters. Suppliers to Messrs. Abrahams' Lead Mines and Mining Companies of Discernment World-wide.

Dear L
Many apologies, but you will find that this order is short by two boxes of the amount that you asked for. This is due to "circumstances beyond my

control" you understand!

Also I would give you a gentle reminder that I have not yet received my share for last month's consignment and should be pleased if you would expedite this.

Yrs truly
M.

Kerensa frowned, the letter still in her hand as she gazed across the room in thought. But surely Cardrew's bought their detonators locally? Smithford's – the biggest manufacturer of safety fuse and explosive devices in the country – had its huge works actually on the outskirts of Camborne itself.

So why was Lennie dealing with a company as far away as Derbyshire? And so secretively? For the correspondents to sign only their initials was highly irregular in business. What bona-fide salesmen would do so? And if they were *not* bona-fide, then they were up to no good. Kerensa's quick brain was racing ahead. What was her husband up to? A rake-off of the profits for each of them? If he was running some sort of racket through Cardrew's, it was possible.

But she had been here long enough, and she could always come again. She riffled through the rest of the papers which all seemed to be similar transactions, and as an afterthought extracted a few of the older letters from the bottom of the pile and slipped them into her apron pocket.

Kerensa carefully locked the drawer and replaced the key in its hiding place. She also locked the door behind her, checking left and right that there was nobody about, before slipping into the kitchen to look around for a hiding place for the letters. Eventually she concealed them in a paper bag underneath the flour inside her bin in the larder, where Lennie would never find them. She was going to savour her new-found knowledge until an appropriate time arose.

'Kerensa!' At the sound of the cook's voice, the girl looked up from the oven where she was checking on the tray of pasties they had baked that morning. 'Take this tray of tea out to the workmen, will you, my handsome?' Molly, flushed-faced and with her sleeves rolled up above her elbows as she kneaded bread dough, went on, 'There's nobody else around – never is when you're busy. Mrs Nance have got all the other girls helping with the laundry because the washer-woman's sick and can't come in today.'

'Of course I will.' Kerensa took the loaded tray and left by the back door. She carefully picked her way across the cobbled yard and down to the former vegetable garden, which was now being relentlessly dug over in its turn. It had rained overnight and the ground was a sea of mud, thick and slippery. As she rounded a corner she could see from the plumes of smoke where the great excavator was at work, on a bank above the level of the garden, ripping up some shrubs and the remains of a stone wall. One man was guiding the digging apparatus from the front, while at the other end the fireman was shovelling coal to keep the huge boiler in steam.

To her surprise, Kerensa could see Jago and Isabella chatting to Richard and Silas, who was waving his arms about and pointing, obviously explaining to them his plans for the operation. But the tray was getting heavier by the minute and she had to look away from them and concentrate on where she was stepping, in order not to slip and drop the whole thing.

Consequently, Kerensa did not notice the great machine begin to slide backwards in an alarming way as some of the loose ground subsided. Nor was she aware that it was gaining momentum as it came plunging down the bank towards her, until she was alerted by a shout from one of the men.

Only then did she look up, see the giant shovel towering over her, the two men on the platform frantically shouting and gesticulating at her to get out of the way. As Kerensa realized the danger she was in, the tray fell from her hands with a crash and she gave a scream of terror, but, as she tried to leap to safety, her feet slipped from under her in the slick mud and she knew she was falling to the ground, right in the path of the machine.

But, at the last split second, she was saved from certain death by a figure who dived towards her with a tackle like a rugby player, caught her waist with both hands and gave her a mighty shove, just as the great machine rolled past and came to a shuddering halt as it met the level ground.

But the giant bucket, out of control now, whipped round on its axis and caught Richard, who had also been running to Kerensa's rescue, a sickening blow to the side of his head, instantly felling him, where he dropped motionless into the sucking mud.

Men sprang from the engine, others joined them, suddenly there were people milling all around, but over and above all the shouting came one single piercing scream of agony. Almost inhuman, like an animal in its death-throes, it was chilling in its intensity. It came, not from Kerensa, who was unhurt and shaking in every limb as she dragged herself upright, but from the second man lying face-down in the mud where she had been standing a few seconds ago. He was unconscious too, and his left hand was trapped beneath the wheel of the excavator. Jago! Oh, God, no! Not Jago! Kerensa fell to her knees again in the clinging mire and wrapped her arms around herself as she rocked back and forth, keening in anguish. Jago! And she could do nothing. Not run to him, not take him in her arms, not even lift his beloved face out of the mud, although he had saved her life.

For there were his family crowding around him doing all those things, and men from the estate were running now with crowbars, with ropes to help the engine men raise the wheel, to tilt the whole enormous weight far enough over and hold it long enough for other hands to gently, gently, slide him out from under it. To raise Richard as well and place both men on the ladders which had been brought for the purpose.

Kerensa could not take her eyes off Jago's still form. Silas and one of the men between them were carrying him towards the house, while others followed with the second casualty. Isabella walked alongside Jago, tears streaming down her face, holding his good hand, while blood dripped from the damaged one in a steady stream, despite all the makeshift bandages which had been hastily applied.

And Kerensa could only stay where she was, frozen with shock, horror and cold. She could not walk with them, could not hold his hand however much she longed to. For she was only a servant. She knelt on in the icy mud, heedless of the penetrating cold which numbed her flesh and crept upwards to numb her brain as well, driving out all feeling apart from a suffocating blanket of guilt.

Because it had all been *her fault*.

CHAPTER TEN

Richard was dead. He had died instantly from that one devastating blow to the side of his head. The servants had been creeping about on tiptoe ever since the tragedy three days before, and a pall of gloom so thick that it was almost tangible hung over the house and everyone in it. How quiet it suddenly seemed, Kerensa thought, without his big, booming voice, hearty laugh and heavy-booted tread on the stairs.

Silas wandered around the house like a lean grey ghost of himself, stooped and dull-eyed. With all the spirit knocked out of him, he had become an old man in the space of one night. Only Grace, whose suffering was as great but whose self-discipline was formidable, hid her grief and held her head high, keeping her tears in check to be shed in the privacy of her own room.

Thanks to her fortitude some semblance of normal life went on, and Kerensa noticed that it was Grace who urged her father into arranging the funeral, which she as a woman could not do, and Grace who attended to all the messages of condolence which came pouring in, along with the constant stream of callers.

So it was to her that Kerensa turned, desperate for news. 'Miss Grace, please. . .' Throwing convention to the winds – for surely this was more important – she just had to ask. They had met in the passage, Grace hurrying towards her parlour with the morning's mail clutched in her hand. 'How' – Kerensa swallowed – 'how's Mr Jago now?'

Grace looked abstractedly at her maid as if Kerensa were a stranger. 'Oh, his poor hand!' she replied and her mouth trembled. 'It's so crushed they can't tell yet how damaged it is. It'll take time, you see, before the doctors can possibly know.'

Kerensa's heart turned over. At the very least this would take weeks, maybe months. And meeting Grace's eyes she was sure they were both thinking the same thing. The piano. Would Jago ever play again?

'He's terribly depressed, of course,' Grace added. 'He shuts himself up in his room for hours on end. Isabella can't shake him out of it, and neither can I. Maybe when the funeral is over. . . .'

Richard was buried on Christmas Eve, when the rest of the world was preparing to celebrate the happiest day of the year. From the back of the church where she sat with the rest of the servants, Kerensa craned her neck to see if Jago was present. Yes! There he was, sitting with the family. How pale and gaunt he looked, his arm strapped up in a sling. Kerensa stifled a sob as the massive burden of guilt descended again and settled even more heavily on her shoulders. One good man dead and the love of her life maybe crippled – all because of her!

Her gaze swept over the rest of the congregation. There was a big attendance, the church was almost full. Not many followed the family out to the interment however, for it was pouring with rain. In the churchyard the great, gloomy yew trees were dripping their own tears onto the huddle of mourners. Clustered around the grave which gaped like an open wound, their responses were muffled, and the minister had to raise his voice to be heard above the squawking of the crows in the branches overhead. '. . . ashes to ashes . . . dust to dust . . . in sure and certain hope. . . .' What memories the ancient words brought back.

Memories of her grandfather's death and its consequences remained with Kerensa for several days as she dragged herself around like an automaton, and she found her thoughts returning to his will which she had never really looked at since, knowing the outcome of it so well.

She'd put it away in her underwear drawer for secrecy – never would she share such painful memories with her husband. Sitting on the bed with her chin on her hand Kerensa thought wistfully how lovely it would be to have someone close with whom she *could* share things, and receive comfort, sympathy and support. Instead of the constant stress which was life with Lennie Retallick.

Kerensa still found release in reading however, continuing to borrow books from the Penhallow library. But Lennie never lost a chance to taunt her about it.

'Pooh – *reading* again?' he had said last time he had come in from work and found her sitting by the range. 'Got nothing better to do than bury your nose in a *book*? My tea ready is it? Or have you been too *busy*?' His lip curled.

Kerensa had been on her feet since six that morning and had just sat down for her first real break of the day. Biting her tongue, she merely gave him a withering look and said nothing as still holding her book in one hand, with the other she passed him the pasty which had been keeping warm on the range beside her. Kerensa knew that the thing which incensed Lennie most was her air of calm detachment and refusal to rise to his baiting. He never lost a chance to try and bring her down to his intellectual level, but if she refrained from arguing, then he had no defence and would eventually slink off somewhere else.

It went against the grain for her naturally spirited nature to remain so passive, but she thought with weary resignation it was better than the constant rowing. Kerensa had known for a long time what a different person she had become from the lively girl she had once been. Nowadays she felt so colourless and washed out that she wondered if one day she might become invisible and vanish completely away. And if anyone would notice if she did.

She opened the envelope and drew the sheets of thick vellum towards her. *This is the last will and testament of me, Joseph Tregoning of Penhallow, near Camborne in the county of Cornwall. I hereby appoint Mr Henry Thomas, of Grylls and Thomas, Solicitors, to be the sole executor of this my will. . . .*

Kerensa skimmed the page and as she reached the bottom her eyes came to rest on the signatures there. Joseph Tregoning. Sarah and William Harris, and the date. Then she raised her eyes from the page and gazed unseeingly out of the window. For that date rang a bell, and she couldn't recall why it should . . . Kerensa nibbled at the ball of her thumb in concentration.

Yes! Now she remembered. That had been the birth date of Sarah and William's youngest child. Little Edith. Sarah had gone home to her mother for the baby's birth, and William had taken some leave to be with her. They had wanted Kerensa to be godmother to the baby, but Mama had said that she was too young. So she had sent a present instead – a coral rattle – Kerensa could see it still.

So – and the realization hit her like a punch in the stomach – they hadn't been in Camborne then, and could not possibly have acted as witnesses. A frown puckered Kerensa's brow. So how could both their signatures be on this document? Somebody must have written them. The solicitors, by proxy? But why? Anyone could act as a witness – they could easily have found someone else. And it would have said 'pp' underneath, for *pro parte* – meaning 'for and on behalf of. . . .' If not the solicitors, then who?

'I can't tell you how much it means to me to have you here.' Jago reached for Isabella's hand with his good one and gave it a squeeze.

They were walking around the grounds, carefully avoiding the scene of the accident. The excavator had been permanently removed, for there would be no more treasure-hunting now. Silas had at last returned to his work at the foundry, a broken man. Nature was taking over the devastation of the garden and already small shoots were springing up to soften the carnage with new green.

'Ah – um – yes.' Isabella paused for a moment, then said, 'Jago – there's something I've been meaning to say for some time, actually.'

Surprised at the unexpected tone of her voice, Jago raised an eyebrow. 'Oh? What's that?'

'I'm going back to London soon.'

His jaw dropped. 'Going back? Isabella, why?' She met his startled expression with a defiant tilt of her head.

'My career,' she said briefly and turned away. 'Jago – I'm *stagnating* in this backwater of yours.' Her hand swept over the scene in one expressive gesture which included the leafless trees, the sodden ground, the grey

deadness of the January day. 'I only came for a few weeks' holiday originally – and then all this happened,' – she indicated his strapped hand – 'so
I felt I couldn't in all fairness desert you, at least until after the funeral.'

Isabella lowered her eyes and scuffed at some dead leaves with the toe
of a dainty boot. 'But I'm not a country person, and I *am* missing London.'
She paused before adding, 'And as it seems now that you – that it's going
to be ... well, a long time before ... or if ... before you come back to
London yourself. . . .' Her voice trailed away.

Jago swallowed, and filled in the words which she had left unsaid.
Before your hand recovers. Before you can play again, *if* you ever play
again! And in a blinding rush of blood to the head as all his own fears and
doubts rose to the surface, he seized her arm and yelled into her startled
face, 'All right then, go! I know you never liked it down here from the
start, but I thought you – that we – *meant* something to each other.'

He flung her from him and turned on his heel. 'Isabella, I was hoping
at one point that we might have a future together. But now that you've
made it perfectly plain that all we shared was our love of music, I can see
you want to be rid of me now that I'm useless as a musician.'

Isabella gasped. 'Jago! I never said. . . .' One hand fluttered to her
mouth.

'You didn't have to: it was written all over your face,' he retorted with
scorn.

'But it's my agent you see – I have commitments, schedules,' Isabella
went on. 'Surely you understand that I can't stay here indefinitely?'

Jago snorted. 'Oh, go back to your city life, your career and your *friends*.
As you pointed out, it's highly unlikely that I shall ever be part of it again.'
Bitterly he added, 'I'm sure that the charming Anton will be delighted to
take my place at the piano – and in your bed as well. It's what he's been
angling for ever since we met.'

Isabella gasped again. 'Oh Jay! Be fair—'

'Fair? You talk to me of fair? When was life ever *fair*?' He waved his
hurt arm at her and winced, then turned his back and marched into the
house as he felt scalding tears rising to form a hard knot in his throat.

Isabella was gone by the end of the week and now Jago could at last see
her for what she was. Older than he had previously thought when he had
been besotted with her. Harder certainly, for she had been putting on an
act all the time that he had thought they were made for each other. Now
he could see that she had only wanted him as a foil to keep up the illusion
of her youth and beauty, and that she would be quite happy to have Anton
take over seamlessly from where Jago had left off. And after Anton there

would always be another, for Isabella needed a slave constantly fawning at her feet as much as she needed air and water.

So Jago withdrew even more into himself and spent most of his time alone. He and his father met only at mealtimes, which they would have eaten in silence if Grace had not forced them into some kind of conversation, for the sake of keeping up appearances in front of the servants.

Without music Jago's life had become a barren wilderness. He went for long walks in the wintry countryside in order to exhaust himself physically, so that he could sleep at least part of each night and keep at bay for a few hours the demons that haunted him. *How many more dreary weeks before they could tell*? This not-knowing was worse than being told he was crippled for life. He couldn't stand it for much longer.

'Oh Dan, I can't stand it much longer!' Grace buried her head in his broad chest and sobbed. 'It's like living in a tomb. Father and Jago hardly speak to each other, nor to me either. I feel so *alone* with no one to talk to except the servants, and not one but you to confide in.'

Dan put a finger under her chin and looked directly into her face. 'What do you mean, *but* me? Grace, that hurts. I've said I'd do anything to get you out of that great house. And I do know what lonely feels like, believe me.' He gave her a hard stare.

Grace, contrite replied, 'Sorry Dan, I know how awful it was to lose both your parents so suddenly. And your sister too. That was really tough. That outbreak of typhoid left so many people with ruined lives. . . .'

'Yes,' he said abruptly. 'But what I'm telling you is, if you would *only* come away with me, we could be everything to each other and neither of us need ever feel lonely again.'

Grace looked up into his beloved face and gently stroked a hand through his beard. It was soft and smooth to touch – irrelevantly she remembered how before they met, she had always thought that whiskers would be prickly. 'Dan, you have to understand that I'm all that the two men have left now.'

She detached herself and they took a few steps hand in hand along the woodland track. 'With Mama gone, then Richard, and Jago like he is, our world has fallen apart and they can't cope with it. How could I possibly desert them as well? I would never forgive myself for running away.'

Dan made a sound of annoyance and shook the small hand. 'Listen to me, Grace Cardrew,' he said roughly. 'You've spent all your young life looking after your family, and they've just taken you for granted. It's high time you looked out for yourself for a change. And more importantly, you're everything to *me* as well.'

She gave him a quick glance and opened her mouth to reply, but Dan cut her off with a raised hand. 'I haven't finished. Just think now, if your father had had his way you would have been married by now to some bloke from the gentry who would have taken you a lot further away – maybe up country – to live. Then they would have *had* to manage without you.' His stormy eyes met hers and he nodded to drive home the point. 'As it is, you've promised to marry me in twelve months' time, so you'll be leaving home then anyway – I'll make sure of that.'

'But by then,' Grace countered, 'things will have moved on and we shall know about Jago—'

'Jago's a grown *man*, Grace,' Dan fumed and his voice rose. 'He doesn't need a nursemaid! He has to fight his own battles like the rest of us. Oh, think of it – we could go abroad – anywhere: America, Australia, South Africa.' He flung out a hand that encompassed the world. 'I can get a job mining in any of those places, maid, and there are Cornish communities too in all of them. You'd feel at home right away. And no one would know whether we was wed or no, nor care neither.'

He tossed her hand from him and his face was set and hard as he glared down at her. 'But of course, that wouldn't do for Miss Grace Cardrew of Penhallow, would it?' His lip curled and the eyes boring into hers had become cold and grey. 'I've always known that I could never be good enough for you,' he added bitterly, 'and that's the *real* reason you're dragging your heels, however much you try to deny it.' He turned abruptly and stepped away from her side.

'Dan, it's not *like* that! It was never like that! Oh, come *back*!' Grace stretched out pleading arms, but he was striding away up the hill with a set to his shoulders that told her more than words how deeply wounded he was. Grace stood helplessly watching his retreating figure until he rounded the bend without looking back, and was gone from her sight.

Kerensa was sitting on a stool outside the kitchen door, plucking a chicken to be roasted later for the day's dinner. It was a calm, mild day and, as she knew Molly would not be happy with her kitchen full of flying feathers, she had decided to remove herself and work in the yard. It was an automatic job and her thoughts wandered as she held the bird in her lap and plucked and pulled, tossing the feathers into a zinc bucket at her feet, for they would be carefully saved and cleaned for stuffing pillows and cushions. Alice Nance would make sure that nothing was wasted. That was what a good housekeeper does, I suppose, thought Kerensa idly.

Her thoughts drifted eventually back to the matter of the will again, and suddenly a revelation hit her like a slap in the face and she had to grab at the bird as it nearly rolled off her apron. *Of course!* She had suddenly remembered the scrap of paper with the names on it. Three names – the same names which appeared on that will. Written repeatedly, as if someone had been practising them. Perfecting the style of handwriting of each individual. Preparing to *forge them*? Kerensa's head began to swim with the enormity of the idea.

And the more she thought about it, the more everything fitted. The vague perplexity of the solicitor who couldn't put a finger on the reason for the change. Because, of course, he wouldn't have known the personal details of Sarah and William's circumstances which made it so suspect. Only Kerensa with her knowledge of the baby's birth knew that. And that knowledge was vital proof. That and the scrap of paper. Written in *Papa's* hand! Oh Papa, what *have* you done? Kerensa's soul cried out in anguish.

But she could see it all now with heartbreaking certainty. Zack had engineered a forgery so that Penhallow would come to him and not to Celia. So her mother had been right all along. Kerensa felt numb. That the father she had loved so much had been capable of such fraud was a bitter pill to swallow. Worse even than his desertion and leaving them in such dire straits – and would she ever discover the answer to that? she sighed.

So, what should she do next? Kerensa absently clasped the chicken in her lap. She could not keep this knowledge to herself; it was too important. For it had been a criminal act. Papa – a criminal! Her eyes began to fill. Oh, how she missed her mother at that moment. Missed the Celia she had formerly been, the mother of Kerensa's childhood. Before – before everything.

The last news from the clinic had been encouraging though. Celia's condition was stable although she was not out of danger yet. However, Kerensa felt keenly the absence of an older woman to turn to for advice, and especially so since her loveless marriage. Oh how tired Kerensa was of taking responsibility and making decisions!

'When you've finished cuddling that there bird,' broke in Molly's dry voice, 'I'll get it in the oven – if you can spare it, that is.'

Kerensa jumped, a wan smile lifting the corners of her mouth. 'Sorry, Moll, I was miles away just then,' she replied, and rose to her feet. 'Yes, I've finished the chicken. Here you are.' She forced her brain to return to the mundane and added, 'I'll go and wash my hands, then chop some sage for the stuffing. Have we got any breadcrumbs?'

For the rest of the day, Kerensa's thoughts were as busy as her hands, and by the time she could leave work she had made a plan. During the walk back to Camborne she decided to take the will and the piece of paper, show them to Nathan Thomas and ask *him* what she should do. He was a solicitor, he would know about these things. So feeling a whole lot better, she returned home to start work again, preparing a meal before Lennie came in.

Fortunately the next afternoon was Kerensa's half-day off and fortunately as well, the solicitor was free. He listened carefully to her story and when she had finished, his eyes narrowed. He removed his spectacles and pinched the bridge of his nose, deep in thought before saying, 'Well, well, Mrs Retallick, this is most surprising.'

Kerensa's attention was riveted to the man's face. Suppose he laughed her to scorn? What if he said that it was all her imagination? A curl of anxiety made her stomach clench and her heart begin to pound as she awaited his reply.

Nathan Thomas replaced his eye-glasses and pulled the documents towards him to scan them again. 'I can't deny that I think you may be right,' he said at last. He does believe me, he does! Kerensa felt her shoulders relax. She hadn't even realized how rigidly she had been holding herself. 'But there's only one way to prove it.' He pushed back his chair and tapped a pen on the blotter as he gazed out at the street.

'Yes?' Kerensa on the edge of her seat now, prompted him.

The solicitor placed his fore-arms on the desk and leaned towards her. 'I would have to send to London, to Somerset House, for a copy of the original will,' he said. 'As you may or may not know – and I should imagine that whoever forged this certainly did *not* know – any will has to be registered there and lodged with them for safe-keeping, in case it needs to be consulted at some future date. As indeed is the case here.' He smiled. Oh, thank goodness there was a way! Kerensa let out all the breath she'd been holding, and gave the man a beaming smile in return.

'It will take time, you understand,' he warned her, as Kerensa rose to leave. She nodded. He cleared his throat and went on, 'And -er- there will be a charge, of course. May I ask, if you don't think it an impertinence, how are you situated now regarding ... ah ... pecuniary matters?'

He remembers the last time I called, Kerensa thought, and he's making sure his fee is safe. 'Perfectly well, Mr Thomas,' she replied with her head up. 'Since my marriage you see—'

'Ah yes.' He relaxed visibly and gave her a thin smile. 'Allow me to offer my congratulations.' He held out a hand.

'Thank you,' said Kerensa and knew that her expression was as bleak as if she had been bereaved instead of wed. 'Perhaps you would let me know when you have any news?'

'Certainly, certainly.' The solicitor bowed over her hand and Kerensa left the office feeling as if her burden had become slightly lighter.

Silas, who had been deep in his account books at the foundry, looked up as Lennie entered the office. There was a comfortable fire burning in the grate to keep out the damp chill of February, and the oil lamp was glowing cheerfully. 'Heard the latest have you?' he asked his agent. Lennie looked blank as he backed towards the grate and held his hands out to the blaze. His wet coat began to steam and Silas added, 'Been an accident over to Dolcoath, so the men are saying.'

'Accident?' Lennie's brows rose. 'What kind of accident?'

'Roof fall apparently.' Silas absently tapped a pen on the blotter. 'Seems they were blasting down at the fifty fathom level and something went wrong. A dozen men trapped down there, so they say. Bad business, eh?

'Blasting?' At Lennie's tone of voice, Silas looked at him curiously. The man's face had paled, and there was an expression in his eyes which Silas could not make out. 'How did it happen?' he asked curtly.

'Don't know any details yet,' Silas replied, and returned to his ledgers. Work was all that he had left now. He had found that if he could keep his mind busy he could tire himself enough to get a few hours' sleep at night.

'I heard there's been an accident over at Dolcoath mine,' Silas said later, when he returned from work. He tossed his hat onto a peg and shrugged off his overcoat. Grace was passing through on her way to the dining-room with a vase of flowers for the table. Not that either of the men would notice if there were flowers or not, but she did. It was a remnant of long ago, when Mama used to insist on a fresh arrangement every day, and Grace had kept up the custom in her memory.

Now she stopped and turned to her father. 'Oh, what sort of accident? How serious is it?'

'Blasting fault, so they say. Don't know many details,' Silas replied. 'But a chap told me as we were leaving the foundry that there's twelve men trapped underground over at Anderson's Shaft.'

'*Anderson's?*' The little vase of snowdrops fell from Grace's hands and shattered on the tiled floor, as she felt all the blood drain from her face. 'That's where Dan works!' She raised both hands to her face. 'I must go over there – I must see if—!'

'Calm down, woman, for goodness' sake,' Silas growled. 'Out of all the hundreds of men that work that shaft, it's long odds that he's one of them. You'll only make an exhibition of yourself for nothing.'

Grace ignored him, as seizing her cloak from the peg, she threw it round her shoulders. 'I must see him – I must make sure he's all right!' Her voice floated back down the hall as she turned to leave, 'We had a row and. . . .'

And I never told him how much I love him, before we parted that day. Now it may be too late – please God it's not too late. Her eyes filling with tears, she left the broken vase and crushed flowers where they lay and stepped over the wreckage. Nothing was going to stop her, nothing get in her way.

'I told you before to give up your obsession with that man!' Silas called after her. 'He's not for you. Grace, do you hear me? I forbid you—' But Grace could have been deaf and blind for all the notice she took of her father.

Silas shrugged his shoulders, all the fight going out of him. He felt drained, weary, and well – what was the use? With Richard gone, nothing mattered any more. He realized that his other two children had always gone their own way regardless of him, so now they could do as they damn well liked. If Grace wanted to make a fool of herself, then let her.

By that time, his daughter had reached the back door and was pulling it open. 'Roberts – stop!' she shouted to the groom, who was about to put away the pony and trap. 'I need that,' she added, as she ran down the steps.

She was out of sight before Silas had reached the drawing-room.

CHAPTER ELEVEN

'Now Mr Cardrew, let's see what we have here, shall we?' Jago, his face pale with tension, restrained himself from snapping at the doctor's patronizing manner and professional smile, and sat like a figure carved from stone. The man removed the plaster and inner strapping and gently raised his damaged hand, turning it all ways and scrutinizing it closely through his wire-framed spectacles.

'Mm, the skin has healed very well, good, good. Does this hurt?' He gently pressed at the base of the fingers. 'Or this?' Jago shook his head. 'Now try to flex the fingers please. Slowly, very slowly.'

The sight of his mangled flesh made Jago's stomach crawl. Red, puffy and shiny with new skin, the fingers were so different from his others that they could have belonged to a stranger. Bent inward at an angle, they were as stiff as those of a corpse and reminded him of the ribs of an old, abandoned hulk which he had seen rotting in a creek somewhere.

Jago gasped as panic seized him – flex them? How? When there's no feeling there at all? I – I can't! But, of course, and he forced himself to breathe normally, they'd been bandaged up for so long that they were bound to be stiff.

He tried again. But— 'Oh God, they won't move! My hand's dead!' He raised his eyes to the other man in horror and tried to speak, but he was so overcome that the words jumbled in his throat.

'Don't worry,' said the doctor with sympathy. 'There's been severe damage to the ligaments, and ligaments always take a long time to recover – longer sometimes than a break. Especially along the joints like this, you see.' He pointed. 'With massage and some special exercises which I can recommend, we'll hope to effect a gradual improvement. Although you must understand that it will be slow.' He looked over the top of his spectacles. 'You will need to be very patient, Mr Cardrew.'

Jago scowled. 'Just answer me one question,' he blurted. 'You must have had cases like this before. Tell me, do you think that I'll ever play the piano again?' A small silence fell, during which Jago could feel every nerve in his body straining, and a clammy sweat breaking out on his forehead.

The doctor had looked away, and was drumming his fingertips on the table top as he obviously sought for the right words. 'My dear young man,' he replied eventually, lifting his shoulders and spreading his palms in a gesture of helplessness, 'only God knows the answer to that one.'

It was what he had left unsaid that hit Jago like a punch in the stomach. For if the man truly believed there was some hope, he would have said so outright, reassuringly and at once. But he had hedged, and from that Jago inferred all that he wanted so desperately to know.

His career was over before it had properly begun. He was to become a cripple for the rest of his life, and would never play properly again, if at all. He looked down at the useless claw that had been his left hand and loathed it. He could not bear to touch it, or have it touch him. He wanted to howl like an animal and scream his outrage to whatever cruel fate had dealt him such a devastating blow.

The doctor had risen to his feet to indicate that the consultation was over and that he had a waiting-room full of other patients, each with their own problems. 'Have a word with my nurse on the way out, Mr Cardrew, and she'll give you the ointment to rub on your hand and a sheet of exercises for you to do regularly. I'll see you again in a fortnight's time, sir.'

Jago hardly heard him but went through the necessary motions of leave-taking like an automaton. Then he left the surgery and turned his horse's head towards the sea and solitude.

Isabella's defection had hit him harder than he had realized at first. Following so soon after his accident, it was as if her departure had taken the last vestige of gaiety and sparkle from his life, and left him in a drab and mundane present, with a future too bleak even to contemplate.

Jago thought wistfully then of Kerensa. At one time he had thought . . . but she was a married woman now, with a child on the way, and had also passed out of his life for ever. He sighed, but having to guide the horse with only one hand needed all his concentration as he came to the rough track along the coast.

It also meant that he could not go for the wild gallop across the cliffs which was what he most needed and wanted. Jago longed to lose himself in the spray and the wet mist which was sweeping shorewards, to howl his rage and frustration into the howling wind, and to pit himself against the savage elements.

When he saw Hell's Mouth looming out of the drizzle he dismounted and hitched the horse's reins over a sturdy blackthorn bush. He looked back towards Camborne but the mist had already blotted out all sight of it. The horizon, too, had vanished. He stood wrapped in a bubble of mist at what could have been the end of the world.

It was certainly the end of the land. Jago stood on the very edge of the chasm, perched between sea and sky, and looked over. Surly waves, grey against the greyer rocks, snarled at him as they punched their furious fists at the land, again and again, clawing out a morsel here, a pebble there, pitilessly eating their way into its very foundations, untiring, relentless.

To Jago, the sight and sound of all that motion was hypnotic. It seemed that the constant whirl and rush of white water was flinging itself up the cliffside with arms outstretched to greet him, inviting him down to share in its tempestuous music, down into forgetfulness. A massive voice boomed in basso profundo from the cave below and the damp wind sang in harmony. One step – it would only take one step – and there would no more anguish, no more worry, nothing. He would become part of this primeval wilderness of thrashing waves and thundering sea for ever. Jago swayed, and held out his arms to embrace the beckoning wind.

A discreet cough came at his elbow. 'Pardon me, sir, but I saw the horse, and then with you standing so near the edge I came over to see if you was all right, like.' The grasp on his arm was like steel. Jago's heart leapt, startled out of his trance, and he swung around to see a brawny farmer looking at him with concern from under his bushy brows. In his other hand he held a shepherd's crook.

'Oh! Oh . . . yes. . . .' Jago struggled for words. How could he reasonably explain why he had been leaning at a dangerous angle over a cliff edge in the rain when there was only one possibility? And he had nearly . . . hadn't he . . . would he have. . . ? He glanced back with horror at the roiling waters below.

He noticed the man's rough clothes and the piece of sacking flung around his shoulders to keep out the weather, and felt ashamed. This man who had next to nothing, who spent his life scratching a living from the poor soil, who could well have turned his back and walked on, had stopped because he cared about his fellow man, and he a complete stranger. Had been concerned for him, Jago Cardrew, who by comparison must seem to be blessed with so much – expensive clothes, shiny boots and a thoroughbred horse which was probably worth more than this man earned in a year.

'Couple of my ewes have strayed and I been looking all over for them,' said the man in a conversational tone. Still keeping hold of Jago's arm he took a step or two back from the edge and Jago had no choice but to follow. 'Lambing time, see. Can't afford to lose none of they. Mind you, Jess'll sniff out where they're to, if they are out here at all. Good girl, she is.' Regaining the safety of the path he let go of Jago's arm and reached down to stroke the head of the Border collie at his side.

'Yes . . . yes,' Jago stammered and patted the animal's rump, totally at a loss for words.

'Trampled down the hedge, they did,' the man went on. Jago gave a shrewd guess that the small-talk was to give him time to cover his own confusion, and was surprised and grateful for the man's sensitivity.

'Canny creatures, sheep, although people don't think so. And this old mist don't make it no easier.' He narrowed his eyes and peered ahead. Then he turned back to Jago and gave him a penetrating look. 'Your horse do look cold and wet, sir, if you don't mind me saying so. Same as what you do,' he added gruffly. 'Maybe you'd better carry on with your ride now, for both your sakes.' He tipped his cap and turned to leave.

Jago's mind was racing. He would have liked to offer the man money to show his gratitude, for he was grateful to him, but knowing the fiercely independent character of the Cornish, was afraid of offending him. 'I will,' he said, 'and I hope you find your sheep safe and well. And – um – thank you,' he said humbly, 'thank you very much.' The man whistled to the dog, waved a hand and they both vanished into the mist.

Grace arrived at the mine at a gallop and with fingers that seemed all thumbs, unhitched the trap and turned the weary pony into a grassy enclosure on the outskirts of the site.

A knot of people were gathered at the pit head, beneath the shadow of the towering engine house from which the beam that powered the winding apparatus protruded. They were clustered around the mouth of the shaft which yawned awesomely at their feet, before dropping sheer into the dark and unfathomable depths of the void which had swallowed up their men.

Mothers, wives, sisters and daughters, some with small children clutching at their skirts, some carrying babies in their arms, all their faces white and drawn with anxiety, stood in an unnatural silence which was broken only by the fretful cries of their young ones.

Groups of surface workers hung about waiting like the rest for news. Grace approached them, ignoring the curious looks from the women who had been eyeing her fine gown and expensive boots, obviously wondering, as her father had pointed out, what a genteel lady was doing in this place at all, and especially under the present circumstances.

'What's happening?' she asked a man who was propped by a shoulder against the wall of the boiler house. An empty pipe was stuck in the corner of his mouth as if he had to have something to suck under duress, like a baby its comforter. He straightened up as Grace spoke, tipped his cap and removed the pipe.

'Nine men are trapped behind a great fall of rock, miss. We don't know if there's any air in there or no, nor whether they're dead or alive. The men are down there trying to dig their way in to them but it's some job, because of all the loose stuff, see?' He spread his hands expressively. 'They're risking their own lives doing it, but it's the only way.'

'Who ... do you know the names of the trapped men?' Grace's heart was thudding madly, and she saw the man give her a closer look then raise his eyebrows.

He must have noticed her white face, for in a kinder tone he said,

'Know someone who could be down there, do you?' Grace nodded.

'Bert,' he called over another miner who was holding a clipboard under his arm. 'Ask him, my handsome, he have got the list,' said the first man in a kinder tone. 'This lady do want to know about someone – see if his name's there, will you?'

The man called Bert bent his six-foot frame down to Grace's level. 'Here we are, miss, this do have all the men what went down on the eight o'clock shift. Who you looking for?'

Grace swallowed on a throat gone suddenly dry. 'Daniel Hocking,' she whispered and the man thumbed his sheet of names. 'Let's see now, um – Frederick Caddy, Henry Truscott and Arthur Laity. They was working together as a pare ... Joe Simmons and his son, Matt.' He ran a dirty fingernail down the list. 'Ernie Waters, Jack Trewhella – ah – here we are – yes. Dan Hocking. I'm some sorry, my handsome,' he added with concern as Grace swayed and put a hand to her face. 'Want a drink of water, do you?'

'You're very kind, but no, thank you, I'll be all right. It was the shock, you see.' Grace sank down onto an upturned wheelbarrow as her legs refused to support her any longer.

A sudden shout from the pit head had the two men running across the rough yard. 'Kibble's coming up,' shouted a woman, as the rim of the huge iron bucket used for hauling the ore appeared at the top of the shaft. A couple of weary men climbed out of it, their faces, clothes and hard felt hats streaked with sweat and the red ochre which was everywhere.

'Quicker this way than climbing all they ladders,' said the first one out, gratefully swigging at the water keg which someone had thrust into his hand. He looked at the ring of anxious faces. 'We can hear tapping,' he said briefly, 'so it do mean that some of them anyhow, are alive.' A gasp went up from the assembled women. 'We do need more candles. And rope. And stretchers for bringing up the wounded when we do get them out.' Men were running to the stores before the words were out of his mouth.

'Leave me take a turn now,' volunteered one of them, 'you two do look fair done in.' He and another bundled the equipment into the kibble and climbed in with a signal to the engine-man to lower away. The whole operation had taken less than five minutes. Now there was nothing more to be done except wait. The patient watchers heaved a collective sigh as the tops of the men's heads disappeared below, and returned to their silent vigil.

Darkness was beginning to fall, and around the site lanterns were being strategically placed where they would be of most use. A group of women, unhampered by children, had taken themselves off to the count-house and started brewing tea. A back-up group of neighbours arrived soon afterwards with baskets of food – sandwiches, buttered splits, saffron buns, milk for the children and anything they could lay their hands on at short notice.

Grace was impressed, and touched to see the way that everyone in the small community was quietly rallying round at this time of misfortune, supporting each other. Then she realized that this was not the first time such a drama had occurred. This sort of situation was an everyday fact of life for these families. For every day their menfolk disappeared into a hot and filthy hole in the ground to face the rigours of hard-rock mining, with its attendant dangers of falls, poor air, floods and blasting.

Grace regarded the women with new respect and moved towards the count-house with them. 'I'd like to help,' she said, to a tall thin person who seemed to be leading the others. 'Is there anything I can do?' The girl looked her up and down. 'You're Miss Cardrew, aren't you? From Penhallow.'

Grace was acutely aware of the stares and the mutterings of some of the others, which came floating across the room and reached her ears whether they had been intended to or not. 'Huh – look at she! What's she think she's doing over here, dressed up in all her finery,' said one voice, low but carrying. 'Playing Lady Bountiful, I reckon – come to see how us poor souls do live. Well, now she do know,' came the reply.

'Yes, I'm Grace,' she replied. 'Please, call me Grace. And I'd like to tell you all why I'm here.' She raised her voice so that it carried around the room. 'I know that you're all wondering.' She stared at the group which had spoken and saw a couple of them shifting their feet and looking uncomfortable.

A silence fell as the others paused in their work and all eyes focused on her. Grace felt herself reddening and lifted her head high. 'I came because the man that I love is trapped underground along with your men. We're all in this together, and I'd be . . . honoured . . . if you would accept me and let me help in any way I can.'

'It's Dan Hocking, isn't it?' asked the tall girl. 'He's your sweetheart.'

Grace turned to her in surprise. 'Y -yes,' she said open-mouthed. 'But how did you know?' The girl smiled and replied simply, 'I know someone who do work for you, see.' She held out a hand. 'I'm Jane – Florrie's older sister.'

Grace took the proffered hand and grasped it warmly. 'Florrie! Oh, what a coincidence!' she said with an answering smile, and added firmly,

'Now give me something useful to do, please.'

The ice having been broken, Grace found that she was soon accepted by the others, as one of them, and in different circumstances she would have enjoyed the experience of being part of a team, of having other women to talk to, of doing a useful job. Under instruction she helped to lay out makeshift beds on the floor for the smallest of the children, then took charge of the water boiler and the huge enamel tea-pots which were kept permanently on stand-by.

A couple of hours had passed before a shout from the pit-head had them running out across the yard again. Grace with one hand to her mouth in both hope and dread, turned down the gas under the boiler, picked up her skirts and ran after them.

'They're bringing some of them up!' a voice called, as the men at the top received the signal to hoist. Carefully they pulled on the ropes and a couple of heads appeared at the top of the ladder, carefully balancing an injured man on a stretcher. The women surged forward until one of the surface men held up a hand. 'Don't crowd round – give them air.' The stretcher-men, relieved of their burden and exhausted after the long haul sank to the ground gasping for breath.

'Who is it, who've they got?' In the flickering light of the lanterns, the women inched further forward. 'Here's another!' the cry went up, but this time it was the kibble that came to the surface. One of the surface men took a look inside, then his expression froze. 'Back! he shouted hoarsely. 'Don't look! Keep they women back out of the way.' Then he was raising both hands in a pushing movement that told its own tale.

The stretcher-bearers who were now recovered enough to speak, swilled down the tea that had been placed within reach and one of them wiped the back of his hand across his mouth as he said, 'They've broke through part of the fall and pulled some of them out – they're coming up one by one if they're fit to be moved. Doctor's down there now, doing what he can.'

He paused for another drink and the second man took up the story. 'There's some lot of them still missing. And Ernie Waters, Jack Trewhella and Daniel Hocking, we don't know nothing about they because they was working as a pare further back, see, other side of the fall. We're still digging, but there's some stuff to shift, I can tell you. It's going to take the rest of the night I do reckon, before we reach them.'

If we do. Grace had sunk down onto an upturned bucket and was holding her head in her hands as it reeled with shock. Please, please she was sobbing inwardly – I'll do anything for him, go anywhere, if only he gets through this. The other women fluttered about her, tending to the injured and comforting the relatives of those who had died, as Grace sat on in a stupor.

She looked up with a start as a hand squeezed her shoulder and met the haunted eyes of the girl called Jane. 'I'm Ernie's wife,' she said simply and, as Grace rose to her feet, they clasped their arms around each other for mutual comfort.

It was five in the morning before all the miners were accounted for, except for the three missing ones who had been beyond the blockage, by which time Grace felt as if she were trapped in some indescribable nightmare, her whole body numb with worry.

Until a sudden shout broke the long silence. As the words 'Kibble's coming up!' rang through the darkness, Grace jerked her stiffened limbs into action and raced towards the great iron bucket as it surfaced. One man standing inside it was supporting Dan's limp form and as it came to a standstill, willing hands lifted him gently out and laid him on a stretcher. The mine doctor then appeared at the top of the ladder. Wiping his brow he said tersely, 'The other two are on their way – next bucket up.'

'Be careful, he has internal injuries,' he said, as Grace reached for one of the big hands, his poor swollen, bruised and lacerated hands, and lifted it up to her cheek.

'Oh no!' she cried, biting her lip. 'Dan,' she whispered. 'Oh Dan, speak to me.' The eyelashes fluttered, lifted briefly, then as if the effort was too much, were still again.

But her voice must have got through, because at last his eyes opened partially, and looked straight into hers before the heavy lids fell over them like shutters coming down. 'Dan, oh my dearest, if you can hear me, try to squeeze my hand.' Grace held her breath and waited. Then it came – the slightest of pressures, like the touch of a butterfly's wing, but it was enough. He recognized me – he heard me – he knows I'm here! Grace was smiling through her tears as the stretcher was lifted and Dan was taken away with the others to hospital.

Grace spent the rest of the night in the hospital waiting-room. Of the other miners, apart from the five dead, four had been blinded, two had to have limbs amputated and one had broken his spine. Five deaths and seven men in the prime of life who would never work again. Grace sat among the dazed and weeping women and bit her nails to the quick as she waited for news of Dan.

And when at last the morning came, the room seemed suddenly full of sunshine as he was pronounced out of danger. 'We've stitched up his face, that was only a flesh wound. But he has a couple of broken ribs which we've strapped up and he's inhaled a lot of dust. Only time will tell how his lungs are affected.' The weary doctor rubbed a hand over his eyes. 'I'm sorry you had to wait so long for news, but there were so many, you understand.'

'Of course,' Grace nodded. None of it mattered any more. For in the light of this glorious day the long, grim hours of the night that she had spent pacing the floor need never have been.

'At the moment he's suffering from shock and exhaustion, so we'll keep him in for a few days. But when he does come home, he'll need looking after for a week or two – he'll still be in a fair amount of pain.' He turned to leave the room. 'Now you go and get some rest yourself, Mrs Hocking,' he added, as he closed the door behind him. Grace blinked and smiled at the understandable mistake. Soon, she whispered, soon.

A week passed, during which Grace spent busily making some plans which she kept to herself until the last minute. Then one morning she tugged the bell-pull and looked up with a smile as Kerensa answered it.

'Ah, Kerensa, I'm so glad it's you. I want us to have a little chat. Please sit down.' Kerensa's eyes widened. Grace swivelled round from the escritoire at which she was sitting and smoothed down her skirt of lavender wool. With it she was wearing a white pin-tucked blouse dotted with tiny flowers, and a cameo brooch. Her hair was piled high on her head in a new and becoming style and her face was glowing with what looked like suppressed excitement.

She looks fantastic, Kerensa thought – she hasn't looked this good since Richard died. And broke off from her thoughts to listen. 'Kerensa, this is going to come as a complete surprise to you, but I hope you'll seriously consider my offer.' Kerensa frowned. What on earth was coming?

'For some time now I have been thinking about a change of housekeeper,' Grace announced. Kerensa blinked in surprise and noticed how her mistress was looking down at her hands and awkwardly twisting her fingers in her lap. 'Mrs Nance has always seemed very efficient in her post, you understand, but we have never really seen eye to eye.'

Grace looked up with a twinkle in her eye now. 'She has always intimidated me, you see – probably because of the difference in our ages, and I could never bring myself to have a confrontation with her.'

Kerensa smiled in quiet complicity. 'I do understand,' she replied.

'So,' Grace said, 'I eventually plucked up enough courage to do so, and I've dismissed her.'

'You *have*?' said Kerensa with astonishment, wondering privately how that interview had gone.

Grace nodded with satisfaction. 'I gave her some excellent references, and it was not quite as much of an ordeal as I expected – as I was dreading!' she laughed. 'And what I wanted to ask you, Kerensa,' she went on more seriously, 'is whether you would be willing to take her place.'

Thunderstruck, Kerensa was at a loss for words as she struggled to take in the implications of this amazing offer. And, as she was still struggling, Grace dropped a second bombshell.

'I very much hope you will agree,' she said, 'because I know that I can trust you implicitly, also that the other members of staff like and respect you, and I need someone I can rely on while I'm away.'

Restlessly she rose to her feet and paced the room as she went on, 'As I expect you've heard from Florrie, Daniel Hocking was badly injured in the mine accident and he needs looking after.' She turned on her heel and met Kerensa's startled eyes.

'So I'm leaving Penhallow to go and live with him. Permanently.'

CHAPTER TWELVE

Kerensa was still too stunned to speak. Whether because of Grace's surprising suggestion regarding herself, or from the amazing news of her departure and the reason behind it, Kerensa was not quite sure.

She looked at the other woman with new respect. Until now she had always thought of Grace as being so meek and biddable, so dutiful towards her father and brothers, that she verged on the goody-goody. But to defy Silas and stand up for herself, to desert them all for the man she loved, that was something else. Would she, Kerensa, have had the courage to do the same were their positions reversed? She would like to think so.

At last she found her tongue. 'Housekeeper? *Me*? But. . . .'

Grace held up a hand as if to fend off any doubts Kerensa might have been going to put into words. 'You're going to say you've had no experience – that it's too much to take on – and that your husband could not be expected to agree, because you would have to live in.'

Kerensa, who had been about to put those very points, smiled at Grace's perception. 'Yes, I was,' she said with a smile. 'So you can see that it really would be impossible.'

'On the contrary.' Grace looked her fully in the face. 'The only valid point there is that of living in, and we can certainly get around that. Alice Nance only lived here because she was a widow and it suited her to do so. With only the two men left now to look after, you would be able to come and go like the rest of the staff. You usually arrive before my father and brother are around, and in any case Cook is quite capable of getting breakfast ready without you having to look over her shoulder.'

Grace arched an eyebrow in amusement as she added, 'Actually I think that she and the others may all be rather pleased to have a little more freedom. From what I've gathered, Mrs Nance was rather a martinet, was she not?'

Kerensa could not help but smile back. 'Well, yes, she was,' she replied. 'And I'd love to do it if you're quite sure. . . .' She spread her palms expressively.

'Wonderful!' Grace clapped her hands together in delighted approval. 'And of course I'm sure. You've never been an ordinary domestic servant anyway, Kerensa, because of your unique circumstances, and your talents have been wasted as a parlour-maid. You'll do very well.' Grace beamed and added, 'There will naturally, be an appropriate rise in your wages. I shall be living at Penponds, so I shan't be more than a mile or two away, and I shall be coming to and fro quite often to keep an eye on things. So you'll be able to tell me if you have any problems.'

Grace rose to her feet and closed the lid of the escritoire. 'Now there are things that I must see to,' she said. 'There is a great deal to be done.' Packing! she thought, and placed her hands to her flushed cheeks as a curl of excitement made her quiver. And telling Father – her stomach lurched at that daunting prospect. She straightened her spine and turned back to Kerensa. 'You can commence your duties from today if that suits you. I shall be leaving here as soon as Daniel comes out of hospital, probably in about a week. All right, Kerensa?'

'Oh, yes, Miss Grace,' said Kerensa, as she struggled to put her whirling thoughts into some semblance of order. 'And thank you – thank you very much.'

★

Silas was sitting in the drawing-room with his head sunk into his chest, deep in thought. Grace had just whirled in and told him of her plans. Had just told him straight and then swept out of the room with her head held high. Before he could even take in what she actually meant. Leaving home! His quiet, obedient daughter – to live in sin with that common miner of hers!

Silas heaved a sigh and the heavy shoulders shook with emotion. A few months ago he would have raged at Grace, stormed and stamped and shouted, forbidding her to see him again. But he had already done that once to no avail, for they had gone behind his back regardless. Oh, what was the use? He felt so tired, so defeated. All his great plans had come to nothing in one brief moment of tragedy, and all his ambitions for his family had been reduced to dust and ashes.

But Grace! He had never seen her so animated, or so determined, and grudgingly her father acknowledged that it must have taken great courage on her part to stand up to him so. Well, well, little Grace. Who'd have thought it – there was a streak of stubbornness in her after all. Silas gave a grim smile and pride raised his head, for she must have inherited that from him. Her mother Evelyn had been as meek and mild as they come, goodness knows, and with that dutiful streak in her too. *That* had eventually caused her death. His lip curled. Pah! Concerning herself with families struck down with typhoid when she could have kept herself out of it.

He sat on as the room darkened with the onset of evening. Maybe he *would* give Grace his permission to marry this fellow after all, seeing as she was so set on it. It would be much better for the family name if they were to be decently wed. Silas reached for the bell-pull. He would call her back and tell her right away.

Kerensa was actively enjoying her new role as housekeeper and the authority it gave her. Not that she was one to suddenly start barking orders at the other servants who up until now had been her friends, but she felt it brought her one step further in her ambition to be mistress of Penhallow. One day.

During her comings and goings about the house Kerensa had seen Jago on several occasions, but always in the distance – vanishing around a corner or a bend in the stairs – walking outside, shoulders hunched, hands in his pockets and eyes on the ground, brooding. Once she heard the far away tinkle of the piano – just a few notes – then the lid was slammed down with a crash followed by silence. Her heart bled for him, for herself, for the hideous quirk of fate which had struck that day and changed their lives for ever.

Kerensa needed to speak to him. Oh, how she needed to. For he had saved her life and she must tell him how she realized that, how much she wanted to give him her heartfelt thanks. And try somehow to apologize, to acknowledge this great burden of guilt which she carried night and day. But how could an apology, however heartfelt and sincere, adequately express her feelings about what had happened? Particularly because as time went on, she began to suspect that Jago was deliberately avoiding her.

At last after much heart-searching, Kerensa decided that the only thing she could do was to write him a note. Ask him to meet her so that at least they could talk face to face. That way she would have made contact, would feel better for having made an effort, and Jago could please himself whether he wanted to see her or not.

Eventually she simply wrote: *Jago – I need to speak to you in private. Please will you meet me in the orchard in an hour? Kerensa.*

She slipped the note in with his morning mail, placing it at the bottom of the pile, beside his plate at the breakfast table, and made sure she stayed out of the way until he would have read it. At the appointed time she was hanging out washing on the lines which were stretched between the apple and pear trees in the orchard, which was one of the places that had been spared from Silas's excavations.

It was a mild day towards the end of February, with a sky the colour of skimmed milk and enough breeze to move the sheet which she had just hung. Kerensa reached for a bath towel. Maybe Jago would just ignore the note altogether. Then, fine, at least she would know. Her mouth turned down at the corners as she thought of what might have been. And the reality of what was.

Kerensa had found that after a few months of marriage, she and Lennie were leading what amounted to parallel lives. He still made her parade to chapel with him every Sunday to see and be seen, but during the week he spent long hours at the foundry, as she did at Penhallow, and the situation was tolerable if she didn't think too much about how her life was wasting away. Kerensa was still a young woman – barely twenty – and felt that the carefree youth she should have had, had been stolen from her. Resentment clouded her brow and she sighed as she pegged out the towel – for she had been forced to grow up at sixteen and there could be no going back now, or ever.

A movement between the trees brought her back to the present. Jago! He had come after all. She felt colour flood her face and her legs weaken, as he ducked his head under the flapping sheet and joined her. 'Jago.' She smiled. 'Thank you for coming. I wasn't sure whether you would want to or not.'

'Kerensa.' He was standing like a cardboard cut-out, his eyes raking her up and down while she took in the gaunt face, the stiffly held left hand and the dull eyes. Her heart contracted in pity as he replied, 'I came purely out of curiosity. I can't imagine that we have much to say to each other. Certainly nothing that warrants a secret assignation like this.' There was no answering smile, just the brooding stare and the clipped sentences. This was going to be harder than she had thought.

Kerensa clutched a tea-cloth in both hands to stop their shaking and took a breath. 'On the contrary – *I* have a lot to say to you, you see. About . . . about that day.' She tore her eyes away from the hand that felt as much a barrier between them as a brick wall and forced herself to find the right words.

'First I need to say thank you for saving my life.' It sounded trite, but oh, how else could she put it?' He gave a curt nod, an inclination of the head which was a bare acknowledgement that she had spoken, no more.

'Secondly, that no words can ever express how sorry I am for what happened – and that I shall carry this burden of guilt with me for the rest of my life.' Kerensa bowed her head, feeling her lips tremble. She bit the bottom one hard. She would not give way to a display of emotion in front of this figure carved out of granite, who was regarding her like something which had crawled out from under a stone.

But as she took in the changed expression on Jago's face, the pegs fell unheeded to the grass. He was holding out both hands towards her and his eyes were soft and gentle, with a hint of bewilderment about them. 'Guilt?' he said, 'Kerensa, for goodness' sake, why should you feel *guilty?*'

Her jaw dropped and her surprise was such that she could only gape at him and stammer, 'Because . . . because it was all my *fault*, of course. I was looking down, trying not to slip – and I didn't see . . . didn't hear . . . until you. . . .' The tea-cloth followed the pegs to the ground as unable to contain her feelings any longer, she raised both hands to her face and covered her eyes.

Kerensa would never know what it cost Jago to keep his hands firmly at his sides and not to gather her to him and stroke that glorious hair, floating on the breeze in a dark cloud, free now of the maid's cap which she usually wore. Not to kiss away the anguish that had been in her voice, in her eyes, and tell her how much she meant to him. Since Isabella's betrayal there had been no one to whom he could turn for comfort, to feel the simple solace of another person's arms, no one even with whom to have a meaningful conversation.

But Kerensa was another man's wife and would soon be a mother as well. Jago glanced at her still slight figure and frowned. She seemed as slim to him as she had always been. Had she lost the child she had been carrying? Could he ask her? How could he put it without seeming to pry?

'Kerensa,' he said gently, 'it was never your fault, any of it. It was a chain of circumstances that had *nothing* to do with you. Look at me.' Kerensa raised her head, scrubbed the back of her hand across her eyes and met his tender gaze. 'You have to believe that. If the finger can be pointed at anyone, it should be at my *father*.' Jago turned away to lay a bent arm against the mossy bark of the nearest tree and pillowed his face upon it. His shoulders rose and fell as if he were fighting against tears of his own and Kerensa saw his throat clench as he swallowed hard.

'Because if it hadn't been for *his* greed and *his* hare-brained scheme,' he said bitterly, 'none of this would ever have happened.' He raised his twisted hand in the air as he turned back to her and his expression of utter anguish tore Kerensa's heart in two.

'How . . . how is the hand?' she asked quietly, as she fought to smother her feelings. 'What does the doctor say about it?'

The stony look had hardened Jago's features in an instant, accentuating the grooves between cheek and jaw and the lines around his eyes, as he replied, 'The doctor sits firmly on the fence and says absolutely nothing. Whether this is because he really doesn't know, or whether he is too diffident to tell me the worst, I can't decide. But I suspect the latter.'

'Isn't there any movement in it at all?' Kerensa having brought up the subject, needed to know all the details for her own satisfaction, however painful it might be to discuss. But her intuition told her that to discuss it was maybe what Jago needed to do, as the first step towards facing up to his shattered life.

'I can pinch my thumb and index finger together, and that's all,' he said through clenched teeth. 'The others might as well be a bunch of dry *sticks*!' he finished, with a howl of anguish, and thumped his good fist against the unrelenting trunk of the apple tree.

Kerensa, torn apart by his agony, was about to step forward and lay a comforting hand on his shoulder before she remembered just in time that she was Mrs Retallick, and his housekeeper, and that such behaviour would be unthinkable on both counts. So she forced herself to remain calm, to encourage, and to show support and sympathy with words instead of actions. 'Perhaps the feeling will return to those as well in time,' she said, 'as it has to the other two. It hasn't been many weeks yet, you know.'

'Don't try to *pacify* me,' Jago growled, 'you sound just like my doctor.' Then as he turned and caught sight of Kerensa's hurt expression he was immediately contrite.

'I'm sorry, Kerensa, truly I am. I know you're only being kind. But I know as well that I shall never play again – and that's all that matters.'

'Jago Cardrew, that's *not* all that matters!' Suddenly Kerensa flared up and all her roller-coaster emotions boiled over at last. 'Playing the piano is *not* the most important thing in the world. You're just wallowing in self-pity! For goodness' sake, you could have been killed! Like . . . like R—'

Suddenly realizing what she had said, Kerensa clapped a hand over her mouth. 'Oh, I'm so sorry. I was carried away then and I . . . forgot my place. Of course it's not for me to . . . I didn't mean to be so presumptuous.' To cover her confusion she turned her back and bent to the washing basket. For a moment there was complete silence, broken only by the twittering of birds in the branches above their heads and the sigh of the wind in the grass.

Then she felt a light touch on her shoulder and whirled around to meet Jago's eyes. To her amazement they were soft, caring and as warm as melting chocolate. Kerensa drew in a breath and held it as he spoke. 'Kerensa, you can forget any ideas about your *place* for ever. I've never thought of you as my servant, so don't think for a minute that such a thing will ever come between us.'

He spread his hands wide, glancing at the damaged one as he did so, and she knew he was trying to express the inexpressible. 'What you said is perfectly true,' he went on. 'I just needed to hear somebody say it aloud, that's all. I required a good jolt to my senses to make me put things in perspective, and I think I can begin to do that now. With you to help me.'

'But. . . .' Kerensa let out the breath on a sigh.

'Yes, I haven't forgotten that you're another man's wife,' he said, as if he had read her thoughts, 'and I can't pretend that I don't wish that things were different. But you're having his child, so—'

'*What*? What did you say?' Stunned, Kerensa gazed up at him in bewilderment. Then she remembered. That day when he'd found out that she was married to Lennie . . . and her expression hardened. 'You always did jump to conclusions, Jago, without waiting to hear the truth,' she said bluntly. And, as she paused, in order to savour the look of embarrassment which crossed his face now, she felt vindicated for that look of scathing contempt which he and Isabella had given her that other day, which had scourged her then and which she had never forgotten.

'You mean you're not – er – not?' His eyes widened.

Kerensa shook her head. 'I never was,' she said firmly, giving him a level stare.

Jago frowned. 'But what did you mean – you said you *had* to get married? Why *did* you marry him, Kerensa?'

Kerensa sighed and pushed a hand through her hair. 'It's a complicated story, Jago, far too complicated to explain now. We've been out here long enough and I shall be missed soon. I'll tell you another time.'

She pegged out the last of the washing with flying fingers and picked up the empty basket. 'Thank you for answering my note,' she said, as she turned to go. Jago held out one hand as if to caress her, but abruptly dropped it to his side again.

'Thank you for sending it,' he said quietly. 'It couldn't have been easy for you.' His eyes rested on hers for a moment, before he swung away and said, 'I'll be seeing you, then – around the house, that is.' Kerensa nodded and watched him stride away between the trees without looking back.

Six weeks after the accident and thanks to Grace's devoted care, Dan had made a full recovery. Grace had not once regretted her decision to leave home to be with him, and they had settled in to Dan's small cottage as if they had always lived there. The village people had taken Grace to their hearts from the day of the tragedy, and there were therefore no pointing fingers nor whispering about her behind her back to upset her, as Silas had predicted.

'I've been thinking, my bird,' said Dan, one day as he came in from pottering in the tiny back garden where he grew all their vegetables, 'that it's about time we made an honest woman of you.'

'Oh, Dan!' Grace turned round from the kitchen range where she was stirring something in a saucepan. Cooking was a new venture for her too, and she was secretly pleased at how adept she was becoming at making simple meals for them both. She replaced the lid and came towards him. 'Do you mean what I think you mean?'

Dan put his arms around her waist and lifted her off the floor, dropping a kiss on her rosy cheek before he set her down again. Then, keeping hold of her hands and looking down at the top of her head he said simply, 'What I mean, Grace my dearest girl, is, will you marry me?'

Grace looked up at his tall figure and all her heart was in her eyes as she squeezed the big, work-roughened hands and brought them to her lips. 'You know you don't have to ask, don't you?' she said tenderly. 'But I'm glad you did. Oh, Daniel Hocking, my only love, I never thought that Father would change his mind like he has, but you know I would have gone ahead and married you anyway, don't you?'

Daniel clasped her to him and rested his bearded cheek on her soft hair, too overcome to speak.

'It was when they brought you up from below and I saw you lying there, that I realized that we'd parted in anger and that you could have died before I had a chance to tell you how much I love you and what you mean to me.'

A couple of tears welled up in the corners of her eyes as she drew away to look him in the face. 'That experience really shook me, Dan, and it made me put things in perspective. In a life or death situation, conventions must go to the wall, because life is too short and too precious to waste in being afraid of what others will think. People matter more than principles.' She dabbed at her eyes with a scrap of cambric and buried her face in his chest.

Kerensa relished the certain amount of freedom which came with her new position and while being careful not to abuse it, and Grace's trust in her, she found herself spending more and more of her spare time with Jago.

They met casually around the house from time to time and after several of the 'accidental' meetings, Kerensa felt sure that he was doing it deliberately. She had also been hearing more often his hesitant attempts at playing the piano with one hand, and pity for him was tearing her apart. So much so that one day when they had bumped into each other on the landing, he coming downstairs as she was going up, Kerensa plucked up courage to tell him about an idea which had been at the back of her mind for some time.

'Jago,' she said, as they stopped at the window looking out over the lawn, green and lush now with fresh grass, 'I . . . I've heard you playing recently and know how frustrating you must find it.' She fixed her gaze on a blackbird cocking a bright eye and patiently watching for worms. Jago gave a muffled snort and muttered an expletive under his breath.

'Oh no, Kerensa,' he said, with the bleakness of a winter landscape in his voice, 'no one else can possibly *know*. You can imagine, perhaps, but only I can know what it feels like in *here*. . . .' He thumped his chest with a fist and his burning eyes seared into her soul.

'Jago.' She placed a hand on his arm, in sympathy, in comfort. How she wished it could be more, she thought. 'Just listen to me for one minute. I've been thinking about this such a lot.' Her hands had begun to shake with nerves and she leant on them against the window-sill, as they both watched the blackbird pulling out a worm which it stretched like an elastic band until it snapped.

'You may not know that I can play basic piano,' Kerensa went on. 'Of course I'm out of practice, I haven't had an opportunity for years, but I wondered if I were to play the left hand for you, whether . . . whether we could make some sort of music together.'

There – she'd said it. Kerensa's voice tailed off and, suddenly self-conscious, she lowered her head. 'If you wanted to,' she added under her breath. 'It wouldn't, of course, be anything like the standard you're used to, but . . . if it would help. . . .'

He was silent for so long that she hardly dared look up in case she had insulted him. But at last she felt a finger under her chin and when Jago raised her face and their eyes met, his expression was so tender that her breath caught in her throat. 'Kerensa, that's the most wonderful offer anyone has ever made me,' he said. 'It would mean so much – even if we only had a little fun. I know I can never manage the serious stuff again. But yes, oh yes! Let's give it a try.' And a broad smile crossed his face. The most genuine smile she had seen since the accident.

Then his face fell and a frown creased his forehead as he said, 'But what will your husband think of it? Won't he mind?'

Kerensa smiled back, her eyes alight with mischief. 'Oh yes,' she replied. 'He'll mind all right – if he gets to know about it. But I don't intend to tell him, and I can't imagine that anyone else will. So what he doesn't know about won't hurt him.' She turned her back to the window and faced him. 'I thought that we might be able to fit in a few sessions between my duties here. What do you think?'

'I think, Mrs Retallick, that it's a wonderful idea and I appreciate your offer very much,' Jago sounded so sincere that Kerensa could have wept for joy. 'Thank you,' he added simply, as she turned at a summons from below.

'I have to go,' she replied. 'Shall I see you in the library after lunch tomorrow?'

Jago nodded. 'Good. That's usually a quiet time for me.' Kerensa picked up the hem of her skirt and went running down the stairs.

'Oh, wasn't that so much better!' Kerensa sat back on the piano stool as she and Jago came to the end of a simple piece of music, having managed to finish together for once. 'It certainly was,' Jago agreed. 'We hardly stumbled at all over that one.' He was looking so much brighter, thought Kerensa. Privately she was convinced that the fun and laughter they had had over their initial halting attempts at playing in tandem, was as good a therapy as the music itself. If one could close one's eyes to the pathos of it all, of course, and the sadness of the former brilliance now so dimmed.

'You play very well,' Jago said. 'Especially for one who's so out of practice.' Kerensa smiled although her eyes were far away. 'I used to have my lessons in this same room, actually,' she added, with such a wistful expression that it was all Jago could do not to put his arms around her and kiss away the hurt. He kept his hands rigidly on his knees as Kerensa went on, 'Playing piano gave me an interest which has lasted ever since,' she said, as she slid her hand up the keyboard in a little glissando and their eyes met in sympathetic understanding.

It gave Kerensa the push she needed to bring up another subject to which she'd been giving a lot of thought. 'I had another idea last night,' she said, taking a deep breath as she swivelled in her seat. 'Well, two actually.'

Jago met her bright gaze and arched a brow. 'Oh, really? Is there no end to these brainwaves of yours?' he replied, with an indulgent smile. 'What now?'

'I'm perfectly serious about this, Jago.' Kerensa had spent the best part of a sleepless night thinking about it while Lennie snored the hours away beside her. She took another breath and plunged in.

'As you've got the full use of your right hand, I thought that you might be able to take up composing. Writing songs, that is. There's a great demand for popular music, you know. Look how successful Sir Arthur Sullivan has been with his song, 'The Lost Chord', since it came out last year. Quite apart from all those lively tunes from the operettas, which he wrote to Mr Gilbert's lyrics.'

As Kerensa paused and nervously cleared her throat, Jago heard the echo of his own voice come back to him. '. . . barrel organ music' he had said derisively to Hal in another time, another place. It felt now like another lifetime. Was this then all he had to look forward to? He realized that bluntly, yes, it was. A far cry from becoming a classical concert pianist, then. But presumably this took skill of a different kind. Maybe it wasn't such a ridiculous idea. In fact, the more he considered it, the better it became, and he found that certain ideas were tumbling around his nimble brain already.

Kerensa was ploughing on bravely despite his lack of response. 'It would be something creative that you could do with a limited use of the piano, but you'd still be making music. I know you like a challenge, and it might be fun as well . . . .'

Silence fell, utter and absolute. She dared not look him in the face, afraid of what she might see there. Scorn again. Or contempt. Anger. Or heartbreaking sadness. She hid her clenched hands in her apron and waited.

'Kerensa.' She jumped and glanced to the side. His eyes met hers and locked, then tenderness flooded through him as he realized what courage and tact she must have had to bring this up, knowing how moody and unpredictable he had been lately. Dear Kerensa, she didn't have to put herself through that, but she had made the effort – for him.

Then like the sun's rays breaking through a dark looming cloud, Jago's face lit up with a beaming smile. 'You are just the cleverest, dearest girl I know. That is an *excellent* idea!' Then, carried away and before either of them had realized what he was about, Jago flung an arm around her shoulders, squeezed her to him and dropped a light kiss on her cheek.

'I would never have thought of it for myself, but that's something I really think I could do,' he went on, his eyes sparkling as the idea took hold. 'It's exactly what I needed – a new direction. You've heard it said that when one door closes another opens, haven't you?'

Kerensa nodded, her palm to the warm spot on her cheek where his lips had touched it.

'Well, that's just what's happened to me. And it was all your doing. I can never thank you enough for this, Kerensa.' He was more animated than she had seen him for months, his face glowing with enthusiasm and she gave a great sigh of relief, for it had been all right after all.

'And the first successful song I write,' Jago added, 'shall be for you.'

CHAPTER THIRTEEN

Grace looked exquisite in a gown of pale blue silk dotted with darker blue forget-me-nots, and she carried a drift of freesias and fern, the scent of which wafted far back into the congregation as she walked down the aisle on her father's arm. She had persuaded Silas to come out of his shell for this one day, and to Grace that meant more than she could say, for it was also a public show of their reconciliation.

She had decided to hold the wedding breakfast at Penhallow, so for the first time in years the house was crammed with people, noise and laughter. The mining families, far from being intimidated by their surroundings and the presence of various businessmen and their wives who were Silas's associates, did hearty justice to the plentiful supply of food and drink. Grace had insisted on hiring a firm of caterers so that her own staff would be free to enjoy the day as well, which meant that the company was an even greater mix of all the classes.

When the toasts to the newly-weds had been drunk, and the speeches made, Jago was sitting chatting with Grace and Dan, watching the company who had been through so much, enjoying themselves on this special day. And a thought occurred to him.

'Grace,' he said, turning a serious face towards her, 'There's something I've been meaning to bring up for a while, and today seems a good time.'

Grace arched a brow. 'Oh? What's that?'

Jago's eyes were still on the chattering crowd as he replied, 'I'd like to see Father compensate these people for all that they've lost. I feel that our family is responsible for what happened and that we should give them a sum of money each to show our support.' He turned dark eyes to his sister's face. 'What do you think?'

'Jay, that's a marvellous idea. Don't you think so, Dan?' She glanced towards her husband.

'Very thoughtful – yes,' he agreed.

'Goodness knows,' Grace said, 'he can afford to.'

'That's what I thought.' A smile lightened Jago's face. 'I'm so glad you both agree.' He drained his glass and rose to his feet. 'I'll put it to him right away, I think. Now is a good opportunity.'

He picked his way across the crowded room towards Silas, and perched himself on the arm of the settee, where his father was drinking whisky and telling some tale to a group of his associates. After a burst of hearty male laughter they drifted away and when the two of them were alone, Jago put forward his suggestion.

Silas's first reaction was outright rejection of the whole idea. 'Good grief, boy, do you think I've got money to burn?' he blustered.

'Oh, come on, Father, since you took over Smithford's, you must have almost doubled your income, and you weren't exactly a pauper before that.' Jago's voice had an edge to it.

'Pah! You know nothing about it. They were asking an astronomical sum before I beat them down, but even so . . .' Jago said nothing as his father hummed and hawed, and at last he saw a calculating look in his eyes as he turned to him and said slowly, 'But – yes . . . you might have a point, boy.' For a magnanimous gesture might stand him in very good stead later on if Cardrew's were to be accused of negligence over the accident. A crafty expression crossed his face. Yes. It would put him in a good light to do that. He would be seen as a public benefactor and therefore above reproach, having done all he could to make it up to the bereaved. If he kept the sum to a minimum – say the least he could reasonably get away with – it wouldn't ruin him and might be money well invested.

'You must have a better head on your shoulders than I thought,' he added. The corner of Jago's mouth twitched at this backhanded compliment. 'I shall make a public announcement. A fitting end to the day, don't you think?' He put aside his glass and rose to his feet as Jago gave a broad grin and raised a thumb in a triumphant gesture towards Grace and Dan who had been watching from across the room.

So as the cheers and applause died away at last, the village families drifted homewards, the remaining guests gathered in the drawing-room for an evening of dancing and entertainment. The furniture had been previously moved to the sides of the room and the carpet rolled up, which made enough space for dancing to the music provided by a small band. Kerensa was sitting beside Lennie in a group of people, and after watching the couples skipping down the centre of the room in Strip the Willow, her foot had begun to tap in time to the lively music.

'Lennie,' she said, putting to one side the glass of punch that she had been sipping and rising to her feet, 'I want to dance. Are you going to partner me?'

She straightened the skirt of her new gown of sea-green taffeta which she knew fitted her slender figure like a glove, and gave a little twirl. Straight and narrow at the front, it flared out from the waist at the back into a fall of tiny frills, and Kerensa thought not for the first time, how wonderful it was to have an occasion to wear something new and pretty. It was as she came to the end of her twirl that she caught Jago watching her from across the room, and stopped dead as their eyes met.

'Certainly not.' Lennie's rasping voice replied. 'I wouldn't dream of making such an exhibition of myself. And I hope you know better than that too, Kerensa. As my wife, I expect you to behave with more decorum.'

'For goodness' sake, Lennie!' Kerensa retorted and tossed her head. 'Everyone in the room is dancing – and if it's good enough for my employer and her new husband, surely it's good enough for me.'

She felt a touch on her elbow and caught her breath as she found Jago standing at her side. 'Mrs Retallick.' He bowed and crooked an elbow. 'May I have the pleasure of this dance?'

'Mr Cardrew!' and Kerensa's eyes were sparkling as she placed a gloved hand on his arm. 'Oh, yes. Yes, please.' And she was swept away and caught up in the crowd while Lennie was left speechless. He watched with narrowed eyes as his wife was spirited away and his look would have cut glass. Jago Cardrew. His lip curled. Everyone calling him a hero because he'd saved her life. Look at him – flaunting that twisted hand of his to prove it. Pah! As for dancing, Lennie had never danced in his life. Mother always said that dancing was the temptation of the Devil – men and women in each other's arms like that could lead to anything.

Kerensa had put her hair up today in a new style and fastened it with a sparkling clip. She had bought herself a new gown too. Lennie ground his teeth in frustration. When he actually felt a twinge of envy for the two moving so smoothly to the lilting music, a flicker of hate flared in his gut and he took a long swig of the punch which he had been imbibing all evening. He would make her pay for this, just see if he didn't. But the polite smile on his public face remained undisturbed.

Kerensa had never felt so happy as she circled the room in Jago's arms. In his formal dark suit and crisp linen he was easily the most handsome man present, and seemed to have shaken off his depression, at least for today. His left hand, even with its poor two-fingered grip, felt warm at her waist, and the eyes looking tenderly down at her were soft and gentle.

Her feet were not meeting solid ground, were they? Surely she was floating above it, Kerensa thought, as she spun on a cloud of music an arm's length away from Jago before he guided her back and into his embrace again. Now her cheek was a hair's breadth from his chest and she could feel the warmth of his body beaming towards her.

'Why did you marry him?' Jago's whisper in her ear broke the spell and Kerensa started and gasped. The rosy cloud had dispelled and bleak awareness of the truth cut through her like shards of ice. 'M-marry him? Oh, yes. I said I'd tell you, didn't I?' She turned her head but Lennie was nowhere to be seen. Gone to bury his nose in another drink, she thought bitterly.

'Let's sit over here,' Kerensa said, as the music came to an end, and drew him into a secluded corner behind a potted palm. There, as the happy dancers whirled past them, she told Jago everything. Of the dreadful choice with which she had been faced, and the sacrifice she'd made. How Celia was still abroad, and how Kerensa was bound to Lennie for the rest of her life.

'Oh, Jago,' she finished, with a smothered sob, 'it feels so good to tell someone.' She looked into his beloved face and added, 'I never had anyone to talk to before, you see.'

Under cover of the cane table where they were sitting, Jago reached for her hand and squeezed it. 'I think that's the bravest and most unselfish thing I've ever heard,' he said solemnly. 'And there was I thinking that you – that you . . . Oh, Kerensa, can you ever forgive me?'

Dark eyes bored into hers, into her very soul, pleading for understanding until she could hardly stop the scorching tears from coming. But stop them she must – this was a public gathering, and soon her husband would be looking for her. 'Jago, after you saved my life? How could I not *forgive* you?' she said in a fierce whisper. 'And that was what I call *real* bravery.'

A detailed enquiry into the cause of the blasting accident had been under way for some weeks. Ministry inspectors and local mining officials came and went, and mine surveyors and representatives of Smithfords spent many hours underground trying to find clues to the mystery.

Naturally, Smithfords with their unsullied reputation at stake, were the most persistent. Tons of rubble was painstakingly cleared and the spot where the fuse had been laid was minutely scrutinized. And eventually their patience was rewarded when pieces of the spent lighter, as they called their own make of detonator, were unearthed and taken back to the laboratory of the works for examination.

Silas and Lennie were sitting at their respective desks in the foundry office, deep in their own work, when a knock came at the door and, as Silas barked, 'Come in', a stranger poked his head around it.

'Mr Cardrew?' He removed his bowler and advanced a few steps into the room. 'Please forgive the intrusion. My name's Richards, John Richards of Smithford and Company.' He flourished a business card. 'I wonder if you could spare me a few minutes of your time, if it's convenient, that is?'

Curiosity overcame Silas's first reaction, which had been to turn the fellow away, assuming he was selling something. But salesmen were Lennie's business and usually made an appointment with him, not Silas. So, he removed his spectacles and stared at the visitor from under bushy brows, 'I can give you just a few minutes, yes.' He pointedly consulted his pocket watch before waving him to a chair. 'This is my colleague, Leonard Retallick.' They exchanged nods, then John Richards folded his long legs and opened his briefcase.

'To come straight to the point,' he said, 'I've been part of the team investigating the cause of the blasting accident at Anderson's shaft.' His glance included both men as he drew forth some charred scraps of material and bent metal, and laid them out carefully on Silas's desk. 'These are the remains of the detonating equipment which was used that day.'

Silas gave a cursory glance and grunted as their visitor turned to Lennie. 'Maybe you would like to come a little closer, Mr Retallick, and take a look as well.' The man's expression was bland but beneath it they were both aware of a hint of steel.

'Of course.' Lennie said, as they grouped around the desk.

'You might think that in something only a few inches long, as well as being half-consumed by fire, there would be little to see,' said John Richards, and glanced up at them both. Two pairs of eyes were riveted on his as he went on. 'As you will know, Mr Retallick,' – he gave a thin smile – 'but Mr Cardrew may not – all the lighters manufactured by Smithford's are inspected very rigorously before being marketed. And one of the most stringent rules is that they must each bear the symbol "P" stamped within a crown, which is a legal requirement.' He paused. 'This proves that they have passed that inspection and have therefore reached the official government "Permitted" standard.'

'Yes, yes,' Silas said testily. 'Get on with it, can't you?'

John Richards gave him a long, cool look. 'And the crux of the matter is,' he went on, 'that this vital symbol is missing from the lighter we have here. The adhesive tape on which it should have been stamped has survived the blast and is clearly quite plain.'

He leaned back in his chair and crossed one leg over the other. 'Therefore, gentlemen, I have to tell you that this detonator was not manufactured by Smithford's but by some other firm.'

Silas sat bolt upright and thumped both fists on the desk. 'But that's preposterous!' he blustered. 'Impossible, in fact. Have you forgotten, Mr Richards, that this firm took over Smithfords some time ago? Tell me, in the name of goodness, why we should go to another supplier when our own vested interest is in this very firm?' His shoulders relaxed and he chuckled softly. 'It would be the equivalent of shooting ourselves in the foot, would it not?' He leaned back in his chair and regarded the visitor with disdain. 'So I suggest, Mr -um -Richards, that you go back to the drawing-board as it were, and think again. For you've obviously made a very big mistake somewhere, ha, ha,ha!' Silas chuckled again and glanced towards Lennie, expecting the smile to be reflected on his face as well. Then he did a double-take in surprise. For, far from smiling, his agent had paled, his expression was stony, and he was looking distinctly uncomfortable.

'If that is the case,' John Richards replied, 'then I'm sure, Mr Cardrew, that you would have no objection if I were to check your storeroom, and have a general look around the foundry?'

'I resent your inference, sir,' Silas growled and glared at him, 'but I'll tell you again I've nothing to hide, so go ahead and search where you damn well like. You won't find anything out of order, I assure you.' He rose to his feet. 'I'll get someone,' he snapped. Silas went to the door and hailed one of the foremen from the shop floor who happened to be passing with a an armful of scrap metal. 'Bert, show Mr Richards around wherever he wants to go, will you?'

The man tipped his cap. 'Yes, sir. If you'd like to follow me, Mr Richards. . . .'

When Silas returned to the office, Lennie had disappeared. He pulled out his watch. It *was* time to leave, but to go off without a word . . . Mm. He settled down and opened the local paper while he waited for John Richards to come back.

Silas was deep in the mining news when the door was flung open without any warning and John Richards appeared on the threshold with a cardboard box under his arm and a self-satisfied expression on his face. He dumped it on the desk under Silas's nose and loomed over him. 'What a surprise,' he said. 'It goes against the grain for me to call any man a liar, but perhaps you would be good enough to explain what *this* is doing in your strong-room.' He stabbed a finger at the box. 'I found it in among the Smithford's stock, tucked into a corner, the only one of its kind.'

'What?' Silas removed his spectacles and leaned forward to peer into the box of detonators. 'What are you talking about – only one? What's the difference?'

'Look at the outside of the box first.' He turned it all ways. 'No label, right? All of ours are stamped with the firm's name. *Then*' – he drew out one of the contents and held it up in front of Silas's face – 'take a look at this. A close look.'

Silas put his spectacles back on his nose and examined the object. About three inches long, it was a harmless-looking metal tube attached to a length of safety fuse, the join between the two sealed with adhesive tape. 'Looks perfectly normal to me,' Silas growled. 'The capsule of chemicals would be inside the metal casing,' he went on, grunting to himself, peering closely, 'and would have to be pinched with pliers to break it before the fuse was lit.' He tugged at the length of tubing where it joined the metal. 'Feels perfectly snug there – so what's the problem?' He raised his head to meet the other man's eyes.

'The problem, Mr Cardrew, is this.' John Richards produced another lighter from his pocket and compared the two. 'Here we have a bona fide Smithford product, *stamped with the "Permitted" symbol*.' He stabbed at it with a finger. 'You see?'

Silas's eyes widened. 'And these are not?' he said. He took another look and his brows rose. The tape joining the two components was plain.

'Precisely.' The other man's voice was cold. 'So, these are obviously sub-standard goods. Which is why one of them went off before it should have done, and caused that tragic accident.' He paused and gave Silas a basilisk stare. 'Do you have an explanation, Mr Cardrew, or not?'

Silas cleared his throat and played for time as his head reeled under the shock. 'I – I'll have to speak to Retallick,' he hedged. 'He's in charge of all this. Give me a couple of days and I'll come back to you on it. Same time again, here, on Friday. All right?' he said gruffly, as he rose to his feet.

'All right. And any explanation of his had better be good.'

John Richards was on his way to the door when Silas stopped him with a raised hand. 'However, you seem to have overlooked one small thing, Mr Richards.'

The other man quirked an eyebrow. 'Oh? And what might that be?'

Silas having recovered some of his composure, rocked back and forth on his heels and gave him a level stare. 'As for calling me a liar, think on this: if I *was* implicated in any shady business, do you really think that I'd allow you to snoop about among my stores?'

The man stared him down. 'Until Friday, Mr Cardrew,' he replied, and closed the door quietly behind him. Silas gave him time to get away, then jammed his hat on his head and left. He slammed the door resoundingly upon his own departure, and headed straight for Lennie's home.

'Oh, Mr Cardrew!' Kerensa regarded their visitor with surprise. There must be some very good reason for Silas to come calling in person; usually people he wanted to see were summoned instead to his presence. She also noticed his flushed face and agitated manner in the split second it took before he spoke.

'Forgive me Mrs Retallick, but I need to have a word with Lennie – something came up at work after he left today.'

'Come through to the parlour and I'll tell him you're here,' Kerensa replied. Once the two men were seated she left the room. She did, however, have the presence of mind to leave the door slightly ajar so that she could stand in the passage and listen.

'You've been up to something!' came Silas's furious accusation. 'And don't try to deny it.' His voice fell to a low rumble and strain as she might, Kerensa couldn't hear every word, but it sounded serious.

Lennie was in turn defensive, truculent and aggressive, as if trying to justify whatever he was supposed to have done. Then she caught the word 'detonators' and, as if a window had opened in her mind, she recalled the locked drawer in the shed and the correspondence with a firm supplying yes, detonators. Risking discovery but reckoning that the two men were too absorbed to come out yet, Kerensa crept closer and put her ear to the crack in the door.

'You've been passing off that shoddy stuff as ours, haven't you – ever since I took Smithford's over?' Silas was spluttering with fury. 'You sneaking, conniving . . . little *rat*! And to think I trusted you, put you in charge of explosives. Dammit, I should have put one up your backside.' Serious as it all was, Kerensa could not resist a smile at the crudity.

'There was nothing wrong with they lighters,' Lennie was blustering. 'Been all right up to now, haven't they? Just because some fool miner didn't prime that one right,' he muttered.

'All these months,' Silas seethed, 'you've been creaming off my profits, haven't you? I wondered where all the money was coming from for your fancy suits and bespoke boots. You little runt! I could strangle you with my own two hands!'

Kerensa risked a peep around the door. Wide-eyed she saw Silas with his back to her holding Lennie by his shirt collar and shaking him like a dog with a rat. Her husband's face was a picture of terror as he swallowed and whimpered, seemingly trying to think of a last-ditch line of defence.

'Prove it,' he said at last, with an attempt at bravado, one hand to his throat as Silas tossed him backwards. 'You haven't got one scrap of proof. Anybody could have put that box there, anybody.'

'Does anyone else have a key to the strong-room?' Silas replied with menace. 'No. I don't need any more proof than that. I'll make you pay for this, don't think I won't. Dragging the good name of Cardrew's in the dirt for the sake of your petty thieving!' He took a few steps and turned back to stab a finger in the air with rage as he went on, 'I'll see you jailed for this, Retallick, and from today you can cease to call yourself an employee of mine!'

Kerensa clapped a hand over her mouth in shock – a shock that was reflected too on her husband's face, as his mouth went slack and his eyes widened.

'Come into the office tomorrow and collect what wages are owing,' Silas finished, 'and after that I never want to see your face in my works again!'

But a crafty look had replaced the shock and fear on Lennie's face now. 'Not so fast, old man,' he said with a sly smile, and Kerensa saw him draw himself up to his full height and puff out his chest. 'I think you might have forgotten something.'

Silas's eyes bulged and he stared at the other man as if he were something unpleasant that he'd encountered underfoot. 'I beg your pardon?' he said distantly.

'I'll put it quite simply,' Lennie replied with a smirk. All of a sudden he seemed to be enjoying himself, Kerensa thought with surprise. 'So listen well, Silas Cardrew.' He took in another breath and said, as if he were playing his trump card, 'Far from giving me the sack – if you don't get me out of this, I'll report what I know about a certain card game that I arranged for you out of the kindness of my heart, a couple of years ago.' He paused and Kerensa saw Silas flinch. 'How you used my knowledge and skill,' Lennie went on relentlessly, 'to fix it so that poor old Zack never stood a chance against you.' He stared eye to eye with Silas. 'And how you *really* came by Penhallow, that fine house you call yours.'

Silas's face was crimson and his eyes bulged as he struggled for words.

'You can't do that!' he burst out. Lennie stood his ground and stared him down. 'Oh, but I can, and I would – never doubt it.'

Silas raised his chin, as he countered, 'You couldn't. Where's the proof? You haven't got any. It's only your word against mine, that's all there is. No one would believe you. No one.' He curled his lip and his eyes flashed as he stabbed the air in front of Lennie's nose. 'You've gone too far now. I swear I'll have you up for slander if you make a word of this known in public.'

'And that's just where you're wrong,' Lennie retorted, his eyes like shards of blue glass. 'Because there are at least two people I know very well who were at the table that night, and who came away when the stakes became too high for them.' He stuck his hands in his pockets and paced the room. 'I had a drink with them afterwards,' he said, 'and they were very uneasy about the way things went. I didn't say anything at the time,' – he squared up to Silas and their eyes met – 'but now I could easily stir their memories and they'd back me all the way. So think on it well, Silas Cardrew, before telling me I'm to be out on my ear tomorrow,' he finished quietly. 'Now get out of my house!' Lennie snapped.

Silas swivelled on his heel and was across the room almost before Kerensa could jump out of the way. By the time she'd recovered, he was out of the front door. And when Lennie emerged right afterwards, she was in the kitchen innocently frying sausages.

'Mr Cardrew's gone, has he?' she said, glancing up. 'What did he want – anything important?'

Lennie paced across the room and looked out of the window. With his back towards her he replied casually, 'No, no – just some unfinished business at the works.' He turned and glanced at the plates standing ready on the table. 'I don't want no tea,' he said shortly, 'I'm going out.'

Kerensa watched as he headed purposefully down the lane towards his workshop. When, shortly afterwards, she saw wisps of blue smoke rising from the field, a shaky smile crossed her face at the thought of him destroying, as he imagined, all the evidence.

Then she sank into a chair as her trembling legs threatened to collapse beneath her. Far from eating a meal, the very thought of food would have choked her. Both body and mind were reeling as she tried to come to terms with all that she had just heard and the enormity of what it meant.

To think that the dreadful accident had been caused by her own husband's greed! Whether directly or indirectly made no difference. Kerensa felt sick. Men had died that day – leaving their wives widowed and their children fatherless, and others were maimed for life. All because of *him*!

And there was the other thing as well. She'd been right about Silas all along. She'd always thought there was some shady business about the way he had come by Penhallow. So he'd cheated at the card evening! Probably made sure that Papa had too much to drink – that would have been simple enough – and then manipulated him into staking Penhallow on a turn of the cards!

The snake! The crafty, underhanded, deceitful *snake*! He and Lennie made a good pair. Kerensa leapt to her feet in fury and clenched both hands into fists. Then her mind started working overtime. What could she do about it? There must be *something* she could do. She paced angrily to and fro, but soon realized that there was nothing, at least for now.

CHAPTER FOURTEEN

'Jago! How nice to see you. Come in, come in.' Grace's smile widened as her brother ducked his head under the doorframe of the little cottage and gave her a peck on the cheek.

'I thought it was about time I came to visit my married sister in her own home,' Jago said, returning the smile. 'How are you and Dan? I haven't seen you for ages.' He sat down on the settle beside the kitchen range and tucked his long legs beneath it.

'We're fine,' Grace replied, pouring a cup of tea and placing it at his elbow before sinking into the rocking chair opposite. 'It was the best decision I ever made, Jago,' she said, turning serious eyes to his, 'to leave home.' The tabby cat which had been sleeping on the hearth rug took the opportunity to jump onto her lap and she stroked it absently as it began to purr with content.

'I miss having you at home,' Jago said, looking over the rim of his cup, 'it's so quiet up there now, you know?'

'I do know,' Grace replied with sympathetic eyes. 'Is Kerensa looking after you both all right? I know I keep an eye on things and she seems very capable, but you would tell me if there was anything, wouldn't you?'

'Of course I would,' said Jago. 'No, everything's fine. How is Dan now really – is he fully recovered?' In such close proximity Jago could see the little worry lines etched on his sister's face which had not been there he was sure, before the accident.

Grace nodded and sipped her own tea. 'Yes, yes he is, thank goodness. But he would never have got over it so soon if I hadn't come over here to tend him.' With a dreamy smile she added, 'He and I were made for each other, Jay, we never have a cross word, you know?'

Jago looked at her glowing face and never doubted it. 'It was a brave thing to do Grace,' he replied. 'I admired you for it then and I'm glad it all worked out so well for you since.'

Grace flushed and lowered her gaze, before changing the subject. 'And what about you?' she asked, brightening. 'Have you had any further news from the doctors?'

Jago shook his head. 'No, and I don't think I'm likely to,' he replied. He paused before going on, 'I want to tell you, Grace, about something I've started doing.'

'Yes?' her eyes widened in enquiry. 'What's that?' Privately she was thinking how much better he was looking – less drawn and with more animation in his face than she had seen since for a long time. 'Well – er – someone – suggested that as I can't play the piano any more . . .' Then noting Grace's startled look he added, 'Oh, I'm not under any illusions, Grace. I've been through hell, I won't deny that, but I have to face the facts and get on with my shattered life somehow.'

'And you talk to me of bravery . . .' There were tears in her eyes as Grace leaned over and gently stroked his injured hand. He gave hers a squeeze in return and said, 'Well, what I was about to tell you is that this – friend – suggested that I should write music – compose tunes that is, instead.'

'What a marvellous idea! Are you going to?'

Jago pulled some sheets of paper from his breast pocket and spread them on his knee. 'I've already started,' he replied, 'I've brought these to show you. I know you can read music from being in the Ladies Choral Society, and I'd like to know what you think.'

Grace held out a hand and he passed them over. She examined the score and hummed quietly to herself as she followed the notes.

'That's really good!' she said, looking up with a smile. 'It would make a lovely song; are there words as well?' She passed the score back to him.

'Oh, come on, Grace, I'm a musician, not a poet!' Jago gave a hearty laugh. 'But I'm glad you like it.'

His sister's brow was creased in thought. Then, 'I've had an idea,' she announced, and stood up so suddenly that the cat gave a protesting yowl and the chair rocked furiously as if also in protest. 'Wait there while I fetch something.' Jago looked bemused as she went racing up the stairs and was soon back with an exercise book in her hand.

'Do you remember – perhaps you don't – that Mama used to write verses?' Grace sank into the chair again and her eyes were bright with excitement.

'Um – well, yes I do, vaguely,' Jago replied, 'I never read any of them though.'

'She was always a bit sensitive about it – afraid people would laugh at her,' Grace said. 'She kept them very much to herself, but she used to show them to me. Some of them were very good, actually. And what I thought was,' Grace went on, 'whether you could set any of these to your music – then you could write real songs that anyone could sing! How about that?'

'That's a marvellous idea,' said Jago, 'but what a challenge.' A slow smile spread across his face. 'It all depends on what those poems are like. Let me have the book to study and I'll see what I can do.'

'What fun!' Grace said. 'I can't wait to hear what you come up with.'

Jago, riffling through the pages said, 'Just don't expect results overnight, will you? It'll take weeks of work even if I *can* manage to put something together.'

Silas had been pacing up and down the hall for some time in an agitated manner, and Kerensa, who had been coming and going about her duties, glanced at him curiously as she passed. She was checking the linen cupboard at the top of the stairs when eventually she heard Jago arrive home, and the rumble of their voices came floating up the stairwell.

'There you are at last!' That was Silas's deep boom. 'I've been looking everywhere for you – where the hell have you been?'

Jago's reply was cool and in a lighter tone. 'Visiting my sister, as it happens,' she heard him say. 'Why? What's the matter? Is the house on fire or something?'

'Worse,' Silas snapped. 'Cardrew's is being held responsible for the blasting accident. John Richards reported it to the police and they're taking us to court. The devil take Retallick! He's going to have a lot to answer for!'

The voices faded down the hall as they walked away. Shock widened Kerensa's eyes. She stood rooted to the spot with her hand on a pile of towels as her notebook dropped unheeded from her hand and her mind began to work overtime.

The letters. Those incriminating letters which were still sitting in their hiding place in her flour bin. They were vital evidence, weren't they? She should really take them to the police. Which would mean betraying her own husband. On the face it that sounded an awful thing to do.

But wasn't he guilty of a terrible crime in which he caused the death of five men? He deserved to be brought to justice. To be punished. And if she were to withhold this vital evidence, surely she could be arrested as well if she was ever found out? Wasn't there something about being an accessory. . . ? Kerensa bit a nail down to the quick as all these thoughts battered her brain like hammer blows in the space of a few seconds.

Could she do it to Lennie? Dispassionately she weighed him up. Her husband. She owed him something for saving her mother's life certainly, but had she not paid dearly for that in the three years since their marriage? She thought of the brutality of their early months, his selfishness, the way he treated her as a trophy to be paraded in public, the coldness of their day to day life and the aching loneliness to which she had been condemned by their marriage.

Should she do it? Kerensa stiffened her resolve and finally made up her mind. Yes. Her duty to the truth was far stronger than any duty she still had towards Lennie. She *would* do it. When the right time came.

'Please, sir, there's someone to see you.' Annie, the ageing spinster who had spent her entire working life at the reception desk at Cardrew's, peered anxiously over her steel-rimmed spectacles as she put her head round the door of Lennie's office.

He looked up and felt the colour drain from his face, as hard on her heels came a policeman. Tall and burly with a luxuriant moustache, he carried his helmet tucked under one arm and his pocket-book in the other hand. 'Mr Retallick.' He nodded briefly. 'My name's Trudgeon. Police Constable Trudgeon.' Annie withdrew her head, and paused for longer than was strictly necessary before she closed the door. However, the policeman waited until she had no choice but to click it shut, then seated himself.

Lennie lifted his chin and looked the other man in the face. He gave a thin smile as he said, 'Constable Trudgeon, this is a surprise. What can I do for you?' The bland expression on his face belied the fact that his heart was thumping so madly that he wondered whether it might even be obvious to his visitor.

'I'd like to ask you a few questions sir, concerning an incident which we are investigating. I'm sure you can spare me just a few minutes?' He looked at Lennie enquiringly.

'Yes, yes, of course,' Lennie beamed. Being addressed as 'sir' had given him a certain amount of confidence and he straightened his spine. They didn't have any proof, couldn't pin anything on him. He'd been too clever at covering his tracks. His brain was turning over rapidly, but no, he couldn't think of a single loophole he'd left anywhere. 'Glad to help in any way I can.'

'Splendid.' Constable Trudgeon crossed one of his shiny boots over the other knee and picked up his notes. 'Now,' he said, clearing his throat, 'as you know, an inquiry has been going on for some time into the cause of the mine accident in which several men lost their lives.'

'Yes, yes,' Lennie said, with a touch of impatience. Why couldn't he just get on with it and come to the point? As if he had read his mind, the other man fixed Lennie with a steely look and went on, 'I have had a report from Mr John Richards of Smithford's, which contains some very disturbing news. News which has led me to you.'

Lennie gulped. 'M-me?' he replied, hating the involuntary tremor in his voice and knowing that the policeman would have noticed it.

'Yes. You are, I believe, in charge of the explosives stores here, and of supplying Smithford's goods to the mines?' Lennie nodded.

'Well, Mr Retallick,' said the constable, rising to his feet and towering over him. 'I'm afraid I must ask you to accompany me to the station, as my superiors will want to put some further questions to you.'

Lennie's jaw dropped. 'You mean you're *arresting* me?' he spluttered. 'But – but . . .'

'Just asking you to come with me, sir, that's all.' The man's face was implacable, and Lennie rose to find that his legs were trembling. 'If you would just get your things and tell your staff that you won't be returning to work today.'

They walked through the town to the police station in Moor Street, not far from Lennie's home. The humiliation of it – people staring, pointing, whispering behind their hands. People from the chapel, neighbours, shop-keepers, all staring after him – Lennie Retallick, pillar of the community, being escorted down the street by a uniformed constable. He could have wept. The whole town would hear about it before the day was over and his reputation would be in tatters.

They kept him at the station for two hours, grilling him about every facet of his work at Cardrew's. How the fuses were made, transported, stored, paid for, until Lennie's head was buzzing and his eyes glazed over. When his interrogator had finished at last, Lennie was so exhausted that he heard him as if in a dream as the man said, 'Right, Mr Retallick, I'm afraid that I have no alternative but to take you into custody to await trial on suspicion of—'

'*Custody?*' Lennie came back to earth with a crash and jumped up, clutching at the table for support as his knees buckled. 'You mean . . . I'm going to . . . to *prison?*' He recovered himself and began to bluster. 'But you can't – there's no proof – not a shred of evidence against me. I haven't done anything . . .' He could hear himself babbling and tried to regain his composure.

'Then in that case sir,' said the other man silkily, 'you have nothing to worry about, have you?' He put away his papers and nodded to Constable Trudgeon who had been sitting behind Lennie. 'Take him away, Constable.'

Kerensa was still deep in her troubled thoughts as she walked home from work that evening. Something else had occurred to her which had stiffened her resolve even further. For given that Lennie had burned all the incriminating material which had been in his workshop, then the letters that she had secreted away would be the *only* concrete evidence against him. And furthermore, if Silas decided to keep quiet about what he knew because of the hold which Lennie had over *him*, then it was doubly important that she should tell what she knew to the authorities, and hand over the letters.

Even putting her personal conscience to one side, at least she owed it to the stricken families to make sure that Lennie received his just deserts. And wasn't there something too, about 'perverting the course of justice'? The worry lines on Kerensa's face deepened as she chewed on her bottom lip.

She was nearing the cottage where she and Celia had formerly lived and was so deep in thought that she almost walked straight past May Spargo who was standing at the gate next door. When she did look up and greet the woman, she saw that her face was alight with what Kerensa imagined, was the latest snippet of local gossip.

'Been looking out for you, I have,' May said, as Kerensa drew level and stopped. 'My dear life, you'll never guess what has happened.' She laid a hand on Kerensa's arm and her bright eyes bored into hers. Kerensa shrugged and replied, 'I don't suppose I shall, May, so you'd better tell me.'

'I only just seen your husband being marched off down the police station!' She folded her arms and gave a nod as she shot this bolt. 'Arthur Trudgeon must have been up to the works to fetch him.'

The woman's eyes never left Kerensa's face as she waited for her reaction, and a look of satisfaction crossed her face when Kerensa's hand flew to her mouth and she exclaimed, '*Lennie*? He's been arrested, then?' Her stomach churned. So, it had come to that already.

'That's what it do look like.' May brushed a smut off her white apron and looked up with irritation at the smoking chimney behind her. 'Carrie Symons said 'tis to do with that there accident down the mine,' she went on. 'Her Joe do work for Smithford's see, and there's all sorts of rumours going round there, she said.'

'I'd better go and see him straight away.' Kerensa swallowed on a tight throat and her black skirt swirled around her ankles as she turned back the way she had come. It was only a few steps to the police station.

She was only allowed to speak to Lennie through the bars of his cell and in the presence of a policeman who listened to every word that passed between them, so their conversation was stilted and mundane. Kerensa gathered that he would be transferred to Bodmin Gaol in the morning to await trial there at the monthly assizes. She went home feeling limp and exhausted.

She unearthed the letters from their hiding-place and put them behind the clock on the mantelpiece, where they accusingly drew her gaze no matter how much she tried to ignore them. How she ached for someone to talk to that lonely evening. Someone older, stronger, to whom she could turn for advice, and for guidance.

But there was no one. There was no way she could involve Jago in this. It was her responsibility and she was going to have to deal with it herself. She would wait until late tomorrow, when Lennie would have been taken away, and give the letters to the police then.

So Kerensa cleared her conscience by walking into the police station the next day, handing over the incriminating documents and walking away feeling as if she had thrown her husband to the lions.

A few days later, Kerensa was passing the closed door of the library when she heard the faint notes of piano music She pressed both hands to her face and listened. Halting, one-handed as it was, nevertheless the tune caught her imagination and soared away with it. It was the kind of understated, repetitive air from which the best songs are created, and there was no way that she was going to pass by and ignore it.

Quietly she turned the china knob and opened the door a crack. Jago's dark head was bent over the keyboard and on top of the piano lay a notebook, anchored by his damaged hand, into which he made a mark every so often. He was totally absorbed and Kerensa was about to withdraw, not wanting to break his concentration, but something must have alerted him to her presence for he started, then twirled round on the piano stool with a look of anger on his face.

'I'm sorry, Jago.' Kerensa spread her hands in apology. 'But I heard the music and it drew me. I just had to creep in and listen properly.' She half-turned away. 'I'll go again – I didn't mean to disturb you.'

'No! Kerensa, don't go. Come over here. You're just the person I need.' Jago's face had lightened and he raised a beckoning finger to her. 'You see, I've been doing what you suggested – trying to write a song. Sit down.' He moved up and made room for her to join him at the piano. 'Now that you're here I'll write down the left hand and you can play it for me.' He scribbled the notes down feverishly on his score sheet and passed it to her. 'There. Try that out.'

Kerensa played it through experimentally at first and Jago joined in on the second run through. When they both actually finished together on a satisfying chord she clapped her hands and laughed in sheer delight.

'It's a marvellous tune, Jago; I love it,' she said with enthusiasm. Then her brow creased in a frown. 'But a song really should have words, shouldn't it? What are you going to do about the lyrics?'

'Ah,' Jago beamed and reached for another book which lay on top of the piano. 'Have a look through these. They were my mother's.' Silence fell as Kerensa began to read and Jago went back to his composing. It was some time before Kerensa raised her head. Then, 'These are wonderful,' she sighed. 'How lucky you are to have them.'

'I know,' Jago said. 'Grace gave them to me – aren't they exactly what I need? That's what set me off really. When I read those poems they began to trigger off tunes in my head. It was quite amazing. Mama must have been really talented and I knew nothing about it.' A hint of sadness crossed his face and he paused for a moment.

'Well,' Kerensa said, lowering her eyes to the book which she still held in her hand, 'I was thinking. You know, now that Lennie's ... um ... away, I've plenty of spare time and I could go on helping you like this.' She raised her eyes and added, 'That is, if you would like me to, of course.'

Jago's face lit up like a beacon as he replied, 'Kerensa, that would be *terrific*! You can't imagine how frustrating and how slow it is to have to do it all one-handed.' She smiled back, gratified by his enthusiasm, and their eyes met and held for a long moment.

For far too long. Kerensa felt herself melting into it as that fathomless dark gaze drew her nearer towards the man at her side. They were sitting so close together that she could feel the warmth emanating from his body and smell the fresh tang of the pomade he used to tame his curly hair.

It was Kerensa who made the first move, afraid of going down the road which beckoned. It was so tantalizingly close that it took more strength than she thought she possessed to turn away, to rise to her feet with some inconsequential remark, and put space between them as if the moment had never been.

She ran a hand through her hair and said the first thing that came into her head. Anything to take the place of what she yearned to say and do, but was forbidden. 'Have you heard anything further about the court case?' She lowered her gaze to straighten her skirt, afraid of what Jago might have seen on her face, then pressed both hands to her hot cheeks.

Jago shook his head. The light had died out of his eyes as she moved away and his face was serious now as he closed the piano lid and leant one elbow on it. 'Not since they put your husband in prison,' he replied. 'We're all just waiting for the trial now. You know that's coming up next week?' His voice was wooden.

Kerensa nodded. 'I suppose your father will be called upon to give evidence,' she replied, 'against Lennie.' And she wondered how Silas would square that with the threatened blackmail.

'Of course he will; being the owner of the firm, the overall responsibility was his, although he didn't actually know what was going on.'

'That was a *despicable* thing that Lennie did!' Kerensa said with vehemence, as she vented her private frustrations in anger against her husband. 'How *could* he, Jago? Put innocent people's lives in danger for the sake of lining his own pockets?'

Jago shrugged. 'He's a weak character – easily gives in to temptation – it happens. But as I said, if Father knew nothing about it I'm hoping it will count in his favour.'

'How can he prove that he didn't, though?' asked Kerensa. 'There's only his own word for it, after all.'

Jago nodded. 'Yes, I know. You're right. I can only go on hoping that they *will* believe him.'

But the matter was not to be resolved easily because the police had brought a charge of manslaughter against Leonard Retallick, and the court decided that he was to remain in custody pending further trial at the next sitting of the quarterly sessions, in eight weeks time. As for Silas Cardrew, he was to be released on bail during the interim period.

Kerensa was revelling in the novelty of having her home to herself, in the peace and freedom which Lennie's incarceration had given her, and in being her own mistress for the first time since her marriage.

She was also for the first time in possession of some money of her own, as since being promoted to housekeeper, she had managed to save a considerable amount of her increased wages, unknown to her husband. Also unknown to Lennie, Kerensa had cleared his wardrobe of the many bespoke suits and shiny boots she had found there, and sold them without a shred of guilty feelings. They had been bought with blood-money, and as such she had no compunction in taking the cash which they brought in and adding it to her savings.

It was during this time that she received a letter from her mother. They had been corresponding regularly ever since Celia had left, and after the first few months when she had been too ill to write, Kerensa had dreaded opening each bulletin from the clinic in case it contained the ultimate news. But gradually over the months her mother's health had improved, now she continued to hold her own and as far as Kerensa knew, she was out of any immediate danger. So today she slit the envelope with nothing more than pleasurable anticipation at what her mother would have to say.

The letter opened with the usual generalities concerning her health, the weather, and chit-chat about people with whom she had become friendly and who held little interest for Kerensa. Then Celia dropped her bombshell.

> *... now my dearest daughter, comes the biggest piece of my news. Maybe it will not come as a complete surprise to you, as you must have noticed how frequently I have mentioned Doktor Gruber's name in my letters to you. Rudi, as I have come to call him, is the physician who has been treating me so successfully since I first came here to his clinic. To whom in fact, I owe my life. And to whom I have now given my heart. For Kerensa – he has asked me to become his wife!*
>
> *Now I realize that this is bound to cause you a certain amount of pain, knowing how fond you were of your Papa, until events went so tragically wrong for us all. But the past is over, time has moved on and I feel that we*

must move on with it. It has been over three years since Zack left us and disappeared without a word, and by law I am permitted to divorce him on the grounds of desertion.

So, after much heart-searching, I have decided to accept Rudi's offer, and I can't tell you how happy this makes me. My only sadness is that I wish I could see you, talk to you and introduce you both, as I am sure you would love him too. He is so kind, so compassionate, with such a sense of humour that we are laughing all the time, which he says is the best medicine of all.

I sincerely hope that you have found equal pleasure and fulfilment in your own marriage, but with such a kind and generous man as Lennie for your husband, I am sure that you must have done, and that makes me think that you will wish the same for me.

So my dearest daughter, after our marriage I shall be making my home permanently in this beautiful country, as Rudi says that to return to the mild damp air of Cornwall would put my health in jeopardy again and would be the worse thing that I could possibly do. Besides, he cannot of course, abandon the clinic.

Write soon Kerensa, and send us your blessing, I desperately need to know that you are happy for me. Until then I remain your loving,
Mama.

The letter fell unheeded from Kerensa's hand as her gaze rested blankly on the net curtains which shrouded the front window from the curiosity of passers-by. She had had no idea. Had not noticed the slightest hint of anything so shattering in previous letters from her mother. So, how *did* she feel about this impending marriage? It would be too selfish not to wish Celia happiness in her new life after all she had been through, and Kerensa did not think she was a selfish person.

But part of her was crying out in resentment at her mother's ignorance of her daughter's true circumstances which, of course, Kerensa had purposely kept from her while she was so ill. Now she could never tell her, for it was too late for that, and she would have to go along with Celia's illusion that she and Lennie were enjoying a marriage made in heaven.

The distance between them, both mentally as well as geographically, was so vast that she would never be able to bridge the gap, and a tear rolled down Kerensa's cheek as she thought wistfully that both her parents were now lost to her, and in their place was an aching void which should have been filled, as Celia fondly imagined it was, by her own marriage.

★

So deeply involved had she been in her mother's news, that Kerensa had not noticed the other letter which still lay on the doormat until she almost stepped on it. As she bent to pick it up she saw that this one as well was addressed to her, and bore the heading of Grylls and Thomas, the solicitors.

It was a simple message, asking her to call at the office at her convenience, and was signed by Nathan Thomas. It jerked Kerensa instantly out of her reverie – what did he want her for? Was it about the will? And was it good news or bad? She would never rest until she found out. Any plans she might have had for the rest of the day, for it was her half-day off, were about to be abandoned. Kerensa reached for her hat and was out of the door in five minutes.

'Ah, Mrs Retallick.' He bowed over her hand, his usually passive face wreathed in smiles. 'I'm glad you could come so promptly. You'll be pleased to hear that I have some favourable news for you.'

'You have?' Kerensa's eyes widened and she returned the smile as her heart began to beat a little faster.

'Sit down, please.' He pulled out a chair and waved her into it. Returning to his desk he sat behind it and steepled his fingers. 'Yes, indeed. I have received the reply from Somerset House that we've been waiting for.'

Kerensa sat up straighter, her heart pounding now. Nathan Thomas opened a drawer, drew out a couple of documents and handed one to her. 'This is a copy of the original will,' he said, and paused while she scanned it avidly. However, not helped by the tension throbbing in her head, it took time to read the clerk's meticulous copperplate script. Then having reached the end, Kerensa read it through again to make sure she was not mistaken in the date. Then she raised troubled eyes to the solicitor's face and clasped her flushed cheeks with her hands.

'So the other *was* a forgery!' She could hardly believe, even now with the proof in front of her, that her father had actually been a criminal. The paper fell to her lap and she bowed her head to hide the tears which pricked her eyelashes. A common criminal – a confidence trickster – a cheat. Oh, Papa, how *could* you? cried the small child of long ago.

But the time for hero-worship was over long ago; she was an adult now, in an adult world where people were not always what they seemed, where they were open to weakness, to temptation, and to deceit.

'It was indeed,' the solicitor replied. 'Your mother was correct all along, in her claim that the house was legally hers – is legally hers in fact.'

Kerensa's eyes widened. 'But, if so, is there any way we could get it *back*?' Her stomach lurched with sudden excitement.

'Er . . .' the lawyer tapped a pencil as he met her steady gaze. 'We can try,' he said briefly. 'Leave it with me, will you Mrs Retallick?'

'Yes, yes. And thank you.' Kerensa brought her emotions under control and reassumed her public face.

'My dear young lady, it's been a pleasure to see a wrong righted,' he replied, and smiled thinly.

Kerensa indicated the will. 'I presume this is mine to keep?' she asked.

'Of course, of course,' he replied, extending a hand as she rose to leave. Kerensa made a rapid farewell and left the building. She needed to be alone to do some hard thinking.

CHAPTER FIFTEEN

The quarter sessions were held over several days in Bodmin, about forty miles from Camborne. On the day of the case concerning Regina v. Retallick, Kerensa intended to rise very early to catch the first train, which would get her to Bodmin in time for the commencement of the sitting. Grace, Jago and Silas had departed the previous day, travelling together in the family carriage, and had stayed in the town overnight.

But, as she attempted to get out of bed that morning Kerensa found that as she put her feet to the ground all of a sudden her head began to swim and she was having trouble in focusing her eyes. She tried closing them again but it didn't seem to make much difference, and by then she had a raging headache as well.

Kerensa slipped back under the covers and tried to get warm, for she was feeling cold right through to her bones in spite of the extra blanket she had grabbed and thrown over herself. There was no way now that she could even manage to lift her head from the pillow, much less travel to Bodmin. Weak tears of frustration seeped from under her eyelids and she slipped into an uneasy sleep, punctuated by strange and disturbing dreams.

Much later, Kerensa awoke drenched in perspiration and so hot that she had to throw off all the covers in order to breathe. Her head was throbbing and her throat dry and parched. She stumbled out of bed and went downstairs, clutching the banister rail like an old woman, to fetch a glass of water. She drank it standing at the sink and refilled the glass to take back upstairs. It must be a heavy cold she thought, as she reached for a soothing powder to add to the water.

She spent the rest of the day and the following night in a semi-nightmare of the crown court, where barristers loomed over her like great birds of prey, their black gowns having become wings and their long noses and pointed chins transformed into sharp and menacing beaks.

By the morning Kerensa's head was no better and she still could not raise it from the pillow. Even trying to do so brought on an attack of nausea and giddiness so severe that she knew that there was no way she was going to be able to leave her bed that day either. She would have to miss the rest of the trial as well.

And she would have to get a message to Penhallow, else no one would know where she was or that she was ill. But how? Kerensa racked her feeble brain, then the clatter of pony's hoofs along the street and the exchange of cheery voices gave her the answer. The milkman. Albert. Of course, he was the same one who called at Penhallow. Kerensa gingerly raised herself, reached for a shawl and, ignoring her churning stomach and the pain gripping her head like a vice, staggered to the window and looked out. The draught as she threw up the sash made her teeth chatter but, thank goodness, there he was. Standing in the cart he was ladling milk from his churn into a woman's jug as they exchanged a bit of light-hearted banter.

'Albert,' she called throatily, 'up here.' As the man frowned and looked to see where the voice was coming from, Kerensa gave him her message and in reply to his anxious enquiry assured him that yes, she would be fine again in a day or two. Then she collapsed back into bed and cried out her frustration in tears of weakness and self-pity.

Hard on the heels of the news that Albert relayed to Penhallow, came Kerensa's first visitor. It was late afternoon and Kerensa was dozing, propped up on a pile of pillows which seemed to be more comfortable for her head than lying flat, when she heard the banging on the front door.

Jerked out of her semi-conscious state, her first reaction was irritation at the disturbance. Then common sense came into play and she dragged herself out of bed and across to the window. 'Who's there?' she croaked, and gasped with surprise when the caller stepped into view and looked upwards. 'Oh, Florrie!' Kerensa called out with relief. 'Stay there, I'll throw down the key.' She crossed to the night stand and retrieved it, then tossed it to her friend. Shivering more from the effort than with cold, she returned to bed and wrapped the covers tightly round herself as Florrie's tread sounded on the stairs.

'I came as soon as I could,' said her friend, sinking onto the chair beside the bed and placing her basket on the floor. 'We was all some sorry to hear you're laid up. How're you feeling now?' she said with concern.

Kerensa looked into her kindly face with half-shut eyes. 'I'm a bit ... whisht ...' she replied, the old Cornish word summing up her feelings exactly. 'It's good of you to come, Florrie.' She managed a weak smile.

'Oh 'tis no trouble. I just finished work, see, so I thought I'd walk over. Looks to me as if you got more than a cold, maid,' said Florrie critically, 'I wouldn't mind betting tis that there hinfluenza what's going round. Heaps of people have got it, so they say.'

'Well, don't sit too close to me then ... don't want you to catch it,' Kerensa croaked.

'Cook sent over a few bits for you.' Florrie indicated the basket beside her, which was covered with a white napkin, 'in case you weren't up to doing much for yourself, she said. We didn't know how you was really, see. Albert only said you was in bed. And I said to Moll that for you to take to your bed you must be bad, 'cos we do know what you're like, don't us? Bundle of energy, you are.' She grinned, and in her weakened state Kerensa could have wept maudlin tears to think what good friends these two were, and how lucky she was to have someone who cared about her.

'Seeing you has cheered me up a bit,' Kerensa whispered, her throat feeling like sandpaper.

'Aw, everyone do always feel worse when they're on their own,' said the other woman. 'Make us a cup of tea, shall I?'

'Oh yes.' Kerensa raised her head a fraction and tried to focus on her friend's face, which seemed to be wavering to and fro. 'Spare the time, can you?' she managed with an anxious look.

' 'Course I can. Haven't got neither chick nor cheeld waiting for me, have I?' Florrie said briskly. Kerensa caught a sudden glimpse of another lonely soul and her heart went out to her friend.

'Shout if you can't find anything,' she croaked, as Florrie clattered off downstairs.

'Haven't heard nothing about that there trial yet,' said Florrie, sipping tea. 'Mr Silas and Mr Jago are still away, see. So with no meals to serve, we got an easy time this week, which is good, because I'll be able to pop round again and see to you until you're on your feet again.'

'Oh thanks, Florrie,' Kerensa replied, with a lump in her throat.

Maybe Florrie sensed something of what she was feeling, because she replied shortly, 'Nonsense, I know you'd do the same for me.' She replaced her cup on its saucer and jumped up. 'Now I'm going to heat up a drop of that soup I got here, before I go. Moll said you won't feel like nothing solid, but her soups are always good and nourishing, so it'll stand by you until you get your appetite back.'

By the time Florrie left she had made up the bed with fresh linen, and Kerensa had drunk the soup and was feeling more comfortable just knowing that her friend would be back the following day.

'You're looking some lot better,' said Florrie on her return, as she brought up a tray and set it on the night stand beside Kerensa's bed.

'It's all thanks to you, Florrie,' she replied with sincerity. She was actually feeling better, she admitted. Her throat was less raw and she could see Florrie's face more clearly, as her friend shook her head.

'Oh, gus on!' Florrie replied in the Cornish vernacular and changed the subject. 'The family's back,' she announced.

Kerensa started and sat up straighter, then winced as a shooting pain stabbed through her head. 'Tell me . . . what . . . what news?' She clutched at the other woman's hand as Florrie having bustled about tidying things away, was now leaning over Kerensa to plump up her pillows. 'Leave that . . . and just tell me.' Florrie did as she asked and perched on the edge of the bed.

'Well, no one have told us directly like, so this is only what Moll and me have overheard between Mr Jago and Miss Grace – I mean Mrs Hocking – see. Because Mr Silas, he've shut himself in his study and I've heard him in there tramping up and down, and shouting at Mr Jago something terrible when he do go in. In some awful mood he is. I only put my head round the door to tell him his dinner was ready and he snapped my head off nearly.'

Kerensa moistened her lips. 'Len . . . Lennie . . . *verdict?*' Kerensa pressed her hand, balling her other hand into a fist in frustration.

'Oh yes,' Florrie replied, and pulled a sheet of paper from her cardigan pocket. 'Asked Miss Grace – I mean Mrs Hocking – to help me write it all down, I did, when she were up to see Mr Silas, so I'd be sure to get it straight.'

She held the paper a foot from her nose and squinted at it. 'Your husband have been found not guilty of manslaughter.'

Kerensa let out all the breath in her body on a long sigh which turned into a fit of coughing. She sipped from the glass of water beside her and dabbed her eyes. 'Thank God. Oh, thank you, God!' she murmured.

'His charge have been altered to – what's that word?' Florrie frowned. 'Can't read me own writing now. Here, maid, you take it.'

Kerensa held out a trembling hand. ' "Nefarious dealings . . . under false pretences",' she read, as she squinted at the rest of it with the letters dancing before her eyes, ' "and conspiring with another for fraudulent gain . . . Sentenced to two years penal servitude".' Two years. She let the paper fall to the covers and closed her aching eyes. It was a fair judgement and a severe enough punishment. Hard labour – yes – at least he would live, and be made to suffer for his crime. It was fitting.

Her thoughts having been miles away, Kerensa now brought them to bear on Florrie again. 'Silas?' she asked.

'Oh, he have been fined a lot of money – damages or something – or court fees was it?' She wrinkled her nose. 'Dunno. Can't remember. But 'tis some lot – that's what he's in such a lather about, see.'

It was over two weeks before Kerensa was sufficiently recovered to return to work at Penhallow, and when she did she was struck by the quietness of the house, and a certain kind of atmosphere about it. And then it struck her. There was no music! That's what it was. Jago's playing had always been there before, the background to her daily duties.

But Kerensa was not the only one to notice the difference. When she mentioned it Florrie replied, 'Tis like living on top of a lighted fuse,' as she poked up the range. She slammed the fire-door shut and went on, 'Those two men are hardly speaking to each other, and when they do they only snap and snarl like a pair of mad dogs. We have to tiptoe about nearly, in case we get the backlash.' She raised her eyes to the ceiling and wiped her hands down the sides of her apron, as Kerensa continued on her way down the passage to the housekeeper's room. She was passing the door of the library when it opened suddenly and Jago appeared on the threshold. She jumped, and her eyes widened as she took in the haggard face and grim frown.

But he greeted her with warmth, as a smile overlaid the gloom and his mobile face lit up with pleasure. 'Kerensa! How are you now? I was so sorry to hear that you were ill. Are you fully recovered?'

'Oh, hello, Jago! Yes – yes, thank you,' she replied, returning the smile and noting the worry-lines that creased his forehead and which had not completely gone away despite the smile. 'I was really disappointed to miss the trial – this illness came at completely the wrong time. Not that there is ever a right time to be ill!'

Seeing him so suddenly after so long had shaken Kerensa's composure. She realized that she was fluttering her hands as she spoke, and had to forcibly restrain herself from babbling inanely at him. She drew in a breath and slowed down as she went on, 'I heard the outcome of it from Florrie, but I don't know any details, and I'm dying to find out what happened.'

'Well, if you can spare a few minutes I'll tell you all about it. In here.' He pushed open the door of the library, and Kerensa decided that the dinner menus could wait a little longer.

'It's good to see you again, Kerensa, I've missed you,' Jago said, indicating the piano. 'Not that I've had much time or inclination for music lately. Father has a lot of problems and there's been so much to think about, I can't tell you.'

Kerensa was listening wide-eyed. 'Problems?' she repeated, as her brows rose.

'I'll tell you all about that in a minute. Sit down. I'll go through it all from the beginning,' Jago said, flinging himself into an armchair. Kerensa did likewise and they faced each other across the empty fireplace. Jago rested his forearms on his knees and leaned towards her, gesturing with his hands as he launched into his story.

'You'll be wanting to know about your husband first.' Kerensa nodded. 'Well,' Jago began, 'he put up a good defence for himself, I'll say that for him. Argued that he had borne no malice aforethought. Oh, he'd read up all the legal terms' – Jago gave a fleeting smile – 'and the jury decided in the end – they were out for a long time over it – that he'd succumbed to pressure from the fellow from Abraham's, with whom he was in league, and that *he* was the real instigator of it all.'

Kerensa was baffled. 'Do you know how this man contacted Lennie in the first place?' she asked, her forehead creasing. 'Who was he, and how did Lennie get to know someone up in Derbyshire?' Still frowning she hung on Jago's every word. There was so much that she didn't understand, and so much that she had never known about her husband.

'Oh, it came out that he – his name's Matthews' – Kerensa remembered the letters signed by 'M' and nodded – 'originally came from Cornwall and that he and Lennie were at school together. Then Matthews went to work at Smithford's as an apprentice, and moved up-country to Abraham's later on.' Jago leaned back in his chair and spread his palms. 'Being old friends they kept in touch, then eventually became partners in crime. Apparently this Matthews was in charge of checking the fuses before they left the factory, and he was removing the ones that were sub-standard and sending them down to your husband. He probably had dealings with other unscrupulous people as well.'

'I see.' Kerensa chewed her lip as she took in all these pieces of the jigsaw. Now at last she could understand it all.

'So that's why Lennie received the lesser charge,' Jago went on. 'Matthews will face his own prosecution, of course, and I doubt whether he'll be so lucky.'

Kerensa drew in a breath and let it out in a long sigh. She was still gazing out of the window, sunk in her own thoughts, when Jago broke in, saying, 'If you've heard the verdict, then you'll know that Father has been fined an astronomical sum of money.'

'Oh yes, I did hear a rumour, but no more than that.' Kerensa jerked herself back to the present.

'He's having to pay the most colossal fine,' Jago said, 'plus all the court charges and the barristers and solicitors' fees, apart from other extras.'

He ran a hand distractedly through his wavy hair, leaving a tuft of it standing on end. His face had become white and drawn now, and the eyes that rested on hers were dark and haunted. 'Father's ruined, Kerensa,' he said shortly. 'It's going to take every penny he has to meet these demands, and I mean every penny. The foundry will have to be sold up, and Penhallow put on the market as well.'

'Sell *Penhallow*?' Kerensa's stomach clenched. 'It's as bad as that?' Jago sighed and nodded.

Oh no, to have strangers living in what she still thought of at heart as being *her* home, was inconceivable. Kerensa felt all the colour drain out of her face until she knew she must be as chalk-white as Jago was. Now she could understand his pallor and something of what he had been going through since the trial.

'The prosecution fellow,' Jago broke into her reverie, 'was just too good for the defence counsel. Ran rings around him, and by the time the case finished he had the judge and jury eating out of his hand.' He clenched a fist and thumped it on the arm of the chair in frustration. 'Defence did his best, brought in several witnesses to testify to Father's good name, but it just wasn't enough.' He shrugged. 'And his fee was enormous as well – all for nothing.' He shrugged as his voice died away and a silence fell in which each of them were sunk in their own thoughts.

When he spoke again, Jago's expression was bleak. 'Of course Father blames me for everything.' He raised his eyes to the ceiling in exasperation. 'If I'd been more this and more that – more like *Richard*, he means,' he added, with bitterness and something like desolation on his face, 'and taken an interest in the business, I would have known there was something going on. That's the way he's talking.

'The fact is, he just has to have a scapegoat and I'm the only one around,' Jago added vehemently, and brought down a fist on the arm of his chair, 'so he takes it out on me. I can't tell you, Kerensa, what these last days have been like.' He ran a hand through his hair again and sunk his chin in his hands.

It was all Kerensa could do to stop herself from jumping up to go to his side and take his head in her arms. But mentally she glued herself to her chair and asked softly, 'So what will you do, Jago, where will you go? When the house is sold, I mean.'

Jago's head jerked up. 'Me? What I'm going to do Kerensa, is to move myself and my piano out of here as soon as possible and go to live with Grace and Dan in Penponds. Grace suggested it, she said I can have their spare room and stay for as long as I like.'

He jumped to his feet and began to pace restlessly around the room. 'Father's going to have to move into the cottage that you and your mother had once, and live on the rents from the others in that row.' His eyes burned into hers. 'Quite honestly I don't care if I never speak to him again. What with one thing and another, Kerensa,' he said bitterly as he glanced at his useless hand, 'I've had enough.'

And what about me as well? asked Kerensa's small inner voice. I shall be out of a job, and, worse, I shan't see you any more. I can hardly come visiting to play left hand on the piano for you in someone else's house. She stifled a sob. She was being uprooted yet again, losing the love of her life as well as the house she loved almost as much, and having to remain tied to an absent husband in a sham of a marriage for the foreseeable future. Not knowing whether to laugh or cry, she realized that today was her twenty-first birthday.

CHAPTER SIXTEEN

After the upheaval of removing furniture and contents from the house for the second time in a few years, Penhallow had been put up for sale and lay empty once more. The rest of the staff had found other positions, helped by good references from Grace, all except Kerensa who felt that she was in limbo and needed a quiet period of reflection before she decided on her next course of action.

So the ghosts of its past were free to drift about Penhallow's deserted rooms, moan around the chimneys in the chilly March winds, and haunt the desecrated ruin of its grounds. The eyes of the house were shrouded in thick curtains and, as week after week passed and no prospective buyers came to disturb its sleep, in the silence and dusty darkness, small creatures endeavoured to make it their own. A bat found its way into the roof space, a family of mice moved into the kitchen, and droves of woodlice, silverfish and black beetles colonized the cupboards and made quiet inroads beneath the carpets.

And while all this was going on Kerensa was biting her nails in impatience as the solicitors took their time in drafting the documents which they were to send to Silas informing him that the house was not legally his to sell, had never been his and that it must revert to its true owner, Celia. Fortunately no buyer came along during this period, although her agitation at last drove her to the solicitor once more.

'But you *must* get it taken off the market!' Kerensa, seated in Nathan Thomas's office yet again, clenched a fist and thumped it on his desk as she leaned forward to hammer home her point. 'Surely it's better to do it now than to wait until some prospective buyer turns up?'

'My dear Mrs Retallick, we are doing what we can as quickly as we can, but if these things are to be done properly, as indeed they must be, it does take time.' A frown creased the solicitor's brow. 'But I can tell you that we hope to finalize in a few days.' And with that she had to be content.

Eventually to Kerensa's enormous relief the man lived up to his word and the "For Sale" boards were removed, allowing her to breathe a little easier. Now she felt that personally she could do no more about it for the time being, as the business had to be left pending official confirmation, which would then be forwarded to Silas.

So, with both the cessation of her employment and Lennie's continuing incarceration, Kerensa had more free time than she had ever had before. Also, together with the money at her disposal, she realized that at last she had the chance to do something she had been thinking about for the past three years. She had wanted so much to go to Switzerland and visit her mother in the clinic, but had never dreamed that there would ever be a way.

Now, however, with the coming together of both Lennie's absence and her mother's plans to get married, it seemed that the chance had come and had only been waiting until the time was right. For what better time was there than to go out for her mother's wedding? Wonderful! Kerensa clapped her hands and her eyes sparkled with excitement even though her stomach was fluttering at the very thought of travelling all that way on her own.

But the fact that she had never been out of Cornwall in her life only heightened Kerensa's sense of adventure, and she spent her quiet days and quieter nights happily engrossed in her plans. Or going over again in her mind the interview with Nathan Thomas which had led to the astonishing revelation about her father. What bitter-sweet news that would be for Celia. She would take the will with her, of course.

Her mother's next letter brought the information Kerensa had been waiting for. '. . . *a May wedding*,' she had written. May! was Kerensa's first reaction – in only a few weeks' time.

I suppose I am a little old for romance, but a spring wedding cannot help but be romantic. Think of me on my special day, my dearest, I do so wish that you could be here too, but know how impossible it would be for you with your busy life. . . .

Kerensa smiled as she folded the sheets of paper and tucked them back into the envelope. What a surprise her mother was about to have. Maybe Kerensa would send a telegram she thought, just before she actually arrived, rather than turn up unannounced, in case the shock was too much for her.

She then set about overhauling her scanty wardrobe. Apart from her working black, she had very little. The dress she had worn to Grace's wedding would come out again for this one, but she would need travelling clothes, a couple of day dresses . . . Kerensa bit her lip as she calculated how much she would need to outlay on clothes and still spend the minimum of her precious savings.

She was still debating this point when, like a fairy godmother, Grace appeared in the kitchen one day when Kerensa was alone, carrying an armful of clothing. 'Ah, Kerensa,' she said, 'I was just wondering whether you could use any of these.' She laid them down on the table-top. 'The fact is, I can't get into them any more since . . . now that . . .' She blushed and came to a stammering halt. 'Well, I suppose I might as well tell you. You see, I'm in – in an interesting condition.'

'Really?' Kerensa's eyes widened and she smiled broadly. 'Oh, I'm *so* pleased!' she said sincerely. 'Many congratulations – to both of you. How exciting!'

Grace nodded, her face scarlet now and indicated the clothes. 'I hope you can wear some or all of these,' she said, 'They'll be out of fashion by the time I get my figure back.' She laid a hand on her stomach and added, 'I thought with your trip coming up . . .'

'Oh thank you so much,' Kerensa replied. 'I was thinking today that I would have to buy some things before I go, but these will help me out enormously.'

When she began to go through the clothes properly, Kerensa was overwhelmed by Grace's bounty. There was a smart walking dress of pearl-grey gabardine with its skirt gathered at the back and supported by a tiny bustle, from which it fell in a cascade of frills to the ankle, another of sage-green grosgrain with cream lace on the yoke and at the cuffs of the tight-fitting sleeves, a practical skirt of navy-blue poplin and a costume of claret-coloured wool jersey with a bell-shaped skirt and a long jacket fastened with tiny fabric-covered buttons. Kerensa tried them on one by one and when she found that they all fitted her like a glove, she was ecstatic. She had never had so many pretty things in her life before and vowed to do anything she could for Grace when she came back, in return for her generosity.

Shortly afterwards she had even produced a guide book to Switzerland from among her possessions and given it to Kerensa. 'It's a few years out of date,' Grace said, 'because I had it left over from when Mama and I went to Basle once for a holiday, but you may find parts of it useful.' She had also gone on to give some advice about a small hotel in London where Kerensa could book a night's stay before boarding the boat train the following day.

When the day of her departure dawned at last, she was so afraid of being late for the train that Kerensa was on Camborne station much too early, clutching her hatbox and umbrella, with her portmanteau at her

169

side and her stomach full of butterflies. Wearing the jersey costume and the flower-decked hat which complemented it, she felt like somebody else, some elegant stranger who had taken her over, and she nodded graciously as a lady might do, to an elderly gentleman who tipped his hat and passed the time of day as he walked by.

Then the train was coming at last, its plume of smoke streaming as it came puffing from under a bridge and round the bend into the station. Kerensa gathered up her things and made for the third class carriages. She was just getting settled when she glanced out of the window at the sound of running footsteps to see a young man rushing for the train, a suitcase under his arm and his overcoat flapping open with the speed of his passage.

Then her heart stopped and she looked again. Jago? Never, it couldn't be! It was only someone who looked like him. She had been doing that a lot recently – seeing Jago's face in a crowd, certain that it was he, until the man turned or came closer and of course it was always a stranger.

But this young man jumped on board as the guard held the door for him, slammed it shut and blew his whistle, and when he came to a halt, panting, in the corridor outside Kerensa's compartment, he leaned against the wall to catch his breath.

It *was* Jago! Her stomach turning somersaults, Kerensa slid the door open and put her head out. His glance slid over her, then away, then back again in a double-take as his eyes widened in astonishment and his jaw dropped. 'Kerensa! It is you!' He took a step towards her as the train began to pick up speed.

'Jago! Oh, what a *surprise*.'

Her expression mirrored his as he looked her up and down and said, 'I almost didn't recognize you! But come on, let's get a seat. This way.' He picked up her portmanteau which she had not yet taken inside and jerked his head down the corridor.

'No,' Kerensa called, running after him. 'I can't, I've only got a third-class ticket,' she said, as she caught him up and laid a hand on his elbow. With a look of impatience he replied, 'Oh, never mind that – I'll settle the difference. In here, look.' And he elbowed open the door of an empty first class compartment.

Kerensa sank with a sigh onto the plush-covered seat, and when she looked around her at the soft carpet underfoot and rested her head on the crisp antimacassar behind her, could hardly believe the opulence of this carriage compared with the third class. A framed poster of St Ives hung on one wall, a gleaming mirror on the other, and there was even a small vase of flowers on the table at the window. She settled back and began to relax.

'I knew you were going out to visit your mother – Grace told me,' Jago said as he lifted their luggage onto the rack. Kerensa noticed that this was not easy for him with only one strong hand, and almost jumped up to help, but knew that Jago would feel bitterly hurt and humiliated if she did. So she clenched her hands together and remained in her seat until he sank down opposite her and went on, 'But for us both to be on the same train, it's amazing. What fun!'

'And you nearly missed it,' Kerensa said smiling.

'I know,' he replied. 'I went to buy a newspaper thinking I had plenty of time. My watch must be slow. Phew!' He shook out the folds of a clean handkerchief and mopped his brow. Kerensa could not take her eyes off him. He was looking better than when she had last seen him, she thought. Not so haggard and drawn. Although there were lines on his face etched there by circumstances, and these would never completely go away, he was looking happier and the twinkle had returned to his eyes.

'Where are you going?' Kerensa asked, taking in the fashionably narrow check trousers and elegantly tailored jacket he was wearing. She noticed he kept one of his kid gloves on over the damaged hand. So, he was sensitive about it in public.

Jago ran his other hand through his wayward curly hair and replied, 'I'm going up to stay with a friend for a few days – Hal Andersen. He and I used to share an apartment when we were students. Haven't seen him for ages, certainly not since – since this.' He scowled and indicated his gloved hand. But after a pause he brightened again and said, 'So we'll both be in London tonight. Where are you staying?'

Kerensa told him and he replied, 'That's not very far from Hal's place. I'll come and see you settled into the hotel before I leave.'

'Oh, thank you, that would be lovely!' Kerensa met his eyes and their gaze locked. And, as they surveyed each other, it was gradually dawning on her that their relationship had undergone an enormous shift. It was no longer that of master and servant – Jago was not her employer now, not therefore one step removed as before. She could meet him on his own level at last, as an equal. So, knowing she was looking her best in her new finery, handed-down though it might be, Kerensa straightened her spine and held her head high.

To break the silence which had fallen between them, she said brightly, 'How's the composing going? Have you written any songs yet?'

'I have actually,' Jago replied, surprising her. 'I haven't had a great deal else to do since I moved in with Grace.' His expression sobered. 'I keep to my own room as much as I can,' he explained, 'because I don't want to intrude on their private life more than necessary.'

He shrugged and went on, 'Dan has made me as welcome as Grace has, and they both say they don't mind my music, but in a small cottage there isn't a lot of privacy for any of us. And now with a baby coming . . .' He spread his hands eloquently. 'Grace didn't know that when she offered me a home, you see.' Jago heaved a sigh. 'So in all fairness to them both, I think I must look for somewhere of my own when I get back. I'll have to give it some thought, anyway.' His eyes met hers again. 'I've missed you, Kerensa,' he said, then after a pause he added so softly that she hardly caught the words, 'and not only for playing left hand for me, either.'

Kerensa's stomach clenched, and to cover her confusion she looked away and said the first thing that came into her head. 'How things have changed for both of us and our families over the past five years,' she remarked. 'My father disappearing, which led to your father moving into Penhallow . . .' But she stopped short of mentioning the true circumstances of *that* move. The time would come when Jago would have to know the full extent of both their parents' deceit, but not yet.

No. Although Kerensa felt as if her father's will was burning a hole in her bag and that Jago must surely see it, they both had enough on their minds at the moment. And deep down Kerensa was fearful of the effect this news might eventually have on their relationship. 'Which brought nothing but disaster from then on for us,' Jago replied, gazing out of the window at the passing countryside.

Was Jago aware that Penhallow had been taken off the market? Kerensa would dearly have liked to know, but she could hardly ask him under the circumstances. It seemed not, or he would surely have mentioned it. But Silas, if he had indeed received the notification yet, was quite likely to be keeping the whole thing to himself, in order to save face and prevent an even worse humiliation than the one he was already suffering.

'Kerensa,' Jago said, half-turning, 'I can't believe that it's nearly two years since Richard died – and this happened.' He glanced down at his hand. 'Then came the mine accident and it was downhill all the way for us after that. My family's been blown apart,' he added bleakly, 'and all our lives utterly changed. It's a lot to get used to.'

Kerensa nodded. She knew that feeling exactly. 'How's your father taking it?' she asked.

Jago sighed. 'I don't think the full extent of it has sunk in yet,' he said. 'He's like a man poleaxed at the moment, lost in his own little world. He sits for hours just staring at nothing, his hands in his lap. It worries me sometimes when I think how he used to be – never still or quiet for a minute. I've tried to talk to him, and so's Grace, but there's just no getting through.'

'It's bound to take time for the shock to wear off,' Kerensa replied in an automatic fashion. For having not seen Jago for a couple of months, she was feasting her eyes on his beloved figure now, and storing up this precious time with him to remember during the lonely days which would face her when she returned home again.

'Have you heard anything of your husband since he was – er – imprisoned?' Jago asked.

'No,' Kerensa replied. 'They're very strict. He's not allowed visitors, or letters either, until he's been there for two months. Then, if his behaviour has been all right, he can have one letter a month after that, and one visit as well.'

At that moment Lennie Retallick was lying flat on his back on his wooden pallet in Bodmin Gaol, looking up at the peeling ceiling and trying to figure out a means of escape from it. During the few weeks he had been locked up, he had made a point of behaving like a model prisoner. Lennie was quiet, biddable, and careful not to cause any trouble. He walked away from any trouble which occurred around him, and set about both ingratiating himself with the warders and being friendly to his fellow inmates. All of which was part of the plan. For Lennie was biding his time until an opportunity arose, and while doing so he was honing his growing reputation for being a 'trusty' or as the authorities called it, a 'star' prisoner.

Eating him up from inside was his seething hatred of Kerensa, which was fast growing into an obsession. He fed on it night and day and thought of little else but getting his own back on her. To think she'd turned him *in*, the sneaking bitch! How could she do it to her own husband? Oh, what wouldn't he do to her once he got out and caught up with her! And get out he would, sooner or later. Of that he was determined. Lennie thumped the peeling plaster of the wall beside him, which was oozing damp in trickling rivulets and swore.

Too furious to relax, he jumped up and began to pace the narrow confines of his cell. Five paces long, by three wide. A small double-barred window too high to see out of. A slot beside the door where a candle, flickering behind glass, gave just enough light to stir the darkness within. The chances of getting out of here were as remote as flying to the moon.

His stomach rumbled. Supper was late tonight. Not that it was much to look forward to – gruel again and a hunk of bread, the same as breakfast. Dinner hadn't been much better, a wodge of potatoes with a piece of fat bacon and a few beans. Apparently it improved according to how long you'd been in, so they said. But he didn't intend to be in long enough to find that out for himself.

And he'd seen that slut making sheep's eyes at that stupid Cardrew son when she thought they were alone. Piano playing! Music! What sort of occupation was that for a man? When here she was all the time with a real man for her husband and did she appreciate him? Oh no, she had to fancy the likes of *him*! Well, when he got out of this place he was going to make them both sorry. Oh yes, they didn't know the half of what was coming to them, he thought, as a sly grin crossed his peaky face.

He *had* to get out. Then he would show them! Show them all that Lennie Retallick was *someone*. A force to be reckoned with. Clever enough to outwit all these uniformed dummies who marched about clanking their keys and shouting orders, thinking themselves so important. Here they came now, he thought, as the door half-opened and a wooden tray was shoved at him through the aperture before it was slammed instantly shut again.

And clever enough to get his own back on a fool woman who thought she could get the better of *him*. The only question was, how was he going to do it?

They alighted at Paddington Station in the early evening, as the sun was setting over the nation's capital. 'It's far too early to go to your hotel,' Jago said firmly, steering Kerensa towards the left luggage office. 'I'm going to show you some of the city's sights first.' As they emerged from the station he added, 'We'll catch a bus down to Piccadilly Circus and walk around from there.'

Kerensa could only nod in reply as she stood bemused by the noise and bustle of traffic, watching as buses, hackney cabs, elegant carriages and delivery drays all thundered along at top speed, regardless it seemed of personal safety, while dashing between the very hoofs of the horses went the crossing sweepers – small ragged boys armed with brush and bucket risking life and limb for a few pence.

Soon she was gazing around her from the open top deck of the horse-bus at the milling crowds and the vast buildings of what appeared to be the hub of the whole world. Everything in the West End seemed so enormous. Kerensa's eyes widened at the sight of the huge emporiums, their windows crammed with every imaginable luxury. She smiled to herself at the memory of Florrie's excited voice telling her how it was, when she had taken her place as Grace's maid, and how disappointed Kerensa had been then. At that time she had never imagined in her wildest dreams that she would get a second chance to see all these wonders for herself.

'Here we are. Come on!' Jago's voice brought Kerensa out of her dream. He was holding out his hand to help her down the stairs as they alighted. 'We'll stroll down to Trafalgar Square and I'll show you the monument to Lord Nelson,' he said. 'Better take my arm through these crowds,' he added, in a matter-of-fact way, 'we don't want to get separated.' He threaded her hand through the crook of his elbow as if it was the most natural thing in the world, and Kerensa's heart gave a lurch of excitement.

That she, Kerensa Retallick, should be strolling through the streets of London, dressed like a lady, on the arm of the most attractive man in the world, was the stuff of fantasy. She almost had to pinch herself to make sure that she was awake and not dreaming the whole thing.

They walked on through some gardens which flanked the river, beneath the soft gas-lighting until they came to a building with large windows and a set of steps leading down to the riverbank. From behind the windows came the clink of cutlery and china, and the murmur of low voices and laughter. 'That's the famous Savoy Hotel,' remarked Jago. 'Well, the back of it, anyway. The main entrance is in the Strand. You may have heard of it.'

Kerensa had not. She glanced up at her companion and thought that this was a side of Jago that she had never seen before. At home in the small town and rural locality where they lived, she had thought she knew him so well, that she was apt to forget that he had spent years as a student away from it. And this confident and knowledgeable man of the city seemed a completely different person from the one who had ridden hell-for-leather across the Cornish cliffs so long ago, with her clinging on for dear life behind him.

Deep in her thoughts, Kerensa had not noticed that the doors of the hotel had opened until she felt Jago beside her stiffen, and his grip on her elbow tightened. Then she followed his gaze and craning her neck to peer between the heads of various other people walking towards them on the path, she saw a couple coming down the steps.

It was fairly quiet here away from the traffic noises, and the woman's tinkling laugh came floating clearly on the air as she turned to her companion and replied to some remark of his. She was dressed in the height of fashion, Kerensa noticed, as they reached the bottom of the steps. Her gown was cream-coloured, with raspberry-pink flouncing on the drift of frills which flared from the high bustle at the back as she turned and the couple began to walk towards her and Jago.

The woman was wearing a matching hat piled high with flowers and feathers, and seemed a good deal older than her escort. It was only as Kerensa glanced up at Jago, about to make some remark that she noticed the expression on his face and that his eyes were riveted on the couple. Then her own eyes widened in shock and amazement. For approaching them along the narrow path came Isabella and Anton.

There was no way that they could have avoided each other, so the men raised their hats and all four stared at each other. It was Isabella who broke the awkward silence which had fallen. 'Well, Jago, this is a surprise,' she said lightly, a thin smile on her lips. 'How are you?'

'Isabella.' Jago nodded. His eyes were hard as he replied with a shrug, 'As you see.' Isabella's eyes flicked instinctively to his gloved hand as he added, 'And you? You're keeping busy, I suppose.' He glanced pointedly at Anton. On the face of it the remark was innocuous enough, but the way Jago delivered it spoke volumes.

Isabella glowered and replied icily, 'Yes, as it happens. We've just been celebrating my opening in *Carmen*. I'm playing the title role of course.' Her chin rose a little higher.

'Ah,' said Jago, and nodded slowly, his eyes never leaving her face. 'Carmen, the fickle and faithless.' He smiled thinly. 'A role to which you are eminently suited. Congratulations Isabella. I'm sure you'll be a great success in it.'

Kerensa's eyes widened as she recognized the insult. She had slipped off her glove for a moment in order to readjust a loose hat-pin, when Isabella half-turned away from Jago to look her up and down. The other woman made a point of staring at her wedding ring, then Isabella looked back at Jago and said, in a voice that dripped vitriol, 'I know you always had this penchant for servants, Jago, but do you really have to flaunt it quite so obviously?'

Kerensa saw Jago's jaw tighten as the two of them stared at each other with mutual antagonism and when he spoke, the tone of his voice would have cut glass. 'At least,' he replied, 'this *servant* does not have the manners and morals of an alley-cat like some so-called *ladies*.'

Isabella's nostrils flared as she clutched at her escort's arm. 'Come along, Anton,' she said with asperity, tossing her head and setting the ostrich feathers fluttering as she dragged him away. 'It's getting late.'

'I'm so sorry about that, Kerensa,' said Jago, through gritted teeth, as he marched her on at such a pace that Kerensa almost had to trot to keep up with him.

'It doesn't matter,' she reassured him and patted his arm. 'Someone like that is just not worth getting worked up about.'

Jago slowed down and half-turned towards her. 'Once I was so sure that I was in love with her,' he said grimly. 'They say that love is blind, don't they? Well, it certainly blinded me, and it took me a long time to realize that she doesn't even know the meaning of the word.'

The moon had risen while they had been too absorbed elsewhere to notice it, and now rode high above the river, looking down at its own reflection in the rippling water. Kerensa raised her head to reply, then her heart turned over as their eyes met and locked. Jago's were dark and stormy, touched with dancing flecks of gold where the light caught them, and Kerensa gave a gasp at the passion in their depths.

'What a fool I was!' Jago muttered, and suddenly his hands were on her shoulders as he roughly pulled her round towards him. He seemed to study her face for a long moment, then as the ground tilted and the moon slid down the sky, he brought his mouth down on hers, crushing her lips in a kiss that mirrored the longing, the frustration and the anguish which had pervaded her own heart and soul for so long. It was agony, it was ecstasy and Kerensa was swept away in the glorious moment, wanting it never to end.

But end it had to, as stark reality intervened like a shutter coming down between them. 'I was so besotted that I couldn't see what was under my very nose,' Jago groaned as he tore himself free and ran a hand over his face. 'And now it's too damn *late!*'

CHAPTER SEVENTEEN

The town of Badensee was everyone's idea of typical Switzerland. Ringed with mountains, the wooden chalet style houses were set about the limpid blue lake and on the lower slopes, where great stands of conifers stood as tall and straight as sentinels at attention. The great mountains which guarded the valley soared high above, their snow-covered peaks piercing a spectacularly blue sky.

There had been an emotional reunion between mother and daughter at the home of Celia's betrothed, who lived with his widowed sister Katya in a tiny red-tiled house in the cobbled square of the town.

After the initial meeting, she and Celia had held each other at arm's length as they both looked for the changes that were bound to be there since they had parted. Her mother was looking amazingly well, Kerensa thought, but with an air of fragility still about her.

'How you've grown up, my dearest!' Celia said to her daughter with tears in her eyes. 'No longer my little girl, but a mature, married woman. I can't tell you what it means to have you here. I'm just so grateful to Lennie for letting you come – and so thrilled that you can meet Rudi at last.'

Kerensa looked at the frail woman beside her and knew she would never be able to tell her the truth about Lennie. For such a shock could well tip Celia over the edge and back into illness, and that Kerensa could not risk. It would be bad enough having to tell her the news of Zack's betrayal, and that *had* to be done.

No. However dearly Kerensa would have loved to unburden herself to her mother, her only living relative, she would keep her anguish buried deep inside her, and assume the mask of happiness at which she had become adept.

Rudi was tall and thin, grey-haired and distinguished-looking, with a narrow face and piercing blue eyes. As he bowed over Kerensa's hand and welcomed her in perfect English, her first impression was that he was someone she would instinctively trust, and she could understand how her mother had fallen for him. Kerensa thought again of Zack and the news of his treachery which she had yet to give her mother, and was thankful that she would have the support of this good man.

The wedding day dawned sunny and calm, and Celia looked enchanting in a turquoise silk two-piece and matching hat. The colour reflected her eyes and was complemented by the still waters of the lake, where they sat on the terrace and drank a toast to the newly-weds after the ceremony was over.

'I'm going to love it so much here,' Celia said to Kerensa, as she showed her round their new home a few days after the wedding. 'I'm only sorry that we shall be so far apart,' she added as her smile faded. 'But of course' – she squeezed Kerensa's hand – 'you'll be able to come and visit again, won't you? Both of you – maybe stay for a few weeks and have a proper holiday. I would love that, because it would go some way towards paying Lennie back for his generosity to me. He as good as saved my life, you know? And without him I would never have met Rudi.'

Kerensa nodded, ignoring the knife-edge of pain that twisted her stomach and changed the subject. 'Mama,' she said gently, 'can we go indoors now? There's something I have to talk to you about. I've been saving it until you had recovered from the excitement of the big day.'

'My dear, how mysterious you sound!' Celia said, as her eyes widened and she turned to lead the way indoors. 'But yes, yes of course. We'll go in here.'

It took a long time to explain the reason for their private chat, and by the time Celia had perused the will several times and Kerensa had come to the end of her story, the shadows were lengthening out on the lake and lights had begun to twinkle in the the houses near the shore.

Celia had been in turn astonished, furious and bitterly hurt. Then, wiping away her tears she said, 'I always knew Zack had a selfish streak but I ignored it because I loved him so much, Kerensa. You can understand that, can't you, now you've a husband of your own?' She raised swimming eyes to her daughter's face. 'I'm sure Lennie has his little faults like everybody does.'

Kerensa had to turn away lest the bleakness of her expression should give her away. Then she clamped her teeth together in order not to collapse into hysteria as she tried to imagine what Celia's reaction would be were she to tell her Lennie's "little faults". That her son-in-law had been swindling his employer for years, had caused the deaths of several innocent men, and was now languishing in Bodmin Gaol.

But she pasted a smile on her face as Celia went on, 'That love is blind is the truest cliché ever written – it is so, so true.' She sniffed and

179

unfolded a lace-trimmed handkerchief. 'But, Kerensa, what a lot of trouble you've gone to in finding all this out!' Kerensa saw admiration in her expression.

'Well, I vowed I wasn't going to give up Penhallow without a fight,' Kerensa replied. 'I love it so much, and I knew you felt the same way. I just had to get to the truth, Mama. It's taken a long time, but Silas will get a letter from the solicitor soon, and then it'll revert to you, just as Grandfather meant it to.'

Celia had been deep in thought, and when Kerensa had finished, she laid a hand on her daughter's knee and said softly. 'I can never thank you enough for this, my dearest. It can't have been easy, and now I have something I want to say to you.' Her gaze was fixed on the twinkling lights across the lake. 'I shall never return to Cornwall on any permanent basis – Rudi has told me that my health would break down again if I did. I need the dry air you see, and Cornwall is so damp and humid it's no good for me.'

She regarded her daughter with serious eyes. 'So, Kerensa, I want you to have Penhallow with my blessing.' Kerensa started and her eyes widened as her mother went on, 'I know you'll love and cherish it and it'll be safe in your care. I never could bear the thought of Silas and his family living there.' She took Kerensa's hand in her own and gave it a gentle squeeze.

'I know you'll never let any other strangers live there. Hand it down, Kerensa, hopefully to your children and grandchildren, as it came to me, and tell them something of the time we almost lost it.' She patted her daughter's hand, then released it as she added, 'So send me the papers to sign and I'll make it over to you legally. Then no one will ever be able to take it from you again.'

The tears came then and flowed in a river down Kerensa's hot cheeks. She flung both arms around her mother's slim frame and they hugged as they had never hugged each other before. 'Oh Mama, *thank you*! I can never thank you enough. And of course I'll love it – I've never stopped doing so.'

And all the way home she nursed the secret that Penhallow was hers, hers alone and at long last. Something she had never imagined, even in her wildest dreams.

'So you see,' Kerensa said to an astonished Florrie, 'Penhallow belongs to me now and no one can ever take it away again.' She was close to tears of happiness as they sat at Kerensa's kitchen table drinking tea.

'But,' said Florrie, practical as always, 'that's all very well and of course I'm thrilled to bits for you. But what are you going to do with it, maid? Thought, have you?' Her forehead creased as she added, ''Tis none of my business, but it must cost a fortune to keep up that huge place.'

When Kerensa did not reply immediately, Florrie glanced at her friend and her expression softened. 'Oh, it do mean a lot to you, I know, but I do call it a white elephant. Sell it off, I would.' She replaced her cup on its saucer with a decisive clink.

'Never! Kerensa said firmly. Then she rose to her feet, gesturing with her hands as she paced up and down. 'I've thought it all over very carefully. In fact, I've been thinking of little else since I came back from Switzerland. And Florrie, I've decided to go back there to live.' She paused and leaned both hands on the table as their eyes met.

'*Live* there?' Florrie squealed, as her green eyes grew rounder. 'In that huge house – on your *own*? My dear maid, mad, are you?'

'It's my *home*,' Kerensa said with spirit. 'The only home I've ever wanted. I'd no more dream of selling it than selling myself. Oh, I know I shall have to look for work – you're right when you say I'll need every penny I can get, but Flo—' She opened her hands and shrugged. 'Think about it. I don't have to live in all of it, do I? Just one or two rooms would be all right.'

Kerensa came to a halt and leaned a hip on one corner of the table as she went on, 'You see, as Lennie won't be out for several years, I thought I might move some of this furniture into Penhallow. Then when he does get released, perhaps we could both live over there.'

She swung one leg to and fro. 'Then he could sell this house, you see – it does belong to him, it's not rented. Then there would be plenty of money to do Penhallow up properly.'

The thought of she and Lennie together at Penhallow was not appealing, but knowing her husband's eagerness for status, she was sure that he would jump at the chance to live in the big house considering his present humiliation.

'Oh yes, well, I see what you mean.' Florrie's face brightened. 'That is a good idea,' she admitted.

Kerensa smiled back. 'I told you I've thought it all out,' she said. 'And there's no time like the present, so I'm going over there today to start cleaning out the place.'

'I'll come over later and give you a hand,' said Florrie with enthusiasm, 'just as soon as I've seen to Mr Silas.' She reached for her coat and wriggled into it.

'Oh Florrie, are you sure?' Kerensa asked. 'That would be lovely, but it's a lot for you to do.'

'Nonsense!' Florrie retorted over her shoulder. 'I'll see you later on, maid.'

Kerensa could not prevent the tears from falling as she turned the key and let herself into Penhallow at last. She stood in the entrance hall and breathed in the smell of dust and neglect as if it were attar of roses. 'It's me,' she whispered, to the crowding shadows. 'I'm back. I promised you I'd come back didn't I? And this time I'm never going away again.' Then as if the house had answered her with a welcoming smile, a shaft of sunlight found its way in through the open doorway and lit up the dusty interior with a stream of golden light.

'Here we are!' a cheerful voice brought Kerensa back to reality, and she turned on her heel to find Florrie behind her.

With the workload lightened by a great deal of chatter and laughter, the wildlife was soon despatched from cupboards and carpets, the festoons of cobwebs swept from the corners of the ceilings, and the main rooms dusted and swept.

So by the end of the week, Kerensa found herself back in her own home. Then followed a kind of limbo where she felt suspended between the past and the future, neither single nor properly married, with her beloved Penhallow the only constant in her solitary existence. And in order to hold on to that she would have to find some employment soon.

At the back of Bodmin Gaol was about half an acre of land which had been turned into a garden, and here some of the star men who had earned the privilege were allowed to work. The vegetables they grew supplied the prison kitchen, and the rest of the ground was given over to flowers and shrubs.

The bulk of the vegetable garden was used for raising potatoes, for they were most widely in demand, and it was here one sunny spring morning that Lennie Retallick with half-a-dozen others, was turning over the soil in preparation for planting the new season's crop.

Thoughts of escape were never far from his mind and, as he straightened his back and rested on his spade for a moment, he glanced around to weigh up the chances. But at the sight of the forbidding fifty-foot walls that surrounded the garden, and the central watchtower which was higher still, his spirits sank. It was going to take all his ingenuity if he was ever going to make it out of here.

So with the patience and cunning of a predatory animal, Lennie bided his time and watched. Watched every vehicle that came and went, making a mental note of their timings and procedures. And eventually he hit on an idea.

Every market-day a cart would arrive to collect the surplus produce. Sacks of vegetables would be loaded up, cut flowers bunched and despatched, at roughly the same time each week, and he decided to make sure that he was one of the men who loaded the cart.

Convinced that this would be the only way of escape, Lennie managed to be working nearby when the cart arrived every week and kept his eyes and ears open. He had actually been up in it one day, ostensibly moving the bags around to make room for more, when he thought his chance had come. The driver had crossed the garden to have a word with the guard, and the other inmates were busy with their own tasks. No-one was looking his way. Heart in his mouth, Lennie crouched down behind some sacks of potatoes and waited. Heard the clump of the driver's heavy boots coming towards him on the path and held his breath. This could be it.

But, 'Retallick!' came a shout and he heard the tread of another pair of boots. 'Where's Retallick?' came the guard's voice, louder this time, and he was forced to rise to his feet. 'What the hell are you doing up there?' growled the man.

'Just coming, sir.' Lennie jumped nimbly down with his heart in his boots. 'Just balancing up the weight of the load, sir.' He smiled.

The man nodded. 'Right. Good man. Back to your work now.'

Oh well, put it down to experience, he thought. Maybe next time. . . .

It was another two weeks before Lennie had another chance. But this time when he turned his head at the sound of a heavy vehicle trundling over the cobbled entrance, he realized that the carter had arrived not only to take out their surplus produce, but also to bring their delivery of seed potatoes.

'Retallick!' came the warder's voice. 'Come and give a hand here to unload – sharpish now,' he shouted, as Lennie was scraping soil from his spade with a sharp stone. Absentmindedly slipping the stone into his pocket, he abandoned the spade and went to stand at the rear of the cart. The driver had let down the tail flap and had now wandered off to chat to the guard, while another of the prisoners jumped up into the vehicle to drag the heavy sacks towards the back. Lennie standing below, reached up and slid them to the ground.

'That's our lot,' said the other man, counting out the bags. 'They others must be going somewhere else.' As he wandered back to his job, the voices of the driver and the guard came drifting over from the far side of the garden where they were standing with their backs to Lennie. And he realized that he was unobserved.

'Got to go,' called the delivery man, 'I'm running late as it is and two more calls to make yet. Next stop Jacob's Farm. Fair distance from here out to the moor and you know old man Jacob, some relation of yours, isn't he? Can turn right nasty if he do feel like it, with his swearing and cussing!' Both men gave a hearty guffaw. 'Don't want to lose his custom though,' called the driver over his shoulder. 'See you again, Tom, when that load of manure's ready – end of next week I expect.'

During this exchange, Lennie had jumped unseen onto the cart, pulled one of the empty sacks over his head and was sitting hunched among the full ones, looking for all the world like just another bag of produce. Thanks be for his small build, he breathed. He who had always wanted to be taller! Lennie held his breath as the man slammed up the tailboard and swung himself into the driving seat. A crack of the whip and the cart began to move, lurching from side to side over the cobbles. Good thing he had jammed himself in the middle of the load, else he'd be thrown out.

Now they had come to the main entrance and the driver was exchanging a bit of banter with the guard while he opened the gates. First the double ones of steel and then the sturdy wooden one beyond that. Get on, get on! Lennie urged silently. But the man wasn't going to stop, and as the cart lurched sickeningly around a sharp corner, the stowaway heard the thud of the heavy door being slammed. They were outside! The first and most difficult part was over and he was on his way.

But as the heavy cart trundled through the streets of the town, Lennie began to wonder if this was an ideal form of transport after all. It was hardly the quick getaway vehicle that he so desperately needed. At this rate, by the time they were out on the country road his absence would have been discovered. Mind you, they boasted that they hadn't had anyone escape from the new prison since it opened thirty years ago, so it might take them a while to organize a search party. Lennie grinned to himself to think that he had been the first one to break out – the first to prove them all wrong. The one who had been clever enough to outwit them! His name would be in the newspaper, he would be famous – or infamous – he didn't care which.

But now there appeared to be some sort of fracas going on and the cart had slowed to a halt. Come on – come on! Lennie urged impotently as a sweat broke out all over him. Get moving, dammit.

They must be caught up in traffic. He knew how narrow the streets were and how busy the town could be. Trust it to be market-day, he cursed, as he heard the squeals of pigs and the lowing of cattle. Then he jumped, as from nearby – it seemed right beside him – a cultured and authoritative voice had begun to shout above the babel. 'Let me through, let me pass! I'm a doctor ... an urgent case ... make way, make way there, I say!'

Lennie greatly daring, fumbled for the sharp stone that he realized was still in his pocket and ripped a slit in the sack just big enough to peer through. The doctor's pony and trap had halted right beside him, its wheels almost touching those of the cart. The man was perched up in front, his Gladstone bag at his side, brandishing a whip above his head and threatening to use it if necessary on the heads of any driver who stood in his way. In the body of the trap Lennie could see the doctor's discarded overcoat and a couple of blankets, which he carried presumably for accidents or emergencies.

It would only take a second to change vehicles. Could he do it without being seen? But there was no time for deliberation – it was the only chance he had, or was going to have once the jam cleared. Taking advantage of the mêlée, Lennie slipped over the side of the cart, put a foot on the wheel of the trap and was up and inside it before he had time to think twice. Burrowing under the blankets he lay as flat as he could and waited for the shouts that would mean he had been seen. But none came. The furore was gradually subsiding as the doctor inched the pony forward and the trap began to move. They were away!

Once out on the open road, the doctor whipped up the animal into a spanking trot and, as its hoofs pounded onward, Lennie wondered where they were going. Anywhere would be fine by him. Yes, this had definitely been the right move, and after his thumping heart had subsided, Lennie gave a self-satisfied grin and tried to make himself more comfortable in the rattling vehicle.

It was a long and uncomfortable drive through seemingly endless country lanes until he sensed by the stillness around them, that they were out on the open moor. Every muscle in Lennie's body was cramped and aching and he was nearly passing out beneath the hot and prickly sacking. By the time he guessed that the trap was turning into a farm lane by the way the doctor was cursing the narrow and rutted track, he was about ready to throw up. Then the sound of a woman's voice came floating out of the house, 'Oh, Doctor, thank goodness ... at last ... I thought you were never coming. This way, quick ... he's took some bad!'

The doctor jumped down, threw the reins over the gatepost, snatched up his bag and, as the voices faded, Lennie deduced that he had followed the woman into the house.

Now for it. But carefully, carefully – this was the tricky bit. Was there anyone else around? Lennie's ears felt stretched with listening and sweat was pouring down his face in rivulets. But when he peered through the hole in the sack, the farmyard was deserted. Now! Heart in his mouth, Lennie ignored his cramped limbs and wriggled out from under the covers. He was sorely tempted to take the overcoat with him, but no, that would draw attention and he could not run the risk. Instead he pulled off the potato sack and took that with him as he leaped over the side of the trap.

He landed painfully in a ditch full of nettles and crouched there until he was sure there was no one about. Then he ran hell-for-leather down over a small field, keeping close to the hedge. Over a stile – keep your head down, for goodness' sake – and he was out on the open moor. He paused to draw breath, head down and hands on his knees as his shoulders heaved, but the sound of a dog barking from the farm he had just left had him running again.

Lennie was physically fit from his hours of manual work and from taking advantage of any exercise time to toughen himself up for just such an ordeal as this, but even so he could run no more. He collapsed in a heap beneath a towering cairn of great stones, burrowed deeper into the cave formed by two flat slabs and lay there unable to move.

He awoke some time later, stiff and cold, and could not for a moment think where on earth he was. The cell walls seemed to have crept in on him and terrified, he sat up with a jerk of alarm, cracking his head on an overhanging rock. Then in spite of the rapidly forming lump, and the throbbing nettle blisters on his arms, Lennie grinned to himself in the darkness.

He was out! He'd done it! Actually done it, just as he'd promised himself he would. Oh yes. His chest swelled, it took more than a few jumped-up dummies in uniform to keep him, Lennie Retallick, behind bars. He was too clever for them, in spite of all their clanking keys and barking orders.

So, what next? Lennie unrolled the potato sack which he had

prudently brought with him when he had left the trap and tried it around himself for size. Good, it was long enough to tie in a knot in front. If seen, he would look just like any farmhand, and it would cover up the broad tell-tale arrow on his shoulder perfectly.

Then he wriggled to the entrance of the cave and peered outside. Twilight was falling and it was vital to put as much distance behind him during the hours of darkness as he could. Lennie stretched his aching limbs and set off.

He was out on the open moor now with nothing to guide him but the stars. Lennie reckoned that if he kept that one big bright one on his left all the time he could steer a straight course, and crossed his fingers that the sky would remain clear until he came to some sort of road.

There was absolute silence all around him. Silence, emptiness and space. After the tiny claustrophobic room where he had been penned up for so long, it was awesome. Lennie looked over his shoulder every few steps in case there was any sign of a light, fearful that by now they would have discovered his empty cell. For as soon as they did, they might well set dogs on his trail. Lennie's stomach churned and he began to run. But running was difficult in this hazardous terrain, no matter how much he urged his pounding legs to go faster. And when he tripped over a rough tussock and landed heavily in a ditch, he was forced to go more slowly. No good ending up with a broken leg in this God-forsaken wilderness.

It was getting really dark now, making it increasingly difficult to see where to put his feet on the rough ground. Pools of stagnant water gleamed in the last sliver of light, boggy places where a man could get sucked down to his death – a horrific and lingering end. Lennie licked dry lips and pressed on, carefully avoiding the patches where flying pennants of bog cotton gave their warning.

He pushed through clumps of stunted thorn-bushes that tore at his legs and arms, he stumbled over clitters of rough stones, which caused frustrating detours which lengthened his long journey even more.

Suddenly Lennie's heart started thumping as madly as if a great flapping bird was beating its wings inside his chest and trying to escape. Two tall figures had loomed up almost in front of him! Only a few yards away and he hadn't heard a sound!

Lennie, as his stomach churned and legs turned to jelly, dropped to the ground and flattened himself, convinced that it was too late. If he'd seen them, it stood to reason that they'd seen him. But complete and utter silence followed. Lennie, flat on his face on the muddy ground, did not dare to raise his head. Why didn't they say something? Come closer? Had they seen him or not? Were they going to wait until he could stand it no longer and was forced to show himself? Sweat trickled down his face and mingled with the mud beneath him. His leg was cramped and a stone was eating its way agonizingly into his shoulder.

At that moment a crescent of new moon hove into view and Lennie pressed himself more closely to the ground, trying to ignore his discomfort. But the pain in his leg was terrible. He couldn't stand it for much longer, he was going to have to move it soon or scream. Whichever way, he was doomed. He groaned, then began to sob. After all he had gone through, worked towards for so long, to be captured in such an ignominious way was unbearable.

Then something inside him exploded and Lennie saw red, as a blind fury compounded of pain, humiliation and wretchedness pounded in his head, and he jerked himself free of the clinging mud. Staggering to his feet he put his hands on his hips and lurched forwards. 'All right – here I am, you bastards,' he roared. 'Don't just stand there – come and get me, damn you!' He took a few more wavering steps before his knee gave way and pitched him headlong towards the waiting figures. And he rebounded from the unyielding shoulders of two hoary standing stones.

Sobbing with relief and weariness and cursing himself for being such a fool, Lennie picked himself up and stumbled on, not daring to rest yet. He had to get as far away as possible under cover of darkness. When daylight came he would find somewhere to hole up and sleep. Meanwhile his burning hatred of Kerensa kept him going when he was ready to drop, and dreams of the revenge he was going to wreak on her stifled the hunger pains in his stomach. Telling himself that each step was bringing him nearer to Camborne and Kerensa, Lennie forced his aching legs onwards.

CHAPTER EIGHTEEN

Lennie had reached home at last. After nights spent tramping the county under cover of darkness and finding bolt-holes in which to lie low during the day, he was actually here.

Well aware that his home was the first place the authorities would look when news of his escape became known, he nevertheless had to take that risk. He didn't intend to hang around here for long. Only as long as it took to get even with his wife.

Lennie was filthy, exhausted and starving. He was clad in a grimy flannel shirt which he had stolen from a washing line and pulled on over his prison uniform, and was now drenched from a recent downpour. He crept stealthily down the back lane behind his home, which seemed to be in darkness. That was good. His little sweetheart was obviously elsewhere – probably in the arms of her lover. His lip curled and he spat viciously into a puddle. But at least he could break in and get something to eat and a change of clothes before he went after her.

The lock on the back door had never been as secure as it should be, and he'd been meaning to fix it just before all this happened. Thank goodness he hadn't. A poke in the right place with the bit of wire which he had wound round it as a temporary measure months ago . . . Lennie grunted with the effort, and there – he was in. Straight into the kitchen, where a faint gleam seeping in from the street-lamps gave enough light to see by. To see that the room was empty. He stood stock-still and his mouth dropped open. Where was all the bloody furniture, for heaven's sake? No table and chairs, no dresser – he made for the larder and flung the door back with a groan. No food either!

Lennie ran upstairs. The bed was gone. One huge wardrobe was all that remained in the room and he wrenched open the doors of that. His clothes! Where were they? All his damn suits? Shoes? Shirts? He gave a howl of rage, forgetting in his shock and fury the need for silence. That bloody woman – where was she? Over to Penhallow of course – where else? God, he'd have the hide off her back for this – flay her alive, he would. Selling off his things as soon as his back was turned! How dare she! But why the furniture? He shook his head as his crazed brain turned over this question and was incapable of coming up with an answer.

But she *had* dared. So what was he going to do now? Lennie balled his hands into fists and pummelled them against the wall. At the very bottom of the wardrobe he spied a moth-eaten old raincoat, discarded long ago, but hidden presumably by the clothes above, it had been overlooked. He seized it with distaste, but he needed something dark and inconspicuous and it would have to do. He wrenched off the sodden shirt and put it on.

Nothing to eat though. His stomach cramped and rumbled loudly. Lennie went downstairs to the sink and drank a quantity of water to persuade it that it was full, then intent on revenge, he let himself out of the house again.

Crazed with a fury verging on madness Lennie crept down the lane to his workshop. In desperation he kicked the door open and, crossing purposefully to the far corner, reached into his secret hiding place, quickly pulled out what he needed and stuffed it into the pockets of the raincoat. He was out of the shed in a few short minutes, climbed a hedge and ran head down until he emerged onto the winding track over the fields which would lead him to Penhallow.

'Oh, Jago! This is a surprise!' Kerensa's heart did the familiar somersault at the sight of him standing on the doorstep, and her hand immediately flew to her hair. It was done up in a kerchief as she had been in the middle of tackling the cobwebs on the landing, and she was also swathed in a large and grubby apron.

She had accepted as much help from Florrie as she wanted to, and together they had cleaned and furnished enough rooms for her to live in comfortably. Now Kerensa was enjoying doing the rest for herself, delighting in being back in her old home and perfectly happy to live there alone.

'I was passing,' he replied, as she held the door open and motioned him to come in. 'I saw the light in the kitchen and thought I would call in and see how you are.' He must have seen her flushed face for he added hurriedly, 'But if it's not convenient, don't worry.'

'Of course it is. I've just been doing some more of the cleaning.' Kerensa removed the apron and kerchief, shook out her hair and ushered him into the parlour. 'I had help to move in and make a few rooms habitable again, but I'm doing the rest in my own time.'

'You work late hours,' he said.

Kerensa glanced at the clock and shrugged. 'I lost track of the time until I noticed that the light was fading. Sit down, won't you, this is one of the more habitable places.' Kerensa smiled. She had been aware of a degree of uncertainty in Jago's manner as he hovered on the doorstep, which was hardly surprising in the circumstances, but now his expression had lightened and he appeared to relax as he returned the smile.

'I heard from Florrie when I went to see Father, that you were living over here. She was quite concerned about you being on your own,' he said, seating himself.

'Oh Florrie. Yes, she's really good and kind-hearted,' Kerensa replied. 'I'm fond of her and she's been a great help to me, but she is inclined to fuss!'

'I really came because I wanted to talk to you,' Jago began, looking down at his lap and twisting his hat round and round. 'To tell you' – he cleared his throat – 'that I – well, that Grace and I—' He looked up and their eyes met. 'Neither of us knew that Father had acquired Penhallow from your family in the way he did.' He shrugged and spread his palms. 'Kerensa, we always thought he'd purchased it legally and above board, you see. We had no reason to think otherwise. But since all this happened, he's been forced to tell me exactly how it was.' His eyes continued to bore into hers as he added with urgency, 'You do believe that, don't you?'

'Of *course* I do,' said Kerensa with sincerity. 'I never doubted it for a minute. I know you and Grace too well to think anything else.' She paused and broke the eye contact. 'But as for your father – well, I'm sorry to say this Jago, because he is your father, but he was quite ruthless with Mama and me, you know, when we had to move out. It hastened her decline and I must say, as we are being honest with each other, that I've never forgiven him for it.' She looked down at her hands. 'In fact,' she went on, 'I spent a great deal of time trying to prove that the house was not legally my father's to wager with in the first place. For Mama's sake, you understand? As it meant so much to her.'

'Yes, I can understand. That's just what Father *is* like, I'm afraid, and why he and I have never seen eye to eye over anything in our lives.' Jago had risen restlessly to his feet and went over to the window where he stood looking out over the darkening grounds. 'Even so, I can't help feeling slightly sorry for him now – although you'll probably say it's only what he deserves.' Jago paused. He thought he had seen a flicker of movement among the trees beyond the lawn and rubbed at the glass as he peered harder. But it was nothing – must have been a squirrel or maybe a cat out hunting.

'He's had to sell that row of cottages,' he went on, turning back to Kerensa, 'all except for the one he's living in. So he has nothing left of his old life.' He spread his hands. 'He's lost the business, his friends have dropped him, Grace and I have left home and with Mama and Richard dead, he's just a lonely old man now.'

Kerensa nodded as she rose to light the gas mantle. She could not work up much sympathy for Silas however pitiable a state he was in. Jago crossed the room again and they both resumed their seats.

'I'm so glad that Penhallow has come back to you,' Jago said, regarding her with a softness in his eyes. 'Do you know, Kerensa, all the time I was living there it never really felt like my home? I always felt that it was more yours than ours, and now I know that it actually was.'

'There's a lot more that you don't know though,' Kerensa said pensively. 'Although this doesn't concern your family directly. But as we seem to be clearing the air of past secrets, I want to tell you about my own father and what he did, too . . .'

Jago listened intently and as Kerensa's story drew to a close, he rubbed both hands across his face and into the silence which had fallen, said at last, 'And you've never heard from your father since he disappeared all those years ago?'

Kerensa shook her head. 'Nothing,' she said and her eyes brimmed. 'Oh, I suppose you'll say that he was almost as much of a rogue as your father, but I loved him so much that for years I wanted to think it was all a mistake. Until I found the evidence. Then I had to believe it. But now, if I only *knew*, Jago' – she spread her hands – 'just whether he's alive or dead, I could accept either one. It's the not knowing that's so awful. It's always at the back of my mind. For a long time I expected him to turn up unannounced as suddenly as he'd vanished, but it never happened.' She wiped the back of her knuckles across her eyes.

'But there we are,' she added briskly, purposely ignoring the hand which Jago laid on her arm, and the sympathy in his eyes. They were too close – nothing could possibly come of it except more trouble. Although every bone in her body yearned to give in, to turn towards him, lean her head on his shoulder for support and for comfort, Kerensa knew that if she gave way in the slightest, she would be lost and there would be no going back.

She jumped to her feet to regain her composure and swiftly changed the subject. 'Come down to the kitchen and I'll make us a cup of tea and something to eat.' As Jago followed her down the passage she said over her shoulder, 'And how about you? Are you doing any composing?'

Jago sighed. 'I'm trying to,' he said gloomily, 'but it's not ideal living in the cottage. I really shall have to find a place of my own soon – I've been putting it off and off because I don't want to hurt Grace's feelings and seem ungrateful for her hospitality. But when the baby arrives I'm bound to disturb it with my playing, and feeling bad about that will hinder my concentration – so as I said, I must do something soon.'

Kerensa had been listening to this tale while she bustled about with kettle and cups and put some sandwiches together, and now she turned to him and said seriously, 'Jago, I've been thinking – how would it be if you moved your piano back here again? You could come over and work when you felt like it, and still carry on living in Penponds. If it would help,' she added looking away and clattering china, suddenly self-conscious, as Jago's face lit up with a huge smile.

'Kerensa, that would be absolutely marvellous! I can't thank you enough. It's a brilliant idea and' – he paused and their eyes met – 'perhaps I could persuade you to play left hand for me again sometimes.'

'Of course I will,' she replied, lowering her gaze and placing their tea on the table, heedless of how much she was slopping into the saucers as her hands shook. Jago didn't seem to notice as he remarked, 'As a matter of fact, when I was in London I showed Hal some of my compositions and he was very encouraging.'

Kerensa smiled as she passed his plate. 'Really?' she said with interest.

Jago nodded and took a bite of his sandwich. 'Actually he persuaded me to take them along to Boosey's – you know, the music publishers? I left several scores there for them to look at – not that I think anything will come of it,' he added hastily.

'Oh how exciting!' Kerensa replied. 'How long will it be before they contact you?'

'I've no idea,' Jago said, 'It's far more likely that I shall never hear anything more about it – I'm not holding out much hope.'

They sipped their tea in uneasy silence and the tension grew as the silence lengthened. Kerensa was desperately searching her mind for something else to say, when Jago glanced at her and said softly, 'Why did you really marry Lennie, Kerensa? I know you told me once that you had to, and I jumped to completely the wrong conclusion. So what was the real reason?'

Kerensa sighed and slowly stirred her tea. 'It's a long story,' she said.

'I'm in no hurry,' Jago replied, regarding her steadily. Kerensa gazed back. She realized that above all she did want him to know, so that there should be no secrets left between them on this day which seemed to have turned into a day of confessions. . . .

'And you managed to keep all this from your mother?' Jago remarked, wide-eyed, as Kerensa came to the end of her tale. 'You mean to say that she never knew the true facts about your marriage and still doesn't?'

'I couldn't tell her, Jago. She was so ill at the beginning that the worry would have killed her.' Kerensa shrugged. 'And as time went on and she was out of the country, it became even more difficult. Oh, I'm no saint – you needn't look at me like that,' she said hastily as she recognized the sympathy in Jago's eyes. Suddenly self-conscious, she glanced away, but he leaned across the table and laid a hand over hers, giving it a gentle squeeze which said more than any words could have done.

'What's that?' Kerensa said, jerking her hand away and sitting bolt upright. 'I thought I heard a noise outside.'

Jago rose and went to the window to peer out into the darkness. 'Can't see anything,' he replied as he came back. He glanced at the grandfather clock in the corner and added, 'Kerensa, I must go, it's getting late. Thanks again for the offer of a home for the piano – I'm really grateful. I'll be in touch as soon as I've made arrangements to shift it over here.'

Kerensa nodded and stood in the open doorway while he unhitched his patient horse, then with a wave he vanished around the corner and into the night. It had begun to rain now, a thick curtain of drizzle which hung in the air and dripped from the lower branches of the trees, but she stayed where she was for a moment, allowing the fresh air to cool her hot cheeks and going over in her mind all that had passed between herself and Jago. If only . . . she thought sadly, glancing down at the ring on her left hand. At that moment it was feeling as heavy as a ball and chain.

Lennie had been lurking in the garden, weighing up the situation and watching his slut of a wife with vicious jealousy. Had seen her laughing and talking with her lover as if she hadn't a care in the world. Had seen them move into the kitchen, holding hands across the table as they made sheep's eyes at one another, and had drooled at the sight of the sandwiches the bitch had placed before him. Sandwiches – while he, her own husband, was starving! But he had bided his time until her fancy man had ridden off, and now the coast was clear. Keeping to the shadows thrown by the trees surrounding it, Lennie began with cat-like stealth to cross the lawn towards the house.

★

Kerensa had turned and was about to go back into the kitchen when some sixth sense alerted her. She glanced over her shoulder and screamed. A menacing figure was looming out of the shadows, dark, terrifying! A tramp? Or maybe one of the rough gypsies from the camp up in the woods. But something about his walk, the way he held himself was familiar. Kerensa clapped one hand to her mouth. 'Lennie!' she gasped, her jaw dropping as she recognized that this tramp was her own husband. She saw the crazed look on his face then, and her stomach turned over as she leapt for the door and tried to close it against him.

Lennie however, had the advantage of surprise and he forced his foot in the aperture, put his shoulder to the door, and easily overpowered her. Kerensa fled across the kitchen, her one thought being that she had left out the bread-knife after cutting the sandwiches. If only she could reach that. . . .

But Lennie was there too quickly, and clamped one grimy hand across her mouth as he seized both her own hands in the other, while Kerensa kicked ineffectually at his shins and tried to fight him off.

'Scream again and I'll kill you,' he said briefly. He threw her into a wooden chair and picked up the knife himself. Waving it in front of Kerensa's face he went on, 'I've waited a long time for this. Oh yes, my darling wife, I'm going to do away with you anyway, you can be sure of that, but it'll be slowly and in my own time. I want to see you suffer first.' He bent forward and leered at her out of bulging, bloodshot eyes.

Kerensa caught a blast of his rank breath as he leaned over her and her stomach heaved. In fact, Lennie stank to high heaven. The lower half of his face was covered in a matted beard, and his greasy hair reached to his coat collar. She turned away in revulsion as he went on through gritted teeth, 'Thought you could turn me in and get away with it, did you? Get me slapped in gaol and you could have a high old time with your lover. That the idea was it?'

'No – no, Lennie, listen to me – it was never like that . . .' Kerensa roused herself. Shaking with fright would do no good; she would need all her wits about her to deal with her crazy husband. Keep him talking, she thought desperately, that's all I can do for the moment. 'Jago and me,' she went on, trying to still her trembling body, 'we're only friends, that's all, Lennie, truly.' And how ironic it was that this should really be the truth, when for so long she had wished with her heart and soul that it could be otherwise.

195

'Pah!' he snorted with contempt. 'You expect me to believe that? After I've just been watching you sitting here, holding hands and drinking tea, cosy as anything? Even shifted all my furniture over here.' His red-flecked eyes peered around the room, 'Mother's things, to make into your snug little love-nest. You've got a bloody nerve – I'll never forgive you for this, you bitch.'

The knife came within an inch of her eyes and Kerensa flinched. 'Take me for a fool, do you? One swipe of this and you won't be so pretty no more. Wouldn't fancy you then, would he? Ha ha, ha!' As the maniacal laughter rang out, Kerensa realized that he was actually deranged, and therefore even more dangerous than she'd thought.

'Oh no,' Lennie was rambling on now, 'I've always been too clever for you. How do you think I came up with enough money to send your precious mother away, eh?' He tapped the side of his nose. 'I earned it with my clever, cunning brain. Did old Silas a favour – earned my reward. He got the house; I got you.' Kerensa frowned. What on earth was he talking about?

'And you never had an inkling, did you?' Lennie went on. 'Some innocent, simple little child you were then.' He took a step nearer and the knife lurched frighteningly close again. Kerensa cringed back against the hard bars of the chair's back. Say something – anything – to distract him, she told herself. She licked dry lips and forced her teeth to stop chattering as she spoke in what she hoped was a calm and conversational tone.

'What did you say, Lennie? I don't understand what you mean.' He took a step back and grinned down at her, showing yellow teeth like those of an animal. 'I don't suppose you do – brains weren't never *your* strong point. But just try to take this in, *if* you can.' He bent and fixed her with his bloodshot stare, wagging a finger as he spoke slowly as if to a backward child.

'Now old Silas, he knew a thing or two, he did. He wanted this here house, see, wanted it badly. And him and me put this plan together. Oh neat, that was.' Lennie smirked. 'I would teach him a couple of tricks with the cards and he'd pull the wool over the eyes of your beloved papa. Oh yes, worked like a dream it did, and poor old Zack never knew nothing!' He cackled loudly. 'Dropped into the trap we set, sweet as a nut, and wagered away the house. Silas cleaned up, I got rich and there we were, laughing.' He cackled again, gloating over the memory.

Kerensa's brain was racing at this revelation. Here was something she could never have imagined in her wildest dreams – that these two had conspired together to hoodwink her father and – her eyes opened wider – that this lout – her husband – had *bought* her with the proceeds. Kerensa clapped a hand over her mouth. Her stomach was churning and she felt sick.

Lennie's expression changed to one of vicious hatred now as he barked, 'Only mistake I made was marrying you, you sneaking bitch! Dropped me right in it, didn't you? Thought you'd get your husband walled up and go dancing off with that milksop Cardrew, that was your plan. But you took on more than you thought when you crossed me.' He thumped his chest. 'Oh yes. And now you're going to pay for it, you trollop.' The knife wavered dangerously as he pointed it at her.

Kerensa swallowed down her nausea and made a supreme effort to keep the conversation going. 'How did you manage to get out of prison, Lennie?' she asked.

'Told you. I was too clever for them,' he said with satisfaction. 'Oh, they couldn't keep Lennie Retallick behind bars for long, oh no.' He puffed out his chest, then paused and Kerensa saw his eyes fasten on the loaf of bread which she hadn't yet put away. Saliva began to dribble from one corner of his mouth.

'Aren't you hungry after being on the run like that?' she asked. 'There's a couple of sandwiches over there, and some bread, if you want them.' She saw him hesitate and the hand holding the knife sank slowly to his side. 'Help yourself,' she went on in a quiet, persuasive tone. 'I won't try to run away. I know you would only catch me again, so what's the point?' The minute he turns his back, she thought, I'll make a dash for it. . . .

But she'd underestimated his cunning. Not in the least distracted, Lennie kept his eyes fastened on her as he sidled over to the table and grabbed the sandwiches, cramming them into his mouth and wolfing them down almost without chewing. He wiped his mouth with the back of one hand and belched loudly.

'Now then,' he said, 'to business!' He tossed the knife well out of her reach and began to rummage in his pocket, eventually pulling out a box of matches. Casually he withdrew one and struck it. But even when he waved the flame to and fro in front of her, Kerensa had no idea what he was going to do.

When he took a step forward to the window however, and held it to a corner of the net curtains, her hands flew to her face and she began to shake. 'No! Lennie – no!' she screamed and jumped to her feet. Her husband however, gave her a vicious kick in the ribs with his hobnailed boot and Kerensa crumpled, clutching at her injured side and moaning, before she fell to the floor with a thud as all the breath left her body.

Afterwards, Jago could never tell what made him pause at the top of the hill and look back over the valley, but when he did he smelled a faint whiff of smoke. Someone having a bonfire, he shrugged, hard luck on them – it's coming to rain. He was turning the horse again when the orange flicker of flame caught his eye and he peered closer through the gloom. It wasn't coming from Penhallow, was it? No, of course it wasn't. He smiled at the thought. As if Kerensa would be having a bonfire! He turned to go, then looked down into the valley again. But wait – it was! *Penhallow was on fire!*

Wrenching the startled horse around, Jago galloped back down the hill the way he had just come, slid from the animal's back before it had come to a halt and tossed the reins over a gatepost. He was about to shout out Kerensa's name and go bursting in, when the bellow of a male voice stopped him in his tracks. Cautiously Jago dropped onto all fours and crept around to the back of the house.

As he peered round the corner at the blazing window and Lennie's figure silhouetted against it, he took in the situation instantly. He doubled back to the front door and crept inside. As Jago approached down the passage to the kitchen, he could see that Lennie had his back to him, and that Kerensa was out of his own reach, trapped as she was in a corner behind the table and chairs. Clutching her arms around her body, she seemed to be in pain, and her face was as white as the tablecloth as she dragged herself to her feet. God, if he'd hurt her he'd kill the little runt!

Lennie, laughing like the maniac he was, struck another match and hurled it at the curtains. The net ones hanging against the glass were blazing away now and the flames had begun to lick at the thicker and more substantial pair, which were taking longer to catch. As Jago stood for an instant planning his next move, there was a terrific crash as the window fell out, followed by showers of shattered glass. Kerensa screamed and covered her face, while into the space blew a gust of wind which fanned the flames in spite of the rain which came with it, and the curtains flared up with a roar.

Through the swirling smoke, Jago had seen Kerensa's eyes widen as she caught sight of him, but he held up a warning finger and with remarkable self-control she had pulled herself together and was keeping Lennie's attention on herself, saying something to him that Jago missed as he bent to snatch up a poker from the fender.

'There she goes!' Lennie chortled, admiring his handiwork as he took a step backwards. 'Not a bad start,' he shouted, above the noise of the crackling flames. 'Now my lovely,' he crooned, swaying in front of Kerensa as he dipped into his pocket again. 'Lennie's got another surprise – something he's been saving up especially. Just for you, you damned lying, cheating, thieving *slut!*' As he raved in a maddened frenzy, Jago crept closer. 'This'll make sure you and your precious house are blown to kingdom come and I'll never set eyes on either one of you again!' Kerensa gasped as she saw that he was holding one of the explosive fuses that were used in the mines. He's going to throw that back in here when he gets outside! She screamed again as Lennie began to make for the outside door.

Then he turned, caught sight of Jago and swore loudly, pausing for an instant. It was enough of a diversion, Kerensa sprang from her place and Jago shouted *'Out! Get out!'* as he brought the poker down on Lennie's head. It was only a glancing blow as he dodged aside in time, but was enough to knock him off balance. As he swayed, Jago swooped on Kerensa and dragged her towards the door. She was semi-helpless from pain and choking on the acrid smoke but willed herself not to pass out, and tried to take some of her own weight off Jago as he struggled through the searing heat.

Dimly through the curtain of smoke she saw Lennie steady himself, one hand to his head as he shouted obscenities at the top of his voice. Then he was staggering after them, waving the fuse high above his head. He made as if to toss it at them both, but before it had left his hand there came a cataclysmic explosion which shook the house to its very foundations, and a piercing scream like that of a tortured animal. *'Down! Get down!'* Jago croaked, and half-lifted, half-pushed Kerensa through the outside door. Coughing and gasping, their eyes red and streaming, he dragged her over the grass.

They had barely reached the safety of the trees before the whole wall of the kitchen began to teeter, then came crashing down to cover the spot where they been just seconds before.

Huddled together, they could only watch helplessly. With the wall down, the huge chimney above began to sway. Beneath its weight the roof folded inwards like an umbrella furling, then the whole lot toppled and came sliding downward, disintegrating almost in slow motion until it fell with a boom like thunder, on top of the rubble which had been the kitchen.

The roaring seemed to last for a long time, as did the clouds of dust, but could only have been seconds in reality. Stunned, the pair stayed where they were until the immediate shock had lessened and they could breathe again, then Kerensa raised her face from Jago's chest where she had buried it as the chimney fell. Swallowing on her dry throat she whispered hoarsely, 'Jago, where's Lennie?'

Jago stumbled to his feet and peered into the driving rain. He took a few steps across the grass, then glanced down. He had stumbled over something soft. 'Don't look,' he snapped at Kerensa who was following, and turned to wrap her in his arms, shielding her from the gruesome sight. For the fuse must have gone off in her husband's hand and the scattered remains were hardly recognizable as human.

CHAPTER NINETEEN

At that moment there came the sound of voices and running feet. Through the driving rain came bobbing the light of several lanterns, as a group of men erupted around the corner of the house. Some carried buckets of water, others brooms and flails, with which they prepared to tackle the blaze. But the combination of falling masonry and the steady downpour had already done the job, and the fire was almost out.

'We're from up the road – over to Magor Farm,' one of them panted. 'Heard some great bang we did, then saw flames shooting up. You all right, are you, sir? And, missis?' He raised the lantern and peered at them, his craggy face full of concern.

'Yes – yes, thanks,' Jago managed. Kerensa shaking with shock could only nod, her teeth chattering too much for speech.

'What the hell have happened here? Begging yer pardon, ma'am.' He nodded towards Kerensa. 'Some mess, idden it?' His jaw dropped as he stared up at the house.

'You'd best get she into the dry,' called out another voice. 'Come on, my handsome,' he added, 'round to the front.' The man stepped forward and as Jago gestured at what lay underfoot, the farmer's eyes widened and he took a firm hold of Kerensa's arm to guide her away.

Jago remained outside to explain what had happened, and Kerensa would have flopped down into the nearest chair and stayed there had not her companion pressed her arm and urged her up the stairs. 'You get them wet things off, missis, before you do catch cold,' he said and his rough country voice was tinged with concern.

Kerensa did so as he clumped downstairs, then reached for a thick wrapper which she tied about her trembling figure, wincing as the sash caught the bruise in her side. Knees pulled up to her chin and her arms wrapped around them, she hugged her aching body. She was rocking back and forth, staring at nothing, when she was roused by Jago's voice calling up the stairs.

'Kerensa! Are you there?' His anxious mud-stained face appeared in the doorway, wet hair plastered to his head. 'Are you all right?' he said with concern as he caught sight of her. Kerensa nodded, but her pinched white face must have told Jago a different tale, for his brows drew together in a frown. 'Look,' he urged, 'you must get dressed and come with me – now. I'll take you over to Grace's for the night.'

Kerensa stiffened and her eyes widened. 'Oh? But—'

'But nothing – you can't possibly stay here.' Jago spread his hands for emphasis. 'Come on,' he held out a hand to her. 'Then I'll come back and help the men board up the house and . . . other things.' His voice trailed off and Kerensa knew instinctively what the other grisly task was. She put a hand to her mouth as her stomach heaved, then beyond constructive thought she rose like an automaton to do as she was told.

Kerensa awoke to the deep rumble of male voices floating up from below and for a moment had no idea where she was. When she fully opened her eyes however and saw the low beamed ceiling above her head, memory came flooding back. Last night! Of course, this was Grace's home and the voices must be Jago telling Dan the tale as he came in from his night shift down the mine.

Now that her head was clear and she was capable of rational thought again, Kerensa began to relive the events of the previous evening, which seemed to her more like a stage melodrama than actuality. Now she had to pick up the pieces of that life and come to terms with what had happened. For Lennie was no more, and technically Kerensa was a free woman. Something she had yearned to be for so long that now it had happened, and happened so suddenly, she could not take it in.

Her reverie came to an abrupt end with a tap on the door, followed by Grace's head appearing round it. Her face lit up when she saw that

Kerensa was awake. 'Kerensa! How are you feeling?' She came into the room and perched on the side of the bed as she looked her anxiously in the face.

'Better, thank you – much better,' Kerensa replied with a smile. 'Quite recovered in fact.' She extended a hand which Grace gently squeezed as she went on, 'Grace, I can never thank you enough for last night. I was in such a state then that I couldn't utter a word. But you and Jago – you were wonderful.'

'Nonsense,' replied the other woman, 'it was nothing. But Jago – how fortunate it was that he smelled the smoke and went back, wasn't it?'

Kerensa ran a hand through her tumbled hair. 'Is that what happened? We didn't have a chance to say much under the circumstances.' And he's saved my life – again! Kerensa's heart turned over at the thought of how differently things could have turned out, for there was no doubt that Lennie, given the crazed state he had been in, would have killed her.

'Jago's just woken up – he's been sleeping on the couch downstairs,' said Grace. 'I don't know what time he came in last night.' She rose to her feet. 'Now, breakfast – I'll bring you up something on a tray.'

'No, no,' Kerensa protested, pushing back the covers and putting her feet to the floor, 'you've done enough for me already, especially in your condition.' She glanced at Grace's thickening figure. 'I'm perfectly able to come downstairs.'

'Are you sure?' Grace regarded her closely and Kerensa nodded.

'Of course. I was only suffering from shock last night. And a bit of bruising where Lennie kicked me.' She gingerly lifted her borrowed nightgown and revealed the streaks of black and blue under her ribs.

Grace raised both hands in horror. 'Oh, the brute!' she said. 'That looks really tender – I'll find some liniment to put on it.' She rose and went back downstairs as Kerensa reached for her clothes and began to dress.

Kerensa arrived in the kitchen to the glorious smell of frying bacon and realized all of a sudden that she was ravenously hungry. Jago was sitting at the table in the window and turned towards her as she entered. As their eyes met Kerensa took in his haggard face and unshaven chin and realized that the events of the night had taken their toll on him as well. She pulled up a chair next to him as Grace put a loaded plate in front of each of them and seated herself with her own buttered toast.

'I can't face bacon in the mornings these days,' she said with a smile, 'although I don't mind cooking it for other people.'

'Jago, what happened at Penhallow after I left last night?' Kerensa said with urgency, as with one part of her mind she noted how well he had adapted to managing his fork with just the grip of thumb and index finger.

'The men went back to the farm and fetched some boards that we nailed to the inner walls to secure the house,' Jago replied with his mouth full, 'and someone fetched the police. They left a man on guard duty until it was light, then came back to remove – well, to clear up the – er – remains.' He avoided Kerensa's eyes. 'And take them to the mortuary,' he finished. Kerensa imagining the scene, swallowed hastily as her food threatened to choke her.

Then into the silence which seemed to have fallen, Grace asked, 'How much damage has been done to the house? Do you know yet?'

'Not for certain, as it was still only just light when I left,' Jago replied. 'But I should say that it's been confined to the back wall. Two walls of the kitchen were completely demolished, and the bedroom above it, along with that part of the roof, but the rest of the house seems to be all right.'

'How lucky that it was a kind of separate wing in itself,' said Grace.

Kerensa nodded. 'It had been built on at a later date than the main house,' she said. 'I must go back there this morning and see it all for myself.'

Jago pushed back his plate and rose to his feet. 'I'll just have a wash and shave, then I'll walk over with you.' Kerensa gave him a grateful smile as he went to fill a copper jug with hot water from the boiler on the range, then disappeared upstairs.

As they strolled along the lanes from Penponds on their way to Penhallow in the warm June sunshine, it seemed to Kerensa that the events of the previous night had been no more than a nightmare. The two days could not have been more different. Swaying in the balmy morning air, drifts of pink and white wild roses decked the hedgerows, and the ditches frothed with cow parsley. Patches of ox-eye daisies and brilliant campion swayed among them and the sun shone benignly down on a world well-washed and freshened by the overnight rain.

Taking in deep breaths of the scented air, she was suddenly brought back to reality as Jago remarked, 'What a difference this is going to make to your life, Kerensa.' She glanced up at the tall figure beside her and wondered exactly what he was thinking. There were so many changes facing her and so much to attend to, that her cowardly brain shied away from even thinking about it all.

She sighed and nodded, trying to get her thoughts into some sort of order. 'I suppose I shall have to arrange the – the funeral first,' she said, with a catch in her voice. 'But I really haven't the least idea how to set about it. Oh Jago, will there be an inquest?' she added and he noticed the apprehension in her eyes. 'I won't have to go to court, will I?' Automatically Kerensa clutched at his arm for reassurance, hardly realizing what she was doing, and Jago bent his head towards her and squeezed her hand.

'There will be, but it will only be a formality. I'm sure you won't be called – it's a pretty straightforward case of accidental death.' Their eyes met as he added, 'Don't worry about it – I'll see to things if you'd like me to, and go with you if the authorities need to ask you any questions. How'll that be?'

'Oh Jago, *thank you!*' Kerensa felt the great burden lifting as she smiled up at him. 'I'd be so grateful if you would.' Softly she added, 'I have so many reasons to be grateful to you, not least for saving my life last night – for the second time.' Their eyes held as Jago shrugged off the remark, and patted her hand. It seemed quite natural then that he should tuck it under his arm, guiding her along as they threaded their way through the maze of tin stream workings, past the churning water-wheels, the clatter of machinery, the shouts of many men at work, then over the plank bridge that spanned the Red River, until Penhallow was in sight.

From the front it appeared unaltered, its mellowed stone gables soaking up the sunshine as it had for a hundred years. But as they rounded the corner and she saw the full extent of the devastation by daylight, Kerensa put her hands to her face and gasped.

Two walls were all that remained standing, their uneven tops looking like a row of broken teeth, and scattered masonry and shards of glass littered the garden for yards around. Kerensa took a few tentative steps inside what had been her kitchen and peered around. 'Be careful,' Jago warned, 'in case more stuff comes down.'

'There's nothing left to come down,' she replied, stifling a sob as she looked around the roofless ruin. But he was poking around on the far side and didn't reply. Kerensa watched as Jago went down on one knee and pulled at a broken floorboard which was sticking up almost vertically, then removed a large chunk of masonry and whistled through his teeth as if in surprise. What on earth was he doing?

At that moment he looked over his shoulder and caught her watching.

'Kerensa – come and look at this,' he said, beckoning. She crossed the room and bent down beside him.

'What have you found?' she asked, peering with surprise as she noticed a hole which had opened up in the floor where the chimney had come down. It was about the size of a manhole or a trapdoor.

'I don't know for sure, but it looks like it could be a cellar or something. Did you know there was anything here?'

Kerensa shook her head. 'Are those steps I can see? Under all the rubble – there.' She pointed.

'Looks like it.' Jago sat up straighter and with a dusty hand pushed his hair out of his eyes. 'Perhaps it was a coal-hole. Anyway, there's too much heavy stuff for us to even think of moving it on our own.' He rose to his feet and brushed himself down. 'I'll get Dan and his workmates to give a hand – he did offer to help out – and then we'll have a closer look.'

'How intriguing!' Kerensa said, her lively mind already trying to imagine what the mysterious hole could have been for, and refusing to accept the notion of anything as mundane as coal. 'What I shall have to do,' Kerensa said, raising clouds of gritty dust as she stepped away, 'is to go back to Camborne to sleep and eat, but I can still spend most of my time over here. I hate that house, Jago,' she said with a quiver in her voice. 'I never felt any part of it was mine. I'm going to put it on the market right away. The sooner it's sold the better. Then by the time anyone wants to buy it, I shan't need it any more because this place will be straight.' Jago nodded as she went on, 'I intend to fix up some temporary means of cooking as soon as I can, then I can stay over here all the time. Have you seen the advertisements for that new stove that works on paraffin?'

'No,' Jago said absently as he removed a couple of bricks from the Welsh dresser which had survived almost intact in the corner of the two walls.

'It sounds really good. They call it a Sootless Kerosene Stove,' Kerensa went on. 'You put methylated spirits round the burner, and the paraffin is in a drum underneath . . .' She stopped in exasperation for it was clear that he wasn't listening.

'This seems to be all right under the dust,' Jago said, 'Although I can't say the same for the china.' Kerensa winced as he collected up the pieces of her mother's willow pattern plates and added them to the rest of the debris on the floor. 'At least when the house is sold you'll have money to do the rebuilding here,' he went on, brushing off his hands and bending to open cupboards and drawers.

★

Dan and a squad of men turned up a few days later and in a surprisingly short space of time had shifted the fallen rubble out in barrowloads and swept the former kitchen free of dust and mess. Those of Kerensa's belongings which were still usable were piled neatly on the dresser and one handy man had repaired the broken pipes and reconnected the water supply.

Meanwhile Jago had engaged a removal firm to shift his piano over to Penhallow, where it took up its former position in the library. 'It looks as if its never been away,' said Kerensa softly, as he raised the lid and played a few notes.

But, Kerensa told herself sternly, she had become too used to leaning on Jago. The time was coming when she would have to live on her own however much she yearned for things to be otherwise.

'It badly needs tuning though,' Jago replied breaking into her thoughts as he looked up with a smile. 'All the moving around hasn't done its insides any good! But that won't take much to arrange.'

'Then you can get back to your composing,' Kerensa replied.

He nodded. 'Did I tell you Grace gave me a book of poems written by our mother? I've been putting some of those to music.'

'Yes,' replied Kerensa, 'I'd love to hear them sometime.'

Jago stood up and closed the piano-lid. 'So you shall. But the best ones of course are with Boosey's at the moment.'

They were interrupted by a shout from Dan, who appeared at the window and beckoned them to come outside. By the time they arrived at the back of the house he was on his hands and knees peering into the 'coal hole'. 'Come and have a look at this,' he said, scrambling to his feet with an air of excitement about him. 'We've cleared all the stuff out, see what we've found.'

Kerensa bent down with Jago at her shoulder as they followed Dan's pointing finger. 'Oh – steps!' she said in surprise. 'Lots of them!' She turned back to Dan. 'Where do they go?' she asked, round-eyed.

Dan shrugged. 'Don't know yet,' he grinned, 'but 'tisn't no cellar, that's for sure.'

'It looks more like a tunnel, doesn't it?' said Jago, peering into the gloom.

Kerensa's eyes were dancing as she smiled back at Dan. His genial face was streaked with dirt as were his huge hands and brawny arms, and his beard was full of dust. 'We must find out where it goes,' she said, and would have gone over the edge there and then if Dan had not laid a hand on her arm to prevent her.

'Careful now, maid,' he warned with the caution of the experienced miner, 'we've got to do this properly. Jim and me are going back to fetch candles and hard hats before we do go any further. You don't know what state 'tis in down there, see.'

'Couldn't have a better man for the job,' Jago said, clapping him on the shoulder. 'We'll clear off out of the way and leave you to it. Give us a shout when you get back.'

It took another half a day of clearance work before Dan at last gave the go-ahead for Kerensa and Jago to come down the steps and into the gloom at the mouth of the tunnel which had been excavated so far. 'The further up we go the clearer it seems to be,' Dan said, handing them each a miner's hard felt hat with a lighted candle stuck to it with a knob of clay.

Kerensa was looking fearfully around at the black, dripping walls which felt as if at any time they could close in around her. Or worse, that they could fall and seal her in this underground place for ever. It would take only the slightest mishap, and this would be her tomb. Even the eerie silence which had fallen now that they had stopped talking was thicker and more menacing than any silence above ground. It was the silence of ages, and redolent of ancient dust.

'All that fallen stuff this end was clogging it up, see,' Dan's voice came booming from in front, echoing in the enclosed space, and Kerensa jumped. She took a few quick steps and clutched at the back of his jacket for comfort, lost in admiration for the men like him who spent all their working life in holes like this.

'I reckon 'tis an old adit, probably from Wheal North up there on the cliff, what would have discharged down in the Red River, see.' He stopped as they came to a fork and the tunnel narrowed. 'And this is where it do join up with the passage from the house, look.' He turned to face them. 'Now this is as far as we've been,' he said, 'and as far as we're going to go from this end. It do get awful narrow as you can see, and I aren't going to risk nobody getting stuck in there.' As he gestured with his hand for them to turn back, Kerensa felt a mixture of relief and disappointment. Although she hadn't known what she expected to find, it was a bit tame just to turn round and go back. 'Jim and me are going to look for the other end of this here from up top,' Dan went on. 'I got a fair idea where it'll come out to, and if I'm right, we'll carry on then.'

It was as they were nearly back at the house, just at the foot of the flight of steps leading up to the former kitchen, that Kerensa raised her head and by the light of her candle caught sight of some lettering scrawled on a flat piece of rock above her head. To see it more clearly she took off her hat and lifted it high. 'Stop a minute, you two,' she called. 'Come and look at this.'

Jago was the first at her side. 'What is it?' He followed her gaze and looked upwards.

'I'm not tall enough to read it properly, but there's something written up there near the roof,' Kerensa said. 'Take this.' She handed him her hat with its candle, as Dan joined them. 'What can you see? Can you read it? What does it say?' Kerensa was jigging up and down with impatience as Jago squinted upward and peered into the half-light.

'Yes. And no. It's very faded. The first word looks like Penhallow. No, *Penhallow's*. Penhallow's something. *T – tr – treas* . . . The rest of that word is completely worn away.'

'*Treasure!*' Kerensa exclaimed, hopping from foot to foot and wishing she were tall enough to see for herself. 'Could it be *treasure* Jago?'

'Well, yes, I suppose it could be,' he said turning towards her.

'What else?' she urged him. 'Can you read the rest of it?'

'Patience, woman,' Dan growled, then grinned at her. 'Give the man a chance!'

'. . . *you have found*,' came Jago's voice. 'That's fairly clear.'

'*Penhallow's treasure you have found!*' Kerensa squealed. 'What? Where? Is there any more writing? Come on, Jago, there must be more than that!'

He grunted and peered closer. 'Yes, there's another line. It goes, *Nature . . . nature's* . . . It looks like *gift* – yes, *nature's gift lies . . . lies . . . all around*. And that's all.' He turned back, handed Kerensa her hat and shrugged.

'*Penhallow's treasure you have found. Nature's gift lies all around*,' she muttered. 'What on earth does *that* mean?' She looked blankly around the passage. 'It says we've found the treasure.' Disappointment was bringing a tightness to her throat. 'But there's nothing here. Oh, no! Someone else must have been here before us and already taken it.' Kerensa leaned her forehead against Jago's shoulder and sniffed. 'I wonder what it could have been.' Visions of gold doubloons and strings of priceless jewels passed through her mind.

An exclamation from Dan brought Kerensa to her senses with a start. She'd almost forgotten he was there. He had been poking about further up the passage, and now gave a great shout which echoed through the narrow tunnel. 'Well I never! Of all the . . .' His voice was muffled as he scrambled on to a lower outcrop of rock and hoisted himself closer to the roof. He jumped down after a few minutes with a huge grin splitting his face and tramped back to the other two, who stood gaping at him as if he had lost his senses. 'I've found it!' he announced.

'What – you don't mean the treasure?' said Jago, and Kerensa clapped one hand to her mouth in disbelief.

'Depends what you call treasure,' Dan replied, still grinning.

'Well, come on, man, out with it,' Jago urged.

'I've only found,' Dan went on slowly, obviously savouring the moment, 'a seam of what looks like almost pure copper. Cropping on the outside of the face, just waiting to be picked out – sweet as a nut. And it goes on for as far as I can see, following the lie of the passage!'

'Copper!' Kerensa's jaw dropped. 'A mineral lode – *nature's gift*! Well, *that* was the treasure Rafe Nicholas meant!'

'Good grief!' said Jago. 'All those years ago, and nobody ever noticed it!'

Their eyes met as Kerensa went on, her quick brain working it all out, 'He must have discovered it when he was using the adit to bring in his smuggled goods. Probably to store underneath the floor of the kitchen. Oh, isn't it exciting!' Tears were pouring down her face now as she laughed and cried at the same time. Jago put a comforting arm around her waist and Dan patted her awkwardly on the shoulder with a fist the size of a small ham.

'You'll be a rich woman, my handsome, time we get all that there ore out,' he said gruffly.

'Oh Dan, do you really think so?' Kerensa snuffled. It was just too much to take in all at once.

A few days later, Kerensa had purchased her new cooking stove and was living permanently at Penhallow again. 'It's all a bit makeshift,' she said to Jago as he called in to see to the piano tuner, 'but it's perfectly adequate for me.' She had set up the temporary kitchen in what had been the dining-room, and given Jago her father's former study for his piano until the library was usable again.

'There's some news, Kerensa,' Jago announced, as he was waiting for the man to turn up. His face was sombre as he said, 'The inquest has been opened and closed. It's all over.'

Kerensa's face tensed. 'And?' she said, meeting his eyes.

'There was no problem – the verdict was accidental death.'

Kerensa let out her breath in a long sigh. 'Oh, thank goodness,' she replied.

'They've released the – er – body for burial,' Jago went on. 'We can see about the funeral now.'

'Oh yes,' Kerensa said, thankful that the whole thing was going to be finished at last. Then she could put the terrible ordeal behind her and get on with her life.

Jago's presence was a lifeline to her at that time. It was he who took all the burden of arrangements out of her hands. Kerensa did not ask to see her husband's remains and consequently never knew exactly what the coffin contained. As far as she was concerned the page had turned on her disastrous marriage, that part of her life was behind her, and she was a free woman again.

'Dan said last night when he came in that he and Jim – and Ernie too I believe – are going up to the top of that field later on to see if they can find the other end of your tunnel,' Jago said, as he arrived at Penhallow one morning to use the piano.

'Oh, good,' Kerensa replied, handing him a cup of tea. It was becoming a kind of routine that Jago would come over in the mornings and work, and they had become used to having a cup of tea together before he started.

'I have to go away for a few days,' Jago said abruptly. He had perched himself on the arm of a chair and was swinging one long leg as he sipped his tea.

'Oh, where are you going?' Kerensa asked in surprise.

'I've had a letter from Boosey's in London. They want to see me,' he replied.

Kerensa noted the repressed excitement on his face. 'They do? That has to be a good sign, surely?'

'I'd like to think so,' said Jago, 'but I'm telling myself not to take anything for granted.' He drained his cup and rose to his feet.

'I should have thought they would send you a letter if they'd rejected your work outright.' Kerensa said. 'So perhaps it really is good news.'

'We'll just have to wait and see,' Jago replied. 'Meanwhile, keep your fingers crossed! I'm catching the midday train, so I'll just put in an hour here today. I've almost finished another score, and I want to take it with me.'

He left the room and Kerensa wandered outside. She hardly liked to admit it but now that she had no commitments and no job to go to, she was finding it hard to fill the days. She had helped Jago out with his music a few times, but their old closeness seemed to have disappeared. Kerensa sighed and turned her mind to practicalities. Once the rebuilding of the house was underway she told herself, and she could get things properly straight again, it would be different.

It was another beautiful summer day and far too good to stay indoors. She would go for a walk. Wandering up the lane behind the house, she followed the rising ground toward the cliffs and the sea. Bushes of gorse topped the hedgerows with leaping tongues of golden flame, filling the air with the scent of coconut, and together with some frothy late blackthorn, looking like fire and ice. The song of larks came falling from the sky in cascades of pure melody, and swallows were darting and swooping among the clouds of midges which hovered over the fields.

Kerensa was climbing over a stile on her return journey when she saw three men in the field and recognized Dan and his workmates. Dan was waving now that he had seen her and was crossing the field with something in his hand. When he came close enough to speak he said, 'Kerensa! We've been looking for you. Went down to the house and all and couldn't find you nowhere. All right are you, maid?' He looked into her face with concern.

'Of course I am,' she replied. 'I went out for a walk and lost track of the time, that's all.' She thought how serious he was seeming, quite unlike his usual jovial self. 'What did you want me for?' she asked.

'We've discovered the entrance to the tunnel,' Dan said briefly.

'You have?' Kerensa's face brightened, then, as he said nothing further, she frowned. 'And?' she prompted.

'And, we found this.' Dan passed over what he had been holding. 'I cleaned it up a bit, see,' he added.

Kerensa said, 'Oh – a watch? A pocket watch! Well, that's interesting.' She looked up, but Dan was scuffing his boots and avoiding her eyes. Nonplussed, Kerensa stared at him. What was the matter with the man?

Then Dan took a deep breath, cleared his throat and said, 'Turn it over, my handsome.'

Kerensa did so. Then clutched at his arm for support as she read the engraved inscription on the back. *To dearest Zack, on the tenth anniversary of our marriage.* A date, then the name, *Celia.* Kerensa gasped. 'Papa! It's

Papa's watch! Oh, Dan, what a find – I can hardly believe it! She looked up at him, her eyes shining with tears. Then her face clouded. 'But I don't understand. How did this come to be in the shaft?'

Dan tightened his grip on her arm. 'Listen, my bird, this is going to be some shock for you,' he said slowly. 'Because the watch weren't the only thing we found down there, see?'

CHAPTER TWENTY

Kerensa knew instantly by the gravity of Dan's expression what else he had found. Her hands flew to her face and she found she was shivering in spite of the warm sunshine. Dan placed a heavy hand on her shoulder and gave it a squeeze. 'You come home along of me now, my bird.' He regarded her with sympathy. 'You don't want to be by yourself in that great house tonight. Grace'll look after you, and Jago's away, so you can have his room, see? Couldn't be better.'

All the time he was talking he was guiding Kerensa down over the field. 'Thank you, Dan,' she replied abstractedly, her voice hardly above a whisper. It would be nice to be with other people tonight. 'But I don't want to be a bother . . . or put Grace to any trouble.'

'You aren't no bother, my handsome.' They reached the road and Dan went on, 'I left the pony and trap down here. Needed it for the tools and stuff. Jim and Ernie left it for me – after I sent them into town see, to tell the – um – police, what we'd found, like.'

Kerensa felt tears pricking the back of her eyes. Poor Papa, staggering around in the dark, lost, bewildered, and then falling. Falling terrified down through the brambles and loose stones that concealed the pit. Had he shouted out, pleaded unheard for help until he lost consciousness? He could have been trapped down there for days.

Dan cleared his throat and when Kerensa, lost in her own thoughts, nodded automatically, he went on, 'I was just on my way down myself when I seen you coming, see. Here we are now. Up you get, my handsome. You'll have to sit alongside of me.' He helped her up onto the driving seat. 'Idden much room in the back.' He jerked a thumb over his shoulder. In the body of the vehicle she could see a couple of scythes, picks and shovels, coils of rope and other clutter.

Kerensa had blessed Dan for his sensitivity in keeping up a steady stream of comforting chat, for she had found speech almost beyond her. Now however, she turned to him as he picked up the reins, swallowed on the lump in her throat and said, 'Dan – how do you think Papa came to be . . . be down there?'

'Dunno, maid, but I'm pretty sure it were an accident.' He clicked his tongue at the pony. 'What was he doing that last day before he disappeared? Know, do you?'

'He'd been playing cards with Silas Cardrew and he was very drunk,' Kerensa said briefly. But of course Dan would have heard all that story from Grace. 'Ah. Yes. That were the night that he gambled with the house, and lost it, weren't it?' Kerensa nodded. 'Well, what I do think,' Dan said, 'is that your Pa was in some state over that, and with him being drunk as well, he wandered about a bit on his way home. Maybe he lost his way – or maybe he thought he would take a short cut across that there field – no one won't never know for certain.'

Oh, *Papa*! How you pulled the wool over everybody's eyes. Cheat, liar, swindler, you were all of these, but you gave me a wonderful childhood, and for that I shall always be grateful. And rogue or not, no one deserves to face death alone in such a horrible place. Did you die instantly perhaps, hitting your head on the rock walls? Kerensa shivered. That would have been a kinder end. But what a place to be trapped in. In pitch darkness, down that slimy tunnel where she too had felt so stifled.

'To think we were so close to him, Dan, weren't we? The other day, I mean, when we went up the tunnel.' Kerensa raised her head and met his kindly eyes. Dan laid a big calloused palm over hers. 'And we never had the faintest idea . . .'

'Try not to think about it too much, maid, 'tis all over now and looking back won't make things no different.' He turned the horse into the narrow village street and stopped outside the cottage. 'Here we are, home. And there's Grace looking out for us.' His wife was coming along the path, holding out welcoming hands as Kerensa jumped down from the trap.

Jago was sitting in the reception room of the music publisher's office, waiting for his appointment with a Mr Clarkson, the sender of the letter. On the edge of his seat and telling himself that of course he wasn't nervous, Jago pulled out his watch, looked at it impatiently, returned it to his pocket and glanced out of the third-floor window at the seething traffic below.

Jago crossed one leg over the other, sighed, then reversed it. And jumped as someone called his name. 'Mr Clarkson will see you now, sir,' announced the elderly receptionist, ushering him into the office.

'Mr Cardrew,' the other man seated behind his desk, rose and extended a hand. 'I'm Geoffrey Clarkson. Do sit down.' He indicated an ancient leather armchair.

'Thank you for your letter,' Jago returned, sinking into the armchair's depths.

'Right, shall we get down to business straight away?' the publisher said briskly, reaching for a sheaf of papers that Jago recognized. 'I've had a good look at these,' he said, glancing up at Jago and meeting his eyes. He paused.

'And?' Jago queried as he held the eye contact.

'And, quite frankly Mr Cardrew, the best one can say about most of them is that they are – well – unremarkable.' He drummed his fingers on the polished desk top. 'Nice enough little tunes in their way, but mediocre.'

Jago's spirits plummeted. But wasn't this exactly what he'd expected? Deep down he had thought as much all along. But he had gone on hoping that perhaps he could be wrong, for a writer is never the best judge of his own work. However, it seemed that in this case he was.

So this was the end of it. All those hours spent laboriously poring over the poems, fitting the notation to their rhythm, trying out the melody one-handed on the keyboard, jotting down the score, all *wasted*! The disappointment was shattering.

'Yes,' the man's voice was droning on in the background, but Jago scarcely heard him, 'these pieces are little different, I'm afraid, from the stuff we get sent in by the sackload every week. So many young hopefuls, you see . . .'

The worst part of it was having to go back to Kerensa and tell her. How humiliating that would be. She had believed in him and he had let her down. Kerensa. He pictured her bright face. She was so sure, and encouraged him so much, never being too busy to play the lower keys when he'd needed her.

This was a bitter blow, and it hurt, but there was no way Jago was going to betray any of this to the man in front of him, and he heard himself replying quite normally. 'Well, I'm sorry to have taken up your time, Mr Clarkson.' Jago rose to his feet and held out a hand for his papers. 'Thank you for seeing me.'

'Wait, wait, Mr Cardrew, you're being too hasty.' Behind his spectacles the man's hazel eyes were twinkling. Jago stared back at him stony-faced. What was so funny, for goodness' sake? Didn't this smirking idiot realize how much time and money he had wasted on travelling all this way for *nothing*?

As if reading his thoughts, Geoffrey Clarkson said, 'Sit down, sit down. Do you really think I would have made you come up all the way from Cornwall when I could have told you that much in a letter?' Jago's mouth opened and shut but no words came out as he backed into his chair again.

'I said, *most* of these.' The man pointed to Jago's work. 'Now tell me, did you write the lyrics yourself as well as the music?'

Mystified, Jago stared at him. 'I – um – no,' he replied. 'They were poems written by – er – someone I knew once.'

'What about this one?' He pulled out a single sheet from the bottom and held it up for him to see.

Jago felt himself redden. 'Ah, yes. That one is different. I did write that myself.'

'I see.' The man regarded him steadily. 'Well, now, Mr Cardrew, I have to tell you that the majority of these works of yours are trite and meaningless compared with this particular one. This has depth and meaning and a powerful melody.'

'It has?' Jago licked lips gone suddenly dry.

The man nodded. 'In my opinion it will appeal to a very wide audience.' He beamed all over his face while Jago could only stare at him in astonishment. 'What do you think of that, young man, eh? Not in so much hurry to get away now, are you?' he chortled.

Jago, who knew he had been getting more and more flushed, now pulled out a handkerchief to mop his brow. Too bowled over to rise to the man's patronizing tone, he gasped, 'I . . . don't know . . . what to think! I'm completely overcome.' For to go from the pit of despair to the giddy heights of jubilation in a few seconds was heady stuff and his mind was reeling.

'Well, before you collapse completely,' said the other man genially, 'you might like to take a look at this.' He opened a drawer and pulled out a sheet of paper. 'I have had a rough illustration done for the cover of your score because – subject to your agreement of course – we should like to make an offer for it.'

Jago's jaw dropped, things were moving too fast. He took the sheet with a trembling hand and glanced at the sketch. And his face lit up with a delighted grin, for this was exactly what he had imagined, when in the darkest days he had poured out his feelings into this song with a flood of emotion that had left him mentally and physically drained. And this piece had been the only one the publisher had looked at twice – when he, Jago, was convinced that he couldn't write lyrics, only music!

'Oh yes, it's good – very good,' he said, handing the drawing back, his head spinning. 'Fine.'

The other man beamed. 'So I take it sir, that we have your permission to go ahead and publish?' he asked, then mentioned a startlingly large sum of money which had Jago's mouth dropping open again. '. . . For sole rights. You agree?' he added, and Jago could only nod his assent. 'I'll get a contract drawn up and send it on to you. And if you have any other work of this standard, we shall always be pleased to consider it,' he finished, as they shook hands and parted.

Jago staggered out of the office, knowing there was a wide grin plastered across his face, and not caring in the least. He felt mentally battered, but so elated that he wanted to run whooping down the stairs like a schoolboy, throwing his cap in the air.

'Oh, Grace, I don't know what I should have done without you and Dan,' Kerensa said a few days after the discovery of her father's bones. 'You've been absolutely marvellous.' She pushed her nightgown into the bag at her feet and looked up as Grace replied.

'Nonsense! Are you sure you're ready to back to Penhallow?' A frown crossed her face as Grace bent to pick up the discarded bed linen, grunting with the effort.

'Oh, I was just going to do that!' Kerensa exclaimed as, holding one hand to her back, Grace tucked the bundle under her arm. 'You must take more care of yourself, Grace,' The other woman waved a dismissive hand.

'Oh, I'm perfectly all right – I just can't bend as well as I used to,' she laughed. 'Seriously, Kerensa, you know you can stay here for as long as you like, don't you? Even when Jago gets back he can have the settee if you'd really rather not be on your own.'

'No, I must go back,' Kerensa replied. 'I'm over the shock now and there are things that need doing.' She sighed and pushed back a stray lock of hair. But Jago! Oh Jago – where were you when I needed you so much? she cried silently. Hanging around London having a high old time with your friends, while I had to cope with another death, another body, another inquest! Soon there'll be another funeral, and in spite of the help I've had from Grace and Dan, it's all been my responsibility, I've had to make all the decisions. It's too much. I feel like an old woman, bowed down with doom and gloom.

'I really must get around to writing to Mama,' she went on, as she picked up a fallen pillow. 'I feel bad that I haven't told her yet, but I just couldn't face it.'

I've been sleeping in your bed, Jago, what would you think of that? It still smelled of you, and every night I put my head in the dent in this pillow that you left behind. I didn't shake it out in all that time, that's how foolish I am ... Kerensa held it to her face and gave it a squeeze before placing it back on the bed. Then she picked up her bag and followed Grace downstairs.

The next day Kerensa was writing her letter to Celia, when she was interrupted by the sound of a horse's hoofs on the driveway. She tossed her pen aside and darted to the window to see Jago rein in his mount and come striding purposefully towards the house. Her heart lurching in the old familiar way, Kerensa gave a quick glance at herself in the hall mirror and patted down her hair before opening the door.

'Kerensa! I ...' He was so shocked at her appearance that words deserted him. Looking pinched and forlorn, the small pale face turned up to his actually seemed to have aged since he had last seen her. 'Are you all right?' he blurted. 'Only you look—'

'Come in, Jago. Yes. No. I mean, I'm not ill.' Kerensa could not prevent the quaver in her voice however much she wanted to. 'But something happened ...'

'I know. Grace told me. I came as soon as I heard.'

Kerensa nodded, then put a hand to her head. All of a sudden the room seemed to be swaying. It must be the shock of seeing him so unexpectedly. All the breath had left her body and there was a surging in her ears like the sound of the sea. 'I'm all right. Really I am,' she lied, tilting her chin as she tried to meet his eyes. Jago, looking at her with concern, saw her begin to crumple and held out his arms just in time to catch her as she fainted away.

When Kerensa came round she found she was lying on the settee, and the first thing she saw as she opened her eyes was Jago's anxious face regarding her. 'Kerensa – oh thank goodness! Don't move,' he said, as she tried to get up. He reached for the cup of tea beside him and gently supported her as he said, 'Here, drink this.'

Kerensa sipped it gratefully, then said, 'Oh I'm sorry – I feel so foolish, Jago. I don't know what came over me.' She felt herself flushing, as much from his proximity as from the tea which was extremely hot. She straightened up and he removed his arm.

'Of course you're not foolish. You've been under huge strain for a long time, you know. And now— Grace told me about your father. Oh Kerensa, I'm so sorry.'

Meeting his eyes, soft and full of sympathy, was too much. She felt tears welling as she whispered, 'Thank you', and blinked them away, shielding her face with the cup.

Perched on the arm of the settee, he was still too close. Kerensa knew that her nerves were all on edge, but surely he could sense the atmosphere as well as she? Oh, *Jago!* she sighed. If only he would either declare himself, or leave her alone, she could cope with it. Miserably she made herself face the fact she had been trying to ignore for so long. That Jago had never actually said he loved her. Not once, even since Lennie's death. So maybe he didn't. Well, she would have to live with that. It would be hard, it would be devastating, but she had faced adversity before. She took a sip of tea and tried to swallow the knot in her throat.

Breaking the silence which had fallen, Jago asked, with an anxious look, 'How are you feeling now?' as he shifted his position and moved away.

'Much better,' she replied, stiffening her spine and returning her empty cup to its saucer.

Looking vastly relieved, Jago smiled. 'Oh, that's good,' he said, then after a moment went on, 'About your father, Kerensa ... I haven't heard any details, I only stayed long enough to hear that he'd been found, then I came straight over here.'

Kerensa looked up and met his gaze as she lowered her feet to the floor. 'I'd like to take you up to the field and show you where he was found,' she said with determination as she rose. 'You haven't seen the other end of the tunnel, have you?'

Jago was staring at her in astonishment. 'You don't mean *now*, do you?'

Kerensa nodded then lifted her chin. 'Yes, I do. I badly need some fresh air, Jago. I've a headache' – she put a hand to her forehead – 'and I feel stifled indoors.' She smoothed down her black skirt – would she never be out of mourning clothes?

The recent deaths had brought back memories of Grandpapa's funeral and how upset she'd been. It seemed such a long time ago. Jago had comforted her then. Up on the cliffs, where they were going now. She remembered that day clearly, it had been one of the milestones of her life. Looking back, it seemed like the last day of her childhood and her first to experience a woman's emotions. She could still remember thundering along the cliffs on horseback with this man, and her feelings had not changed since.

Kerensa brought herself back to the present and moved across the room. Jago continued to looked dubious. 'Are you sure you're up to it?' he emphasized.

'Of course I am – don't fuss!' she said, her frayed nerves snapping. Instantly regretted her loss of control, she said, 'I'm sorry, Jago. Thank you for the tea and everything. I really do appreciate it. It's just that I seem to be all on edge today.' Kerensa sighed and tried to pull herself together.

They took the familiar track which wound up behind the house, only this time instead of climbing the stile, Kerensa led the way through a field gateway and over the short-cropped pasture. The flock of sheep paused momentarily in their nibbling to raise curious yellow eyes to the intruders, then went back to their peaceful chewing.

'Is this the place?' Jago asked, as they approached a clump of stunted blackthorn bushes and a clutter of loose stones. Kerensa nodded. She approached the edge of a cleared space and peered over. A temporary grating had been placed over the sheer drop into pitch darkness which lay below. Before that had been done there would have been nothing to prevent anyone, human or animal, from falling to certain death. Jago took one look and swore softly to himself.

Kerensa covered her face with her hands. 'At least he wouldn't have survived long enough to suffer,' she whispered, as tears squeezed out between her fingers. Her questions had been answered and for that at least she was grateful.

'No, I'm sure he wouldn't have known anything about it,' he said grimly. 'Come on, Kerensa, let's get away from this place.' He placed an arm around her shaking shoulders and guided her back to the path.

'Up to the cliffs, Jago, please. I don't feel like going back yet.' He nodded and they walked in single file, each preoccupied with inner thoughts, along the narrow track and over the stile. The derelict ruin of Wheal North engine house loomed briefly above them, before they were out on the cliff track and making for the sea. Kerensa rubbed the back of her hand across her eyes and realized that the tears had brought a kind of relief. Her headache had cleared and in seeing where he had died, she felt she had laid Zack's ghost more convincingly than she would at the funeral still to come.

The sun on their backs was getting hotter as the day wore on and Jago had removed his brown linen jacket and thrown it over his shoulder, where he held it dangling from one finger. They came to the edge and sat down in a nook formed by a rocky outcrop dotted with brilliant gold lichen. Far below, the churning water was benignly blue today, but scattered black rocks still crouched like predatory beasts, their jagged teeth waiting for the winter storms, when they would be a death trap to shipping blown off course. But up here the wind sang through the heather, and the turf was speckled with the creamy cups of fragrant burnet roses.

'I'm glad we did that,' Kerensa said softly, her eyes on the sea, then turned towards him with the first real smile Jago had seen on her face that day. It filled out the hollows and lightened the shadows below her eyes. Then, as a thought obviously struck her, the smile vanished and she turned to him with a look of consternation. 'Jago! I'd forgotten! Oh, I'm so sorry – I've been so sunk in myself I haven't asked you!'

'Asked me what?' He put on a puzzled expression but could not prevent his eyes from twinkling, for he knew perfectly well what she meant.

'About your news of course! Did you have a good trip? Was it successful? What did the publishers say? Oh, how could I have forgotten!' Kerensa clapped a hand to her forehead, contrite.

'Understandably, in the circumstances.' Jago shrugged broad shoulders beneath the white shirt, its sleeves rolled to the elbows. 'But to answer the first question, yes, I certainly did—'

Kerensa broke in, her eyes full of excitement. 'Do you mean . . . it was successful? The songs . . . they really liked them?'

Jago's beaming face was answer enough and she clasped her hands together as her voice rose in delight. 'Oh well *done!*' she exclaimed. 'Tell me all about it.'

'There's quite a bit to tell,' he said, 'but briefly, yes they're going to publish. Just one of the songs that is, but they made a very generous offer and were quite enthusiastic about it. Seem to think it might become very popular, in fact.' He raised shining eyes and met Kerensa's jubilant face.

'Wonderful!' she exclaimed, then frowned. 'Only one song? Which one's that?'

Jago shook his head, avoiding her eyes. 'You haven't – er – actually heard it.' he said. 'It's one I wrote ages ago, before Grace ever gave me the book of poems.'

'Oh, I see. And what did they say about those others?' she urged him, but Jago was looking out to sea.

'They weren't very keen on them at all,' he said, in a low voice.

'Oh?' said Kerensa, deflated, and waited for an explanation. When none came, she prompted, 'Well, when can I hear this one that they do like so much?'

Jago seemed to come back from a long way off, then suddenly jumped to his feet with a decisive air, seized her hand and pulled her after him. 'Right now,' he replied. 'It's time you did. Let's go.'

Back at Penhallow they went straight to the piano and Jago handed her a score-sheet. 'This is the music,' he said. 'I'll show you the words after we've played it. Are you ready?' When Kerensa nodded, he sat on the piano stool and moved up to make room for her beside him. She studied the score, then ran a hand over a few keys, humming to herself.

'Right, now,' Kerensa said, when she was ready and they began playing together.

The melody was haunting, ethereal, and had the hairs at the back of her neck prickling as it touched some chord deep inside her. It soared to a pitch that was exquisitely beautiful, but sang of a sadness which brought a lump to her heart and moved her almost to tears.

Now she knew why the publisher had seized on this song and disregarded the others. They bore no comparison. When the last notes rose up the scale like a question unanswered and died away on a troubled chord, Kerensa turned to Jago with tears streaming down her face.

'Why didn't you tell me you could write like that!' she demanded. 'And why didn't you ever show this to me before?'

Jago closed the lid of the piano and leaned his elbows on it, supporting his chin in his hands, head bent. Then he took a deep breath and swivelled round to face her.

'Kerensa, I wrote this when I was in a black pit of despair not long after the accident.' He glanced briefly at his left hand. 'I was looking back and, I suppose, yearning for what might have been.' He paused and cleared his throat, then lifted one of her hands. 'I was going over my life, right from the beginning. And I came to the point where I realized that I fell in love with you when you were sixteen and your grandfather had just died.' His dark eyes were burning into hers and Kerensa swallowed hard as her head began to swim. Nothing could have prepared her for this shock. Just when she had resigned herself to . . . it was too much to take in.

'I don't suppose for a moment you remember when I met you on the

cliff and you'd been crying – a little figure in a black dress just like this.'
He lifted a fold of her skirt.

Kerensa nodded, 'But I do,' she said. 'I've never forgotten it either.'

Jago regarded her with wonder in his eyes. 'But things happened,' he
went on, bending his head to glance down at his hands. 'You were still a
child, then as time went on I met Isabella and thought I'd fallen in love.'
His face darkened and he thumped a fist on the piano. 'By the time I realized how wrong I'd been, you were married to Retallick.'

Jago paused and spread his hands, palms up. 'And since he died I've
always felt quite simply that I had nothing to offer you. I was too proud, I
suppose, to come to you as a penniless man with a crippled hand.'

'But—' Kerensa broke in, but Jago went on, 'Even more so when the
copper lode was discovered on your land and I realized that you were
going to be a wealthy woman. But now' – he rose to his feet and to
Kerensa's surprise, held out another sheet of paper – 'now I can give you
this and I hope you'll understand.' He pushed it into her hand and
abruptly left the room.

Kerensa's brows rose as she looked after his fleeing figure, then turned
to the paper Jago had thrust at her. It was the printed score of the song
they had just played, its title displayed in a tasteful surround showing a
surging sea, with towering cliffs and wheeling birds above. 'A Song on the
Wind', she read, and opened it to find that on this sheet the words were
written beneath the notes.

I send a song on the wind,
And the sea-breeze will waft it to you.
Through the star-studded night
And the day's dawning light
I send my song on the wind to you.

I send my heart on the wind, and the sea-birds will bring it to you.
Through the heat of the noon-day sun,
In its blaze till the day is done,
I send my heart on the wind to you.

I send my soul on the wind, and the sea-spray will toss it to you.
Through the storm and the falling rain
The thunder will speak of my pain,
As I send my soul on the wind to you.

222

I send my love on the wind. My love, heart and soul is for you.
It will ride on the wind's sweet breath
Till eternity conquers death,
So I send my love and my song to you.

It was only as she closed the sheet with tears streaming down her face that she noticed the tiny dedication written across a corner. 'For Kerensa, my strength, my inspiration and my only love – forever.'